A Wish in Manhattan

Mandy Baggot

Bookouture

Published by Bookouture

An imprint of StoryFire Ltd.
23 Sussex Road, Ickenham, UB10 8PN
United Kingdom

www.bookouture.com

ISBN: 978-1-910751-49-7
eBook ISBN: 978-1-910751-48-0

ACKNOWLEDGEMENTS

Thank you to my wonderful agent, Kate Nash. You always have my back and I'm so glad I have you in my corner!

Thank you also to my great friends, Rachel Lyndhurst, Susie Medwell, Sue Fortin and Linn B Halton. You ladies are always there for me, giving me hugs and kicks up the bum! Here's to getting together more often and having oodles more laughs and wine!

A big thank you to all my Facebook friends and Twitter followers and my amazing street team, The Bagg Ladies. If it wasn't for your constant support I wouldn't be reaching the number of readers I am. Every tweet, mention, share or review is so appreciated!

Finally, a mention has to go to David Spencer (Squid) and Joseph Garrett (Stampy Longnose) – the Minecraft YouTubers who kept my children entertained for a lot of the summer holidays when I was editing the book. 'Welcome to another Let's Play video …' became music to my ears. Thank you!

To my two beautiful, clever, funny, cheeky daughters,
Amber and Ruby.

You two helped inspire the character of Angel and
this book wouldn't be the same without your input.

Mama Child is so proud of you both and I love you very much!

CHAPTER ONE

McDonald's, Winchester Street, Salisbury, Wiltshire, UK

Hayley Walker had quit her job. She had *quit* her job. What had she been thinking? Escape was the answer to that one. Finally ridding herself of sweaty Greg and his desperate attempts to fold and press *her* at the dry-cleaning firm. But now, an hour after the deed had been done, she was starting to realise she should have thought a lot less about escape and a lot more about money. Or rather, her lack of it. And exactly what she was going to do after Christmas. Throwing in the towel had been a knee-jerk reaction. A desperate leap. Was she going to live to regret it? Part-time party planning wasn't going to bring home the bacon or the expensive cereal with the free books.

'Do they have Yorkshire puddings?'

Hayley looked up from her phone-tapping and faced her nine-year-old daughter, the eater of the expensive cereal with the free books. Angel had half a cheeseburger hanging out of her mouth and she was trying to ram in the straw of her Diet Coke too. Hayley hadn't heard exactly what she'd said, something about pudding. She was too busy wondering if she had time to search the job section of the local paper before they left the country whilst also running through the whole travel itinerary in her head. Bang went her hopes of new clothes for them both for this trip. What was going to be on-trend this winter? She'd never really believed in the tweed phase. Maybe, if she didn't sleep, she would have time to make alterations on what they *did* have in their wardrobes. She put the lid on her thought box and focussed on Angel.

'Angel, manners in a restaurant please.' Hayley pulled the cardboard cup away.

She watched Angel's eyes spiral upwards, then around, taking in every inch of the McDonald's. No matter what her daughter's look was saying, it *was* a restaurant. Serviettes made it so and it was the only restaurant Hayley could afford right now. Even more so after today. She sighed. This McDonald's was *their* place, mum and daughter bonding over burgers. It was a constant, familiar, and familiar was comforting when she was about to throw them both halfway across the world.

'Well? You haven't answered my question.' Angel exaggerated the words for all she was worth. 'Are. They. Going. To. Have. Yorkshire. Puddings. In. New. York?'

Hayley put her phone on the table. She didn't know the answer. But it was obviously important to Angel. More important to her daughter than the fact she had never been on an aeroplane before and she had to sit still for eight hours and she was about to discover a whole new country. Who would have thought Yorkshire puddings could be so critical?

'I don't know,' Hayley said. 'But I can find out.' She smiled at her daughter.

'Google it,' Angel came back.

'What, now?'

'Free Wi-Fi in McDonald's. You always say that.'

Angel sucked at her drink, eyes bulbous like marbles.

At the moment there was nothing better than *free*. A bubble of pride bounced off Hayley's insides. She watched Angel biting down on the straw with her perfect teeth, her cheeks a little reddened, her mousey brown hair set in two pigtails with tinsel woven into the bobbles. Angel was the best thing she'd ever done. The only real, satisfying thing she'd achieved and she'd done it, for the most part, on her own. She swallowed down a knot of emotion and sucked at her own drink.

'I can't wait to meet Uncle Dean's new boyfriend,' Angel said.

Hayley started to choke on the liquid in her mouth and dragged the straw out. Her phone fell out of her hand and into the cardboard tray of chips she hadn't touched yet. 'What?'

'We Skyped last week when you were staring at those forms on the internet for *hours.*'

Angel was right, all Hayley had done the past few weeks was fill in forms. She thought she needed a visitor's visa. From what she'd read it would have been easier to send them the blood of a unicorn and spoilers for the next season of *Game of Thrones.* If only someone had mentioned ESTA to her before her head had got so close to exploding. New York – a Christmas holiday to Angel and an important mission to Hayley. She had spent the past two months straining her eyes to burning point on late night internet searches. Now it was time for the hunt to get up close and personal.

Hayley swung her attention back to Angel.

'He's called Vernon. Vern for short and they met at some really cool party Uncle Dean got invited to.' Angel flicked one of her pigtails. 'Will we get to go to really cool parties?'

Hayley's mind was working overtime. Her brother had a new boyfriend he hadn't mentioned. Did they do Yorkshire puddings in America? Could she get hold of a unicorn? Luggage scales – she definitely needed to get some luggage scales. SHE HAD NO FULL-TIME JOB!

'I don't know, Angel. We're going to have a lot to do when we get there and …'

'That's pretty close to a yes.'

'Are you going to finish that burger?'

'Are you going to eat your chips?' Angel put her tongue into the bottom of her mouth and poked it forward, tilting her chin.

'You know making that face is like swearing in America,' Hayley warned.

Angel changed her expression and looked at her mother with only slight scepticism.

Hayley pointed a finger and grinned. 'Gotcha!'

'That's not fair!' Angel screeched. She reached across the table and stole a chip from Hayley's tray, popping it into her mouth.

Hayley smiled, picking up a chip herself and dunking it in ketchup. Fries were about as uncomplicated as you could get.

Hayley looked out of the window onto the street. It was already dark, the sky blue/black with menacing grey clouds converging above the city skyline. People were wrapped up in wool coats, passing by, rushing home from work or to late night shopping, their breath visible in the freezing air. In just a few days, she and Angel would be leaving it all behind and travelling thousands of miles across the ocean for Christmas in the Big Apple. Minus temperatures in double figures and streets full of Santas, Michael Bublé music and candy canes.

Hayley watched a woman pushing open the door of the restaurant and she reached forward across the table to tap Angel on the arm.

'Fashion alert at three o'clock.' Hayley made the tapping more insistent. 'Angel Walker, tell me what you would do for this woman with nothing but a scarf and a hair clip.'

'Oh, Mum, really?' Angel looked at the woman heading for the counter. 'I think she looks fine.'

'Purlease! Cream boots with that grey coat?'

Angel sighed. 'What colour is the imaginary scarf?'

Hayley grinned. 'What colour do you think the imaginary scarf should be?'

'Red?'

Hayley shook her head, screwing up her face in disapproval. 'Brown?'

'Uh-uh. One last go?' She watched her daughter look the woman up and down, assessing.

'Spots!' Angel exclaimed.

Hayley clapped her hands together. 'Yes! I'm thinking a bit of Dalmatian print, clipped onto that coat like a drape. She would go from faux-pas to fashionista in a second.'

'Are we going to tell her?' Angel asked.

Hayley laughed and shook her head. 'No.'

It was just a game now. Something to occupy the designer side of her brain. It was all she'd ever wanted. Making creations to grace the catwalks, seeing the clothes come to life, delivering the finished products to high-end stores all over the world. She swallowed as she looked back at Angel. It seemed like a lifetime ago. And it was. Her life had changed beyond recognition. She'd gone from spending her nights cutting up fabric and laughing with friends over bottles of Lambrini, to night feeds and nappy changing. The only fashion she'd ended up dictating was her baby girl's, despite attempts to pass off puke stains as *en vogue*. She'd chosen to become a mother and mothers made sacrifices. What else was there to say?

'Vernon has a dog called Randy,' Angel blurted out, interrupting her thoughts.

A chip lodged in her throat and Hayley had to cough. 'What?'

'I think he named him after that judge on *American Idol*.'

Hayley sighed. 'Let's hope so.'

Balmoral Road, Salisbury, Wiltshire, UK

Angel had sung the Michael Bolton version of 'Santa Claus is Coming to Town' on repeat since they'd left town. Now they were parked up and the song was just reaching its final crescendo. Usually Hayley would have joined in – she had almost perfected the hair flick and the high gruff voice – but she was still panicking about the amount she had to do before they left. It helped that she didn't have a job to maintain any more. How wrong did that sound?

Giving in to the first drink with manager Greg had been her biggest mistake. Him not taking no for an answer the second, third and twelfth time of asking couldn't be put on her, but the getting too close beside the dry-cleaning steam machine had been the last straw. Fondling business suits and stain-covered cocktail dresses for six months was definitely enough. Her options were now open, which would have scared her more had she not been squirrelling away money from a second job as a party planner. Things had been busy on the run up to Christmas, she'd even scored some extra cash giving some of her richer clients fashion advice. With a clear diary for next year and just enough funds to cover this trip, she could now concentrate on what was important. The search.

Hayley screwed her eyes tight shut and gripped on to the steering wheel. Despite her bravado with Angel, she was excited and terrified in equal measure about this trip. In the far corners of her mind, heightened by the fact she was now unemployed, this trip to New York had all the makings of an escape plan. It could be a chance to see how the land lay over there, how Angel took to the US life. Her throat tightened just thinking about it. She and Angel, starting afresh, new horizons, doughnuts the size of dinner plates and cruising every floor of Barneys.

Hayley opened her eyes. It would only be window shopping for now, with her finances as they were. She looked to Angel. Her daughter had pulled down the visor and was pouting to herself in the vanity mirror like she was about to pose for a selfie.

Unfortunately, Hayley wasn't like her ridiculously clever brother, Dean, who had been headhunted for his position with Drummond Global. She had no extraordinary skills to offer the US. Just a hard work ethic and … well, just that. She and millions of others were all looking for the same sort of change. New York, paved with gold, a concrete jungle where dreams could come true.

'Shall I put it on again?'

Angel had turned in her seat and was now looking at Hayley, her finger poised on the button of the in-car CD player.

'No! Not again.'

Angel let out a laugh that made Hayley's skin prickle. Right now her daughter seemed innocent and unburdened but Hayley knew better. She knew what Angel was thinking and hoping for before she went to sleep each night and she was going to do whatever it took to solve it. New York could hold answers for them both.

'Come on, let's go and show Nanny your new coat,' Hayley said, opening the car door.

She stepped out of the car and shut the door, putting her hands into the pockets of her coat. The trees on the street cast dark shadows against the orange glow of the streetlights. Frost was starting to coat the windscreens of the parked cars and half a dozen houses had flashing and blinking Christmas lights on their brickwork or hanging from their eaves. Outlines of decorated Christmas trees were just visible behind net curtains and Hayley sucked in the quiet of the English suburb, turning her attention to a cat jumping up onto a neighbouring fence. Her whole landscape was about to change for a couple of weeks. Was she ready for all that could bring?

She watched Angel run up the path, the bag containing the new bright red duffle coat clutched in her hand.

Hayley took another moment, leaning back against the car and surveying the house she'd grown up in. It hadn't changed in twenty-eight years. The small, black, iron gate was still half off its hinges, the grass trimmed neat but the rose bushes overgrown. It was a hotchpotch, some things working, other bits uncared for. It had been a little like that with the people inside. Dean had been thoroughly nurtured, was still cared about; she had been left to garner weeds. For someone relatively self-sufficient it hadn't been a problem, until she got pregnant and her dad died.

The cold wound itself around her and she internally shook. She didn't resent her brother. She loved him with every fibre of her being. But as soon as Angel had come along things had deteriorated. Her mother just didn't look at her the same way. There were awkward silences, guarded help, emotional detachment. Rita had been there for her in every practical way possible, but that was where it ended. Money and advice had been handed out rather than love and support. Even now it still felt a bit hollow.

'Mum!' Angel called. 'Nanny says if you don't come in now I'll have to shut the door. It's letting all the heat out!'

Hayley rolled her eyes and braced herself. She had to be positive, smile and, most important of all, not mention that she'd lost her job.

'Red? I thought you were going to get her pink. You said you were going to get her pink.' Rita Walker didn't hold back. Hayley watched her mother turn her head, directing hard eyes her way.

Angel stopped twirling around and stood still, her arms held out stiff like an insulted scarecrow. The joy in her new coat instantly shattering at Rita's remark.

'We tried on nine coats in eight different shops. Angel liked this one and to be honest I was losing the will to live by then,' Hayley responded. Why did she always feel like she had to defend all her decisions? She slumped down onto the sofa, just missing a pile of *Home & Country* magazines. Why her mother had ever signed up for that monthly subscription she would never know. Their home was, and always had been, far more *Britain's Worst* than *Downton Abbey*.

'You gave up you mean.' Rita sniffed. 'Made do.' She reached forward, picking up her fine bone china teacup with the chip on the rim.

Hayley nodded. 'It was a bargain too.' She pitched her voice just right. 'Nothing like a *charity shop* bargain.'

She had never seen her mother move faster. She was up and out of her reclining chair quicker than a fighter jet taking flight.

'Take it off, Angel.' Rita tugged at the sleeve of the coat, shaking the girl's arm in the process. 'Quickly.'

'Nanny! You're hurting!'

'Mum, stop. I was joking.'

Angel wrenched her arm back and hugged herself.

Rita turned her body to Hayley then settled herself in an angry stance. 'Why would you say something like that?'

'Why would you go on about it needing to be pink?'

Hayley watched Angel clamp her hands over her ears. She'd been backed into a corner again. Rita was good at that but it was unfair for Angel to be caught in the middle. They had a couple of nights staying here because the landlord was redecorating their house while they were away and the firm needed to start early. She should try and maintain peace and tranquillity and ignore the jibes directed her way. It wasn't as if she wasn't completely accustomed to it by now.

'Shall I make a pot of tea?' Hayley offered, getting to her feet.

'I've made a shepherd's pie. Angel, you must be starving,' Rita said.

'Oh, we've had dinner already,' Angel replied, spinning around again.

'Oh?' Rita queried.

Hayley practically ran for the kitchen, waiting for the words to come from Angel's mouth.

'We went to McDonald's.'

Hayley could almost feel the temperature drop. Just two more sleeps. Two more sleeps and they'd be heading for America.

CHAPTER TWO

Drummond Global Offices, Downtown Manhattan, USA

Oliver Drummond let his eyes wander. Mackenzie, the head of his legal division, had her voice pitched at boring the second she opened her scarlet lips. *Settlement. Management. Negotiation. Collaboration.* And his very least favourite *strategise*. Strategising wasn't in his nature. He was a doer. He acted, instinctively, and, more often than not, impulsively. He didn't mull things over, that's what he paid other people to do. By the time his employees had strategised the ass out of everything, all that was left was for him to do was give the green light. He wanted the finish line. The winning touchdown. He had no interest in the bits in between. Creation and completion were his fortes. And if people had a problem with that mantra, well, they knew what they could do.

Oliver turned his head back to the dozen or so people sat at the boardroom table on the eightieth floor of Drummond Global and nodded at Mackenzie. He had no idea what she'd said but he was confident in her ability to get the company out of whatever mess she'd been called in to deal with. He'd make an effort to find out. He should know, if only the bare bones of it. He put the end of his steel ballpoint in his mouth, pressing it to his lip. He'd been so focussed on the Globe over the past few months he'd let everything else slide. The Globe was going to change things. The tablet wasn't just going to alter the lives of its consumers, it was going to reinvigorate his passion for the company. And he'd get right into the professional zone on other projects today ... as soon as he got rid of last night's hangover. He was blaming his best friend Tony for every last shot of that.

He shifted in his executive leather chair at the head of the table as a twinge pinged like an elastic band in his chest. He gritted his teeth together, trying to ignore it. He didn't have time for this. He would not allow it to exist in his world. He turned his head to the floor-to-ceiling windows overlooking Downtown Manhattan. Snow was falling, spreading its whiteness over the tops of neighbouring buildings, raining down towards the ground. He focussed his hazel eyes on the flakes, watching their journey until they disappeared out of sight. Right now he wanted to be one of them. Weightless, drifting, silently floating through the air, oblivious to anything around. A layer of white hung from the neo-Gothic roof of the Woolworth Building, while shards of ice dripped from what he could see of the frontage of Broadway. Outside, the city was turning into a winter wonderland; inside, there was an avalanche waiting to happen.

The distraction of the winter weather wasn't enough. The pain was still there. It was an ache that seemed to increase in magnitude with every passing second. He fought the urge to grimace, holding his jaw in place as the monotony of Mackenzie's voice continued in the background.

It could definitely be muscular. Maybe he'd pulled something when he was working out. And how crazy were those dance moves Tony had forced him to do last night? He swallowed, putting a hand to the dark grey tie at his throat, slackening it off a little.

'Oliver.'

The direct tone and the force at which his name hit his eardrums drew his attention back to the table. Clara, his PA, was giving him one of her *special* looks. The eyebrows were up in her mahogany-tinted hairline, her head tilting downwards, glasses sat halfway down her nose, shoulder pads widening. He'd just about deciphered this look to mean *get your head back in the room now or I'm going to quit.* Somehow she knew that scared the crap out of him.

Oliver adjusted his body in the chair as another shot of pain hit his chest wall. This wasn't good. Was this how it started? No, he needed to banish that thought from his mind just like he had all the other times this had happened. He *wasn't* his father. He *wasn't* his brother. This was *not* touching him. He swallowed. He didn't believe that. He was always going to be next.

He directed his gaze to the brassy statement necklace laying just above Clara's fifty-something décolletage. It paid homage to everything that was bad about the eighties. Where did she get these things? A smile broke on his lips. This was good. Focussing on Clara's poor taste in accessories was really working. He leaned a little nearer to her, ignoring the thud of his heart and the perspiration at the back of his neck. Then the reflective fake diamonds started to blur his vision. He tipped slightly, nudging Clara's elbow with his hand. The papers she was holding fanned to the floor in spectacular fashion.

Mackenzie stopped talking. Oliver straightened up quickly, blinking desperately, his face coated with an expression he hoped signalled solidarity and comradeship. He nodded his head as Clara dipped to recover her documents from the carpet.

Oliver cleared his throat before speaking. 'Do carry on, Mackenzie.'

'What was going on in there, Oliver? If I wasn't old enough to be your mother I'd have thought you were trying to hit on me,' Clara said as they headed from the boardroom.

'I apologise. I was bored and I couldn't look at Mackenzie. She's hankering after another date and the last time I took her out she drank me under the table.'

Clara turned and looked at him, wearing the school principal expression.

'I know, I know, and I'm done mixing business with pleasure,' he stated.

'So, you're confident you know everything there is to know about the proposed takeover of Regis Software?'

The long strides he was taking meant she was following him at running pace along the corridor. Deftly, he swept left, heading towards the bank of elevators. He needed to get back to his office, take a breath. He paced with urgency before remembering Clara could barely walk in her shoes at the best of times. He slowed.

'I kick-started the project, Clara. My father and Andrew Regis weren't just old friends. They were like brothers. He came to every birthday party I ever had until I got too old for clowns and piñatas.' He stopped, pressing the stainless steel button to call the lift. He tried to hide the bob of his Adam's apple. He had no idea of the latest content in the Regis Software contract. He had set it up, he had banged out the basics of the agreement … what had happened then? It was nowhere near final stages, was it? What exactly had he missed?

'So, bearing that in mind, after dinner and drinks you decide to ship out?' Clara had her bluntest tone on now. If he didn't know her background already he would have guessed at prison officer.

Oliver filled his lungs to their maximum capacity and turned to look at her. 'I don't know, Clara, has something happened I don't know about? You're my PA, if you know something then it's your duty to tell me.'

She adopted a confused expression as she looked back at him. 'I don't know anything.'

'Then I ask the question … am I not the CEO of Drummond Global?'

Who was he trying to sound like here? Donald Trump? King Midas? He watched Clara swallow away her resolve. She did a good job, no, scrub that, she did a *great* job. So why was he intent on making her feel small in this moment? He moved his tongue in his mouth and swallowed away the bitter taste. He was attacking, fighting instead of fleeing, because she'd backed him into a corner. If he wasn't careful he would lose his edge.

'I'm not my father, Clara.' He stopped talking, the breath suddenly catching in his throat. He tried again. 'And I don't need to get involved in every minute decision there is. It's a more modern approach.'

'I'm well aware of all that, Oliver.' Clara paused before carrying on. 'I'm worried about you, that's all.'

'Please don't do that.' He moistened his lips. The pain was back now, only a lot worse. His heart was beating like the corps of a military band. He could no longer fill his lungs. Breaths were coming short and sharp. He tried to recover. 'I … I don't pay you to worry about me.'

A vice-like grip wrapped itself around his heart and squeezed, unrelenting. Where was the damn elevator? The steel of the lift door just in front of him started to warp and bend in his vision. The internal glass windows to his left and right bowed and refracted the morning sun hitting the building from behind them. The walkway was suddenly getting sauna hot.

'Oliver, are you all right?'

He opened his mouth to speak but his jaw was tightening. Everything was being squashed and compacted like garbage in a city truck.

'Oliver,' Clara repeated.

The words he wanted to say just wouldn't come. Clara's necklace spun around in his vision and before he could do anything else his body dropped to the floor.

CHAPTER THREE

Balmoral Road, Salisbury, Wiltshire, UK

I met someone last night at this really cool club called Vipers. Michel De Vos!!!! An artist!!!! He looked a bit like Johnny Depp and he was foreign too. Exotic!!!! I think Dean would probably fancy him. We danced and talked and he told me all about his paintings and photographs. He's going to be exhibiting at these cool galleries – New York Life and the Tilton. New York is giving me all these completely amazing opportunities. You just don't bump into sexy artists in Wiltshire.

I can't remember the hotel we went to. It began with 't' I think or it could have been 'the' something. It was nice though. Like a Hilton. And there were chocolates on the pillow. I ate them all and he didn't mind. And then he kissed me and I kissed him and we did EVERYTHING … twice. And I lay there thinking this is one of those perfect moments I'll remember forever. Me, in New York with an artist called Michel.

In Dean's old bedroom Hayley snapped her ten-year diary closed. She'd read enough. The memories were good but the feeling they left her with didn't feel nice, it felt … dirty. She pushed the diary onto the bookshelf between a Jill Mansell and

a Jilly Cooper. Not content with how it looked she set a toy elephant and half a dozen fairground Gonks in front of it.

'Mum!' Angel called from the other bedroom.

Hayley pushed two Gonks closer together so the diary was
no longer visible and checked how it looked. Obvious because
of the furry guardians? Or invisible?

'Mum!' Angel called again.

'Coming!'

Hayley couldn't help the smile forming on her lips when she
got to the other bedroom. Angel was diligently putting things
inside her suitcase, her pigtails bouncing as she moved from
drawers to case and back again in the smallest bedroom of the
house.

Angel turned, a thick dictionary in her hands. 'I do have
twenty-three kilos, right?'

'Yes but, Angel, seriously? A dictionary?'

It was a hardback. She could see Angel struggling to even
hold it in one hand.

The reply came quickly. 'It's my favourite.'

Her daughter had a favourite dictionary. Why didn't she
know this? It was a proud mother moment despite how much
it weighed. Hayley sat down on the edge of what had been her
childhood bed. The duvet cover with swirls and graffiti logos
on had long since been replaced by something clean-lined, neutral and perfectly prim – ideal if ever the Queen or Mary Berry
needed a bed for the night.

'They do have books in New York you know.' Hayley patted
the duvet next to her.

Angel put her hands on her hips and struck a surly pose.
'Does that mean I can't take my favourite dictionary?'

What did you say to moves like Beyoncé from a nine-year-
old?

'What if I want to know what *sidewalk* means?'

'You know what *sidewalk* means.'

'That's not the point.' Angel stuck her head forward like an ostrich getting interested in prey. 'There will be things in America I might not understand.'

'They speak English, Angel.'

'American English is very different to British English. They practically never use a "u" in anything and they prefer "z" to "s".'

'See how much you know already,' Hayley quipped.

'I *need* my dictionary.' Angel pouted better than Naomi Campbell.

'Your *British* English dictionary.'

Angel let out a growl akin to an irritated beast on a nature documentary. Definitely more bear than ostrich. 'I bet you're taking that massive diary.'

The words pinched but Hayley did her best not to let it show.

The diary she'd just hidden was practically an undetonated grenade. She didn't know why she even kept it. Most entries these days were a couple of lines, sometimes only a few words.

> *Angel's tooth came out when she ate the yellow Quality*
> *Street. Mother made another crack about single mothers*
> *– she'll be asking Denise Robertson to give me advice*
> *soon. Greg bought me a sausage roll from Greggs, it would*
> *be funny if he wasn't expecting his sausage to be rolling*
> *around somewhere near me and the trouser press.*

Hayley forced a smile. 'I'm not taking it.' There was no way she could take it now.

Angel plumped herself down onto the cover, crossing her legs underneath her body in a show of flexibility to rival an experienced Pilates class attendee. 'You should get a new diary.'

'What for? There's nothing wrong with the one I have.' The one she hoped to God Angel hadn't been reading. Along with the random sentences of life events she'd been writing in there this year, there were nine other years, including the very beginnings of Angel's existence. And it was *those* entries that were the most controversial, as well as being the most helpful when she had been researching their upcoming trip.

'You should bring your ideas book then. The one with all your drawings and designs and the bits of material in,' Angel suggested.

Her ideas book. She'd had so few ideas lately she'd turned the back of the book into notes for her party planning exploits. Most people wanted the packages set out on the website but occasionally, every now and then, someone would ask for something a bit different and then she pounced on it, like a hungry lion who'd been starved for an age.

'What would I need that for?' She swallowed.

'To note down all those designs you give people.' Angel smiled. 'Like that woman in McDonald's. Imaginary scarves.' She wafted a hand in the air. 'Berets and buckles. There's going to be so much inspiration in New York.'

Hayley smiled, enjoying Angel's enthusiasm. 'You're changing the subject, young lady, when we're meant to be getting ready for our trip,' Hayley reached out her fingers and nudged Angel's ribs, tickling.

'Stop it!' Angel squealed.

'Sorry, didn't hear that.'

'Mum!' Angel screeched, falling backwards on the bed and trying to get away from the attack. 'You'll make Nanny come up here and you know she doesn't like to be interrupted when she's watching *Coronation Street*.'

Hayley removed her hands with the speed of a mousetrap mechanism. The last thing she needed was her mother on the warpath.

Her eyes went from Angel to the thick book laying on the bed. She picked it up and opened it.

'Ah, here's a word I might need to get familiar with.' Hayley cleared her throat. 'Bodega – a cellar or shop selling wine and food especially in a Spanish-speaking country.'

Angel snapped the dictionary shut and claimed it back. 'I hope we're not going to spend all our time searching for fizzy white wine.'

'No, once we've established our local seller we'll be loyal.'

Angel crossed her legs again, placing the dictionary in the middle of her lap and fixing her eyes on Hayley. 'Do you think Nanny will be OK on her own at Christmas?'

There was deep sincerity in the question. Angel loved Rita. She was the only other person who had always been there for her. And she *had* been there. In body, if not in spirit.

Rita wasn't coming because she had a hospital appointment on Christmas Eve. She'd been waiting over six months to see one particular consultant about her ongoing arthritis that she didn't dare reschedule. Hayley felt guilty for two reasons. The first was that perhaps she should be here to take Rita to the appointment and the second was that it had been a perfect excuse to not invite her on the trip. She swallowed as the last thought hit home.

Hayley put her arm around her daughter and drew her into her body, kissing the top of her head. 'I think Nanny is going to be just fine on her own. Haven't you seen the salmon head in the freezer? And she's hidden Bendicks at the back of the larder.'

'Are those the minty dark chocolates?'

'Yeah, the ones she usually keeps by the side of her chair under deep security at Christmas.'

'If I have more than three they make my mouth spicy.'

'Reasons Christmas is going to be better in New York number 49. Not having to share chocolates with Nanny.'

'But we will have to share them with Uncle Dean, Vernon and Randy.'

'Are you sure Randy's a dog?'

'Yes …' Angel paused. 'Well I heard something barking in the background on Skype. And there was definitely a leather collar on the coat rack behind Uncle Dean.'

Hayley swallowed. 'Dogs are allergic to chocolate,' she said quickly. 'Just like Nanny's allergic to clothes from the charity shop.'

Angel let out a sigh. 'Nanny's a good person. She's just different to you that's all.'

That simple sentence from the lips of her offspring cut deep. Because it was the truth. Her mother wasn't an ogre. She hadn't beaten her, or deprived her of material needs, she just hadn't ever been spontaneous with emotion. That didn't make her bad. They were just opposites.

'Sorry,' Hayley said in little more than a whisper.

'So, can I take my dictionary?' Angel batted her eyelids up and down, poking out her bottom lip and looking suitably like a cast member of *Annie*.

Hayley sighed. 'You can take the dictionary as long as you promise not to take that ancient old Christmas storybook. I can't take another year of Alfie falling into the toymaker every night for a week.'

She looked at Angel, waiting for her to relinquish the dictionary. Her daughter's face was expressionless.

'OK.'

'OK?' Hayley checked. 'Are you sure? This must be one special dictionary.'

'The dictionary comes and, for being an awesome mum, I think you should have some fizzy wine,' Angel said, checking her watch. 'It's past eight o'clock and it's nearly Christmas.'

'Quick! Where's the nearest bodega?' Hayley smiled. 'Come on, it's late. Let's move the case off the bed and tuck you in.'

She strained to pick the case up lengthways but managed to slide it down onto the floor without losing any contents or banging the floorboards too hard. It was a double *Coronation Street* night. When she straightened herself back up, Angel was slipping down under the covers, eyes wide open, but the first signs of sleep showing. She yawned.

'Time for sleep,' Hayley said, brushing a hand over Angel's hair.

'I don't really mind if they don't have Yorkshire puddings in New York you know,' Angel said.

Hayley looked at her daughter's expression. There was concern in her large blue eyes. She didn't want that. Whatever life threw at them none of it should ever come to rest on Angel's shoulders.

'I have good news.' Hayley smiled. 'Google tells me they *do* have them and they're called popovers.'

'Really?' Angel looked less than convinced.

'Really. And the best news of all is they sell them in a ready-made mix.'

Angel broke a smile then and clenched her fingers into excited fists.

'Reasons Christmas is going to be better in New York number 84 – they have Yorkshire puddings.' Hayley grinned. 'So, let's recap. We know what a bodega is and we can probably pick up the Yorkshire pudding mix while we're getting the fizzy wine.'

'Mum!' Angel said, swiping a hand at Hayley's arm and laughing.

She kept the smile going but inhaled a long breath and watched the happy expression restored on her daughter's face. This trip was all about Angel and she didn't even know it yet.

Hayley leaned forward, kissing Angel's forehead. 'Go to sleep now. No reading up on George Washington or how many types of squirrel there are in Central Park.'

'Only one, the grey squirrel and they're in decline. Apparently …'

Hayley put a finger to her lips and Angel stopped talking.

'Time for sleep now but tomorrow I want to hear all about the little critters.'

Angel smiled. 'Night, Mum.'

'Night, Miss Mensa.' Hayley went to the door turned off the light and stepped onto the landing.

She waited a few seconds, just wanting to stay in this happy bubble before everything in their lives changed, and then she heard the softest of voices.

'Dear God, or Father Christmas, it doesn't matter which … If you're listening I really, really want to find my dad.'

CHAPTER FOUR

St. Patrick's Hospital, Manhattan, USA

Oliver felt as if he had the contents of a toolbox in his mouth. Every single spanner and a dirty wrench. A horrid, metallic taste tainted his tongue and the flesh on the inside of both cheeks. It was making him nauseous – as was the chattering machine next to the hospital bed that was recording every movement of his heart. All the doctors arriving en masse when he'd been admitted had since disappeared. He was prostrate on the bed, the sensation in his chest now nothing more than a numb ache, Clara tapping on her phone next to him. Worry was etched on her forehead. He couldn't be here anymore. He hated these places and he needed to get back to work, get to the bottom of all that was going on with Regis Software. He tried to move into a half-sitting position.

'Oliver, don't you dare move. The nurse said you need to lie completely still.' Clara clamped a hand to his forearm, dropping her phone into her lap.

'I just need to see what this damn machine is saying and then I can get out of here.' He craned his neck. 'What's it saying?' He tried to focus his eyes on the graph shapes appearing on the screen.

'It's saying if you don't lie still your personal assistant is going to get the meanest nurse she can find,' Clara retorted. 'Try to stay calm.'

'In this place?! Are you kidding?' He flopped back down.

He didn't need to read the graph to know what it was saying. Those humps and bumps, the lines rising and falling, they only meant one thing. *Heart attack*. He knew without any shadow of a doubt. It was his destiny. It wasn't a case of 'if' but 'when'. It was genetic, written in family history. This was what the male Drummonds had in their future. Heart problems and eventually … death.

That realisation weighed on his shoulders like an unmoveable snow drift. Maybe this year was it for him. Time out, nothing else, not even making thirty. Like his brother.

'It's not a heart attack.'

Now his PA was apparently a mind reader, although clearly no physician. Oliver stared up at the ceiling, looking into the pattern of the off-white tiles, a string of cheap silver tinsel hanging lamely from one crack. It looked like someone hated Christmas just as much as he did.

He wasn't going to meet Clara's eyes. The woman was just trying to keep his spirits up. That's all people knew how to do in situations like this. She knew his family story. She knew the inevitable ending.

His tightened chest had definitely slackened slightly, but it wouldn't stay that way. It would take him over again, when he wasn't ready, another time, another place.

'When my first husband had his first heart attack he turned the colour of a well-ripened plum. Then, when he hit the floor, he was paler than a hockey mask.'

Oliver swallowed away a sick feeling burning his stomach. He wasn't sure he wanted to hear this.

'His second heart attack was different. Sweating, confusion … he said it was like having a wrecking ball on his chest.'

'Was there a third?'

Clara nodded. 'Oh yes, the third one killed him.'

He'd heard all he needed to. There was no escape from this death sentence and now he just wanted out of here. He began ripping the monitors off his chest and flailing up to a sitting position. 'Don't tell me any more.'

'Oliver, put those back on.'

'I can't be here.'

He was just pulling the very last round sucker from his chest when the door opened and a dark-haired woman wearing a white coat and carrying a clipboard entered the room. She was beautiful. Asian colouring, cat-like eyes, full lips. Oliver toyed with the sticker in his hand like a kid being caught with his hand in the candy jar.

'Mr Drummond, sorry I was called away.' She looked at his fingers holding the sensor that was supposed to be flat on his chest. 'I see you got impatient.' The corners of her mouth lifted in a wry smile.

He watched her walk confidently to the machine. She pressed some buttons and began making notes on her chart.

'I'm sorry, Doctor. I told him to keep still but he isn't the best at following instructions,' Clara spoke up.

The doctor finished writing before looking up, smiling at Clara and clicking off her pen. 'I have a lot of patients like that.' She looked to Oliver. 'Nearly all of them male.'

He swallowed. This was a woman in control. It was intoxicating and, for a second, he felt completely disarmed. He needed to find his rhythm here. He gripped the buttons of his shirt and began to fasten them together. He was still here, alive. His heart hadn't beaten him in this round and he wasn't going to be throwing in the towel that easily. It was just like NFL. He'd never stopped giving his all for that. He needed to remember that feeling.

He set his hazel eyes on her. 'So, what's the verdict, Doctor? Am I going to be well enough to take you out to dinner tonight?'

And there he was. Back in the game. There was amusement in her expression as a smile reached her lips, a glint of acknowledgement in her eyes.

'For God's sake, Oliver.' Clara exhaled a breath of annoyance.

The doctor's eyes looked him up and down, from his leather shoes, up through his designer trousers, to the tailored shirt he was just finishing doing up. 'You had a panic attack.'

Her words crushed his libido like a snowplough clearing the streets. He was shaking his head without even knowing it. A panic attack? Panic. Weak. Desperate. *Small penis.*

But just what was he thinking here? This was a good thing. It *wasn't* a heart attack. This was *great*. He blew out a breath.

'Your symptoms are a classic case of hyperventilation,' the doctor continued.

'No,' Oliver shook his head. It may not be a heart attack but he was damn sure it wasn't panic either. Panic wasn't in the Drummond nature. 'It wasn't like that at all.' He looked to Clara. 'I wasn't gasping for breath like some sort of asthmatic and I wasn't panicked.'

'Mr Drummond, it isn't like most people think. Hyperventilation is a complex reaction the body makes when it needs to try to get you to slow everything down.'

He shook his head again. This did not compute. Whatever had happened was everything to do with his family history and nothing to do with being a lightweight.

'I don't do slowing down, Doctor ...' He scrutinised the identity badge hanging from a lanyard around her neck. 'Doctor Khan. I run a global business.'

'Oliver,' Clara had her calming voice on now. It was the tone she used when she thought he'd gone too far in a meeting, when he'd made one heated comment too many. Well, he hadn't in this case. He wasn't going to listen to some junior doctor tell him the pain and his collapse was due to something excited teenagers got at a Taylor Swift concert.

'Mr Drummond, I can only imagine the sort of pressure you're under at work. People in your position, under that amount of stress on a regular basis, you're susceptible to all kinds of health issues that aren't always immediately apparent.'

She might be beautiful but he wasn't going to let her tell him this was to do with panicking. He had never panicked in his life. He wasn't even sure he knew how to do it.

'You're aware of my family history?'

'Yes. I did a quick review of your file. Would you like me to …'

He cut her off. 'You're sure it wasn't a heart attack.' It wasn't a question so much as a statement.

The doctor nodded. 'Your blood pressure is slightly elevated but everything else is completely as it should be. For complete peace of mind my suggestion would be to—'

He raised himself up off the bed, standing to his full six feet and picking his tie from the counter. 'Thank you, but if I'm not dying today then I think we're done here.' He smiled at Doctor Khan, regaining his composure and control before dipping a hand into the pocket of his trousers.

'My card,' he said, offering it to her. 'If you want to take me up on the dinner offer.'

He could almost feel Clara raise her eyes to Heaven.

CHAPTER FIVE

Mancinis Restaurant, 10ᵗʰ Avenue, Manhattan, USA

When you'd had your life flash in front of your eyes everything was magnified. The times this had happened Oliver could only count on one hand, but he knew there would be more to come. It was as inevitable as Christmas and the start of a new year. But, for now, in this moment, there was simply clarity. It was a chance to take stock, to re-evaluate, every encounter enhanced.

Oliver raised the delicate stemmed wineglass to his nose and savoured the aroma of the Merlot within. Oak, deep, dark berries, aged to perfection: the most expensive red wine they had on the list. He closed his eyes and put the rim of the glass to his mouth. He let the wine touch his lips first, before opening them up and allowing the liquid to reach his tongue. It was smooth, dense, like a velvet wrap had coiled itself around the flesh.

He finally swallowed the wine and replaced the glass on the table, surveying the rest of the restaurant. It was full and from his vantage point he could see people being turned away at the front door. That's what his status in the business community had bought him. A regular table at one of the most exclusive restaurants in the area from just a phone call, no matter how late. Except he was alone. He'd called Tony, asked if he wanted to continue where they'd left off the night before, but apparently his invitation wasn't quite as tempting as a night with a Polish girl called Erica. He didn't blame his friend. Hell, if Doctor

Khan had taken him up on his dinner offer he wouldn't have called Tony in the first place.

Oliver looked out the window, half-hidden by the heavy, gold-flecked curtains and a string of expensive-looking Christmas bells. The snow was coming down faster now and, as the temperature dropped, it was starting to layer up on the sidewalk. A couple, wrapped up in scarves, hats and gloves came into view. The woman, dark hair flying out from under her hat, screamed as the man hit her with a snowball. Their forms bobbed and swayed in front of the red and green lights of a flashing Christmas tree on the adjacent building. Oliver watched the woman bend to the ground and start to gather as much powdery white stuff as she could scrape up to counter his attack. She threw, but her aim was off and the ball hit the windscreen of a parked car. Shrieking, as her partner chased her again, they ran off up the road. He was still watching the situation play out when he heard someone clear their throat.

Oliver turned his attention back to the restaurant and looked up to see a waiter stood next to him, dressed in the Mancinis uniform of cream tuxedo with a maroon waistcoat and matching bow tie.

'I apologise for disturbing you, Mr Drummond, but I wondered if anyone was joining you for dinner tonight,' the waiter asked.

Oliver nodded his head. Yes, that was exactly what he needed to get over the earlier hospital drama. His mind wandered back to Doctor Khan. She had virtually prescribed stress relief. Maybe it was time to follow the doctor's orders.

'Absolutely, Ricco.' Oliver let his eyes roam around the restaurant, falling on the other patrons. He looked away from the couples holding hands across the table, the businessmen, the over forties. Who was left? There was a group of four women half a dozen tables away from him, two blondes, two brunettes. They weren't too loud, they hadn't started eating yet and each of them was impeccably dressed. Then he spotted her. Sitting at a table in the very corner of the room, just close enough for him to see everything he needed to see. Hair the colour of honey, fingers wrapped around a glass of white wine, black day-to-night dress.

'Ricco, send a glass of your best champagne to the lady over there and ask her if she'd care to join me?' He nodded in the direction of the corner table.

'Yes, sir.'

Before the waiter turned to depart Oliver spoke again. 'And Ricco,'

'Yes, Mr Drummond?'

'We'll both have the salmon.'

'Very good, sir.'

Oliver sat back in his chair, took another sip of wine and waited to see what would happen. He didn't really need to watch. He was certain of the outcome. After all, what woman would refuse free champagne and the opportunity to dine with a billionaire?

His chest creased suddenly, making him sit a little uneasy. Straight away the fear flooded his every part. He swallowed, trying to home in on the background music of instrumental Christmas schmaltz he couldn't stand. It wasn't working and he could feel his head starting to throb. No, this was not happening. He wasn't going to give into it no matter what 'it' was. *It's a heart attack. Your number is up. You're going to die.*

He shook his head, trying to dislodge his subconscious. The beautiful doctor's diagnosis began to run over his mind again as he tried to focus on Ricco, approaching the honey blonde with a glass of champagne on a silver tray. He didn't have time for stress, or death. He had to fight, not give up like his father and brother had done.

Oliver pulled in his stomach and sat up in his chair ignoring the twinge in his pectoral muscles. He watched the woman accept the glass the waiter was offering and seek him out. She raised the glass a little, a bashful smile on her lips. He swallowed down the pain. He wasn't going to let it get in the way of his evening. He was in.

Her name was Christa. She was in New York for two nights and this was the second of them. It was perfect. She was staying at the Bryant Park Hotel, her boss had reserved the table and she was visiting for a conference. She was in cosmetics, nail polishes and something called acrylics for a national company named Cuticle. She talked a lot and after her third glass of champagne her Idaho accent really came out. She was just the sort of distraction he'd needed.

'Sorry, Oliver, I'm boring you. You don't want to hear about French manicures and the latest in Gelish.' Christa put her glass down on the table, nearly toppling it over in her haste.

'I never knew it was so complicated,' he responded. 'But I have to admit, if we're being really honest here, nails aren't the first thing that attracts me to a woman.' He kept his eyes on her and was rewarded with her gaze and a soft smile taking over her mouth.

'Is that so?' She placed her hand on the table, smoothing the linen cloth with her fingers. 'Are you gonna tell me what *is* the first thing that attracts you?'

She looked coy now and it was relaxing him. He leaned forward a little. 'Well, Christa, what do *you* think it is?' He was teasing and from the look on her face she was enjoying every minute of it.

'Is it a smile?' she guessed. 'Maybe the eyes?'

He waited a few beats, carefully filling her glass up with champagne. 'No.' He shook his head, a smile playing on his lips.

'Do you have a thing for blondes?' Christa picked up her glass, took a sip of the liquid inside.

He shook his head, sat back in his seat, his eyes still fixed on her. This was the part he liked best. The questioning, the innocent expectation, the not knowing what was going to happen next. He was as exhilarated here as he used to be on the football field, as he sometimes was when he was closing a deal at Drummond Global. He'd not closed many of those recently. He drummed his fingers on the table, pushing the negative thought away. This was *his* time. Here was where he did his living, with no boundaries. Here, his short life expectancy just didn't exist.

He moved a little closer still. 'It's an aura,' he said in no more than a whisper.

He could see she was transfixed, almost hypnotised by the sound of his voice. Her right elbow was resting on the table, her hand at one of her small, gold heart-shaped earrings. He didn't feel guilty about the little white lie. After all, she was going to get as much out of this as him, if not more.

'An aura,' she repeated, softly.

He nodded, leaning in to the table, sliding his hand past the condiments. His fingers were mere inches away from hers now.

And then Christa laughed, the sound erupting loud and hard. 'That's so funny.' She sipped at her wine, a little spilling over her lips. 'An aura!' She returned the glass to the linen cloth and banged the flat of her hand down on the table.

He was thrown, just for a split second. This usually got them every time whether they really believed it or not. She was supposed to be flattered, feel special. He had to turn this around. He smiled.

'What? You don't think it's true?' He eked out a small laugh of his own. 'You think I spin this sort of line to every woman I meet?'

'I'm not dumb enough to think otherwise,' Christa said, swigging more champagne. 'But ...' She put her glass back down on the table and inched her fingers closer to his. 'I don't really mind.'

Oliver wasn't sure about this change in proceedings. He was always the one in charge, the one calling the shots. He didn't know how he felt about Christa making the first move. He widened his smile. It was time to make his move.

He made the connection, slipping his fingers in between hers and linking them tight. He heard a small gasp leave her lips. It was time.

'Make a wish,' he whispered, his eyes demanding attention from hers.

'What?'

He could see the breath was catching in her throat, her chest rising and falling so softly it was barely moving at all.

He wet his lips before continuing. 'If you could have one wish, right now, tonight, what would it be?'

A titter of a laugh escaped from her and he could tell there was nervous excitement behind the logical part of her that was trying to say this was madness.

'You're crazy,' she responded.

'Make a wish, Christa. If money were no object.' He squeezed her hands. 'If you could do one thing, go one place, something you've always dreamed of, what would it be?'

She shook her head then, the honey-blonde waves shimmering in the half-light. 'You are certifiable.'

'I'm serious,' he said.

She smiled, shaking her head once more. 'Well, in that case, I've never been in a helicopter and I've always wanted to see New York from the air, like in the movies.'

A result. Slowly he slipped his hand into the pocket inside his jacket and drew out his cell phone. 'Finish your champagne and I'll make the call.'

She almost dropped the glass to the floor.

Christa's screams as the helicopter dipped down over the city were like food to his soul. She was clutching his arm so tightly it felt like the bone was turning numb. But, despite the vice-like grip on his limb, the pain in his chest had gone. Even as he thought about it, nothing happened, no twinges, no aches, nothing. It was like he was free from it all. That's what happened when you lived in the moment. You could almost forget everything else.

Christa's eyes were on stalks, watching the sparkling lights of the Empire State Building, the Chrysler Building and Trump Towers, as they flew around the boroughs. The Empire State, one of the Seven Wonders of the Modern World, its iconic Art-Deco style tapering up to almost meet them in the sky never failed to impress at night, particularly from their vantage point. Circling some of the most well-known buildings in the city, almost close enough to touch … he could see how it made Christa feel. He knew she was experiencing something she'd always wanted to do, a life's dream – because of him. That meant something. It was one wish she would never forget making, because it had come true.

'This is amazing!' Christa shouted above the roar of the engine.

Oliver nodded his head, took her hand from his arm and linked their hands together. 'So, what do you want to do next?'

She turned her head away from the cityscape for a moment and directed her gaze at him. Smiling, she replied. 'I think I'd like you to see the inside of my hotel room.'

'I thought you'd never ask,' he answered, edging towards her.

CHAPTER SIX

Heathrow Airport, London, UK

'Is Dean meeting you at the airport?' Rita asked, shaking a Fisherman's Friend into her hand before popping it into her mouth.

'I don't know yet,' Hayley said, pushing the cases a few more inches in the queue for check-in.

'What? You've not arranged it?' Rita's voice was shrill. 'You're going to be arriving at night. You have to have someone waiting for you.'

'I just didn't want to bother him straight away when we can easily get a cab.'

They were going to be staying with Dean. His large, expensive, beautifully decorated bachelor pad was going to be their home for the holidays. Without this offer there would be no way this trip would be affordable. But the truth was, as soon as Hayley started asking more of her brother he would give it and then some. Dean was generous to a fault and the whole trip would be taken completely out of her hands. She didn't want that. This was her and Angel's adventure, even if it had to take place on a shoestring budget.

'A *cab*.' Rita said the word like it would be driven by the leader of a terrorist organisation.

'Yes, Mum. And it will be fine. It will be just like the one we used to get here, only smaller and yellow, probably driven by someone who talks more Brooklyn than Billericay.'

'But why would you do that?' Rita continued.

This was why she'd wanted to leave her mother back in Wiltshire. A pleasant goodbye at the broken gate, air kisses and hugs neither of them really meant, then away. Liberty. That sounded mean. Hayley swallowed and offered her mother a smile, deciding to change tack

'Angel, do you have any more George Washington facts you'd like to share from your special dictionary?'

'He was born in Virginia and he didn't have any children,' Angel said, thumbing the pages.

'I expect Dean has company cars at his disposal. He needn't have come in person.' Rita unzipped her patchwork leather handbag. 'I'll give him a call.'

'No!'

Hayley surprised herself with the volume of her voice. She put her lips back together and tried to subconsciously tell her body not to let the colour red she felt hit her cheeks. The couple in front of them did a surreptitious glance backwards. There was only one thing for it.

'Sorry.' She let out a breath. 'Sorry, Mum, I shouldn't have shouted. It's just we're running a bit late and flying is so stressful.'

Rita screwed up her nose. 'I don't know what's stressful about sitting doing nothing but watch television for eight hours.'

The sentence *well you should know* was at Hayley's lips but she pressed them shut and said nothing. After all, her mother thought this was just a Christmas trip, a few weeks in the Big Apple and then home again. Rita knew nothing of the mission or Hayley's crazy dream, the itch that New York could be an opportunity not just a vacation. Unless her mother had been reading her ten year diary. She shuddered. If that ever happened she'd be booking a one-way ticket around the world and never coming back. She was starting to regret not bringing it with her.

She only hoped the cheap, ugly toys would do their job and keep it from being found. There would be no stopping the flipping of pages if Rita discovered it. There was no such thing as privacy where her mother was concerned. Your business was her business but only because she wanted to have an opinion on it, not because she actually cared.

Angel piped up. 'Actually the flight time is seven and a half hours and one of the films is Alvin and the Chipmunks.'

'Great,' Hayley said. 'Annoying, singing rodents. That should pass the time and soothe the stress right out of everybody.'

'Anyone would think you're not looking forward to this holiday,' Rita said.

She was obviously making too much out of this and her mother's relentless questioning wasn't helping. She had to make it out of the country without a whiff of anything other than Happy Holidays plans.

'Don't be silly. Of course I'm looking forward to it. It's snowing there, isn't it, Angel?' Hayley grinned at her daughter.

'Yes, minus four degrees and set to get so cold you could throw a pan of boiling water in the air and watch it turn to snow before your eyes.'

'I'm not sure throwing pans of hot water around is something to be encouraged,' Rita said seriously, directing her gaze at Hayley.

'It's all over the TV,' Angel said.

'So is that awful woman who sings about snakes and that's definitely not a good thing.'

Hayley furrowed her brow at her mother. 'Do you mean Nicki Minaj?' She shuddered again. 'Because I hate to tell you this but she's not actually singing about snakes.'

'Did you know snakes don't have eyelids,' Angel asked, hugging her dictionary to her chest.

'How did a conversation about snow turn into this?' Hayley looked desperately at the rows of people ahead of her. 'And why won't this bloody queue move?'

'If you're getting anxious here, you wait until you see the queues for taxis at JFK,' Rita said.

Hayley spoke through gritted teeth. 'I *have* been to New York before.'

Rita shot her a look. 'How could I forget?'

Hayley swallowed and moved her eyes to Angel who was regarding them both, sensing the atmosphere but not knowing the cause.

'You're right,' Hayley said quickly. 'But we're British. We're experts at queuing and waiting our turn. If all else fails I'll act all foppish and bumbling like Hugh Grant and wait for someone to take pity on us.'

Angel let out a tinkle of a laugh while Rita just continued to look sour. Only Hayley knew the puckered lips were all for her and nothing to do with the Fisherman's Friend.

'Mum, we're going to have to go through security because we have a gate allocated already.'

Hayley watched Rita fuss around Angel. The hair was being pressed into place, the red coat – still a bone of contention for her mother – was being fastened up tight, her cheeks cupped, kind words being expressed.

'Now,' Rita started. 'Remember to look both ways very carefully when you cross the road because they drive on the right.'

'Yes, Nanny,' Angel said with sincerity.

'And don't have a hot dog from one of those street vendors on the corner of everywhere. There's a reason they don't have a shop.'

'Yes, Nanny.'

Hayley immediately craved the biggest hot dog they could find from the grungiest looking guy the second they got there. 'We have to go.'

'All right!' Rita barked. 'Can't I have five minutes to say goodbye to my granddaughter?'

And your daughter. Hayley chewed her lip and tried to dismiss the words that bit. It was good Rita cared so much about Angel. She checked her watch again.

'I hope your hospital appointment goes OK, Nanny,' Angel said. Rita would be fine. A neighbour was going with her to the hospital and she had a year's supply of after dinner mints and an arctic roll.

'Freda and I will have a pensioner's lunch at the coffee shop there.' She put her hands on Angel's shoulders. 'Don't forget to give your Uncle Dean a kiss from me and tell him how much I miss him.'

The golden child. The one she put up on a pedestal as high as the Chrysler Building. Hayley cleared her throat, hoping to dislodge the bad feeling.

'I hope you have a lovely Christmas, Nanny. I'll call you,' Angel said, smiling at her grandmother.

'Oh don't you worry about me, Angel. I'll have one of those meals for widows and single people from Marks and Spencer.'

Hayley closed her eyes. If she mentioned getting out the electric fan heater or watching *Pollyanna* she was seriously going to lose it.

'Right then, off we go,' Hayley said, pulling Angel towards her by the fabric hook on the back of her rucksack.

'Bye, Nanny,' Angel chirped.

Hayley felt her mother's eyes on her but didn't know what to do. Hugging always felt so awkward and air-kissing was even worse. Guilt was now winning out over everything else.

'Bye, Mum. Happy Holidays as they say in New York.' Hayley stepped forward, ready to embrace her mother with everything she had. Instead she impacted on Rita's foot.

The noise that came from her mother's mouth was akin to a cat having its tail trodden on. A yelp and a stagger had Angel rushing to her grandmother's side.

'Sorry,' Hayley breathed. 'Sorry, Mum.'

'Are you all right, Nanny?' Angel asked, concern etched on her features.

'Yes …' Rita let out a jagged breath. 'Nothing the chiropodist can't fix I don't expect.'

Hayley didn't dare move her feet a second time. 'Well, if you're sure you can make it back to wait for the taxi driver then we'll head off.' They really couldn't wait any longer. And the emotion just wasn't coming.

'Bye, Nanny,' Angel said again.

Hayley put her arm around her daughter and, drawing her close, she simply waved a hand.

CHAPTER SEVEN

Drummond Global Offices, Downtown Manhattan, USA

'Good morning, Mr Drummond.'

It wasn't a good morning. He felt like shit. Christa had turned out to be the most insatiable woman he had bedded in over a month. His mouth was dry not only from the champagne but also from the humidity of the hotel room heating she insisted on turning up to simulate the temperature of a rainforest. That had been just one of the fantasies she'd wanted to act out. Some of the others involved food from the room service menu he never wanted to see again.

He forced a smile at the blonde receptionist and noticed for the first time that she wore glasses. Did he know her name? Had they dated? He wasn't sure he wanted to know the answer to that last question.

'Good morning,' he responded, heading for the bank of lifts.

As he waited for one to arrive he looked through the glass doors to the street outside. The snow had stopped overnight and only a fine dusting remained. It was business as usual on the street, taxis, bike couriers, shoppers, workers, guys on roller-skates like they were auditioning for *Starlight Express*. Icicles hung from the building signs, there was a glaze of frost on fire hydrants and lampposts and the corners of billboards were streaked with a sprinkling of white.

The bell chimed and the silver metal doors slid open. He stepped inside and hit the button for the eightieth floor. It struck him then, as the elevator began to rise, that he had no idea what was in his schedule for the day. How had that happened? Maybe Clara was right. Had he dropped the ball lately? He checked his watch. It was a little after nine. He hoped there was nothing for at least an hour or he might have to send out for mouthwash.

The elevator finally came to a stop and when the doors opened there was Clara. She was wearing maroon, another statement necklace at her throat, but the expression on her face was one of concern.

'Good morning, Clara,' he stated hesitantly.

'We have a problem,' his PA said without prelude.

'Have you called Mackenzie?' he asked, beginning to walk along the corridor towards his office.

'It isn't a legal problem,' Clara said. 'It's—'

He interrupted her. 'I didn't have a nine o' clock appointment, did I?' He powered on past the other offices towards his room at the very end of the walkway.

'No, but, Oliver wait, listen to me before you go in there,' Clara rasped as she broke into a jog, chasing him.

He put his hand on the door but stopped, turning to look at his assistant. Her face was the colour of an overripe strawberry and there were beads of perspiration above the beads of the necklace.

'Your mother is in there,' Clara whispered, pointing at the office door.

He creased up his face in the hope his ears were as dry and deficient as his throat. 'Sorry, Clara, could you say that again?'

'Your mother is in your office,' she repeated.

It was his turn to perspire. He could feel the collar of his shirt getting a little tight, his body reacting to the statement in the way it always did where his mother was concerned lately. He wanted to run, or at least turn on his heel and head back down the corridor to the bank of elevators. He could call Tony. They could head out to play golf. Blast away his hangover and his worries on the fairway, spend a couple of hours in the nineteenth hole. He blinked, coming back into reality.

'What do we do?' The words were out of his mouth before he thought about how infantile he sounded.

'What do *we* do? Oliver, I told you this would happen if you kept ignoring her calls.'

Clara was gesticulating at him, her hands flying about to get her point across like a desperate shadow puppet act. And she was right of course. She had warned him several times that if he didn't call his mother back she would turn up at his penthouse or here. And there wasn't a lot he could do about it. He might control the company but she was also a member of the board. This was as much her building as it was his. But he knew already her visit wasn't about the business. No, this was definitely personal.

He inhaled a long breath and put his hand to the tie at his throat, straightening it, ensuring it gave away nothing about the night before. Straight away the twinging in his chest began. He almost welcomed it. If the Grim Reaper took him now he wouldn't have to deal with this conversation. He closed his eyes, holding his form steady.

'Make us some coffee, Clara. I've got this.'

And then he just stood, his hand on the door, listening to Clara's dull footsteps on the carpet as she powered off to arrange the drinks. He was making far too much of this. It was his mother. He loved his mother, very much. He pushed the handle down and opened the door.

Stepping into the room, he watched her stand from the seat opposite his desk. He took in the black patent court shoes, the bright orange designer shift dress, the matching wool jacket over it, and her perfectly coiffured blonde hair. Nothing out of place. Cynthia Drummond was fifty-five but still looked mid-forties.

'Mom,' he greeted, striding across the floor towards her, arms open.

He embraced her fully, letting her hug his body to hers like she always did. He drew away first.

'This is a surprise. You should have told me you were coming. I would have been more organised,' Oliver said, moving behind his desk and sitting down. He picked up his pen and rubbed his thumb over the barrel.

'Nonsense, Oliver, you would have found a reason not to be here,' Cynthia said, sitting back down and picking her Gucci handbag up off the floor. She placed it on her lap.

He let out a laugh. 'I wouldn't have done that.' The words came out a little too quickly.

'You've been avoiding my calls,' Cynthia carried on.

The second she said the sentence all he could see were the pile of yellow notes Clara had been sticking to his desk for the past couple of weeks. He swallowed. 'It's been very full on here and ...'

Cynthia cut him off. 'I know what this is about, Oliver. It's what it's always about.'

It didn't sound like she required him to give an answer. He sat still, his thumb working overtime on the pen until it started to hurt.

'It's December isn't it. You're always like this in December,' Cynthia said. It didn't sound like she wanted to be interrupted.

He put the pen down on the desk and picked up his baseball stress ball, squeezing it in his palm. 'I don't know what you mean.'

'One word.' She paused for a breath before continuing. 'Christmas.'

He felt the hairs on the back of his neck raise up like she'd said something really offensive. Why did he have such a problem with the word? How could nine letters make him want to crawl under his desk and not come out until it was all over?

'I need to know if you're coming home.'

His mother's voice started to fracture just a little and it got to him. He squeezed the stress ball harder.

'I thought you could spend some time at the house. Sophia and Pablo miss you.' She stopped for a moment, as if to recollect. 'And so do I.'

He squeezed the ball until it disappeared into his palm completely. Christmas wasn't the same without his father and brother. The family home in Westchester wasn't the same. It was cold, empty, bereft, despite his mother's attempts to make it into some sort of stately show home. There were new drapes every second month, urns of flowers everywhere, any frill and frippery to fill the gaps. And he definitely wasn't being blackmailed by her use of the housekeeper who had been around since he was a teen and her ten-year-old son who played a mean game of hockey.

'Mom, it's always difficult around Christmas, you know that.' He put the ball down and laid the flats of his palms on the desk. 'I'm in the middle of a hard negotiation right now that's going to go right down to the wire.'

'I know all about the Regis Software merger, I *am* a member of the board.' She let out a sigh. 'I'm not asking you to take the next two weeks off work, Oliver. I'm asking for one day, maybe a couple of nights.' Cynthia unfastened her bag and removed a handkerchief. 'Bring Tony if you have to.'

'Tony's going to Italy,' he responded.

'With his family?'

'I guess.'

'Because family's important.'

'Mom, don't get upset,' he said as she dabbed at her eyes.

'You're giving me no other option.' She sniffed. 'Since your father passed …'

'Stop.'

It was one short word but he'd said it with enough power to call a halt to anything.

Oliver sprung from his chair. He headed towards the full-length windows, leaning one arm against the pane of glass, looking at the buildings surrounding the Drummond offices. The pain in his chest was making itself known again as he tried to concentrate on the metal and steel in his sightline. The Chrysler Building. Art Deco like the Empire State but completely unique with its ornate arches leading to the spire at its pinnacle. Spikes of industry, sharp shards of ironwork – the ache in his torso stabbed harder.

His mom had no idea how he felt. None whatsoever. It wasn't just the memories, it was his future, or rather his lack of it. She may be living without a husband and her eldest son, but he was living with a ticking time bomb. He didn't want to be her crutch. She had to get used to loneliness because it was going to happen to her again. And this time there would be no one left. He squeezed his eyes tight shut, blocking out the wintery cityscape.

'Oliver, if we don't ever speak about your father and your brother it will be like they didn't even exist.'

He could hear her tears now but he couldn't turn around and face her. He couldn't have this conversation. He leaned his weight heavily against the window, letting it hold him up, bear his strain for just a moment. He kept his eyes closed and all his deepest memories, vivid pictures from the past, rushed his brain at once.

His father, Richard, tall, thickset, with a sweep of dark hair that had always taken some taming. Eyes that had constantly twinkled, in fun, or shining with a new idea or a triumph to share with the family. Heavy jowls that vibrated when he talked, and that smooth, commanding voice that had issued instructions to his employees as brilliantly as it had given praise and encouragement to his children. Richard had been comfortable in any role. Dressing up as one of Santa's elves for charity, speaking at the funerals of their friends and family or negotiating million pound software contracts. He had been much loved and much admired.

Just like Ben. Oliver's big brother. The tall, strong, dark-haired boy he'd grown up with and had looked up to. Ben wasn't just the image of Richard, he had replicated their father's professionalism and poise perfectly. He'd inherited that instinct and ability to adapt to any situation he found himself in. Or, sometimes, situations he'd found Oliver in. One time involved trespass and the police when their parents were out of town. Ben had cooled the police officer down as effectively as throwing a cold bucket of water over him. Nothing had fazed him.

They'd lost Richard just last year, right before Christmas, and Ben had died five years before that, just three days before his thirtieth birthday. Just like their paternal grandfather. And that was the Drummond curse, a genetic fault. Richard had made it to sixty-five. And that made him the exception. The lucky one. Which meant, to Oliver, that his days were numbered. He turned thirty in just a few months.

'Come home for Christmas, Oliver. We'll have turkey and I'll arrange a tree.'

Now he'd let these memories in there was no stopping them. All he could see, cluttering up his mind, were images of his father, his brother and him from their last Christmas together.

They'd had far too much turkey dinner then had wrapped up in four layers of clothing to descend upon the neighbourhood, throwing snowballs, sledging, and making snowmen with the kids. Not an agenda or an iPad in sight. Laughter, red cheeks, hot breath in the air and running until their toes went numb.

He couldn't lose it here. He couldn't let her know how it affected him. He was the one who had held the business together while the rest of the world gave in to their grief. And that's why he was an emotionless stalwart. Because caring was pointless and would only do more damage in the end.

'I can't,' he stated coolly.

'Oliver …' Cynthia started to counter.

He turned then, facing her but not looking at her. 'I really can't, Mom. I'll be working.' He knew his voice was cold but that was what this situation required him to be. He clenched the muscles in his jaw.

'On Christmas Day? Really?'

'The business doesn't ever switch off.' He held his stance.

'The offices have never opened on Christmas Day since your grandfather founded the business.'

'And he dropped dead two weeks later.'

'Oliver!'

The exclamation was shrill, the same tone she'd used on him when he was a kid getting into things he shouldn't. He should apologise. His words were uncalled for. It was a low blow when she was already emotional. His mother was getting to her feet but he wasn't going to stop her. This needed tough love. He had to be cruel to be kind

'If you won't spend Christmas Day with me then you leave me with no other choice,' Cynthia said, slipping the handbag over her shoulder then rolling the tissue inside the sleeve of her jacket.

This didn't sound like a better option. This sounded like she was about to launch a grenade his way. He met her gaze then and waited for her next words.

'It's the Christmas fundraiser for the McArthur Foundation coming up. As well as organising the whole event and sweet-talking the local dignitaries for donations, they've also asked me to speak this year.' Cynthia took two steps towards the door. 'Thank you for nominating yourself in my place. I'll email you the details.'

She couldn't do that to him. She wouldn't.

'Mom, I can't,' he said. He dug his hands down into the pockets of his trousers to hide the tremor.

A chill settled on his skin as what she'd said started to sink in. Talking in public was what he did. But about technology. About the company's work, implementation and progress, lines of strategy. Not about anything personal. The McArthur Foundation fundraiser was a sparkling, twinkling, barrel of Christmas affair. There would be tables of notable Manhattan businessmen and women, probably the mayor and the police commissioner, but much worse than that, families of people affected by the cause the money was being raised for.

'No, Oliver, you can. And you *will*.' She put her hand on the door. 'You might be able to let me down without a second thought, but you will *not* let down that charity or betray our connection to it.'

Cynthia whipped open the door and very nearly bowled into Clara carrying the tray of coffee.

'Oh, Mrs Drummond I was …' Clara started.

'I can't stay I'm afraid, Clara.' Cynthia cast a look back Oliver's way. 'I don't want to take up any more of Oliver's precious time.'

He swallowed the pebble of emotion in his throat and dropped his eyes to the floor. Could this day get any worse?

CHAPTER EIGHT

Drummond Global Offices, Downtown Manhattan, USA

Oliver had been staring at the figures so hard they were all merging into one big numerical mess. He had structured and re-structured these figures for the Globe so many times. He strained his eyes, forcing them to look harder at the chart in front of him. They actually ached, hurting from overuse. He sat back in his chair and pinched the bridge of his nose with his thumb and forefinger. If he was truthful to himself he'd had a headache ever since his mother had left the office that morning. He'd bumbled his way through a lunch meeting, Cole having to do most of the work to get the client onside, and then he'd spent the rest of the day holed up in his office looking at figures and proposals he should have looked at weeks ago. Now he was trying to direct his focus on the thing he cared about most at the moment, the launch of his tablet. He picked up his pen, held it over the report for a second then dropped it back to the desk. It was no good.

The only thing on his mind was the damn McArthur Foundation fundraiser. And how he was going to get out of it. Because that's what he had to do. There was no way he was going to let his mother put him in that position. The charity stuff was her thing, not his. She liked it. She spent half her life doing it. He, on the other hand, detested the emotion of it all. If people wanted to donate money to a cause then good for them, but he didn't see the need for dressing up in tuxedos and ball gowns to show how well-meaning you were. Blatant publicity seeking like that had never been his bag.

He grabbed up the baseball stress ball and squeezed it tight in his hand until his knuckles turned white. He released his grip just as the door swung open. Clara came in, almost dropping the files she was holding.

'Oh, Oliver, you gave me a scare. I didn't realise you were still here.'

He looked at his watch. 'What are you still doing here? It's almost seven.'

'I had a couple of things to finish off while it's quiet.' She put the files into his in-tray. 'These can all wait for the morning.'

'Then you should go home,' he said, putting the ball back on the table.

'I will if you will,' Clara said, folding her arms across her chest.

'As fun as it is to play parlour games with you, I'm not really in the right frame of mind.' He let out a breath and picked up one of the files she had just delivered.

'The meeting with your mother didn't go so well.'

'It was fine. She was just being a mother and I was playing the son role very badly. Same old.'

'She told me you've refused to go home for Christmas,' Clara said, adjusting her stance. 'That you said you were working.'

'I will be.'

'Why? We're not open for business.'

'Believe it or not, Clara, there's a great deal of stuff that goes on in the background here.'

'Nothing that can't stop for Christmas Day.'

'Maybe some of us don't want to stop for a sentimental overdose of carols, candy canes and candles at midnight.'

'You heard what the doctor said yesterday.'

Why wasn't she giving up? He just wanted to be left alone. Wanting to spend one day in December doing something different to everyone else shouldn't be a crime. And he shouldn't be constantly judged for it. 'The doctor saw the business suit and made a call based on that.'

'Oliver, it was a bit more than that.'

He shook his head. 'Is there a point to this conversation?'

'Well, that depends.'

She was looking at him with an expression that said *I'm going to treat you like a naughty schoolboy until you start listening*.

'On what?' he asked.

'Whether you want my help with the McArthur Foundation fundraiser.'

He stood up then, shaking his head and moving towards the bank of windows. 'She told you that too.'

'She's worried about you, Oliver, and so am I,' Clara continued.

He looked out at the Manhattan skyline, lights shining bright as the sky turned black. He could just see the inky tidal movement of the Hudson River, ferries creeping back to the docks. The snow was falling again, thick flurries settling over the thin layer left from the previous night. Here he was, viewing the most incredible scene, an enviable setting and all he felt was trapped.

'Don't waste your energy on me, Clara. I'm a lost cause.' The words were out before he'd even thought about it. Did he really believe that? And if he did, did he really want Clara to know? She was his personal assistant not his counsellor.

'Phooey!'

'I'm twenty-nine, Clara. You do the math.'

'If I thought you were going to drop dead so soon I would have left before you became the CEO.'

'No you wouldn't. There isn't another employer in the city who pays more.'

He heard Clara's exhalation and regretted not thinking again. He didn't change position. If he kept focussing on the outside she might just leave.

'And that's why you think I work for Drummond Global? Why I work for you?'

There was definite resentment in her tone now. He'd done that. Just by making a stupid, flippant remark.

'It's why most other people work here.'

'If that's what you truly believe, Oliver, then you have even bigger problems than I thought.'

He nodded to himself. He didn't need to be told that. He was just a screw-up waiting to die. He turned around just in time for the slam of his office door to tell him he was pretty much burning his bridges with everyone.

His phone vibrated in the pocket of his trousers. Pulling it free, he checked the display. He pressed to answer and put it to his ear. 'Hey.'

'Hey, Drummond, what's happening in the financial sector? Gone into oil yet?'

Tony's Italian-Brooklyn accent managed to get a smile from him.

'Has papa started serving fries with those pizzas?'

'That's low, man.'

'You started it.' He looked out at the lights of the city, finally feeling an internal thaw.

'Listen, you up for something tonight? I'm cooling my heels and fancy heating them up a little.'

'Things not go so well with the Pole?'

'Tonight's a brand new adventure just waiting to happen, man.'

Oliver smiled, loosening off his tie. 'Give me an hour.'

Brooklyn Bridge, New York

'Can we stop? Please! Can we stop, Uncle Dean?'

Angel had had her face pressed against the darkened windows of the limo since they'd left JFK Airport. As predicted, Rita had called Dean, probably in the advert breaks of *The Chase*, and given him all the details of their flight. They'd been made to feel like felons having their photos and fingerprints taken before they were allowed into the country, then Dean had been waiting in the arrivals lounge, their names in Sharpie on a cardboard sign bordered in red tinsel. Why he'd thought he needed a sign Hayley didn't know but it had made Angel squeal with excitement and Hayley's stomach had fluttered with a mix of longing and love for her brother as he'd gathered her up in a hug befitting of a missing relative found on *Surprise Surprise*. After an almost eight hour flight and looking rough, the last thing she wanted was to be stood next to Holly Willoughby.

Angel had been wrestled up onto Dean's shoulders only until he realised just how much she'd grown since his last visit home. He'd dropped her down to the ground, clasped her hand instead and led the way outside. A sea of yellow taxis had greeted them and a line of weary travellers waiting their turn for a ride. The limousine waiting for the Walker party was a welcome sight although Hayley was never going to admit that to her mother.

'Gabe, can you pull over?' Dean called to the driver. 'My niece wants to stop.'

'Sir, I wouldn't recommend doing that. Some of the other drivers told me the cops are getting hot on cars that pull over on the bridge.'

'It's OK, Dean. She doesn't need to see everything this second. We can walk the bridge tomorrow or something,' Hayley said.

'No, Mum. I want to see it now. Please, Uncle Dean!'

'Pull it over, Gabe. We see a cop car, we'll jump back in and outrun them like an episode of *Blue Bloods*. How does that sound?' He grinned at Angel and offered his hand for a high five.

Hayley watched their hands connect, the utter joy taking over her daughter's features. This was all so exciting for her. Seeing New York for the very first time *was* special. It was Angel's first moments here, ones she would remember forever. Just like she had. The smell of the city – it's living, breathing heart, its electricity – the feeling that you were right in the midst of something that was constantly evolving. She'd stood on the Brooklyn Bridge at eighteen with her whole life stretching out before her. Wishes, dreams, a blank canvas to fill up any way she chose. She remembered stretching her arms above her head and feeling the breeze filter through each finger. Freedom, a foreign country, dollars in her pocket and a few weeks of indulgence before she knuckled down to college. And then there was that one night, way too much vodka and a Belgian called Michel.

The car pulling to a stop made Hayley come to. Angel was already tugging at the door handle before the brakes had fully engaged.

'Wait, Angel. You have to be careful.' She had visions of Angel stepping into traffic and being mown down. 'There are a lot more cars here than at home.'

Angel let out a hiss of annoyance. 'I'm not sure that's actually true. Most people here use the subway.'

'OK, Miss Smarty Pants, have it your way. Fly out of there, but be prepared to get up close and personal with a van load of Krispy Kremes,' Hayley bit back.

'Hey, it's OK. She's just excited,' Dean said, sitting forward on the seat. 'I'll look after her.'

Hayley let out a sigh. Why was she so jumpy? The guy from airport immigration had set her on edge like he was a mind reader, privy to her innermost thoughts. He'd asked a million questions – who she was visiting, how long for, her plans for the holidays – and then Dean had been there. Calm, confident, gorgeous Dean, who she loved with all her heart but who just seemed to do everything a whole lot better than she did. Including managing her daughter. Her parenting skills were all she had since fashion dreams had been given up. She thought she was doing OK but Dean, clever, industry-led Dean, was just such a natural with his niece. And Angel adored him, bonding again immediately. Was this because a male figure in her life was a novelty? Or because it was something she craved? Would this be what it would be like with her father in her life?

Angel opened the car door, slipping out and stepping up to the metal and wire barrier. Hayley heard the 'wow' before her daughter's feet even hit the snow-covered tarmac. She followed Dean and Angel out of the car and joined them at the edge of the bridge.

And there was that view. Straight out of the movies. A scene so well-known but so completely different when you saw it for real, when it was that close.

High-rise buildings towered up from the banks of the Hudson River, shards of light bouncing off the water, reflecting in the ripples of the tide. Squares of yellow and rectangles of orange and white lights came from the tall, slim blocks across the river.

Firm, foreboding but somehow also welcoming. Snow speckled the view, large, slow-moving flakes drifting in the breeze.

'Which is the highest building, Uncle Dean?'

Hayley looked to Angel. She had her feet up on the first rung of the metalwork, leaning out, but her brother was directly behind her, his body close, his arms holding Angel steady. Snowflakes were settling on their hair. There were moments, like this one, where she saw elements of Michel in her daughter. It was something about her profile, the shape of her nose and definitely her eyes. Hayley continued to watch Angel with Dean. One night ten years ago had never mattered more than it did now.

'That's the One World Trade Centre. It stands at one thousand seven hundred and seventy six feet and has a hundred and four floors.'

'Wow,' Angel said.

'See, it's there,' Dean said, pointing across the water.

'How many steps does it have?' Hayley asked.

'I don't know that, but I do know it has elevators,' Dean responded, grinning at her.

'Mum didn't really want to know. She was trying to be funny,' Angel told him.

'I know, Angel. She did it all the time when we were growing up.' He tickled Angel's ribs until she had to jump back down onto the road. 'So, are you hungry?'

'I am. We had chicken on the plane but that was hours ago,' Angel answered.

'How about Chinese? I know this great little restaurant,' Dean suggested.

'Oh, we don't need to go out anywhere,' Hayley began.

'My treat,' Dean said.

'Yes!' Angel did an air pump.

'Well, why don't you hop back in the car and we'll go and get us some dim sum and fortune cookies,' Dean said, opening the door for Angel.

Once the excited nine-year-old was back in the car Hayley let out a sigh that had her shoulders rolling. She clutched hold of the ironwork of the bridge but quickly let go as her fingers froze.

'Are you going to tell me what's wrong?' Dean asked, putting a hand on her shoulder.

She hadn't known her brother was so close. The comfort almost brought tears to her eyes and she realised in that moment just how much she missed him. He'd been here, in New York, since she was seventeen and only now did she grasp just how much that had challenged her. He was her big brother, the only one who had never judged or asked too many questions.

She forced a smile but she wasn't sure it had met her eyes. 'I'm fine.' How could she even begin to tell him everything that was wrong? It was easier this way.

He shook his head. 'Come on, Hay, you've never been able to lie to me since the day you hid your Barbie's dresses just so I couldn't put them on Action Man.'

She couldn't help the laugh escaping. 'I didn't understand back then.'

'Making soldiers cross-dress just seemed natural,' Dean said in a camp voice. 'I'm sure I wasn't alone.'

She looked her brother up and down. Brown brogue shoes, dark blue designer jeans, clean shaven, with his short brown hair gelled up to perfection. His blue knit coat was collecting snowflakes and it was almost exactly like the last time she was here. Younger, more excited, but still vulnerable.

'What is it?' Dean said in no more than a whisper.

Hayley shook her head and forced a smile. It wasn't the right time. She wanted to be closer to having answers, find a trail and be heading towards a result before she let anyone in on it. 'It's so good to see you.'

And then her cheeks hit the wool of Dean's coat and the flakes of white mushed up against her skin as he embraced her hard. She breathed in the scent of his cologne, savouring all the memories it brought back. Fun, laughter, simple, uncomplicated times.

'You're in New York, Hay! New York! My adopted home town! And it's Christmas time!' Dean swung her about in his arms like she was a fabric doll. Then he held her away from him, hands planted on the side of her reddened cheeks as he swayed her head from side to side. 'I have a whole list of things for us to do. We're going to finally get you in a horse and cart. We're going to go skating at the Rockefeller Centre. Vern is going to get us tickets for something on Broadway.' An ecstatic sigh left him. 'It's going to be the best two weeks of your life!'

Hayley took back control of her head. 'Who's Vern?'

For a second the wind was taken out of Dean's sails but then he laughed and clamped a hand on her shoulder. 'Nice try. Your daughter never keeps anything secret. She must have told you about Vern.'

Hayley smiled. 'She might have. But I definitely need to know more about Randy. Please tell me it's a dog and not a pet name.'

CHAPTER NINE

Asian Dawn, South William Street, New York

'You going to eat that or stare at it like it wants to buy all your shares?'

Tony shovelled in a mouthful of beansprouts and pulled at Oliver's plate with his spare hand. His black hair bounced around his forehead as he devoured the food on his plate, spatters of juice speckling his olive skin.

Oliver shook his head at his friend. 'Really? Just because I don't eat like a starving woolly mammoth?' He pulled the plate back towards him.

Tony was right though. He had ordered food he didn't even want. After the heated debate with Clara, his brain was fried. He hadn't been able to concentrate on the Regis Software merger paperwork and the stress ball had been given the pounding of its life. He needed to unwind. He was coiled so tightly in every area of his life and now he had his mother on his back. As if he didn't have enough going on. Maybe the doctor was right. Maybe a rapid physical dismantling could happen at any time. A breakdown. *Or a heart attack.*

He picked some noodles up with his chopsticks and put them to his mouth, hoping the ingestion of food would quell the panic, soften the ache in his chest wall. He chewed slowly, trying to savour the subtle flavours, concentrate on just the eating, nothing else. His eyes moved to the other patrons, enjoying the fine food and the unique ambiance of the restaurant. Red paper lanterns hung from vantage points around the room, elaborate Chinese plates and ornaments adorned the walls and each table had a delicate, fresh orchid in its centre with a glowing tea light candle.

'So, what's happening in your world?'

Oliver turned his attention back to Tony. 'Ah, you know, the usual.'

'Really? Because Momma heard they called an ambulance for you yesterday.'

Oliver threw his napkin to the table and inhaled a breath. 'All of my staff have signed a confidentiality clause.'

'And most of them eat at the family restaurant. What can I say?' Tony lifted his shoulders nonchalantly.

He would identify the employee who was sharing information and make sure they were reprimanded. Reports of ill health, Chinese whispers through the city, would do the company no good whatsoever.

'Well? I'm waiting here,' Tony said, his brown eyes fixed on him.

He swallowed. 'There's nothing to tell.'

'No?'

'No.' He didn't sound convincing and he knew Tony wouldn't be fooled.

He dropped his eyes to his plate of food, considering what to say next, if anything. He heard Tony suck in a breath and a chink of glassware made him raise his head.

'Well, you're here so you didn't die,' Tony stated.

'I admire your powers of observation.'

Tony shook his head. 'I don't understand you. We've had this conversation so many times. You said you weren't going to let this thing take over.'

'It's kind of hard not to.'

'Pa!' Tony waved a meaty hand in the air. 'We all know the worst that could happen. You could keel over right here right now, your head in black bean sauce, stomach empty, unfulfilled …' Tony lowered his voice a notch. 'Not been laid in forty-eight hours …'

'Actually it's a little under twenty-four.'

'Last night?' Tony asked, eyes wide. 'Man, you're good.' He took a swig from his beer bottle. 'So what's the problem? You made it out of the hospital instead of being transferred to the mortuary, it's all good.'

'My mom wants me to go home for Christmas and, if I don't, she's going to make me speak at the McArthur Foundation fundraiser.'

'That cold slab at the mortuary is sounding tempting,' Tony teased.

Oliver put down his chopsticks and picked up his beer bottle. 'You don't understand what it's like. You have a million cousins, nieces and nephews for Christmas, I have my mom, the shroud of death hanging over the place and Pablo quizzing me on the NHL which I never have time to watch anymore.'

'What d'you want me to say?'

'I don't know. That I'm not being a Grade A jerk. That I have every right not to want to spend that day in December that way.' He was getting agitated just talking about it. He shifted in his seat as an uncomfortable current of pain ran up his left arm.

'Look at it this way. What scares the crap out of you the most? Spending a few hours stuffing yourself full of turkey with your mom? Or standing up in front of a room full of New York's finest, talking about your dad and Ben?'

Oliver flinched and tried to hide it by picking up his chopsticks and spearing a clump of noodles. He knew the answer to that. The public affair scared him a lot more than visiting home for the day, but both scenarios were going to open up closed wounds and remind him what he was living with.

'I don't know,' Tony said, sitting back in his chair. 'I could kill you now instead. We could order up a bottle of Scotch and go out with a bang.'

Oliver couldn't help the corners of his mouth twitching. Only Tony could turn his death sentence into a joke. His friend had been making him laugh since 1989. Tony's parents' Italian restaurant, Romario's, had been the Drummond's Friday night out since he was old enough to eat solid food. It was one of the few places he'd visited with his father and brother that he still went to. There wasn't room for grief amongst the larger-than-life personalities of the Romario family.

'Seriously, man, if *I* knew I wasn't going to make old age I wouldn't be wasting a second worrying about it. I'd be living it.'

'I *do* live it,' he countered.

Tony snorted. 'In between panicking about it.'

There was that word again. *Panic.* From the mouth of his best friend.

'Order some more drinks,' Tony said. 'And I promise, you drop here and now, I'll keep every secret you ever told me for at least a month after the funeral. After that, it's open season and capitalising on every talk show this side of the seaboard.'

The car stopped outside the Asian Dawn restaurant and Angel's jaw dropped at the sight of the frontage. There were china painted dragons, ivory-coloured statues and two flaming torches at the door. Strings of tinsel adorned the dragons' necks, a garland of gold-coloured candy canes hung over the doorframe and, fixed to the wall, was an image of Santa Claus holding the reins to his sleigh, which flashed on and off in stages of red, white and green.

Angel opened the car door and jumped out onto the pavement, running up to the nearest ornate dragon. As she got out too, Hayley watched her daughter smooth her hands over the pottery mane, fingering the swirls and dips in the masonry.

Angel turned then, looking at her. 'Can I have anything I want?'

This restaurant looked like something out of a James Bond Shanghai scene. Everything about it signalled top dollar. She'd be lucky to afford a tip let alone a meal.

Hayley opened her mouth to speak.

Dean beat her to it. 'Of course you can.'

'Do they have ice cream?'

'Only the best ice cream in Manhattan.'

'Dean …' Hayley started as Angel headed to the door. 'This place looks lovely but it also looks like somewhere Kim and Kanye would come to be seen.' She let a breath out. 'It looks expensive and …'

Dean reached out, putting a hand on her shoulder. 'It's on me.'

'You can't do that the whole time we're here, Dean.' She locked eyes with him. 'And I don't want you to. It isn't fair.'

Dean smiled. 'Tonight is my treat.' He patted her shoulder. 'Come on, let's fill you both up with New York's good stuff.'

Hayley smiled. She had to admit the thought of sweet and sour chicken and the best ice cream in Manhattan was more than a little tempting. And if she ran into Kimye … well she'd maybe suggest that Kim's colouring went much better with gold than red.

Tony let out a belch. 'So what was she like?'

Oliver creased his brow at the question. 'Who?'

'Miss Less-Than-Twenty-Four-Hours-Ago'

Christa. This one he remembered the name of. 'If I'm honest, a little bit creepy.'

'Yeah?' Tony shifted his body forward in his seat and looked increasingly interested.

'She made me pretend I was a lemur.'

Tony laughed out loud, a sound that echoed the whole way round the restaurant and back again like an audible boomerang.

'It's not funny,' Oliver hissed.

'I don't see the issue.' Tony wiped his face with his napkin.

'It works in your perverted world maybe.'

'Did you get her number?'

'Absolutely not.'

'Shame,' Tony grinned. 'I would have been any animal she wanted me to be.'

Oliver shook his head at his friend as Tony's mobile phone erupted into life.

'Hey,' Tony answered, shifting back in his chair. 'Momma, no, I can't.' He rolled his eyes as he looked to Oliver. 'Momma, Ivano does this every second week …' He continued the conversation in loud Italian Oliver had no hope of ever translating even if he did know some of the language.

Oliver toyed with his food and finally lay down his chopsticks in defeat. He just wasn't hungry and he sensed what was coming. Tony ended the call and picked up his beer bottle, downing the contents.

'I've got to go,' Tony announced.

'Trouble at the restaurant.'

'Another one of Ivano's diva moments. He's walked out. Momma needs help in the kitchen.'

'You're going to cook? You hate cooking,' Oliver reminded him.

'Sshh, you're ruining my rep. All Italians love to cook.' He took his wallet from his trouser pocket and began pulling out bills.

Oliver waved him away. 'Forget about it.'

'Don't pull the billionaire card again, you did that the other night and I know how much I drank.'

Oliver smiled. 'I can't take it with me, can I? Go on, get out of here. Go and whip up some pasta with Momma.'

Tony paused. 'On one condition.'

'Go on.' Oliver looked sceptical.

'Woman at my six o'clock all on her own.' Tony nudged his head, indicating a booth behind him. 'She might be in need of some wish fulfilment.'

Oliver tilted in his seat to get a look. Long chestnut hair almost to her waist and a red dress that showed off every curve. He had to admit he liked what he saw. But unlike last night, he was conflicted. The trip to the hospital *had* affected him. He didn't know if he had it in him tonight.

'Call me with the details tomorrow,' Tony said, grinning.

'I'll see you,' Oliver said, waving a hand. He watched his friend depart then blew out a breath before beckoning the waiter to him.

'Yes, Mr Drummond.'

'Would you please send a glass of your best champagne to the lady at that table over there?'

'The lady in the red dress?' the waiter queried.

Oliver nodded. 'She is dining alone, isn't she?'

'Yes, sir, she is.'

'Fine. When you take over the drink, ask her if she'd like to join me for dessert.'

'Very good, sir,' the waiter said, backing away from the table.

'Oooo can we sit near the lobsters? Did you know lobsters can live for up to seventy years?'

The young girl's voice was British and far too knowledgeable for the age she sounded. Oliver turned his head and watched the girl, a tall man in his mid-thirties and a brown-haired woman enter the restaurant and head towards a vacant table to his left.

'If any survive more than seventy days in this restaurant I'd be surprised,' the woman of the party answered. He watched her brush the snow from her coat then remove it, laying it over her arm as the man pulled out seats for them.

Family. Looking forward to Christmas. All the things he couldn't cope with. Except the child. He didn't have any experience of that. Wouldn't. Living with your head in a noose made you discount certain agendas.

He turned his attention back to the waiter and the woman in the red dress just across the walkway from him. The glass of champagne was being offered but the woman was waving it away. This didn't look good. And despite his uncertainty, he didn't want to be rejected. He hoped the waiter would direct the woman's attention his way so he had a chance to work his magic.

Right on cue, the waiter stepped back, indicating Oliver. This was his chance.

'No one's allowed to eat this one!'

It was the child's voice again and despite the woman looking his way, he was drawn to turn his head to see what she was doing. She was kneeling up on her seat, her fingers at the glass of the tank that housed the live menu.

'Do not give it a name.' That sentence came from the mother and it provoked his lips into a smile.

'I'm going to call him Lyndon. After Lyndon Baines Johnson, the thirty-sixth president of the United States.'

Oliver smirked. This kid sure knew her presidents.

'Fine. I'll have anything off the menu that hasn't been christened,' the woman said.

'Mr Drummond.'

He snapped his head back as the waiter addressed him from his left.

'The lady doesn't drink champagne,' he began. 'But she said if you would like to join *her* for dessert you'd be very welcome.'

'Is that so?' Oliver said, leaning a little to get a better view of the woman in red. She was definitely worthy of his time and moving seats would get him away from the audible intelligence of a child who looked no more than ten.

He cleared his throat, dropping his napkin to the table and picking up his beer. He needed to get away from the happy family with the knowledgeable child, no matter how amusing she was. Mom and Dad could have been poster models for the American Way. Any minute there would be laughter and cosy hand-holding.

He swigged at the liquid in his bottle, deliberately setting his eyes on his playmate across the room. She was looking back at him, assertiveness coming out of every pore, but her eyes said something else as well. The look written there was telling Oliver she was open, ready for adventure, excitement. She was flattered by his attention but she wasn't a pushover. This was going to be much more sophisticated than impersonating jungle animals.

He stood then, his eyes still on her. He addressed the waiter. 'I'll have the lychee ice cream.'

'I'm going to have smoked chicken with wild rice noodles and some pan-fried pork buns,' Angel ordered. She slapped her menu back down on the peach-coloured tablecloth.

Hayley smiled and rolled her eyes. The appetite her daughter had definitely inherited from her.

'Sounds good to me. Hay?' Dean asked, looking to her now.

'I daren't have lobster,' she responded, earning a wrinkle of the nose from Angel. 'I'll have the three chilli chicken.'

'Oh shit,' Dean exclaimed, putting his hand to the side of his head and turning in to the table. 'Shoot! I mean shoot, sorry, Angel.'

'What's the matter? Is the chilli chicken not good?' Hayley asked.

'No, it's my boss. He's sitting just over there,' Dean said. He hitched his head back. 'But don't look.'

It was pointless following the statement up with a *don't look*. It made her want to look all the more. Hayley was seeking out some mid-fifties ogre of a businessman, all Rolex watches, port-filled belly, cigars on the table. She didn't see anyone like that. In fact she wasn't even sure who Dean was referring to.

'I don't see anyone,' she said, still staring. 'Where?'

'Stop looking. I don't want to have to speak to him,' Dean responded.

'Oh, Uncle Dean, is he really mean?' Angel asked, leaning her elbow on the table and looking enthralled.

'I don't understand. I thought you loved your boss. I thought you went to dinner at his house and … didn't you go away for a weekend with his family in the spring?'

Dean shook his head. 'This isn't Peter Lamont. I love Peter. Peter's the head of development. This is *the* boss. Oliver Drummond,' he stage-whispered. 'The CEO of Drummond Global.'

That had her attention. Hayley looked again, trying her best not to appear too obvious.

'Table at the back, with the woman in the red dress,' Dean said.

And then she saw him, just a couple of tables to their right. Leaning back in his chair, white shirt, no tie, grey trousers, a confident smile on his face as he chatted to his dining companion. He wasn't at all what she would imagine the head of a huge worldwide business to look like, not that she knew any others. He was young, maybe a little older than her, and he was hot! Definitely more billboard than ogre. His hair was short and tawny in colour, cut simply. He had a strong nose, an even stronger jawline, and his hazel eyes she seemed unable to look away from. This guy had *charismatic* written all over him. No wonder he was an industry leader.

'He's such a jerk,' Dean stated.

'Why?' Hayley asked, watching as Oliver talked to his date. He had the kind of mouth models would kill for. Full lips but totally masculine, the sort you could look at for a long time and just imagine roving all over you. She swallowed.

'Honestly, I wouldn't know where to start,' Dean said.

Hayley snapped her eyes away, the spell broken.

She was still trying not to think about persistent Greg and her handful of other failed dates since Angel had been born. It didn't stop her looking back though. She wet her lips. 'Is that his girlfriend?'

Dean was forced to turn his attention in his boss's direction. He snorted. 'That will be someone he picked up tonight. There's a rumour he pays them. I guess that's one way to get rid of your billions.'

'He has billions?!' Angel's voice came out a little too loud and her eyes went out on stalks.

Dean continued. 'His father was such a great man, an inspiration to the whole consumer electronics and computer software industry.'

'Did he have billions too?' Angel asked.

'Uh-huh. He took the company into the global arena, from just a small firm with big ideas to a huge company with no limits.'

'And, let me guess, junior is mucking it all up,' Hayley said. Perhaps junior had different priorities too.

Dean shook his head. 'No, he's good at what he does. He flatters and uses his father's old-school network to the company's advantage, but, in my book, if you can't remember the names of the people you employ, can't spare a *good morning* or a smile now and then …' Dean stopped, focussing his attention on Angel. 'Listen to me. Going on about work when we have Chinese food to order.'

'Shall we call the waiter?' Hayley suggested, finally turning her attention away from Oliver.

She couldn't remember what she'd intended to order because, for some reason, food was the last thing on her mind right now. Reasons Christmas is better in New York number 35 – eye candy at Chinese restaurants.

CHAPTER TEN

Asian Dawn, South William Street, New York

Oliver watched her lick the ice cream from her spoon with all the experience of a Brooklyn hooker. Maybe that's what she was. Did it matter? That's what the rumour mill thought anyway. He put down his own spoon. She smiled then and, ravishing the stainless steel one more time, she placed it into her bowl.

'So, are we staying for coffee? Or are you going to take me somewhere a little more intimate?' his companion asked.

She was possibly the most forward woman he'd ever propositioned. Any soupçon of inner vulnerability had completely disappeared between their eyes meeting and her sucking the silverware like a porn star. He wasn't sure he liked it. He wasn't sure he wanted this now it was being laid out for him. It was all too easy. Too brazen. He swallowed. What was his problem? Easier was better, wasn't it? Nothing difficult, just sex, a quick fix, no flying off in helicopters or trips to Vegas.

A skipped beat of his heart alerted him to the fact the woman – what was her name again? – was waiting for an answer. He'd lost all concentration, his tongue was parched and his glass was empty.

She leant forward, making sure her ample breasts met the table and rose up in the confines of her dress. 'Shall I call us a cab?'

It didn't really sound like a question. An internal punch to his heart had him squirming in his chair. He could feel his breath catching in his throat, adrenaline flooding his every sense. He could feel the blood flowing fast and hard through his entire body, his fingers were growing tight, his vision clouding.

He put his hand on the table to steady himself as he stood. 'Please excuse me, for one minute.'

Without saying anything else, he headed in the direction of the restrooms.

'Did you know that the word *noodle* actually comes from the German word *nudel*? That's n-u-d-e-l.'

Hayley was watching Angel trying to use her chopsticks. Most of the noodles – or *nudels* – were falling off the two prongs as soon as she'd got them anywhere near on.

'Do you want a fork?' she asked as Angel grabbed the strands between her lips and sucked.

Angel shook her head and sucked harder. Maternal pride coated Hayley's insides as she watched.

'She gets her brains from me, you know,' Dean said, nudging Hayley's elbow and smiling.

'Are you calling me stupid?' Hayley said in mock crossness.

'I wouldn't dare. Not when you're holding chopsticks *and* a fork.' Dean eyed the leftovers on her plate. 'If you don't eat that chicken, you know I'm going to have to.'

Hayley put her cutlery down and pushed the plate towards him.

'I didn't mean … take it back,' Dean said, his fingers shifting the china across the cloth.

She shook her head. 'No, it's fine. I've had enough.' She just wanted to get back to Dean's apartment now, put her head on the pillow and let the exhaustion sweep over her. Tomorrow she would face what she'd come here to do. Tomorrow, after two months of virtual searching for Angel's father, she was going to begin the physical search. Starting with one of the galleries he'd mentioned exhibiting at all those years ago. Thank God for the ten-year diary containing all the information she'd needed to make a start. She'd remembered the name of the hotel too. It didn't begin with 't'. It was the Shelton. She'd phoned them twice, both times getting the client confidentiality spiel. Bribing the receptionist hadn't worked either. She also suspected they probably didn't keep records of guests for ten years. She just had to hope turning up at the galleries was going to get her more results than the phone calls and emails.

Angel's mouth hung open as the waiter walked past, a lobster on a silver platter heading for a table near the door. 'It's Lyndon,' she announced, tearing up.

'No,' Hayley said quickly. 'It can't be. There were about twenty lobsters in that tank.' She turned to observe the bubbling water, green weeds wobbling in the current. There were definitely fewer crustaceans than there had been. 'Look, there he is.'

She pointed at a lobster bearing the closest resemblance to 'Lyndon' – although they all looked the same to her – and hoped for the best.

Angel shifted in her chair, getting up onto her knees to get a better look inside the water. 'No it's not.'

Nothing could get past her daughter but now a crisis was looming. Hayley looked to Dean for help.

'Hey, Angel, tomorrow afternoon, when I get back from work, shall we go and see Vern and Randy?' Dean asked.

Angel was still eyeing the remaining lobsters in the tank, seemingly scrutinising them, checking every mark, the position of the elastic bands on their pinchers. 'I guess so,' she said half-heartedly.

'Want to see a photo?' Dean offered. He reached into the pocket of his jeans and pulled out his phone.

'I think *I'd* like to see a photo,' Hayley said.

'Of Randy?' Dean asked.

'No, of Vernon, the guy I had to hear about from my daughter.'

'Oh, I don't have any of him on this phone,' Dean said quickly.

'You have more than one phone? When did you join *Sons of Anarchy*?'

'This is just my phone for ...' he hesitated.

'For pictures of dogs?' Hayley offered.

Dean ignored her comment and reached to put the phone under Angel's nose. 'There he is.'

For a second Hayley thought Angel wasn't going to move her eyes from the water tank. But as the waiter headed towards it, his hands in rubber gloves, ready to pluck another lobster from the water, she slipped back down onto her chair and turned her attention to Dean's phone.

'See how cute he is,' Dean said, swiping to another image.

'What type of dog is he?' Angel asked, calling Greenpeace about the sea creatures all but forgotten.

'He's a Pomeranian.'

'Is he fully grown?' Angel asked.

'Yes, they're a small breed.' Dean smiled. 'You should see Vern with him. It's like a giant taking a mouse for a walk.'

'So he's tall then. Is that all I'm getting?' Hayley said.

'You'll see him tomorrow.'

'Can we take Randy for a walk tomorrow? Can we go to Central Park?' Angel asked, leaning her head sideways and batting her eyelashes.

Hayley stood up, placing her napkin on the table. 'While she goes full on child actress, I'm going to go to the toilet.'

'The *bathroom*. We're in America now,' Angel corrected.

'Fine. I might even turn on a faucet.'

Oliver splashed his face with water and looked at his reflection in the mirror of the gents' bathroom. He was pale, his hazel eyes a little bloodshot. He held out a hand, stretching it into the space, seeing what happened. It was trembling. Not an obvious shake like someone with Parkinson's, but a visible tremor. He clenched his fist and closed his eyes. What was he doing here? After his close call at the hospital, his run-in with both his mother and Clara, he should have left with Tony and headed home.

But going back to the penthouse alone, biding time, thinking, wondering, worrying, that wasn't a life. That's why he did what he did. Here, with this woman, with Christa last night. Because being with someone, being part of the intricate fabric of New York, was better than the alternative. Wondering when you were going to die and who would care if you did.

He shook the water from his hands and smoothed the rest into his hair. Looking at his reflection again, he swallowed. He had two choices. He either rode this feeling out, went back to the table with whatever-her-name-was and enjoyed a night of carnal desire he really wasn't in the mood for. Or he escaped out the back door. There was really only one option.

The cool air from the corridor lifted Hayley's hair as she moved through the door from the restaurant. As soon as she had been to the toilet, she'd suggest skipping dessert and calling the driver. Angel had to be running on adrenaline alone right now. It was something like three o'clock in the morning in the UK.

She stopped walking the second she saw him. She widened her eyes, getting them used to the half-light in the hall, making sure she *was* seeing what she thought she was seeing. It was Dean's boss, the hot Mr Meanie, struggling to open the fire exit door at the end of the corridor. What was he doing? Was he a smoker in need of a nicotine hit? It seemed desperate if that was the case. He was pushing and pulling like his life was at stake.

She knew what she should do. She should disappear into the ladies' toilets and pretend she hadn't seen. Whatever he was doing was none of her business and she shouldn't be standing there appreciating the fine cut of his trousers as he leaned against the metalwork. She subconsciously took a step towards the ladies bathroom. And that's when he turned around.

She could see his top button was undone and half the bottom of his shirt was untucked from his trousers. His hair was wet and, even from this far away, she noted his unsettled breathing.

'Are you OK?' she asked.

He spoke first. 'I, er, can't seem to get the door open.'

He looked awkward, one hand on the handle of the door, the other drooping at his side. She wasn't sure what to do, but now he'd addressed her she couldn't just leave.

'Do you *need* to get it open?' she asked, wondering what a billionaire was doing trying to break out of the back entrance.

He nodded. 'Oh yes. I really do.'

'Why? Is there a fire?' She took a tentative step closer.

'More of a fire*fight,* if I'm honest.' He pushed at the door again. His breathing was ragged and he looked unsettled. 'It's necessary to take evasive action.'

Hayley took another few steps towards him. 'And you can't use the entrance you came in by?'

He stopped manhandling the door then and turned to face her. He furrowed his brow. 'You're English.'

'Yes. And you're so obviously on the run. Who is it? The mafia? The Triads?'

He smiled then and the beginnings of a laugh fell from his lips. He shook his head at her. 'If only it were that simple. I'm actually off to change into Spandex and save the city like Superman.'

Thinking about him in Spandex did worrying things to her insides. She swallowed, watching him look her up and down. From her boots that had seen better days, to her jeans she'd been wearing for the last three seasons, then to the green-coloured long-sleeved top that had definitely shrunk in the last wash. She was as far from Galliano as it was possible to be.

'Ever needed to sneak out on an unsuitable date?' Oliver asked her.

Her mind went to Greg. Over-tanned, teeth over-whitened, breath over-garlicked. She could relate to many occasions she'd wanted to slip out of his sight. But this was not what she'd been expecting. He was about to abandon a woman at a restaurant. That did not sit well with her.

'You're sneaking out on a date?' she clarified.

'Well, kind of, not exactly a pre-planned engagement but …'

'And you're not going to tell her you're leaving.' Her hackles were rising fast.

'I've settled the bill.'

'Wow, that's heroic. Very Superman.'

'It isn't like you think,' Oliver said, pulling in another ragged breath.

'No?' It seemed exactly like she thought.

'She's not a date in the normal sense.'

She raised her eyebrow and took a half step backwards. 'I think I'm going to just back out of here, pretend you haven't insulted the whole female population and let you get on with the great escape.' He might have eyes the colour of cashews but this behaviour wasn't acceptable in her world.

'Please …'

It sounded like a desperate plea. She stood still.

'Listen, this is the first time I've done this. She's just …' He let out a breath and paused for a second. 'Anything I say is going to sound insulting to you, so please, just help me open the door, I can go and you can forget we ever met.'

He really did sound agitated and keen to make a rapid exit. Hayley wondered what his date had done to make him want to flee so badly.

'Is that a promise?'

He held up his hand. 'On everything I have.'

She stepped forward and leant against the door, pushing down on the steel bar with all of her force.

'I do have to say that my male pride is going to be significantly injured if you open that door.'

'I'll feel I've let down the women of Britain if I *don't*.' She shoved at it. 'I've decided the woman in the red dress is going to be a lot better off without you.'

'Whoa, that hurts.'

Hayley pushed, pressed and shunted, all at the same time and the door whooshed open, taking her with it. Her feet hit the snow-covered concrete of the alleyway outside but she held onto the door, steadying herself. The snow was falling thick and fast and the night was as black as tar, its air ice-cold.

'Well, it's open.' She looked back at him, standing just inside the doorway, his eyes still on her.

'And I feel like the biggest dick,' he replied.

There was no humour in his tone and when she met those nut-coloured eyes she realised just how jaded he looked. There was exhaustion written over every part of him, the tense shoulders, the tight jaw, his hands clenching into fists. Maybe Mr Meanie had a lot more on his mind than being civil to his workforce. Maybe he did have a good reason for running.

'Thank you,' he said sincerely, stepping out and joining her on the snow.

She waved her arm out. 'So, there you go, wide open alleyway. You'd better get a move on, save the city.'

'I guess I should.'

Snowflakes were circling down, catching in his hair and landing on the shoulders of his shirt, seeping through the expensive material. The mighty fine bone structure could be admired now he was so close. A Jason Stathamesque layer of light brown covered his jaw, those full lips pink with cold, his chin firm.

He shivered. 'So, what do I call the English rose who rescued me tonight?'

He sounded more confident now, his eyes bright, standing a little straighter.

She smiled. 'Given that you're still acting like you're on the run, I don't think I can share such personal information.'

'That's very wise. But if you won't tell me your name I'll just have to call you Bridget Jones.'

'Is that really the best you have? How about Emmeline Pankhurst, the leader of the Suffragette movement or Margaret Thatcher, one of Britain's greatest Prime Ministers?' Now she sounded a little like Angel.

'What would you like me to call you?' Oliver asked.

'I thought you promised I'd never have to see you again.'

'Fingers were crossed behind my back.'

She couldn't help but smile. 'Sneaky. Just the sort of behaviour I'd expect from someone abandoning their date.'

'There are extenuating circumstances, I promise.'

Hayley thought for a moment then spoke. 'Seeing as you say you're Superman, you can call me Lois.' She nodded. 'I've always had a bit of a thing for Clark Kent.' Wow, where had that come from? Was she flirting?

'Lois,' Oliver said. 'Yeah, that works.'

A shiver ran over her, the velvet notes of his voice making her insides rumble. She held out her hand to him. 'I *would* say it was nice to meet you, Clark.'

'Why don't you?'

She swallowed as he took a step closer to her. He *was* completely gorgeous. But he was *ditching* a date, running out of a back exit and leaving without saying a word.

'It was nice to meet you, Lois,' he said, taking her hand in his.

Hayley broke the connection. 'Well, goodnight. I'll leave the business card I just pilfered from your pocket for your date.'

She watched the horror coat his features and he reached a hand down to pat the pocket of his trousers. And then he smiled, obviously realising she was playing him.

'You're good,' he responded.

'Yes, I am.' She waved a hand. 'Goodbye, Clark.'

She turned and faced the door to head back into the restaurant building. Hearing his footfalls in the snow, she glanced back, watching him jog away from her, moving through the snow and kicking up puffs of white dust as he disappeared into the dark.

Hayley shook her head. New York City. In Gotham with Superman. This place was all kinds of crazy. She closed her eyes and breathed in the night, internally cursing herself for flirting with him. It would come back to bite her. Her karma would be jet lag hitting hard in the middle of the night. She opened her eyes, directing her vision up the dark, dank-looking alley leading to the main street. Perhaps Oliver Drummond's karma for abandoning a date would be freezing to death on the jog home without a coat.

CHAPTER ELEVEN

Oliver Drummond's Penthouse, Downtown Manhattan

Even after a shower, Oliver still couldn't get warm. Dressed in sweatpants and a long-sleeved Knicks top, he entered the lounge room of his penthouse, heading for the Scotch. This was his bolthole. A luxury bachelor pad with one of the best views in the city. It had every convenience on the market. Wide screen, surround sound, HD, MP3 and Dolby. Even the washing machine could play music. He had to have something to make that chore bearable. From the expensive wool carpet in the bedroom and the solid oak floor in the rest of the apartment, to the mood control spotlights in the ceiling, it was the crème de la crème of city living.

He took a drink. Bailing from the restaurant had been stupid and he'd left his suit jacket at the damn table. He didn't think there was anything vital in any of the pockets – he had his wallet and phone – but he couldn't be sure. He'd called Asian Dawn but he'd got the engaged tone on each occasion. At the end of the day, he had other suits. Maybe it wasn't worth the aggro. His biggest worry was it containing contact details the woman in the red dress could use to get hold of him.

He poured himself a tumbler of the amber liquid, his hands shaking. When the glass was half full he quickly swigged back a mouthful. The burn hit the back of his throat and he relaxed a little, leaning against the solid oak sideboard.

Cradling the glass against his chest he turned to look out of the floor-to-ceiling windows, taking in the view of Central Park. He could see everything from here. The lights from the iron lamp posts, the pond, the bridge over it, that vast patch of green – now heavily speckled with white – appearing like an oasis in a grey desert.

He had been stupid to go out with Tony tonight. He'd gone out looking for something – anything – as some sort of punishment by proxy for Clara and his mother. It served him right for ending up at a table with someone keener than a teenager in an Apple store.

Oliver walked over to the windows and stood close, watching the constant stream of snowflakes drifting past the glass. A thickening stack was piling up on his balcony. Like the big fat layer of misery he was living in.

He hated the fact that everything in his life was pre-ordained. It was his lot, because of who he was, just like with the company. That wasn't his dream, it was his father's and Ben's. And now it was his burden to bear whether he wanted it or not. Along with the short life expectancy he probably wasn't helping with the Scotch. Perhaps Tony was right, drowning himself in bourbon would be a relatively painless way to go.

He closed his eyes remembering his dream, the one so different to Richard and Ben's. Football. He'd been nothing short of the best, destined for a career with one of the big teams. It had felt so good being able to strike out on his own, a job path all set, a future secured that didn't involve the family business. And then it had just been ripped away from him, snatched right out of his hands, his trail turning back towards Drummond Global after all. He hadn't wanted it. He'd wanted something of his own, not just a legacy to fulfil. And that was where the Globe came in. By creating something that was going to revolutionise the tablet market he was finally going to get his moment. It wasn't winning the Super Bowl for his team but it was the closest he was going to get.

Oliver slugged back some more whisky and watched the lights reflecting from the other buildings' windows. It was time for change. It was time he took full ownership of his role. There was no shirking it so he may as well make the most of it. His mother and Clara had both clawed their way into his psyche today but only because he had let them. Why should he feel so freaking guilty about not wanting to go home for Christmas? Why was he letting himself get cornered into situations? He couldn't do the church and the carols and the celebrating Jesus' birth because it meant nothing to him now. What had God ever done for his family except wipe half of them out?

Tomorrow he was going to go into the office and make everybody remember who the boss of Drummond Global really was. And he was going to prove to himself that that boss didn't wear a designer dress suit or a statement necklace.

Dean Walker's Apartment, Downtown Manhattan

Angel had fallen asleep in the back of the car as soon as it had set off from the Chinese restaurant. Now, laying in a pinker than pink bed in one of the spare bedrooms of Dean's apartment, she was barely awake as Hayley brushed her hair.

'Do we have to do my hair?' The words were hardly audible through a giant yawn.

'If we don't do it now it will be in knots in the morning and you'll moan and groan and I'll get cross … it's just easier if we do it now.' Hayley ran the brush through her daughter's brown hair. 'You can close your eyes.'

She watched Angel's eyes shut and her shoulders relax.

'So, did you enjoy the Chinese food?' Hayley asked.

'Can we go there again?' Angel asked, lips barely moving apart.

'I guess so. But we're in New York now. There are thousands of other restaurants we can try.' She smiled. 'Reasons Christmas is better in New York number 9 – much more than Pizza Hut, McDonald's and Nandos.'

She ran the brush through Angel's hair again. In this moment, when it was late, when her stomach was full and her brother was in the kitchen making hot chocolate, what she was here to do really hit her. She was going to make her daughter's wish come true. She was going to scour New York until she found Michel. The nights of fruitless searching on the internet were not going to eat away at her resolve. He was out there, somewhere, and Angel wanted to know him. It was up to her to fill that void and she was determined to do it by Christmas.

She stroked the brush down Angel's hair again, the bristles jerking slightly as she hit a knot.

'Is it still snowing?' Angel asked.

Hayley stopped brushing and reached one hand towards the window. She stretched and parted the curtains. Chunky white blobs were flying past the glass, changing direction with the wind. Her eyes were drawn across the street, to a window opposite with the lights on and the blinds open. A couple were in their living area, standing by a table. A decorated Christmas tree, white lights blinking, illuminated the space. Hayley watched as the man passed the woman a wine glass. He moved his lips, saying something, and the woman threw her head back, laughing like he'd told her the funniest joke in the world. It was an almost magical connection. One she had no concept of. She closed the curtain, shutting out the scene and the winter night, and went back to brushing Angel's hair.

'It's still snowing,' she informed her.

'Good,' Angel yawned again. 'I didn't want to wake up and for it all to be gone before I've had a chance to make a snowman.'

'I think,' Hayley started. 'That we should make a snow *character*.'

Angel eased her eyes open. 'Like what?

Straight away her brain told her Superman. She shook her head, dislodging the notion. He was not a character to bring to mind. And Superman's eyes were blue not pistachio speckled with chocolate flakes. She swallowed before replying. 'Like Bart Simpson.'

Angel's eyes opened wider. 'How about a snow *president*.'

'Good luck with Abe Lincoln's hat.'

Angel smiled. 'Oh, Mum, you're so funny.'

'Now I really know you're tired.'

Angel let out a sigh and Hayley put the brush down on the bed.

'What's the matter?' Hayley asked.

'You know how I'm not sure I believe in Father Christmas anymore.'

'Yes, and you know I told you if you don't believe you won't get any presents.'

'Yes, well, what if something I asked for can't be bought … or made?'

Hayley stilled, wishing she still had the brush in her hands. This was the conversation she'd been waiting for since October. The very first time she had heard Angel's night-time request for someone to magically bring her father to her had been on the last night of half term. And it had made her cry because Angel had never asked her outright about him.

'Well,' Hayley began, 'if it's something that can't be bought or something that can't be made by the toymaker then you have to believe in something else.'

'What?' Angel asked.

'Wishes.' Hayley swallowed. 'You have to believe that wishes can come true.'

Angel screwed up her nose. 'But that's like believing in magic.' She tutted. 'Although Dynamo is a very good magician, I do know it's not real.'

'Wishes aren't like magic. Wishes, well, they're a bit like dreams. And dreams aren't magic. They're something you long for, something you can work towards.'

Angel was staring at her like she was a lunatic.

'So, say my dream was to win the National Lottery. I wouldn't have a chance of achieving that dream unless I bought a ticket. And if I bought a ticket every week for the rest of my life I'd ...'

'Still die poor?' Angel offered.

Sometimes Angel was too clever for her own good. 'Perhaps the lottery wasn't a very good example. Let's say my dream is to marry Prince Harry.'

Angel slapped a hand over her eyes. 'Mum, you're far too old for him. You'd have a much better chance with Prince Andrew.'

'I think I might be a bit old for him too, if you believe the rumours.' Hayley sighed. 'All right, not Prince Harry or Prince Andrew then, how about ... Jude Law.' She waited for any immediate objections. 'Not too old, not too young, handsome, has children ...'

'Mum!'

'Well, if my dream was to marry Jude Law I'd have to ...'

'Do something with your hair,' Angel answered.

Hayley put a hand to her hair and opened her mouth in shock. 'What's wrong with my hair?'

'Let's get back to Jude Law. He's growing on me.'

'I think I want to know what's so wrong with my hair that Jude Law wouldn't want to marry me.'

Angel put her fingers out, slipping them between the strands of Hayley's brown hair.

'You should get it cut,' Angel announced. 'Short. Like Anne Hathaway.'

Hayley examined the ends, split, dry and in need of help. She wasn't going to find anyone as cheap as Brenda back home, but maybe she'd try if she was a living, breathing fashion alert as her daughter seemed to be suggesting. She cleared her throat.

'Back to the question.' She took hold of Angel's hands. 'If my dream was to marry Jude Law, I could, theoretically, stalking laws allowing, put myself in his world. But obviously not until I've had my hair seen to.'

Angel smiled. 'But he still might not marry you.'   .

'No, but I could do everything to make it happen. From being in the right place at the right time, to believing it was possible.' She squeezed Angel's hands.

'But what if you don't know where the thing you asked Father Christmas for is? Or how to find out.'

Hayley released one hand, placing it on her daughter's head and smoothing down her silky hair. 'You have to trust in your wish, Angel, that's all I'm saying.'

All her daughter had to do was ask and she would tell her what she knew. But she sensed she wasn't ready. Either that or she was worried what her asking would do, concerned about how it would make Hayley feel.

'Lie down and close your eyes. And when I'm out of the room make your wish,' Hayley said, standing up. She eased Angel back onto the pillow, stroking her hair.

'Night, Mum,' she said, her voice breathy as sleep started to overcome her.

'Goodnight, Angel.'

CHAPTER TWELVE

Drummond Global Offices, Downtown Manhattan

Today Oliver was untouchable. Today nothing was going to get to him. Not the chest pains, not his employees who didn't understand the complex nature of his position and definitely not his mother's threats about Christmas. He was going to be that business magnate all the newspapers said he was. A worthy successor to his father's throne. Not the son who had ruined one career and was playing around with a second.

He had a macchiato in his gloved hands and the streets weren't too snow-ridden thanks to the constant stream of citizens ploughing through. Horns blasted and brakes squealed as a large guy trying to carry a Christmas tree swayed into the road. The flags hanging from the buildings either side of him battled against the harsh wind and two men pedalling rickshaws fought against the elements, their passengers huddled up under blankets. Oliver smiled to himself. This morning he was going to take control and get a buzz going about the Globe.

Taking a swig from the cardboard cup with his name written on it, he pushed at the doors to his building. Standing on the matting just inside, the coffee caught in his throat.

Right in front of his eyes, to the right of the long stainless-steel reception desk, three men in coveralls were erecting a Christmas tree. A *real* Christmas tree at least ten feet tall. The scent of pine and greenery whooshed up his nose uninvited.

What the hell was this doing here? He blinked hard and refocussed. No, it was still there. He gritted his teeth together. This had to go. He couldn't have that monstrosity staring at him every time he entered and exited the building. When they had it upright, it would be bedecked. Gold, red, silver bells, stars and those damn jolly Santa Clauses. It wasn't going to happen.

He closed his eyes. He needed to keep hold of his resolve, own the day. Without even looking at the women behind the desk waiting to greet him, he marched towards the bank of elevators. He'd show the season of goodwill exactly what he thought of it. Goodwill was exactly where the tree was heading.

Dean Walker's Apartment, Downtown Manhattan

Someone had drugged her. That was the only explanation as to why her brain didn't feel connected to any other part of her and why her limbs were as heavy as solid rock.

Hayley turned back the bright turquoise duvet cover that was over her and attempted to slide out. Planting two feet on a sheepskin rug, she stood and hit her head on a glitter ball-style lampshade.

She let out a groan and put her hand to her temple, mussing her bed hair over her eyes. As she came to and the room came properly into focus, she realised where she was. New York. Her brother's gigantic apartment, where everything shouted out his love of sparkles and flamboyance. There was a signed, photo of Elton John in a gilt frame on the turquoise wall and below it a sculpture of Liberace, a pink feather boa around his neck. She shook her head, smiling. Her brother was such a stereotype.

She staggered to the door, almost getting her fingers caught in a decorative gold swag on the handle, and pulled it open. The smell of syrup enveloped her and the sound of Frank Sinatra was coming from the kitchen.

She made her way along the hall.

'Angel Walker, you're meant to get at least some of the ingredients into the pan!'

Hayley stood in the doorway taking in the scene before her. Angel had a jug in her hand and Dean was in charge of a large pan on the state-of-the-art hob. Last night she'd barely been able to take in the details of Dean's home. Now, in the morning light, she saw just what an amazing pad Dean had. This kitchen/dining/living space was the jewel in the apartment's crown. With chocolate brown chenille sofas, rugs, perfectly placed knick-knacks and a fifty-inch plasma TV in the lounge area, a ten-seater contemporary dining table with a chandelier over it and then, this fabulous kitchen. It spoke of Dean's success, a success Hayley had always been proud of, if not a little jealous.

'Hey, good morning,' Dean greeted, spotting her leaning against the doorjamb.

'Good morning.' She waved a hand attached to a floppy arm. 'I think I'm still on English time.' A yawn took over. 'Actually, scratch that, I *know* I'm still on English time.'

'We're making pancakes,' Angel announced.

'So I smell.' She made her way over to the breakfast bar and hauled herself up onto a stool.

'D'you want some coffee?' Dean offered, taking a step back from the cooker.

She looked him up and down, from his immaculately polished brown brogues, his snug fit suit trousers, to his pale blue shirt and accompanying waistcoat. Suddenly, in the pyjamas she was wearing, with her terrible hair, she felt like a poster girl for *The Big Issue*.

'Can I be really English and have tea?'

'I've got orange juice with bits in,' Angel said, holding aloft a glass.

'Sure,' Dean answered, going back to tending the pancakes. 'Breakfast, Darjeeling, Earl Grey or Rooibos?'

'The first one,' Hayley answered. 'I can do it if you tell me where the tea cupboard is.'

'You sit there. You're my guests.' Dean, spatula in one hand, reached his other towards a bright red cupboard to his right, opening the door.

'We're not really guests, Uncle Dean, we're family,' Angel reminded him.

'I know you are but you're on holiday. You're here to relax, take it easy and enjoy. Besides, I have to go in to work this morning so you'll be doing the tea-making for yourselves until this afternoon.'

'Ohhhhhh,' Angel said, sounding disappointed.

'Angel, not everyone gets to have school holidays,' Hayley said, picking up a fruit she didn't recognise from the sequinned bowl on the breakfast bar.

'I wish I did.' Dean served some pancakes up onto a plate. 'But I'll be back about three and we can go and see Vern and Randy like I promised.'

'Yay!' Angel exclaimed.

Dean put the plate of pancakes on the breakfast bar then lifted Angel up onto a stool, pressing a fork into her hand. She used the other hand to steer her New York guide book towards her.

'So what d'you think you'll do today?' Dean asked, pouring hot water into a floral teapot.

'We could go to the Empire State Building and then we could visit the Statue of Liberty and the Guggenheim museum and …' Angel started, eyes like marbles.

'Whoa! Hold that enthusiasm. Mum is going to need a New York minute to get over the jet lag,' Hayley interrupted. 'And New York isn't just tourist attractions, you know. When I came here last time I tried to take in the local culture. The sounds, the scents ... the galleries.'

The very first place she wanted to go was the gallery at the top of her hit list. New York Life. She just wasn't sure how to pitch it to Angel. Telling her about the search was going to get her hopes up. She wanted to have some sort of sniff of hope before she told her daughter what she was doing.

'But we're only here for a few weeks and I want to ride on the ferry too and visit the New York Public Library and ...' Angel carried on, flicking over a page in her book

'Angel, I promise, we will do all those things but ...' Hayley began. Her head was starting to throb.

'Did I mention I have an Xbox?' Dean said, diverting Angel's attention as he poured the tea.

'Do you?' Angel's eyes were wide again. 'Dylan at school has an Xbox and I played it when I went to his birthday party. Do you have Lego Batman?'

'You can download any game you like.'

'Cool.'

Dean put a fine bone china cup full of tea in front of Hayley. 'So what d'you say? Mum gets a long shower while you fight off the Joker and Penguin and then you can head out and suck up the big city.'

Hayley mouthed a thank you and put a finger through the delicate drinking vessel, bringing it to her mouth like it contained a life-preserving potion. 'So, have you got a busy day ahead?'

Dean nodded, a mouth full of pancakes. 'Oh yeah. Thanks to a panicky text from Peter at seven a.m.'

'What's happened?' Angel asked.

'Oliver Drummond has called a meeting for the whole design and development team at ten.' Dean shook his head. 'I can't tell you how many meetings like this we've had. He will have been over the specifications of the Globe again and decided to tweak something that doesn't need tweaking and me and my team will have to go back to the drawing board just to satisfy his ego.'

'He sounds horrible,' Angel said. She drank some of her orange juice.

'Maybe the meeting won't be like you think. It might be a good thing,' Hayley suggested.

'He's delayed the sign-off for months now. Before too long the project just won't be viable and me and everyone else working on it will have wasted so much time and money.'

'What exactly is the Globe?' Angel asked.

Dean smiled. 'It's like the iPad, only better because ... I helped design it.'

'Wow!' Angel said.

'Listen, I promise, no matter how this meeting goes I'll bring one home and show it to you later.' Dean got down from his stool and hurriedly finished his coffee. 'I've got to go, get the heads-up on this meeting.' He smiled at them both. 'Anything you want, anything you need, eat it, drink it, play with it, treat this place as your place, OK?'

'OK,' Angel replied, putting her hand out for a high five.

Dean connected his hand then bent to kiss Hayley on the cheek. 'Have that long shower and don't do too much.'

'Angel, did you hear that? We aren't to do too much.'

'Did you know Solomon Guggenheim's first collections of paintings were displayed at the Plaza Hotel? Can we go there too?' Angel raised her head out of her book.

'Sounds like we *are* doing too much,' Hayley said.

'See you later. I'll be back by three. Enjoy the Guggenheim.' Dean waved a hand as he headed out the door.

'Please tell me it has a café.' Hayley picked up her teacup and put it to her mouth again.

Angel nodded her head, looking up again. 'It does. And they sell fizzy wine.'

'Perfect,' Hayley answered.

Angel smiled. 'Did you bring your ideas book to New York?'

'I did.'

'So maybe we could go to some fashiony places too,' Angel suggested.

'Maybe,' Hayley answered.

'Oh no, fashion alert. Uncle Dean's forgotten his jacket.' Angel's eyes went to the dining area.

Hayley looked at the tailored grey suit jacket hanging over the back of the chair. Stylish, expensive – everything Dean had was top of the range to her bargain basement.

'Can we drop it in to him?' Angel asked.

'Are we going to have time between all this culture?'

'We might have to miss out the fizzy wine.'

Hayley slid down from the stool. 'Going for a shower. Make the Xbox game quick! Reasons Christmas is better in New York number 89 – there's so much to do!

CHAPTER THIRTEEN

Drummond Global Offices, Downtown Manhattan

How was the chick in the red dress? Did she have a favourite animal ;)

Oliver smiled and shook his head at Tony's attempt at text humour. Ten o'clock was nearing and he was nervous. He worked the fingers of both hands over the pliable material of his stress ball, trying to grind out the tension. He leant forward in his chair and pressed a button on his phone.

Two rings. Three rings. Impatience coursed through him. Where was she? *Four rings.*

'Oliver,' Clara finally spoke through the connection.

'Where were you, Clara?' he barked.

There was a short hesitation before the answer came. 'I was collecting your mail.'

He shook his head in frustration. 'Could you come to my office?'

'Would you like the mail?'

'Is it ready?'

'Not quite.'

'Look, forget the mail, just come in here.' He ended the call and stood.

This week he had let situations get the better of him. He'd given in to his medical condition and, in the aftermath, he had dwelt on it all way too much. Today, and every other day going forward, was going to be strictly business, emotion free. The second he dropped his guard, even just a centimetre, he lost sight of the big picture, what he wanted. And, for the most part, all that was was to be left alone. No questions, no complications and no promises.

He paced now, his irritation fuelling every step. How long did it take to walk the corridor for God's sake? Perhaps he ought to suggest she wore shoes she could actually move in. There was a knock on the door and then it was pushed open, Clara appearing a little flustered and distracted, her leather portfolio in her hands.

'I need you to take a letter,' he barked before the whole of her had entered.

'Of course.' She bustled in, heading for the chair opposite his.

'It's to Luther Jameson. The usual address.' Oliver began to gather speed as he walked up and down in front of the windows showing off the Manhattan skyline.

'Luther Jameson?' Clara asked.

He turned to look at her, saw her pen poised over her pad, hesitating.

'Is there a problem with that?' He ground his teeth together, just waiting for her to dare to oppose him.

'No, I …' Clara began.

He cut her off. '*Dear Luther. I was sorry to miss you at the golf club last month. I hear a good time was had by all and a considerable sum of money was raised for the McArthur Foundation. Unfortunately, due to prior commitments, I will be unable to attend the fundraiser on …*' He paused, turning back to Clara. 'Add the date in there whenever it is. *But, to go some way towards an apology I enclose a cheque for $25,000 in addition to Drummond*

Global's annual donation. I hope you have a successful and lucra-tive night for the charity and I wish you and your family a wonder-ful Christmas.' Oliver let out a sigh. 'He isn't Jewish, is he?'

Clara kept her eyes fixed on the notes she was taking.

'Clara, is the man Jewish? Does he celebrate Christmas?'

'I'll check.'

'Send it out today, I'll sign the cheque.'

Clara was unmoving.

'That's it,' Oliver said, walking back to his desk. 'You can go now. I've got a meeting with design and development at ten.'

Clara got to her feet, hugging the portfolio to her chest. 'Oliver …'

'There is one other thing,' he interrupted. He breathed in hard. 'I don't know who organised that monstrosity of a Christmas tree in the lobby but I want it gone. Today.'

He sat down in his chair and put his hand on the mouse next to his keyboard. This was how a day should be started. Controlled, conducted, nothing left to chance. Long may it continue.

Boardroom One – Drummond Global Offices, Downtown Manhattan

As Oliver arrived at the boardroom door he could hear the hub-bub of voices. He strained his ears, trying to catch snippets of the words. He could imagine what they were saying. They all thought he had called them here to pull apart the latest version of the Globe. All the revisions it had been through had been necessary. Since he'd started on the project, he knew he wanted to create something to really rival Apple. Lots of companies had tried but he was going to be the one to succeed. Because, despite what some people thought, he *did* know this business. His father had made sure of that.

Thinking about his father his mind harked back to a time when they'd sat in the house together dismantling a Dell. Ben was away at camp and Oliver had planned to be out playing football but a deluge of rain had put paid to that. Instead he and Richard had taken out the screwdrivers and taken apart the computer. He'd watched his father, saw the excitement in his eyes, the concentration on his brow as each section was carefully disassembled and inspected. Richard had encouraged him, advising him on each component, telling him how each one worked and their relationship to each other in the overall operation of the machine. It had been more than a lesson in electronics that day, it had taught him everything about his father's vision and passion. The insurmountable drive Oliver struggled with on a daily basis. Why couldn't he commit like his father had? Because he didn't have a long future ahead of him? His father had known that too and he'd carried on regardless, fearless to the end. Or maybe because it wasn't that first dream. The football career at his feet. The path he'd chosen not the one that had been given to him. He swallowed. At least he *had* a path. How short it was going to be was anyone's guess.

As if sensing his thoughts his body reacted, his chest tightening, forcing him to stand taller to iron it out. Oliver put his hand on the door and pushed it open.

All conversation stopped the second his shoes hit the carpet of the room and he made his way to the seat at the head of the chrome and glass table. It was time to get some respect back.

'Good morning everyone,' he greeted, putting a folder on the table and keeping his eyes there.

'Good morning,' came the mumbled reply from the dozen individuals present.

He flicked open the folder then looked up, his eyes glossing over all the team members. 'So, the Globe.'

He could sense the tension in the air. It was as if it was electrically charged, just waiting to crackle apart if he dismissed this prototype again. He had been harsh over this, he knew, but it had been necessary. You didn't just mock up a product to rival one of the world's biggest companies in five minutes. It had to be right. More than that, it had to be perfect. And even perfect didn't mean they stood a chance. It was a cut-throat business. It would be scrutinised by the best in the industry, compared to its counterparts. There was no way it was going to fall short on his watch.

He picked up the controller on the table and pointed it at the flat screen panel behind him. Displayed for the whole room to see was a graphic he'd prepared earlier. There was the seven point nine inch smooth-lined rectangular tablet moving around in a slow circle, showing off its curves as well as a beauty pageant contestant. One by one the features and specifications began to appear next to the rotating piece of technology. 32mb as standard, Wi-Fi and free 3G, a camera to rival the best on the market, Spotify free for six months, free unlimited cloud storage, apps from a large online partner site.

Oliver clicked the controller again and stopped the spinning tablet and held the specifications where they were.

'I know you've spent a great deal of time on this product. And I also know how many setbacks there have been.'

He could almost hear the collective groan, even though there was nothing but silence. They were looking at him, their faces blank, not giving away any of their feelings. But he knew. He knew his holding back of this product had caused conflict within the company. He also knew this team had spent hours, days, weekends and family time trying to get this project completed.

But he had pushed hard because Drummond Global and Oliver himself couldn't afford to produce anything less than acme.

'But setbacks are all part and parcel of creating something like this. Something revolutionary.' He spread his hands out. 'So, who thinks this product is ready for market?'

He put the question out there but he knew no one would answer. After the months of toing and froing, they were all too concerned about losing face to risk putting themselves out there.

But then a hand went up. A dark-haired man seated at the middle of the table had raised his hand in the air. This was unexpected. But not necessarily unwelcome. The man looked vaguely familiar. Had he worked with him closely before? If he had he didn't remember his name.

'Please, stand up. Tell everyone here why you think the Globe is ready to go into production,' Oliver invited.

The employee got to his feet, pushing his chair back a little as he created more space. 'This latest model incorporates all the great concepts of Apple's iPad but with more. We've made it 32mb as standard with the fastest processor on the market driving it. We haven't compromised on style, design or functionality. There's really nothing else we can do to make it better without having to increase the price points we've fixed on. Sure, in six months we might be able to come up with a faster processor but, right now, this is as good as we can make it.' The man paused for a second. 'Plus, I've been using one of the models for a week now and there's no way I'd go back to my other tablet.'

Oliver watched as the employee's face took on a glow as he came to the end of his speech. The man put his hands into the pockets of his trousers and looked slightly awkward, as if not knowing whether to keep standing or to sit down.

'What's your name?' Oliver asked.

The twitching of his comrades, the turning heads and shifting in chairs told him they were expecting harsh words not a 'what's your name'.

'Dean Walker, sir.'

He nodded. 'Good.' He pushed a button on the controller and revealed the final wording on the screen behind him.

The Globe – launching March 2016

'Dean Walker, you're in charge of making this happen.' He picked his file up from the desk. 'I'll get a date set for the next briefing.'

He nodded at the team sat before him then headed from the room. The door hadn't even closed when the collective cheer went up. Oliver smiled. Back in the game.

CHAPTER FOURTEEN

New York Life Gallery, Upper East Side, Manhattan

Hayley felt sick. Here they were standing in front of a gallery she had heard about ten years ago from the lips of Angel's father. Holding hands with the product of that union, her precious daughter, she took in the red brick exterior. The United States flag hung from a white pole at its centre, and an inch-thick covering of snow blanketed the frames and sills of the windows. A small brass sign declared it was the New York Life Gallery.

'This doesn't look as impressive as the Guggenheim,' Angel said, folding her arms across her chest.

'Don't judge a book by its cover. A grand exterior doesn't mean the finest exhibitions. Usually the ugliest-looking kebab vans make the best kebabs.'

'Have you been here before? The last time you came to New York?' Angel asked.

'No,' Hayley let out a breath. 'And I wish I had.' She caught herself quickly. 'It's meant to be good. Which is why I wanted us to come here.' She squeezed Angel's hand. 'Come on, let's get out of the cold, and I promise, if there's anything resembling an unmade bed or the contents of someone's bedpan, we'll leave.'

'What's a bedpan?'

Now Hayley was here she wasn't sure what to do. There was a man in the first section of paintings that looked like he was in charge. Hayley couldn't help but notice his tie didn't entirely match with his shirt – spots and stripes had never been a thing. She sighed. She just needed to busy Angel with something. A painting with, what looked like over a hundred small flowers on it gave her an idea.

'Ooo, I've heard if someone correctly counts the number of flowers on that painting over there there's a prize,' Hayley announced, pointing to the picture. This subterfuge was to keep her from getting caught up in this search too soon. It was for her own good. Anyway, what parent didn't tell their child a white lie every now and then?

Angel's eyes lit up. 'What sort of prize?'

'The chocolate kind,' Hayley said.

'Is there a time limit?'

'I don't think so.'

'That prize is mine,' Angel said, striding towards the painting with victory written all over her face.

The second Angel had left her side Hayley sidled up to the suited man a few yards away. As she got closer she saw a lanyard around his neck stating he was 'Carl'.

'Good morning,' Hayley greeted. 'I'm wondering if you can help me.' Her eyes darted to Angel, wanting to make sure she was fully occupied before she carried on. 'I'm looking for a friend of mine. I called and I emailed a month ago but no one got back to me … because I'm sure you're very busy.' She paused, gathered herself. 'He's an artist. We've lost touch and I can't seem to track him down online.' She began to unzip her rucksack. 'The last time we saw each other he mentioned this gallery and I wondered if you might remember him or have a record of him if he's exhibited here.' Hayley pulled out a photograph. Usually kept in the ten year diary it was starting to look dated and was a little worn around the edges. 'His name is Michel De Vos.'

Her heart was pumping like an overactive engine piston, driving the adrenaline around her body. Whatever this man said next was going to be make or break. She watched him observing the photograph, giving it his full attention, taking her and her request seriously.

'I don't recognise him, ma'am, and the name isn't familiar to me,' he finally replied.

Disappointment flooded through her but she held onto her breath and her resolve, not ready to give in to any emotion just yet. 'Have you been here long? At this gallery, I mean. He may not have exhibited recently. Maybe someone else here recognises the name,' she suggested.

He passed back the photograph. 'I've been here almost twenty years now.' He smiled. 'I'll tell you what I'll do. I'll email the other members of the gallery cooperative we're connected with, see if any of them can help.'

'Would you?' Hayley exclaimed. 'That would be brilliant.' She looked to Angel who was still staring at the flower painting, her mouth moving silently. She would buy her the biggest bar of Hershey's she could find.

'No problem. If you let me have your details.'

'And, how long would that take exactly … to get an answer from the other galleries?' The very last thing she wanted to sound like was someone searching for the one-night stand she'd had ten years ago. People weren't willing to give out information if you reeked of desperation. But she needed a timeline. She only had a couple of weeks and every second counted.

'I'll email today,' Carl assured kindly.

'Thank you, that's wonderful.' She crossed her fingers behind her back. 'Could you mark it urgent?' she added.

Her email address and mobile phone number given to Carl, Hayley joined Angel in front of the painting.

'Don't speak! I'm almost done ... almost done ... one hundred and sixteen, one hundred and seventeen ... one hundred and eighteen flowers!' Angel gasped for breath and looked at Hayley.

'Ooo so close. It was one hundred and twenty three,' Hayley responded.

'What? No, it can't be! I checked! I counted them twice!'

'Maybe the artist lost count,' Hayley suggested. 'Come on, I'll buy you cake at the Guggenheim.'

The Guggenheim, Upper East Side, Manhattan

It had taken Hayley almost twenty minutes to get Angel inside the building. The cylindrical white structure of the museum rose up from the street like the spiral inside a shell, so unlike everything built around it. Even to the untrained eye it was a stunning building, clean, curved, giving a hint to the artistry held inside the walls.

Hayley hated to admit she was slightly more interested in the chestnuts being roasted over a barrel just outside. Despite eating a large bowl of pink maize for breakfast she was still hungry and the cinnamon, spice and marzipan infused air everywhere was making her crave Christmas treats. Heavily iced fruit cake, mince pies, Terry's Chocolate Orange. Would they find that in a bodega?

'Did you know Solomon Guggenheim was a very successful businessman before he started collecting paintings?' Angel's eyes were still in the guidebook Hayley had had to purchase.

As they began to walk through the atrium Hayley's eyes were on the newspaper in her hands. Right now, thinking about the life history of Solomon Guggenheim and looking at paintings of odd shapes and sculptures you needed to turn your head upside down to understand wasn't what she wanted to focus on. Half of her mind was still back in the New York Life Gallery, the other half was staring at a cheesy advertisement.

Desperately Seeking Domestics

Majestic Cleaning Services are looking for hygiene operatives to join their expanding company. Must be English-speaking. Hygiene experience preferred but not essential. Contact Ms Rogers-Smythe

There was a phone number. She swallowed. A small job would help tide them over here and give them a bit of a head start when they got home and she had to search for new employment. She shook her head. Was she mad? She couldn't just apply for a job, could she?

But apart from her part-time party planning, she was officially unemployed and a few weeks in New York couldn't have come at a worse time. This advert could be the answer.

Her phone buzzed from her bag and she stopped walking, swung her rucksack off her shoulder and retrieved it. She looked at the text message. It was from Dean.

Mum called. Said u got here OK. She said make sure Angel keeps her coat dun up. Left a jacket on dining room chair. It's Oliver Drummond's. He left it in Chinese last night. Forgot 2 bring it. Can u drop in 2 the office?

It was Oliver Drummond's jacket she had squashed and creased down into her rucksack. Perhaps she should have cut the sleeves off to teach him a lesson for deserting that woman last night. Being a billionaire, perhaps he didn't even wear clothes twice. Maybe they were just as disposable as his dinner companions.

'There's an exhibition of paintings from Wassily Kandinsky,' Angel said as they moved up the ramp. 'Apparently Solomon Guggenheim has over one hundred and fifty of his paintings in his collection.'

'He must have liked him. What did he paint?' Hayley asked.

'Paintings,' Angel answered with a grin.

'Ha ha, funny girl.'

'Ooo look at this one up here!' Angel jogged ahead, starting up the spiral path.

Now was her chance. With Angel preoccupied with paintings, but in plain sight, she could call Majestic Cleaning. She hesitated. Should she? They probably wouldn't even offer her a job. She could just call and see what they had to say. And if they offered her a job? Well, the trip to New York hadn't been cheap and there was Christmas too. Angel needed presents to unwrap and she couldn't solely rely on Dean's hospitality. She stopped walking and tapped onto her phone. The empty search box was just waiting for her to key in a number. Her thumb hovered over the icons. Her eyes were back on the newspaper in her left hand. She could treat Dean and Angel to a night out maybe. A cleaner's wages probably wouldn't stretch to somewhere like Asian Dawn but she could probably stretch to a diner.

Watching Angel standing in front of something that looked like a badly drawn steam train, she hastily tapped out the number before she could overthink it. She waited to be connected.

'Good morning, Majestic Cleaning.' The voice sounded like a cross between the Queen and a well-connected baroness but with a definite American twang.

'Oh, hello.' Hayley cleared her throat, wondering why she felt the need to speak with a cut-glass accent. 'Is that Ms Rogers-Smythe?'

'This is she.'

'Hello, Ms Rogers-Smythe. My name is Hayley Walker. I've just come across your advert in the New York Times.'

'You're English!'

The exclamation sounded like Ms Rogers-Smythe had discovered an alien life form.

'Yes. Is that going to be a problem? I'm here for a few weeks and …'

'No problem! No problem whatsoever.'

'Good,' Hayley breathed out. 'That's good.'

'Would you be able to attend the offices tomorrow? At nine?'

'Well, I …' Her eyes went to Angel who was inspecting a sculpture that looked like a warty frog. She took a deep breath. 'Yes, of course. That would be fine.'

'Oh jolly good. I'll text the address to this number.'

'Great.'

'Lovely, I look forward to greeting you tomorrow. Toodle pip!'

'Toodle pip,' Hayley responded.

She cursed herself as she ended the call. *Toodle pip*. Why had she said that? And how was she going to explain to Angel she was visiting a cleaning firm?

Hayley watched her daughter dipping her head at the warty frog, shifting closer and inspecting its ears. Angel was enjoying every second of this trip already. If only she could get her the icing on the Christmas cake. Her father, gift-wrapped. Maybe Carl from the gallery had already sent the email. Perhaps there was someone in another gallery already typing a response with

Michel's details attached. She just had to keep looking and keep hoping. She walked the ramp to join Angel.

'Not a patch on Kermit is he?' Hayley said, nudging Angel's elbow.

'His name is Roderick P. Frog and he was sculpted by Henry Von Elderstein.'

'Oooo a blind artist,' Hayley said, running her hand over the frog's bumpy head.

'Mum!' Angel exclaimed.

'What?'

'The sculptor isn't blind and you're not appreciating its unique style.'

'To be honest I've got pots you made at pre-school that look better than this.'

Angel scowled. 'You aren't having fizzy wine until we've been in every section.'

'I hope they do very large bottles.'

They didn't do large bottles and everything on the menu was expensive. Hayley watched Angel biting into her slice of carrot cake while swinging her legs from the high white leather stool she was perched on. They'd looked at pictures, information screens, sculptures, models and even some living art for over two hours. And Angel had provided a running commentary from the guidebook the whole way round, so much so that a couple of Japanese tourists walking behind them had ditched their audio and relied solely on the enthusiasm of a nine-year-old. Here she was worrying about getting a job as a *hygiene operative* when her daughter had already carved out her own career as a museum curator.

Hayley took a sip of her cappuccino and turned to the view outside. Even with a layer of snow over the ground of Central

Park the paths were filled with joggers, walkers, people going about their business as usual. It wouldn't happen in England. In England, a couple of flakes of the white stuff and the whole country fell apart. Cars skidded, buses stopped running, schools closed and people hid under their duvets. New York wasn't just a different city, it was a whole different world. But it was a world she definitely wanted to get to know better. She turned back to her ideas book, open on the table in front of her. Warty frogs and pigs with multiple tails weren't something to inspire the fashionista in her but perhaps the architecture of the building was. She smoothed her pencil over a page.

'Do you want to share?' Angel asked, pointing to a portion of cake on her plate.

Hayley shook her head. 'No, you go for it. I have plans for hot dogs and roasted nuts.'

'I wish Uncle Dean could have come with us today,' Angel said, crumbling part of her cake with her fingers.

'He's going to finish early, remember? So you can go crazy with the dog.' Being English she felt she couldn't say Randy too much in public. She drew a little more, curving a neckline like the exterior of the building.

Angel clamped her hands over her mouth Macaulay Culkin style. 'We forgot to phone Nanny!'

Hayley looked up from her book and replicated her daughter's look but with less of the sentiment. She hadn't forgotten, she had avoided it. 'She's fine. She texted Uncle Dean.'

'I feel bad,' Angel said, propping her head up on her elbow on the table.

'Don't feel bad. It was my fault I didn't remember to remember.'

'You mean you forgot.'

'Something like that.'

'Do you think Nanny would have liked this museum?' Angel asked.

Hayley smiled. 'I think she would have moaned about the toilet facilities and the prices and she would have hated that painting of the dustbin.'

Angel laughed. 'Shall I send her a postcard of it?'

Hayley closed the book and put her pencil down. 'Angel Walker, that's something I would do. And if you turn out like me, Nanny will call the vicar and get you exorcised.'

Angel frowned. 'Like make me go running?'

'Ah ha! Special dictionary required. E-X-O-R-C-I-S-E-D'

Angel picked up her rucksack and dug her hands inside.

Hayley smiled, picking up her coffee cup.

'Exorcise. To free a person of evil spirits.' Angel grinned and waved her fingers across the table. 'Wooooo!'

'Attagirl. Want to ride the subway?'

'But we haven't finished here yet!' Angel folded her arms across her chest. 'I want to see a piece called Grosse Fatigue.'

'Just imagine me with bed hair and mix it together with fizzy wine and jet lag.' Hayley grinned. 'I'll show you tomorrow.'

CHAPTER FIFTEEN

Drummond Global Offices, Downtown Manhattan

Oliver was buzzing. Getting the fundraiser off his back first thing had set him up for the rest of the day. The meeting with the design and development team had been the cherry on top. Now the only thing hanging over him was the takeover of Regis Software. Maybe Clara had been right. Maybe he had taken his finger off the pulse with respect to that. Perhaps he needed to do more. He'd had an email from Mackenzie this morning saying the lawyers were dragging their feet over some moot point.

What would his father do? He shifted in his seat as that thought went through his mind. Why was he thinking that? Hadn't he been telling everybody he wasn't his father, that he was his own man? He shouldn't need an eighties businessman's guidance to manage a twenty-first-century company. Did he really need or want this merger? What were the benefits for both companies?

He picked up the phone on his desk and pressed a key. He waited for Clara to answer. 'Clara, could you get Andrew Regis on the phone?'

Outside Drummond Global Offices, Downtown Manhattan

Hayley's eyes went from the dark grey street, the snow having been worn away, through the chrome and glass entrance doors and upwards, scanning the many floors to the spiral top of the offices.

The building of Drummond Global was like a real-life Lego construction, only made of metalwork and windows, not plastic bricks. It was a complete world away from the architecture of the Guggenheim. *This* was industry. People inside this multi-million-dollar organisation were all part of important decisions, deal-breaking negotiations, creating and selling vital technology. Dean was a global hardware genius, fitting right into this high-stakes world. It was another universe when compared to fresh-pressing and stain removal at the cutting edge of the dry-cleaning industry.

'Is this where Donald Trump works?' Angel asked, her eyes following her mother's, her hands occupied with a giant hot dog. Hayley had devoured hers in thirty seconds and moved on to a pretzel that hadn't taken much longer to finish.

'No,' Hayley said, her eyes following the line of the building and back down again. 'This is where Uncle Dean works.'

'Wow, it's huge,' Angel said through splutters of bun.

'Yeah, it is.'

The sound of 'Jingle Bell Rock' came bursting out of a boom box on the sidewalk, a breakdancing reindeer busting some moves. Hayley reached a hand out to Angel. 'Come on.'

'Hot-dog hands,' Angel said, shaking the bread-covered sausage up and down and following.

'We won't be here long. We'll just leave this jacket for Mr Meanie and we'll go and get milkshakes.'

Angel answered with an indecipherable noise through sausage chomping.

Hayley pushed at the door and the warm air from inside buffeted her hair as she passed through the entrance. She heard another *wow* escape from Angel's lips as they stepped into the foyer.

It was the grandest office Hayley had ever been in and looked more like a high-tech hotel. There was a cream tiled floor that had been polished so well you could almost use it as a mirror, a central terminal with a bank of screens dominated the rest of the area and at the far end of the room was the reception desk, a sculpted metal affair with three women – scratch that, three models – in matching grey and pale blue uniform sat behind it.

'Fashion alert at twelve o'clock,' Hayley whispered to Angel. 'Grey and pale blue. What were they thinking?'

'They need some tangerine in there,' Angel replied. 'Or some deep plum.'

'Nice work.'

'Wow! Look!'

Before she could say anything else, Angel was skating across the slick floor. Her daughter stopped just in front of a giant Christmas tree. It was easily three feet wide and its star topper almost touched the ceiling. The annual spruce in Trafalgar Square had nothing on this. Then she creased her brow at the scene. Two men in overalls were working deftly with the swags, baubles and bells but it looked like they were taking the decorations off rather than putting them on.

'Don't touch anything,' she called to Angel.

She went up to the reception desk, undoing the zip of her backpack as she moved. Smiling at one of the blonde-haired receptionists, she pulled the jacket out of her bag. Angel arrived at her side.

'Hi, good afternoon. Could I just leave this for Oliver Drummond?' Hayley draped the jacket over the desk and watched the receptionist's friendly smile turn into misunderstanding.

'He left it in a restaurant last night and I'm just returning it.'

The receptionist didn't look like she wanted to take ownership of the jacket or do anything about it. 'I'm afraid Mr Drummond is out right now.'

'That's fine. I don't need to see him. I'm just dropping off the jacket,' Hayley said. She pushed the item a little nearer the receptionist.

The woman nodded and then picked up the telephone. 'I'll just give his PA a call.'

'That's OK, I don't need to see anyone, honestly. I'm just doing a favour for my brother.'

'Clara? I have someone here for Mr Drummond.' The receptionist paused for a moment. 'With an item of clothing.' She then looked at Angel. 'And a child.'

What on earth was going on? Why couldn't she just leave the jacket and be on her way? She should have just said the jacket was for Dean and let him sort it out. She was stuck now, waiting for a personal assistant who probably had a heap of important computer stuff to get on with.

'Thank you,' the receptionist said into the phone before replacing the receiver. 'Clara will be right down. Would you care to take a seat?'

Hayley let out a frustrated noise and moved towards a selection of dark grey leather sofas that looked like they'd been manufactured out of *Jurassic World* models.

'Your face is all red and blotchy,' Angel remarked as they sat down. She started to finish her hot dog.

Hayley put her fingers to her cheeks, feeling the heat there. An errand for Dean was going to make her look like a stalker. One of those obsessive types that wanted to drink the victim's pee or roll in their bed sheets to be close to them. Actually the rolling in the bed sheets held a certain appeal.

The only saving grace was Oliver Drummond was out. He need never know she was here. She could be any anonymous woman with a child bringing back a jacket he'd mislaid.

The entrance doors opened, an icy breeze whipping through into the reception and, along with it, the man whose jacket she had on her lap. There he was. The rich guy she'd helped escape down an alley. Oliver Drummond. He was unbuttoning a black woollen coat as he entered, revealing a well-fitting charcoal-coloured suit. Highly polished leather shoes were on his feet, but her eyes quickly moved upwards, over the width of his chest, his brown-blonde hair spiked and scattered with snowflakes and those unmistakeable eyes.

'That's him!' Angel stage-whispered, hot dog bun specks falling from her mouth.

Hayley swallowed, watching him make his way across the floor, another man at his side, engrossed in conversation. She needed to stop looking at him. If he turned his head, even one inch, he would see her. And then it happened. He looked to the bank of sofas where they were sitting and their eyes connected. She felt the look deep in her belly and hated herself for it having any effect at all. Drooling over Channing Tatum was one thing, this, especially when the business pin-up was only metres away, was another. Just as quickly as their eyes had met he turned back to his companion, still walking to the elevators at the end of the room. He'd dismissed her. Looked and then looked away. He really was the fickle philanderer she'd first pegged him as. Unwanted disappointment struck.

'Did you know Oliver Drummond is one of the richest men in America?'

'I've told you lots of times before, Angel, money isn't everything,' Hayley snapped. She was annoyed at herself. How fickle she was!

'I know. Uncle Dean says he's nearly always miserable,' Angel followed up.

'Yes, well, right now I know how he feels.' What was she doing with this damn jacket? She should have strode across the reception area and thrown it at him. Then he might have remembered her. Not that she was bothered that he hadn't.

Hayley got to her feet the second she realised a woman wearing a black business suit that was a little too small for her, a coral statement necklace at her décolletage, was heading past Oliver Drummond and his companion towards them. A poker straight expression was on her face.

'Hello,' Hayley greeted, gathering the jacket in her hands. 'I'm sorry about all this. I just …'

'Hello. I'm Angel.'

Hayley watched as Angel held her hand out to the woman, a beam of a smile on her face.

The woman reached out, took Angel's hand in hers and shook it. 'Hello, I'm Clara, Mr Drummond's personal assistant.'

'Wow,' Angel said, as if she'd just announced she was the first female Pope.

Hayley pushed the jacket towards Clara. 'I think the receptionist got the wrong end of the stick. I don't want to see Mr Drummond I just … my brother works here, and Oliver … I mean Mr Meanie … Drummond, sorry, Mr Drummond, he left this jacket in a Chinese restaurant last night.' She shook her head at the scenario. 'He forgot it this morning … Dean, my brother and … he asked me to drop it in.'

'Chinese food again, huh?' Clara remarked, folding the jacket over her arm. 'One day he's going to turn into a deep-fried noodle.' She smiled at Angel who grinned, all eyes and teeth. At least one of them was functioning like a normal human being.

'Right, well, we'll be going. Come on, Angel,' Hayley said, grabbing her daughter by the sleeve of her coat.

'Did you know that as well as being one of America's richest men, Mr Drummond is also one of the world's most eligible bachelors?' Angel piped up.

Hayley wanted the ground to swallow her up. For someone who was so intelligent, Angel had no idea what might not be appropriate in polite conversation.

'I didn't know what it meant at first but then I Googled *bachelor* and ...'

Hayley put an arm around Angel and stifled her into her coat. 'We'll be going now.'

Clara smiled. 'What was your name again?' The question was directed at Hayley.

Hayley stroked Angel's hair, pressing her face into her side as her daughter attempted to struggle her mouth away to freedom.

'Lois,' Hayley croaked. Angel let out a stifled noise that sounded like a gagged hostage.

As she turned them both away from Clara and headed rapidly to the door, she was already cringing. She didn't let Angel go until they were outside, sucking in the frozen winter air.

'Why did you do that?' Angel moaned, rubbing at her lips with her fingers.

'Why did *I* do that? Why did you come out with the top ten amazing facts about her boss?'

Angel shrugged. 'I only know two.'

'Thank God for that.'

'You were acting all funny,' Angel carried on. 'And why did you say your name was Lois?'

Hayley pointed down the street. 'Oooo look, a bodega! Let's see if they have Yorkshire puddings and a Terry's Chocolate Orange.'

CHAPTER SIXTEEN

Drummond Global Offices, Downtown Manhattan

Oliver splashed some water onto his face, letting the beads of moisture take away the heat there. The conversation with Andrew Regis today had been a little odd. When he'd tried to get out of the man exactly what the outstanding issues with the merger were, Andrew hadn't had much to say.

Oliver stood up, palming his face, letting the excess water fall into the square basin in front of him. He looked at his reflection in the mirror, catching the last drips off his chin then planting his hands down on the bench, steadying himself.

He'd suggested another meeting to iron things out, talk about the future for the companies and then Andrew had hit him with it. Talk about the past. Tales of his father's avant-garde approach to business back in a time where firms were struggling, the economy was in a sticky patch and unemployment figures were higher than ever. Weekends in the Hamptons and barbecues on the beach. Andrew had brought all those images flooding into focus and, along with it, every ounce of pain, regret and anger Oliver felt. Plus the giant sceptre of fear that was always hanging over him.

There had been times, wonderful, care-free times, when death hadn't lurked in every corner of the Drummonds' lives. There had been laughter, so much laughter, a childhood Oliver wished he'd been more appreciative of at the time. Their beach house at the Hamptons had been sold but he still remembered everything about it. The way his mom had decorated it in a nautical, seaside theme. Cool blues and greys, driftwood sculptures on the dresser, photos in bare wood frames, shells and sand in pots, nothing uniform. He and Ben had spent endless days on the sand, chasing each other, chasing girls when they were older, and running after every last sunset before they had to come inside. Then it was movies with popcorn, wrapped up in striped rugs, their hair still wet, sand sharp between their toes. Richard always wanted comedy so he could laugh out loud. Cynthia preferred romance so she could cry. Ben liked action movies and if Jackie Chan was in one he'd loved it even more. Oliver had never minded what they watched as long as they were all together.

He swallowed back the memories and stared at himself. What was he doing? Looking for all the answers like they were etched on his face? There was nothing there except the eyes he'd inherited from his mother, the long straight nose of his father and the hard, tense jaw which was all his own. He needed to get it together. Just because it was *that* time of year again, didn't mean he could fall apart.

He sucked in a breath, trying to ignore the pull of his chest wall and the spasm of an ache that happened when he straightened his shoulders. He shrugged them up and down, trying to release the tension. Maybe it *was* stress. Perhaps it was better to believe he was weak than face the notion he was going to drop dead at any moment. He scoffed. Tony would be chastising him if he was here now.

As if the reminiscing hadn't been enough, Andrew had also mentioned the McArthur Foundation fundraiser. The businessman had bought two tables and he was taking his top performing employees. Oliver remembered opening his mouth to tell Andrew he wouldn't be attending but something had stopped him from committing to the sentence. It was plain and simple guilt over his non-attendance, over his mother's disappointment and disapproval, over everything in his damn life right now. Fucking guilt he shouldn't have to bear. At this rate, guilt was going to kill him sooner than any heart attack.

His suit jacket was lying across his desk when he got back to his office. He approached it, gingerly, with caution, as if it might contain an incendiary device. Who had put this here?

Only now was he able to put two and two together. Slowly it was all falling into place. He'd seen her. Earlier today, when Cole had been giving him a running commentary on a charity project they'd been looking into. He'd looked for just a second, acknowledged an attractive woman sitting there and a girl eating something. Then he'd looked away again. It had been Lois. The woman who had rescued him from a night being eaten alive by the woman in the red dress. Why hadn't he paid more attention?

The door of his office opened and Clara stepped through.

'Oh, I'm sorry, I didn't realise you were back in here.'

'Clara, did you put this here?' Oliver asked, holding the jacket up.

She nodded. 'Yes, a woman brought it into reception.'

'Did she leave her name?' Oliver asked.

'She did,' Clara said. 'If only I could remember what it was.'

He folded his arms across his chest. He knew what Clara was doing. She had picked up on his shift in body language from fractured to intrigued and she was spinning this out.

'Do you want to work the whole weekend?' he asked.

'You wouldn't dare.'

'Try me.'

Clara toyed with one of the beads on her necklace. 'Her name was Lois.'

He smiled, shaking his head. She still wasn't giving up her true identity. Even under his PA's scrutiny, he couldn't stop the flicker lighting up his eyes. This was interesting.

He made a grab for the stress ball, closing his fingers around it hard. He nodded at Clara. 'What was it you wanted?'

'The latest contract for the Regis Software project. Mackenzie emailed it. It came in after your phone call with Andrew Regis.' She placed a file on the edge of his desk. 'And here are the supporting documents.'

Clara was still standing by his desk, scrutinising his every nuance. His shutters rose back up.

'Is that all?' he asked her.

Clara smiled and headed for the door.

Central Park, New York

'Come on, Randy! Here, boy!'

Angel went haring off through the falling snow, chasing after a dog that looked as if it had had its hair professionally styled. The mutt was more pampered and preened than Hayley. She pulled at her hair self-consciously, tucking it into the collar of her coat.

The park was like a winter wonderland. All the grass, trees and bushes were coated with white powder, making them look like a picture-perfect snow globe scene. The air was chilly and snow had started to fall again, already thickening the few inches laid the night before. Outside the park the high-rises towered over the vast island garden like giant gatekeepers. It was like nowhere else on Earth and, with every step Hayley took, it brought back memories of her last visit.

She'd been as slim as she'd ever been then, slim enough to feel cool and comfortable in skinny jeans. She'd lived in her jeans and a pair of black platform boots with diamantes and buckles. She must have looked halfway between a biker and a party girl. Her hair cut in a no-nonsense bob, she'd felt like she could own the world if she wanted to. She had dreams, aspirations, ideas that could fill her book ten times over, and nothing was going to stop her.

She had laid out on the grass of Central Park, her eyes in the sky, watching the clouds drift from the roof of one high-rise to another, letting herself become part of it all. New York was going to charge her passion and inspire her. It was the city of dreams and she was going to grab at every possibility it offered.

She sighed. Too much grabbing in the wrong place had set her off on an entirely different course. 'So, Hayley, did you enjoy your first night in New York?'

The question came from Vernon, Dean's boyfriend. The dog's appearance hadn't been the only shocker. She could only imagine that was why Dean wasn't keen on showing her photos of his boyfriend the night before. Vernon was tall, like her brother, but he was older – a *lot* older – at a guess at least fifty. He had the salt-and-pepper hair and brown eyes of George Clooney, with a tanned complexion that hinted at an Italian heritage. When they'd first met, he'd hugged Angel straight away and kissed Hayley on both cheeks. He was easy and relaxed, warm and open. She wondered why her brother thought she might have been judgemental – she wasn't their mother! What were numbers anyway? As long as he treated Dean right, nothing else mattered.

'We were both suffering a little from jet lag and I had to watch my daughter burst into tears over the death of a lobster.'

'Lyndon,' Dean added.

Vernon looked bemused.

'You really don't want to know,' Dean said, linking his arm through Vernon's and smiling. He looked to Hayley. 'How was the Guggenheim?'

'Interesting. I'm not entirely sure I understood every piece, but Angel sucked it up like the little sponge she is.' Hayley kept her eyes on her daughter, watching her ruffling the dog's mane of fur. Her daughter was having a ball in New York already. A warm glow invaded Hayley's chest as she continued to look across the park. This was what she wanted. Her daughter laughing, happy and carefree.

'Well, I hate to talk business but you'll never guess what happened today,' Dean said, scuffing up some snow with his shoe as he walked.

'Hold up, let me guess … um, your tyrannical boss told you the Globe isn't anywhere near ready and it's back to the drawing board?' Vernon said.

The mention of the tyrannical boss shifted Hayley's stomach lining as the jacket incident came to mind. She put her hands in her pockets. She really needed to buy some more gloves.

'Would you believe it if I said it was the complete opposite?'

'You're kidding me,' Vernon said in shock.

'It gets even better,' Dean continued.

'You're getting a pay rise?' Hayley offered.

'Not quite that good. I'm in charge of the project.' Dean wore a grin from ear to ear.

'Dean, that's amazing news.' Vernon stopped walking and clapped his arms around him.

'I'm lost. Explain please,' Hayley said, feeling a little left out.

'Oliver Drummond signed off on the Globe today. We're launching in March and it's my job to coordinate the whole thing, to make sure it happens,' Dean explained, still smiling.

'That's ... so cool. It is cool, isn't it? It's not going to be too much for you? Have you got enough time to take it on?' Hayley asked.

'Hay, I've been waiting so long for something like this. As much as I like Peter, he hasn't exactly been pushing me towards running projects like this. It's a huge opportunity,' Dean told her.

Of course it was. It was what her brother was good at. Managing. Being utterly competent and clever. He was in his element. And he was such a lovely person he deserved every ounce of his success. Unlike her, with her lack of full-time job and a mission to track down an ex-lover.

She broke, bursting into heavy, hot tears.

'Hayley?' Dean said, as Hayley turned away from him, her hands up to her face.

She was so embarrassed, yet she couldn't stop. 'I'm OK,' she forced out, as thick, wet streams fell from her eyes and almost froze on her cheeks.

'I'll catch up with Angel,' she heard Vernon say softly.

She felt Dean take a step towards her and she wafted her hand in the air. 'Don't hug me. I'm being an idiot.'

'You're not being an idiot,' Dean said in a consoling voice.

'I am. It's the jet lag, that's all, or maybe looking at paintings of pigs with three tails.'

'Are you sure? Has something happened at home?'

Hayley shook her head, turning finally to face him. 'Nothing's happened. I just ...' She stopped.

'Tell me, Hay, please,' Dean begged.

She looked across the park at Angel. She was throwing a stick for Randy, getting encouragement from Vernon. She needed to talk to her daughter, properly. She deserved to know the truth now. She raised her eyes to meet Dean's anxious expression.

'I quit my job and Angel wants to find her father.'

There. She'd told someone. A slight lightening of her shoulders occurred and she blew out a breath as if she'd been holding it in her whole life.

It was Dean's turn to exhale. 'Well, you know what I think about your job? I think you can do better than a dry-cleaning company. I'm glad. And you'll find something else. Hey, maybe this is a chance to pick up your college course again? Get back into fashion?'

Hayley thought about her ideas book with the beginnings of a couture dress shaped like the Guggenheim. It was hardly Vivienne Westwood.

'So what has Angel said about her father?' Dean asked.

'Nothing. I mean, she hasn't spoken to me about it at all. And half of me wishes she would and the other half hopes she doesn't.'

'Then how do you know she wants to find him?'

Hayley sighed, remembering the very moment she'd made the decision to come here.

'Because she made a wish to God and Father Christmas. And I was standing outside her bedroom door.' Hayley paused. 'I heard her. She tagged it onto the end of her prayers, Dean. She said, if Father Christmas or God were listening, there was only one present she really wanted …' The emotion was trying to get the better of her again. She took a breath. 'She would like to meet her dad.'

This time when Dean moved to comfort her, she let him. She buried her face into his woollen coat, sniffing hard to control the tears. Dean's hand was in her hair and she let his warmth and his love wash over her for a moment.

'This was always going to happen, Hay. And to be honest, she's so bright, I'm surprised she hasn't asked before now.'

'I know.' She lifted her head up. 'And that's half the issue. She hasn't actually *asked*, Dean. She's made a wish she thinks I don't know about. Because she feels she can't talk to me about it.'

'And that's why you're here this Christmas,' Dean added in.

She nodded. 'I've been trawling the internet looking for him and there's nothing! And today, before we went to the Guggenheim, we went to a gallery he mentioned.' She shook her head. 'Nothing again, but the man was nice. He's going to email some other people.' She stepped back from Dean's embrace, wiping at her eyes. 'Sorry, I think I dribbled on your coat.'

'Don't worry about it.'

'Sorry,' Hayley said again, her gaze falling back to Angel and Vernon who were chasing Randy round and round in circles.

'Stop apologising,' Dean said. 'You're not Superwoman. You can't do it all.'

Superman. She sighed, banishing thoughts of hot billionaires she had no time for or interest in.

'So you have *no* idea where he is?'

She shook her head. 'No. I mean I've searched and searched for weeks. Nothing on Google, or Facebook either.' She sighed. 'I basically could get a job with the CIA for all the background checking I've been doing.'

'Do you want me to help? There are definitely other sites I know we can try,' Dean suggested.

'I know nothing about him, Dean. I don't even know if the name he gave me was real. That's why I'm here. Because this place, this city, is the only connection we have.' She threw her arms up, indicating the expanse of land and buildings surrounding them. One city. But one of the biggest cities in the world and she had to try and find a man she'd only spent one night with. She was also ignoring the part of her that was saying he could just as easily be in Kuala Lumpur or Acapulco.

'Well, whatever you need, I'm here for you,' Dean told her, sincerity coating every word.

'I know,' Hayley responded, sniffing the emotion away. 'Thank you.'

'So what are you going to do?'

Dean made sure Angel was pre-occupied with Randy before he asked the question.

'Well, my master plan was to go back to the places I went with him. Show his photo, ask around. He said he was an artist, I can phone the half of the galleries I haven't already contacted.'

'Do you *know* how many galleries there are in New York City?'

'Yes, of course I do. I've spent the last two months calling and emailing them.' She let out an irritated sigh. 'I tell you what, Dean, shall I go and ask Angel? She's bound to know. She could probably even tell me what year they opened.' She brushed the snowflakes off the front of her coat with a sharp, annoyed motion. She'd been harsh and Dean wasn't saying anything in response. 'I'm sorry.' She moistened her lips. 'I was going to try Vipers, the club where we met.' She looked up at Dean. 'But I'd need you to watch Angel for me.'

'Are you going to tell Angel what you're doing?'

Hayley shrugged. 'I don't know. What do you think? I'm worried if I say anything at all I'll get her hopes up and then if I don't find him …'

'Well, in my opinion, every child has a right to know who their father is.'

That comment turned her stomach over. She agreed, but her default position as a mother was to always protect her child. If she opened this box with Angel, there would be no putting the lid back on.

'I guess I didn't think through the talking it out with her bit,' Hayley admitted.

Dean swung an arm around her, drawing her close to him. 'It doesn't have to be turned into an episode of *Jerry Springer*. You just have to sit her down ...'

'Remove the special dictionary from her hands so she can't look up the phrase *one-night stand*.'

'Hay, is that what you're worried about? How she came into this world?'

'I don't know, maybe.' She sighed. 'I just don't want her to think she isn't special because I wasn't in a relationship. And... I don't want to think I was *that* girl. Stupid, naïve... she's meant to look up to me.'

'She isn't going to think any of that,' Dean said. 'Look at her.'

Hayley shifted her gaze to her daughter, holding out her hand to Randy, controlling his moves with a wave of her finger, lips moving as she spoke to the dog. She was her everything.

'There isn't anyone on this planet more special than that bundle of cute intelligence,' Dean told her.

'But I've let her down,' Hayley said.

'How so?'

'Because I should have found a keeper not a shaggy-haired artist who charmed me with his foreign accent.'

'I have to admit, I've been charmed by my fair share of those too.' Dean smiled.

'I wasn't thinking that.' Hayley laughed, easing the tension. 'So, I want to hear all about how you met Vernon.'

'Looks like George Clooney, doesn't he?'

'A replacement because the real one went and got married?'

Dean shook his head. 'Oh no, he's so much better than the real thing with his gorgeous hair and puppy-dog eyes and the way he ...'

'I really don't need to know what you get up to.'

'I was going to tell you he can cook.'

'Oh my God, he *is* better than the real George Clooney!'

Dean smiled and took hold of her hand, squeezing it against the wool of his gloves. 'Oh by the way, thanks for dropping the jacket in today. Angel's been the talk of the building.'

'Uh oh.'

'The "world's most eligible bachelor" comment tickled Clara Fortaine.'

'One day that girl is going to get me arrested,' Hayley replied. Looking across at Angel darting through the snow, her eyes sparkling, cheeks rosy, her breath hot in the air, she knew there wasn't a thing that girl could do that would stop her going to the ends of the Earth to make her happy.

CHAPTER SEVENTEEN

Drummond Global Offices, Downtown Manhattan

Why did he do this to himself? Oliver had the McArthur Foundation website up on his PC screen. His intention had been to check the list of sponsors attending the fundraiser just to update himself on who was on board with the project. What he was doing now was reading the heartfelt stories from families the charity had helped. It was torturous. It brought back memories of Ben. It physically hurt how much he missed him. And every day it hit him how much better suited Ben would be to this role than he was. Ben had been the dream son. The more academic one, who passed his driving test first time and won the spelling bee. Ben had been kind, thoughtful, doing anything for anyone. Oliver had been the brat. He'd always thought of himself first and everyone else a good while later. Because he hadn't needed to be the good son. That was Ben's job. Ben had the halo and it was pointless to even try to compete. Football was the only thing Oliver had had. The only thing he'd shone at. The only area of his life he owned. He swallowed. That's where he should be now. Playing professionally, living the life he was destined for, not slipping into his dead brother's shoes and living out *his* destiny. The Globe was going to make the difference. The Globe was going to be the game changer. It was about putting his stamp on things, feeling differently and not living in the shadow of ghosts.

He clicked his mouse onto another page and there he was, staring back at him. Ben. His mother had no doubt got the photo uploaded. It was the photo their father had taken when Ben had won the prize for innovation at the annual Manhattan Chamber of Commerce awards. A piece of software Ben had created had changed the way not only Drummond Global worked, but businesses across the world.

Ben smiled out at him, joy etched on his face, life seeping from every pore. Oliver had been there that night, sat with the family, clapping his brother to victory. He had been so proud of him but jealous in equal measure. His brother might have had a short life but he'd got his dream.

The door of his office opened and Clara breezed in. He hurriedly minimised the screen.

'Have you given up on knocking, Clara?'

'I'm sorry. When you told me you weren't working late tonight I presumed you wouldn't still be here at eight p.m.' She slipped some files into his in-tray.

'And what are you still doing here? Has husband number two left you?'

The expression that filled every inch of her face told him that his attempt at a joke hadn't gone down so well.

'I was just packing up,' Clara said, turning her back on him and heading for the door.

'Hey, wait up a second.' He stood up and his movement or maybe his words made her stop. 'You haven't explained why you're still here.'

She faced him again. 'You don't need to concern yourself with the answer, Oliver. I turn up on time every day and I work late. I am the model employee.'

'I'm not saying you aren't.' He tried again. 'Have I missed something?'

She shook her head. 'No.'

'So everything is OK in the house of Fortaine?'

'Oliver, this has never been something we talk about.'

He nodded his head. She was right. He had always drawn the lines very succinctly. Emotional attachment of any kind was time and effort wasted. But Clara had worked for him since he'd taken over, for his father years before that. For business purposes he should know a little of what was going on in her personal life, shouldn't he? If she was distracted at home it might make her distracted at work. He drew in a breath. He'd started this now, there was no going back.

'I know we don't. But I'm asking you now. What's going on?'

The question was broad enough to draw out a response. He put his hands on the back of his chair, pressing the leather underneath his fingers. He could see Clara was struggling with this. Why had he said something so flippant without thought?

'I don't know if he's going to be there,' she admitted through a tapered breath.

Oliver didn't know what to say. He hadn't expected Clara to be so honest. Now he was way out of his area of expertise. Flattery was the extent of his talent with women. Comforting was never part of his agenda.

'We're going through a difficult patch at the moment,' Clara elaborated.

She was wringing her hands together, pushing and pulling at the skin, and he didn't know what to do. He was no good with stuff like this. It freaked him out.

'Is there anything I can do?' It sounded pathetically weak and a little insincere. But it was all he could come up with.

'I don't think there's anyone else. I mean, who would put up with him? He's lazy and ungrateful and his psoriasis is very bad at the moment,' Clara continued.

Oliver moulded his fingers into the fabric of the chair a little more, trying to work out how to make this situation he'd created a whole lot better. Should he let her talk? Just stand there and listen? Weren't people supposed to feel like a weight had been taken off just by talking their load away? That's what the therapists had tried to tell his mother anyway.

'It's been like this since he lost his job.' Clara sighed. 'He worked for that company for twenty years and in the end it counted for nothing.'

He moved quietly, coming around his desk and pulling out the seat opposite his desk. He didn't need to do anything else, Clara was already lowering herself down into it.

'It does something to a man,' Clara continued. 'When you give everything you have to a role you love, dedicate yourself to a company like that and then all you've ever known is just taken away so fast.'

She was struggling to hold back the tears now. This was a big deal to her. When had she started struggling so much? He hadn't noticed anything at work. Or was that merely because he hadn't been looking? Because he was always so blinkered by what was going on in his own life?

Clara carried on. 'I've tried to get him to look for something else but he just can't see past the stigma of being made redundant. Because he thought he was never going to work any place else, he thinks he *can't* work any place else.'

Oliver racked his brain trying to remember what it was Clara's husband did. He didn't even recall his name. Mike? Mark?

Then it was like Clara came to and she turned her head, focussing on him.

'Oh, Oliver, I'm so sorry.' She got to her feet. 'I don't know what I was thinking. You don't want to hear about all this. And I shouldn't be bringing it into work.' She got to her feet, straightening her jacket.

'You haven't been bringing it into work.' He paused. 'And I asked.'

'I know but …'

'Why don't you have tomorrow off?' Where had that idea come from? He had never done that in his life before and the absolute shock on Clara's face told him she thought he was ailing for something.

'No, that's ridiculous. I'm fine,' she insisted.

'I know you're fine. I'm just suggesting you take a day, spend some time with …' He really couldn't remember her husband's name.

'William,' Clara offered.

'Yes. Just take a day, Clara.' He swallowed. A feeling he wasn't familiar with began to take a stranglehold on him. It was the McArthur Foundation website. Looking at that had turned him into a ball of weakness. He put a hand on one of the buttons of his jacket and fastened it up.

'Are you sure?' Clara asked, her voice soft and full of vulnerability.

'Yes, I'm sure.' He threw an arm towards the door. 'Now get out of here, get some takeout, go home.'

He watched her take one step and then she stopped, looking back at him.

'And what are you going to do?' she asked.

'Me?' What was he going to do? He'd been riding the crest of business success earlier. He wished he'd never opened the stupid website. It had killed his mood. He couldn't let that happen.

'I'm going to go home, get a shower, call Tony and head out into the bright lights of the city.'

'No more Chinese food,' Clara said as a warning.

'Perhaps Spanish tonight.'

Clara took a breath and gathered herself. 'Thank you, Oliver.'

He waved a hand quickly, almost desperately. He couldn't handle any more sentiment. 'Go home.'

She smiled again and headed towards the door. Just as she was about to cross the threshold Oliver had an urge to stop her, to ask her if she'd finished the letter to Luther Jameson. He hadn't signed the cheque yet. He could change his mind. He could give the McArthur Foundation fundraiser his support. He could speak there, he could take *his* load off.

As the thought of standing up in front of a function room of people soaked into him, he felt his heart convulse and he had to swallow down the nausea. Clara waved a hand at him and it was all he could do not to throw up. He couldn't do it. He wasn't changing his mind. It was inconceivable and that was the way it was going to stay.

CHAPTER EIGHTEEN

Vipers Nightclub, Downtown Manhattan

'I shouldn't have eaten so many burritos.' Tony let out a belch, one hand on his chest.

'You think?' Oliver said. 'I'd guess it was the two sides of fries that really did it.'

'Why didn't you stop me?'

'Because both of us having heart attacks and going together might be kind of cool.'

Tony swiped a hand out, catching Oliver on the shoulder. 'Asshole.'

Oliver smiled. The music in the club was thudding through his body, banging his ribcage, pulsing through every internal organ and he was relishing it. He wanted this buzz, he needed to be part of this life. People filled the dance floor, their bodies moving to the sounds of Bruno Mars and Jason Derulo, swirling under glitter balls and bright white Christmas lights. Garlands decked the windows, tinsel hung from contemporary art on the walls, the holidays were coming and everyone here was hungry for it. Except him. Because he didn't want anything to stop. He needed to be busy, vital, involved in the fabric of something, to stop himself from thinking too much. Like today when he'd clicked on that website and given Clara the day off. *Weak.*

He put the bottle of beer to his mouth and let his eyes rove over the clientele. They were spoiled for choice here. There was a group of women to their right joining the dance floor. Despite the snow outside, they were dressed to impress in figure-fitting dresses that didn't leave much to the imagination. The blonde of the party looked Oliver's way, sending him a mere hint of a smile. He raised his beer bottle a little, just to show interest. She moved her hips in time to the next track as it came through the speakers and he admired what he saw. Tonight was going to be a good night. He could just feel it.

'I'm seeing this,' Tony said, nudging Oliver's ribs with his elbow. 'Why do they always notice you first?'

'Don't knock it. It means they get to notice you at all.'

'Hey!'

'Come on,' Oliver said, stepping towards the group of ladies.

Dean Walker's Apartment, Downtown Manhattan

'Did you know that Central Park was originally opened in 1857?'

'Did you know if you don't put that guidebook down I'm going to start eating your pizza,' Hayley said, playfully.

They were sat around the large dining table eating pizza Vernon had made from scratch in about ten minutes. It was the most divine-tasting base Hayley had ever had and it seemed her brother's partner was turning out to be a catch in every department. If only she could meet someone like that instead of being set upon by the likes of Greg.

Hayley drained the wine from her glass in one mouthful then took a look at her watch. It was almost ten o'clock and she couldn't help feeling that Angel should really be in bed. It was the second late night in as many days and coupled with the jet lag it didn't bode well for tomorrow. She also had plans of her own for tonight. Plans that didn't involve the company of a nine-year-old. Vipers nightclub.

'What was your favourite animal at the zoo?' Vernon asked, topping up Dean and Hayley's wineglasses.

'Oh I loved the sea lions,' Angel announced. 'Did you know that sea lions can stay under the water for up to forty minutes?'

'I didn't know that,' Vernon answered.

'The longer you know Angel, the greater your life's knowledge will be, trust me,' Hayley said, picking up a piece of pizza.

'The only thing Mum is an expert on is *EastEnders*,' Angel piped up.

Hayley put a hand to her chest and looked shocked. 'You've burned me! I also happen to be an expert on hits of the year 2000.'

'That takes me back. 2000, pleather before it was pleather and Madonna's "Music",' Dean said.

'I concur. I graced a few dance floors to that one,' Vernon joined in.

'You never did!' Dean said, smiling.

'Just because we haven't been out dancing yet doesn't mean I can't,' Vernon said.

'OK, Fred and Ginger, no spats at the dinner table,' Hayley said.

'Did you know Madonna is afraid of thunder?' Angel said, sipping from her glass of Coke.

'What? You've made that up,' Hayley said.

Angel shook her head. 'I read it somewhere.'

Hayley nudged Vernon's arm. 'See what I mean? Child genius.'

Angel smiled and looked at Dean. 'We met Mr Meanie's personal assistant today, Uncle Dean.'

'I've heard all about it,' Dean replied.

'And we really don't need to hear any more,' Hayley added. She screwed her face up at Angel, pushing her tongue forward in her mouth and jutting out her chin.

'Isn't that a form of swearing in America?' Angel asked loudly.

'So what did you think of the offices?' Dean asked.

'It's massive! How many floors does it have?' Angel asked.

'You mean you don't know,' Hayley teased.

'Eighty. And it's quite a workout if you take the stairs,' Dean answered.

'Do you have to rehydrate at the top?' Angel held her empty glass aloft. 'Can I have some more Coke?'

'I'll get you some,' Vernon said, rising from his chair.

'Oh, Angel, go with him. He has trouble with the ice machine,' Dean encouraged.

'OK. Vern, can we let Randy out of the spare bedroom when we've finished eating?' Angel asked as she got up.

'As long as you keep him away from the cushions,' Dean answered.

'There we go,' Vernon said. 'As long as he stays away from the precious fripperies.'

Hayley couldn't help smiling. The two men sounded like an old married couple. It was nice. She hadn't seen Dean this happy or settled before. She waited for Angel to make it to the kitchen area then put a hand on Dean's arm.

'So could you watch Angel for me tonight? So I can go to Vipers and ask if anyone remembers Michel?' Hayley's heart jumped into her throat. 'It is still there isn't it?

'Yeah, it's still there but …' Dean started.

'I know Vernon is here and everything, but it's late, she'll be asleep the second her head hits the pillow, I promise.'

Despite having no luck in the gallery today her stomach was fizzing with anticipation about visiting Vipers. The place she'd met Angel's father. There was a chance, maybe a small chance, that he might even be there. Just because ten years might have gone by didn't mean *everything* had changed.

Dean looked over at Vernon and Angel laughing as crushed iced spurted out from the refrigerator.

'See, she's being a doll and Vernon likes her *and* I finally got her to part with the dreadful Christmas book she made us read every December.'

'I don't have a problem with minding Angel, Hay, I'm just worried about you. I know you're doing this for Angel but are *you* really ready for it?' Dean asked.

Hayley sucked in a giant breath. She was trying to do everything but think about whether *she* was ready for it or not. She just had to be. This wasn't about her.

'I don't know. I wasn't ready for the end of *Spooks* but I had to deal with it all the same.'

Dean was looking at her, seemingly scrutinising every nuance. She tried another smile and picked up her wine glass, sipping at the contents.

'I don't think you should go there on your own,' Dean said.

'I promise I won't go off with any suspicious-looking characters and come back pregnant.' Hayley held her hand up like she was committing to the Girl Guide promise.

'That isn't funny.'

'No, I know but I *am* doing it for Angel.' She sighed. 'I have no secret yearning to see Michel again.'

Now Dean was eyeing her with suspicion.

'Why are you looking at me like that?'

He sighed. 'Well, how many boyfriends have you had since Michel?'

'Come on, I've got a nine-year-old daughter.' She looked over to the kitchen. Vernon and Angel were making artwork out of the glass of Coke with a paper umbrella, straws and fruit.

'So there's been nobody?'

'I'm not particularly comfortable having this conversation with my brother.'

'Hayley …'

'There's been a few, OK. A couple of dinners and a couple of nights at their places.' Her mind went to Greg. 'A desperate colleague who wanted to iron out my creases and so much more.'

'What?'

Hayley sighed. 'There's been no one special enough to meet Angel.'

'Because?'

'Not because I still hold out hope of reuniting with someone I knew for half an evening, one night and half a morning ten years ago.' She huffed out a breath and dug her fork into a baby tomato.

'Listen, don't get me wrong, I think you're right about focussing on Angel but …' Dean began.

'Look what Vernon made me!' Angel held aloft the fluted glass of Coke festooned with every embellishment imaginable. Saved by the bell – read Coke.

'We thought it went with Uncle Dean's cushions,' Vernon remarked, retaking his seat.

'Funny guy,' Dean said, a smile at his lips.

'Do you like it, Mum?' Angel asked, sitting back down and showing Hayley her glass.

'I think it looks worthy of a nightclub,' she answered, defiant eyes shifting to Dean.

CHAPTER NINETEEN

Dean Walker's Apartment, Downtown Manhattan

Hayley looked at herself in the gold-edged full-length bedroom mirror. The navy blue wool knit dress would have been perfect for the North-Pole-like climate outside but would have baked her under the nightclub strobes. So she'd hacked off the long sleeves. With the arms gone, she'd tidied up the cuts until it hung from her like it was always meant to be that way. One of Angel's bright white flower hair clips was now positioned on the front as an appliqué and her hair had been tamed as far as it could without the aid of a professional stylist. The reflection declared her almost Rachel Rileyesque and that would have to be enough.

She reached down to the bed to pick up a small silver sequinned clutch bag. Her mother had bought it for her when she was sixteen from a fancy shop you only dared step in for a treat. It was a rare occasion where the two of them had actually got along.

Hayley smoothed her hand over the magnetic clasp then pulled it open. There was just enough room for money, a key, a credit card or two, lipstick, powder and perfume and the only photo you possessed of the father of your child.

She drew out the photo she'd shown Carl at the gallery earlier, pressing the corners a little flatter. There she was, looking young, vibrant, her highlighted hair looking glossy and conditioned, her smile wide, joyous, like someone high on life or maybe someone just full of tequila.

And there, next to her in the photo, was Michel. Michel De Vos. A Belgian artist – or so he'd told her – hoping to make it big in the metropolis. She'd admired his chocolate-brown eyes as well as his accent and she'd listened intently as he talked about his plans for the future over a seemingly never-ending bottle of sparkling wine and a few vodkas thrown in for good measure. They'd danced and they'd sung loudly and completely out of tune and then he'd asked about her.

Hayley sighed and sat down on the bed. Running her fingers over Michel's dark hair in the picture, she remembered everything they'd spoken about that night like it was a favourite DVD she'd watched time and again. She'd told him all her secrets. Her ambition to be a fashion designer. How she wanted to finish college, get some work experience with a fashion house in London, work on other people's designs until she got a chance to deliver her own.

And he'd listened, looking at her like she held the world in her palm. He'd called her an artist too, said she was going to be making clothes for Hillary Clinton before she knew it. She'd laughed and said she was hoping for someone more like J.Lo.

Fashion designer. It was almost laughable now. She'd got herself pregnant, listened to her mother's disappointed *I told you so's* and got a job at a factory that made Wellington boots.

Was Michel still an artist? Did he get to pursue *his* dreams? She wasn't sure she really wanted to find out. If he had, she would be jealous. If he hadn't, she would be disappointed. But this wasn't about her. It was about Angel.

She slipped the photo back into her clutch bag and fastened it up.

Vipers Nightclub, Downtown Manhattan

'Any second now and they're going to be back over here,' Tony said, his eyes fixed on the group of women moving to a David Guetta song.

Oliver leaned on the dark wood and surveyed the dance floor from their vantage point. The beer was slipping down well and at last he felt himself start to loosen up. This was good.

'So, how are we gonna play this?' Tony asked, his mouth at Oliver's ear.

'What?'

'I said, how are we gonna play this?' Tony repeated twice as loud.

'I heard what you said I just didn't know what you meant.'

'Well, is it gonna be the double dating thing or the singular attack?'

'Safety in numbers,' Oliver answered.

'Yeah but you usually end up with both of them.'

He shook his head. 'That happened *once*.'

'And I'm not letting it happen again.' Tony loosened the top button of his shirt then ran a hand through his thick black hair. 'See ya!' He waved a hand and strode onto the dance floor, his head bobbing and bouncing like an excited emu.

Oliver laughed, watching his friend sidling up to the object of his affection.

'I know who you are.'

The blonde-haired woman he'd paid attention to earlier was suddenly at his side, the heat from her body unavoidable.

He straightened up. 'You do, do you?'

She nodded. 'Uh-huh. You're Oliver Drummond. I've seen your photo in the *New York Times*.'

'And where have I seen you before? A billboard maybe?' he flirted, putting his beer bottle on the shelf in front of him.

'That's cute,' she responded. 'So, are you here on your own?'

He looked over one shoulder and then the other, then turned back to smile at her. 'Theoretically I guess I am now.' He widened his smile. 'But with a capacity crowd I'm sensing potential.'

'Want some closer company?'

'You haven't even told me your name,' he responded.

'Buy me a drink and I might let you in on that.' She smiled with confidence and he nodded, returning the sentiment. She was good. She was practised and a player. She could get his day back on track. And his night.

'What would you like?' he asked her.

Just walking through the front doors of Vipers brought so many memories flooding back.

Hayley stepped into the main room of the club and the music enveloped her. A heavy bassline kicked in, a track she recognised, and suddenly she was transported back ten years.

Her very first New York nightclub. She'd felt so grown-up in her neon pink mini-dress with her glossy hair and dollars destined to be spent on enjoying herself. Dean had pulled her onto the dance floor to something by Whitney Houston. She'd swirled and twirled and got tipsy on vodka within the hour. Her relationship with alcohol had been the most longstanding one she'd had. Some things didn't change. Even this place hadn't changed much. The dark woodwork she remembered, the mirrored tiles she didn't and the walls without mirrors were now painted a sultry plum. It looked like a classy boudoir, with just a dash of decorations to let patrons know that Christmas was coming.

She paused where she stood, taking in the fashions, seeing what the nightclub-goers of 2015 wore. There were hot pants and tight jeans, little dresses with sequins and sparkle. The men wore smart jeans or suit trousers, more shirts than T-shirts – Vipers had got a little more upmarket. Reasons Christmas is better in New York number 45: Anything goes in the fashion stakes. And that was one of the things she loved about the city most. The non-conformity, the ability to express yourself, be different and unashamed. *Freedom.* Maybe she was thinking too hard with her ideas book. Perhaps she just needed to relax into it a little more.

Michel had certainly been relaxed the night they'd met. She remembered exactly what he'd been wearing that night. Faded denim jeans, the hem fraying over his retro Converse. His T-shirt had fitted him perfectly and he'd known it. And it had borne a slogan. She'd had a definite thing for slogan T-shirts back then. It had stated simply, *I Shoot People*, and then had a sketch of a camera below. It had appealed to her childish sense of humour. And if she was honest she would still find it funny.

Hayley headed for the bar, almost able to taste the cranberry vodka. It was busy and she joined the throng of individuals waiting for one of the bar staff to give them attention. Dying of thirst was a possibility, judging by the disgruntled groans every time a server took an order from someone who had skipped the line.

Hayley raised a ten dollar bill in the air, waving it in the direction of a passing barman.

'I find a hundred dollar bill works better.'

She spun round, looking at the owner of the voice. Oliver Drummond. *Clark.* Dressed in dark grey trousers, a pristine white shirt open at the neck, those eyes still the colour of cased pistachios. His musky cologne drifted up her nose as her gaze refused to move from him.

'Hello, Lois,' he greeted.

She forced a smile. So he recognised her now, did he? 'Why, Superman, I did think about calling, but wasn't sure the need for a vodka cranberry was dire enough to require your services.'

'I think it depends just how desperate the drinker is for it.'

'She had a couple of glasses of Italian wine she couldn't pronounce the name of an hour ago.'

'I'm surprised you didn't call 911.' Oliver raised his hand and the barman immediately stopped right in front of them, waiting for orders.

'A bottle of Bud, a white wine soda and a vodka cranberry,' he ordered.

'Whoa, stop. No white wine chaser for me,' Hayley said quickly.

He smiled. 'It isn't for you.'

'Ah, already replaced the woman from last night.' She smiled wider. 'Are you going to get to the end of the date with this one?'

He didn't respond to the question. 'Thank you for returning my jacket.'

'Oh, it was nothing.' She paused, raising her voice a little louder over the music. 'Actually, it wasn't nothing. I'm pretty sure your receptionist thought I was a conquest bringing in your love child.'

He wasn't sure whether to smile or grimace and he was pretty sure the look he'd ended up with didn't make the most of his features.

He watched Hayley's mouth open like a cartoon character. 'Wow, you mean that's actually happened.'

He nodded, handing the barman the money for the drinks. 'A couple of times.'

'Whoa.'

'And I hasten to add that none of the children were mine.' He smiled then and passed her a tall glass filled with red liquid.

'Good to know,' Hayley said, nodding.

'So, you're meeting someone here?'

She shook her head. 'No … just checking out an old haunt.'

'You've been here before,' he stated the obvious.

'Years ago.'

He watched her eyes drift to the glass of white wine he was holding. Shit, he'd forgotten all about the blonde.

'I'd better let you go and give that to your date,' Hayley said, as if mind reading was her speciality.

'It isn't a date,' he answered quickly. He wet his lips.

'Is that how you justify it when you bail out early?'

'That was a one-off.'

'Business then?' She lowered her voice, inching her head closer into his personal space. 'Something about the Globe?'

He reeled back then, shocked by her words. What did she know about something so confidential?

'I have no idea what you're talking about,' he answered swiftly.

She knew about his business. Their encounter at the Chinese restaurant hadn't been coincidental and neither was this. His hackles were raised now, suspicion rife. Was she competitor or press?

'Sorry, it's none of my business,' she spoke fast. 'It's just putting my brother in charge of the project practically made his year.'

His face wrinkled in confusion until everything sunk in. That's where he had seen Dean Walker before, at the Chinese restaurant, with Lois and the chattering nine-year-old child. Relief flooded his insides and he watched Hayley's eyes widen.

'Ha! You thought I was from Apple, didn't you? Luring you into buying me drinks so I could get the inside scoop on the next big thing.'

He shook his head. 'Of course not.'

She laughed. 'You went as white as if I was carrying Kryptonite in this handbag.'

He tried to recover. 'How do I know you're not?'

She raised her hands. 'I come in peace. No substances poisonous to superheroes and no Mob connections, I promise.'

He really wanted to get rid of the white wine. He looked to the blonde across the dance floor. There really was no competition. This English girl was fun and feisty. He liked the idea of a challenge.

He cleared his throat. 'Just stay right there and give me one second.'

CHAPTER TWENTY

Vipers Nightclub, Downtown Manhattan

What was she doing? She was watching her brother's billionaire boss, one of the world's most eligible bachelors, give someone the brush off … again … for her. Her heart was thumping hard. Was she completely out of her mind? She had learned her lesson about starting a relationship in this nightclub ten years ago. It was not somewhere to begin anything. It was jinxed. And she was not in the market for anything. Not drinks with completely unsuitable men. No matter how hot they were. And he *was* hot. Every inch she could see … and probably all the inches she couldn't see but could imagine. This was craziness.

She moved then, quickly, heading across the floor towards a tall, shaven-haired man in his forties wearing a white shirt, his body the width of a Sherman tank. He was chewing gum and had an earpiece in. A doorman might remember Michel. He could have been working here ten years ago. She slipped the photograph out of her clutch bag.

'Excuse me,' she shouted above the music.

He leant forward, lining up the ear without the earpiece to her mouth.

'I was wondering if you might have seen this man.' She offered out the photograph. 'He used to come in here, a lot I think, and … I'm looking for him.'

The doorman took hold of the photo and squinted his eyes at the picture.

'You his wife?' he asked.

'No … of course not,' Hayley responded, guilt coating her tone anyway.

He handed the photo back. 'I'm not sure. I see a lot of people, sweetcheeks.'

'I realise that.' She sighed. 'It's just … really important I get in touch with him so …' She pushed the photo back into his line of sight. 'If you could have another look.'

The doorman glanced back towards the photo and shook his head. 'He's not familiar to me, sorry. You should ask Artie, on the bar.' He sniffed. 'But he's not on tonight.'

Hayley tightened her grip on the glass she was holding and forced a smile onto her lips. 'Thank you.'

She turned away and saw Oliver heading back towards her. He had to negotiate several groups of people. If she moved now she could be out of the door in seconds. She could disappear into the night like he had from the alleyway at the back of Asian Dawn. But that wasn't in her nature. Besides, she was starting to think there was a bit more to Oliver Drummond. An ogre-like control freak wouldn't have just given her brother the head role in the launch of their new lead product.

And why shouldn't she enjoy herself for an hour or so? If a billionaire wanted to buy her drinks who was she to stop him?

He neared, navigating the groups of people quickly. She would have one drink. And then she would move on to showing the bartenders the photo of Michel.

He was smiling as he approached and she felt its warmth settle on her. He spread out his hand, indicating the tables to their left in the quieter area of the club.

'Shall we?' he asked.

'Lead the way, Clark.'

'So, billionaire businessman, how does that happen?'

He smiled, watching her take a long sip of her drink, all bright eyes and enthusiasm.

'Haven't you seen *Fifty Shades of Grey*?' he answered.

She looked up then, a blush on her cheeks as her eyes met his. 'I'm not sure explaining Christian Grey's *business* position was the aim of that movie or the books.'

He leaned forward in his chair, holding her gaze. 'What do you want to know?'

He watched her swallow, wet her lips.

'Whether any of the rooms in your house are red now.'

He laughed, pure, deep and unfettered. His stomach contracted with the motion, unaccustomed to it. He adopted a more serious look before responding. 'And if they are?'

'Each to their own, but it's not for me. I went to an Ann Summers party once and got a little jittery when they said some of the items were refurbished.'

He smiled. Honesty. No game-playing. This was refreshing.

He took a swig of his beer. 'I inherited the company from my father.'

'Old money. So, I guess that makes you a duke?'

'Not that I'm aware of, but that would be kind of cool.'

'And different from the whole Superman dress up. Do you really do that by the way?'

He grinned, lacing his hands around his beer bottle. 'Only on weekends.'

'In the red room.'

'And I thought that was going to stay my secret.'

It was her turn to laugh then and he delighted in the way she gave into it, her cheeks rising up, her eyes narrowing in pleasure. Suddenly his libido was on high alert. He fingered the paper label on the bottle, picking at a strip.

'Unfortunately the day job gets in the way of the saving the city full time.' He smiled. 'Without the aid of tight costumes my father helped to revolutionise the computer industry in the 1980s. I spent a lot of my childhood watching him solder motherboards together.'

'Is that a good thing or a bad thing?'

'Back then I would rather have spent my time watching NFL.'

'And now?'

He nodded. 'Yeah, pretty much still feel that way for the most part.'

'So you're not all work, work, work, then?'

Now the unease rolled into his shoulders as he thought about the job he did. The billions of pounds he played with, the employees he was responsible for. It was a burden. He didn't love it like his father. He wasn't exceptional like his brother. He was doing his best but he was hanging everything on the Globe. Failure wasn't an option. He had to make that work or he didn't know what came next.

He smiled, regaining his composure, hopefully before she had even realised it had diminished. 'All work and no play isn't my style.'

'If only your staff could hear you now.'

The vodka and cranberry was doing strange things to her tongue. She liked to talk but she wasn't usually this good at shooting herself in the foot every time words fell out of her mouth.

'Was my name bandied around the dinner table along with the wine you couldn't pronounce the name of?'

The tone of his voice had an edge to it and she quickly shook her head. 'No, of course not. Dean isn't like that.' She hurried on. 'He's a hard worker and he's the most intelligent person I know. And he's very discreet. Completely discreet. Always has been.' She hoped she had salvaged this.

'Hopefully he won't be discreet when he brings the Globe to market. I want more press than a red carpet event at the Oscars.'

'And I wouldn't mind one of the dresses.'

Her fingers went to the hair clip on the front of her dress then across to the cut-off shoulders she hadn't had time to hem. She cleared her throat. 'None of those in my luggage. Anything with Swarovski crystals would completely eat into the baggage allowance.'

He smiled, seemed to drop his eyes to Angel's hair clip on her dress. It had looked funky in the mirror at Dean's apartment, now it felt trashy. Not that she cared. Because she was completely disinterested in men. This man in particular. Who was rude and abandoned dates and was definitely not giving her any kind of hot flush whatsoever.

'So, you're just visiting?' he asked.

'I think so …' She wet her lips. 'I didn't mean that,' she corrected. 'I meant to say, yes.'

He looked quizzical then.

'I've got a return ticket for just after New Year.'

His gaze was unsettling her now. She pulled at a petal on the hair clip. 'School starts back in January.' She swallowed. 'You know I have a daughter. The one your PA probably told you went on and on about you being an eligible bachelor.'

She really needed to stop talking now.

'And she was getting very talkative about the lobsters at the restaurant the other night,' he said.

Hayley looked up, a smile on her face. 'You heard that?'

'To be honest it was pretty hard not to,' he said with a wry smile

'Yeah, she's loud and opinionated and too clever for her own good.'

'What's her name?'

'Angel,' Hayley said.

'It's pretty.'

'I think she would rather be named after someone from history now she's nine. Every day I wait for the forms to change her name to Boudicca.'

Oliver laughed hard and her insides took note. He had a nice laugh, it wasn't false or pretentious, it was warm and genuine. She had trouble believing this man was the mean tyrant who ruled with a rod of iron. Not that you could tell anything from a laugh. She clamped her lips to her glass.

'So, talking of names …' he started.

'Yes, Clark.'

'I can't carry on calling you Lois.'

'Why not? Don't you like an air of mystery?'

'You know *my* name.'

'Not all of it.'

He sat back in his chair and looked confused. 'What?'

'I don't know your middle name.' She sucked at her drink. 'If you're almost a duke you have to have at least one middle name. I think it's royal law or something.'

Oliver shook his head vehemently but he was enjoying every second of this repartee. He couldn't remember the last time he'd engaged in anything like it. Most of the time, when he was looking for some female distraction, it involved small talk he needed to put no effort into. *Say they look nice. Ask about their job. Flatter them.* Here, with Lois, he was fully in the moment, not because he needed to prove he could be, simply because he *wanted* to be. A ripple ran through him. That thought scared the shit out of him.

He moved, leaning his elbows on the table, shifting forward in his seat and looking directly at Hayley.

'OK, so are we doing a deal here? Because I'm quite the negotiator.'

'You must want to know my name really badly.'

'Maybe I do.' Did he? They'd only had two conversations.

'You first,' she said as the music lowered and a softer track began to filter.

'Which one d'you want?'

Her mouth formed a small 'o' and he couldn't help his lips, moving upwards in a grin at her reaction.

She licked her lips, rolling the straw in her drink between her thumb and forefinger. 'I think I'm going to have to have both. Don't tell me there are more than two.'

'Just two.'

'Phew.'

'But if you want them both you're going to have to give me your first name *and* something else.'

She folded her arms across her chest. 'Just because I don't have two middle names? What sort of negotiation is that?'

'The only one I'm willing to agree to.'

'And …' She paused to suck a little harder on her drink. 'What's this other thing you want?'

He had said the words so many times. Maybe too many times. Yet, somehow this time, he really wanted to know. He stripped another piece of label from the beer bottle, his eyes not leaving hers. He took a breath. 'If you could make one wish, what would it be?'

'Is one of your middle names "genie"?'

'I'm being serious.'

'Me too.'

'Neither of my middle names until you answer.'

The way he was looking at her was making her insides squirm like she had a belly full of snakes. Was he for real? Her hands straight away went to her silver clutch bag, settling over the clasp. She could tell him she wanted a dress like Lady Gaga's or even to *make* a dress for Lady Gaga, that would be giving him something real. But it wouldn't be the truth. Because there was only one thing she wanted at the moment. And was she really about to share that with Dean's boss?

Hayley took a deep breath, closed her eyes and let the words come out in a rush of breath.

'My name's Hayley and I wish to find the guy I had a one-night stand with ten years ago.'

She flicked open her eyes to gauge Oliver's reaction. He was looking back at her, no emotion evident, his fingers toying with the paper he'd ripped from the bottle.

Her heart was hammering in her chest as he still made no move to respond. What was there to say now? She had turned flirtatious banter into Desperation Central.

He took a swig of beer from his bottle and placed it back down on the table. 'Richard and Julian.' He nodded. 'Now we're even.'

CHAPTER TWENTY-ONE

Vipers Nightclub, Downtown Manhattan

Oliver watched Hayley now, stood on tiptoes at the bar, showing off the photograph she'd pulled from her purse a few minutes before. *Michel* from *Belgium* – or so the guy had told her ten years ago. He hated him already, which was, of course, completely and utterly irrational. He didn't know him. But *Michel* had known her. Lois. Hayley. The so-called artist, with the scruffy dark hair, had become intimately acquainted with her after just one evening together. Why was that pulling at him? Hadn't he been intimately acquainted with a number of women that quickly? He swallowed. Almost every woman he'd ever been with. So why was he judging her?

This was madness. What was he even doing here with her? Why had he homed in on her instead of taking up an evening with a simple fling – get in, get out, have fun – the blonde who knew what she wanted?

He swallowed down a mouthful of beer. He could leave. He'd made her no promises, he'd just bought her a drink. But that would be running out on two dates-that-weren't-dates in two nights. That was serial behaviour. A pattern. He didn't do that. He'd told *her* he didn't do that. It would make him into a coward. *Weak.* His heartbeat thrummed and he blinked heavily.

Oliver watched her showing off the photo to staff. He should find Tony. That's what he was going to do. His friend could be in just as much of a fix as he was. Or not. If Tony was getting on well with the brunette, he wouldn't want Oliver butting in. He could call. So why wasn't he moving? Why couldn't he keep his eyes off her? He didn't get invested in women. Investment was never on the table.

He watched her turn back around, her face flushed, her hair bouncing with every stride she took. He blew out a breath as she neared. It wasn't too late. He could still make his excuses.

'They didn't recognise him,' Hayley stated, slipping back into her seat. 'But the doorman earlier said there's someone called Artie who has worked here for a lot longer and he might be able to help me.'

He found himself nodding his head but had no idea what he was agreeing to or sympathising with. He didn't feel peachy with anything about this development.

'But typically he's not working tonight.' Hayley sighed as she pushed the photo back into her purse.

'That's that then,' Oliver finally spoke.

She raised her eyes in response to the flat tone of his voice. Despite all the encouraging things he'd said when she'd elaborated about Angel's wish, he didn't understand at all. And why should he? Despite knowing his two middle names he was a stranger.

'He's working next on Friday,' she said.

'Right,' he answered.

She carried on. 'And I have lots of other art galleries to try.'

'Good luck with that.'

She narrowed her eyes at him. 'Is there something you want to say? You look a little uptight.' She swiped up her drink. 'Was my wish not what you were expecting?'

'If I'm honest, no, it wasn't.'

'So what reply do you usually get? Wait, let me guess.' She adopted a pose, leaning back in her seat, the back of her hand held against her forehead. 'I wish for … something from Tiffany's and a night in a bridal suite with you.'

She watched him fidget as if he disliked what she was saying. She was obviously bang on the money. *Money.* His billions he could flaunt however he chose. That's what he'd been expecting. A wish he could buy.

'I just don't understand why you would waste your time trying to find someone who's not been in your life for ten years.'

He *did* have an opinion. And, from his stance and pallor, it appeared he was very uncomfortable about the whole Michel situation.

'I'm not doing it for me. I'm doing it for Angel,' she responded.

'So you say.'

'What!' She couldn't help a laugh escaping.

'She's had her whole life without a father, why the interest now?'

Her mouth sprung open in shocked surprise. Now her fight and flight responses were well and truly triggered. Who did he think he was analysing the timing of her daughter's request? He knew nothing about the situation. She shouldn't have told him any of this. The hazel eyes didn't look so attractive when they were narrowed in accusation.

'Thank you for the drink.' Hayley stood, picking up her bag.

'You're going?'

For a fleeting second he almost sounded like he was back to that person she'd enjoyed playfully sparring with. But she mustn't be fooled. He thought she was an idiot for being young and getting pregnant by a stranger. And maybe she was, but she didn't need it rubbed in her face. She had a mother who had done that most of her life. This had been a stupid mistake. She should have just had one drink, sat on a bar stool and quizzed the bar staff … alone.

'It was nice to meet you,' she responded. 'Maybe ask the blonde what her wish is. I suspect it could lead to your red room.'

She smiled at him, then, with her head held high she marched to the exit doors.

Oliver sat there feeling like he'd been given a beating. Yet, she hadn't bruised him with her words, hadn't raised her voice, just made it very clear he'd overstepped the mark in his responses. And he had, he knew that. Because he'd turned all Neanderthal over a man she'd met years ago, and he had no clue what it was like being a parent. He had asked what her wish was, had really wanted to know, and then when she'd told him, been as honest as a person could be, he'd thrown it back at her. *Jerk*.

He pushed his bottle of beer to one side, stood up, slipped on his coat and rushed towards the exit. He couldn't leave things like this, for reputation purposes only, obviously. He'd apologise. He'd offer her his courtside seats at the Knicks. No, that wouldn't impress her. Did he want to impress her? He hadn't done such a great job so far.

One of the doormen bid him goodnight but he didn't respond. He put his hand on the door and pushed his way out into the night.

The icy wind wound itself around him as he staggered out into a flurry of snowflakes. His only thought was catching her up and apologising. And what then? What was his grand plan after that?

He didn't stop to think any more. He quickly looked left then right, trying to pick Hayley out from the groups of people on the street fighting the wind. A hint of long brown hair and the cream colour of her coat had him hurrying off right.

His heart was racing and the snow battered his cheeks as he ducked to try and avoid the full force of winter.

'Hayley!' He barely recognised his own voice. It sounded needy and desperate.

Was the hair and coat he was chasing really her?

He tried again. 'Hayley!'

She stopped walking the second she heard her name travelling through the biting breeze. Oliver Richard Julian Drummond. What was he doing following her? By now she'd assumed he would be drinking another beer with a random, asking them what their deepest desire was. She turned around, looking down the street.

There he was, moving at a jog up the pavement towards her, the snow coating his dark woollen overcoat, flecks of white in his tawny coloured hair. Why had she stopped? There was nothing he could say that would excuse his reaction in the nightclub. She should turn around again, head off. But it was like her shoes were stuck to the snow on the ground.

He was within a few yards now, his pace slowing as he neared. She bit her lip, his proximity, the chiselled jawline and full lips affecting her. Her stomach gave a roll like a plane in an aerobatic display.

He stopped opposite her, his body visibly shaking with the cold. He pulled at the collar of his coat, as if he was trying to close off every gap to the elements.

'I have to get back,' Hayley said quickly. 'I don't want to leave Dean with Angel too long.'

'Sure,' he responded. 'Just let me apologise.'

She folded her arms across her chest, the wind circling her body, blowing up her hair and finding its way into every exposed inch. 'There's no need.'

'There's every need.' He put a clenched hand to his mouth and cleared his throat. 'I was behaving like a spoilt child and I offended you.'

Hayley's stomach took a dip. His words made a mark. He hadn't needed to catch her up. He had *wanted* to. How did that make her feel? Tingly was the answer, tiny, dancing sparks of heat were doing a Zumba class inside her. But that was all just circumstantial. He was a user of women – she'd seen it first-hand – and she was not in the market for being picked up.

She shook her head at him. 'Buying me a vodka and cranberry doesn't entitle you to pass judgement on me. If I'd had any idea, I would have bought my own drinks.'

'Ouch,' he answered, his eyes on her.

'If you'd had to hear your daughter asking so desperately to meet her father, you'd be here doing exactly the same thing.'

She was becoming way too impassioned now. But it was bursting out of her. The quandary she'd been in about coming to New York, her love for Angel, how stupid she still felt about falling for the first guy to buy her wine. This time when she shook her head it was at herself. She stamped the snow off her shoes.

'I'm sorry.' He put a hand to his hair, shaking the flakes from it. 'I was being petulant.' He paused. 'And to be honest, I was thinking selfishly.' He took a breath. 'I don't know why but …' He swallowed. 'I didn't want to think about you spending time with an artist from Belgium.'

His words spiralled through the space between them, out of control, refusing to settle. What did that mean? She met his gaze, her body's engine pumping a rush to each nerve ending. His eyes were unrelenting, holding hers captive, making it impossible to look away. What was happening here? It was like her body was conspiring against her. Every sense was rising up, awake and alert, setting off a chain reaction that started in her toes and moved like lightning through the rest of her body. She couldn't breathe, her stomach was being sucked in as if stuck in the middle of a vortex, her chest had contracted on an inward breath and her eyes were static … on him.

And then the gap was closing. She didn't know if she was moving or he was moving or whether they were both inching forward in unison. All she did know for certain was she felt a little bewitched, out of control, completely not in charge of her own will.

His body was so near now, his face close. She could see every eyelash outlining those beautiful hazel eyes, every tiny dot making up the fine layer of bristle on his jaw, the way his lips curved so gently, so sensuously.

Her brain was incapable of logic. All it was processing was his presence and exactly how that was making her feel. It was like mice had invaded her stomach and were chasing each other around in circles. And she hated it as much as she was relishing it. This was not in her plan. This was reckless behaviour, just like ten years ago. This was her brother's boss. She'd had two conversations with him. One was by a fire exit when he was running out on a date. The other involved cranberry and vodka. This was Christmas spirit in overdrive and she needed to stop now, reclaim her common sense.

His hot breath entwined with hers, mixing together in the freezing night air and, as the seconds ticked by, Hayley was spinning faster and faster towards something she didn't understand. All she knew, as her body moved of its own accord, was it was going to happen.

And then their mouths met in an urgency like no other she'd experienced before. His lips parted hers, the kiss binding them together as the snow floated down around them. Any annoyance at his earlier selfishness had evaporated in the heat of the moment and all she wanted to do was hold onto this feeling, hold onto him, for as long as she could.

Hayley closed her eyes, bringing her hand up to his cheek, letting her ice-cold fingers graze his jaw as his mouth swept over hers.

A car horn sounded and she broke away, a shiver running through her body. Reality finally kicked in. What was she doing? The same nightclub. Another man she barely knew. This was only her second night in New York and she was kissing someone! Someone who had challenged her quest to find her daughter's father. She was officially certifiable. It had to be the wine she hadn't known the name of mixing with the vodka or the jet lag.

She took a step back from him. 'I have to go.'

'Go?'

The surprise in his voice pulled at her. She shouldn't have kissed him. She shouldn't have let him kiss her. It didn't matter who had started it. She was going to finish it.

'Yes, I have the Belgian artist's daughter to worry about and ...' She was backing away so quickly snow was puffing up around her feet with every movement. 'It was nice to see you again.' She made to turn away.

'Hayley, wait,' he called.

She waved a hand. 'Goodnight, Superman.' She was leaving while she'd managed to regain control of her senses.

CHAPTER TWENTY-TWO

Drummond Global Offices, Downtown Manhattan

Oliver had been in the office since before six a.m. He'd dictated four letters and read through two reports before Manhattan started to wake up. Now he was stood at the floor-to-ceiling windows taking in the view.

People like ants, racing up the sidewalks, crossing the streets, moving with purpose through the latest snowfall. Yellow cabs lined up in traffic, cars with Christmas trees strapped to their roofs, school buses, bicycles, all going somewhere on the straight roads between the high-rise buildings. He sucked in a breath. *Hayley.*

She was all he'd been able to think about since she'd left him in the street last night. They had kissed. He had kissed her like he hadn't kissed anyone in a long time. With his heart. He shook himself, moving away from the window and heading back to his desk. And then she'd fled. That was, without a doubt, a good thing.

He sat down in his seat, stretching his arms out and linking his fingers behind his head. He had apologised for his unwarranted reaction to her wish but it wasn't enough. He should have done more. He moved in his chair, bringing his arms down, one hand finding the mouse. It wasn't too late. He could do something to redeem himself. He minimised Dean Walker's employment record and fired up Google. He started to type intently.

A knock on his office door directed his attention away from the screen.

'Come in.'

The door opened and there stood a blonde-haired woman who looked vaguely familiar. Did she work for him? What was her name?

'Good morning, Mr Drummond.' She stepped forward.

'Good morning.' He had no idea what this woman was doing here. He moved his hand to the phone, a finger hovering above the button for security.

'Mr Drummond, Clara asked me to fill in for her today.'

Shit. He'd forgotten he'd given Clara the day off. And Clara had known he would forget and had arranged cover like the highly efficient individual she was.

'Good, right.' He moved his hand away from the phone. 'So there are some dictations waiting to be typed and I'll let you know when I have something else for you.' He looked back to his PC, hovering the mouse over the search box.

'Sir, I think you should be aware of today's news.' The woman held a broadsheet out towards him.

'Thank you, just leave it on the desk.' He usually read news on his phone while he stood in the queue for coffee. This morning the only thing on his mind had been a woman who drank vodka and cranberry.

'I really think you should take a look, Mr Drummond.'

He raised his eyes then, saw the concern and urgency in hers. 'What's your name?'

She shook her blonde hair off her shoulders and moistened her lips. 'It's Kelly.' She placed the paper onto his desk.

'Well, Kelly, what is it in the news that's so important I need to drop everything and read it now?'

He watched her disposition flake before his eyes. Today wasn't a good day. Today he was cranky. Because he hadn't had enough sleep and he'd been given the brush-off by a woman who intrigued him.

'Well, sir, you're on the front page.'

The cramping in his chest took a hold as all the things it could be came to mind. The McArthur Foundation? A reporter he'd spoken to about health concerns and technology? The Globe? He was getting palpitations now just thinking about the fall out if news about the Globe had leaked to the press already. His rivals would have a field day if they got their hands on that.

He slipped his fingers over the newspaper and dragged it across the desk towards him, his heart bumping an unhappy rhythm.

Whatever perfume Kelly was wearing started to infiltrate his nose, mouth and eyes. It was nauseating. He turned the paper around until it was straight in front of him. Then he unfolded it. The headline took his breath.

One Wish in Manhattan

There was a photo of him from a business dinner he'd attended a month ago. His eyes roved the report, picking lines out as a sick feeling rose in his stomach. *Serial single... granting fantasies... death of his father... Christian Grey... modern day genie... Regis Software.*

He knew straightaway who had done this.

As the first flush of anger filled his body, his mobile started to ring, the display flashing on and off in his peripheral vision. Tony's laughing face taunted him. He snatched the phone up and pressed to answer.

'What d'you want?' he snarled.

'I see you're making headlines, man. Your wish-making secret's out. I'm wondering what your play is gonna be now. I'm thinking mind-reading. The mystical power of thought. That would get them every time.'

He closed his eyes. He wasn't in the mood for his best friend's lousy sense of humour and he was starting to perspire. Kelly was also just standing in front of his desk like a spare part. His left hand started to shake and he clenched his fist tight.

Oliver's vision started to blur as he tried to focus on the framed 2014 business infographic at the very end of his office. The pie charts and graphs all started to merge into one as his breath quickened and someone sat a sack of rubble on his chest.

'Mr Drummond, are you OK?'

It was Kelly's voice but it sounded so far away. He opened his mouth to speak but had nothing.

'Oliver? Are you there?' Tony's voice called from the mobile.

The phone fell from his hand.

En-route to Majestic Cleaning, Manhattan

'Ow! You pinched my arm!' Angel exclaimed, frowning.

'Sorry, we just need to get a move on. Reasons Christmas is better in New York number 44 – street entertainers. Look!' Hayley said, pointing. She dodged left as a bicycle mounted the pavement, zipped right to avoid a man dressed as Santa Claus pushing a shopping cart. There was Christmas music on repeat coming from every store and people dressed in costume holding charity buckets on the sidewalk. Snow White and seven dwarves danced in a circle while a man in a very tight fairy outfit showed off far more than his gruff voice tackling 'The First Noel'.

She'd woken up late and now only had a couple of minutes to reach the office of Majestic Cleaning. Dean had left early for work, Vernon and Randy had left even earlier and the only choice she had was to take Angel with her.

Angel quickened her pace, her mouth descending on the bagel she was holding. 'Where are we going anyway? My guidebook says the best time to see the Statue of Liberty is in the afternoon.'

The noise of the city was so distracting. Was she supposed to cross over here or carry on? Which way was north? Hayley narrowed her eyes against the winter sunshine, squinting for a street sign.

'Mum, you're not listening.'

'No, I'm not. I'm trying to work out whether we have to cross the road.'

'The street.'

'That dark grey thing there, lines of cars, slush and ice ...'

'I was just saying, that in America you should say "street" not "road".'

'Well, actually, where we're going I need to sound as English as ... as ...'

'Emma Watson?'

Hayley turned to Angel. 'Yes! Yes, exactly. Emma Watson.' She took hold of Angel's bagel-free hand. 'I think it's this way. It can't be far now.'

'So, where did you go last night?'

Hayley swallowed. Last night. She'd done nothing but think about Oliver since the second she'd arrived back at Dean's apartment. What the hell had she done? Why had her sense deserted her? How had she let her obviously fickle body have control over her brain? The strongest coffee Dean's machine could make had numbed her shock a little.

'I went to… catch up with a friend.' She wasn't about to tell Angel the real reason she was scouring a nightclub. Not yet anyway.

'You have a friend in New York already?'

'Sort of.' She should have known saying she had a friend in New York was going to further her daughter's interest.

'You really should say "kind of", being as we're in America.'

'And you, young lady, should really stop lying to your mother at nine years old.'

A rouge appeared on Angel's cheeks as they continued to walk. 'Uncle Dean said he wouldn't tell you.'

'You told me, no, you *promised* me you hadn't brought "Alfie and the Toymaker" with you.'

'I don't think I actually said those very words.' There was a brief contrite look then the expression changed to a smile. 'Vernon loved it.'

'That's good to hear because he'll be the only one reading it to you.' Hayley stopped, turning to her left. 'OMG, this is it.'

In front of them was a plain black door, a small brass plaque attached to the middle of it stating 'Majestic Cleaning'. There was a bell on the doorjamb. Hayley went to press it but hesitated. Did she really need to do this? She closed her eyes. She needed the money. She needed to be prepared for whatever happened with the search for Michel. Was she really not going to take that flight home if they hadn't found him by New Year? She swallowed. Money gave you options that was all she wanted right now.

'Majestic Cleaning,' Angel read aloud.

'Yep,' Hayley responded.

'Is this where we have to be?'

How was she going to explain this to Angel? She couldn't believe she had got this far without more questions.

'What are we doing here, Mum?'

The voice was so soft and concerned she didn't know what to say in response. She took her daughter's hand and pushed at the door with the other. 'Let's just go inside out of the cold.'

'I don't think Uncle Dean needs a cleaner. His apartment already has shiny everything.'

They'd climbed the stairs and to the left was a white wooden door with a brass doorknob on it. From behind it there was the sound of a woman on the telephone, talking very slowly and eloquently, like she was describing a ten thousand pound vase on *Antiques Roadshow*.

Hayley raised her hand and knocked.

'Come!' a voice called.

Hayley turned to Angel. 'Could you wait here?'

Angel looked like she'd just told her to play on a motorway. The girl stuck her hands on her hips and looked even more affronted. 'What's going on?'

'Nothing.' Hayley knew she was going pink. 'Just wait here, don't you move anywhere, OK? Not one inch. And I promise when I'm done we'll go to the Statue of Liberty.'

'Come in!' the voice called again.

She gave Angel her very best pleading expression. 'I'll be five minutes.'

Giving Angel no chance to say anything more, Hayley put her hand to the doorknob and pushed her way into the room.

The smell of lavender took her breath from her lungs. She didn't dare breathe for fear of coughing. A woman no more than her own age stood up and came around the desk. She was wearing a maroon-coloured uniform, pleats in all the right places. Her hair was the colour of polished walnut set into a bun and just visible under a tricorne hat. A whiter than white blouse was buttoned up high on her neck, then came flawless skin and glossy lips.

'Hello, I'm Rebecca Rogers-Smythe,' the woman greeted. 'You must be Ms Walker.' The woman held out her hand.

'Hayley.' She realised she had emphasised her British accent as she gave Rebecca's hand a solid shake. Emma Watson would be so proud.

Rebecca let Hayley's hand go and looked her up and down from her winter boots to her hair that was flecked with snow. She realised then she probably should have made more of an effort. She could have added one of Dean's fancy door swags to her coat or some silver buttons. Too late now.

'So, what experience have you had?' Rebecca asked, pointing to a floral embroidered carver chair as she returned to her desk.

'In cleaning?' Hayley asked, sitting down and gripping the arms of the chair with sweaty palms.

'Here at Majestic we like to call it hygienic maintenance.'

'Sorry.' She swallowed. 'I've worked in several office buildings and a local hostelry. My last job was in a dry-cleaning … establishment.'

'And you could provide references?'

'Yes.'

'We never deal with spills on wool.'

'No?'

'If there is any sign of vomit or defecation you do not touch anything, you call me.'

The tastes were in her mouth already but she managed to nod her head. It was actually hard to get a word in.

Rebecca let out a breath of what sounded like relief. 'I don't usually take people on without a thorough vetting procedure, but I had an employee leave two days ago and I cannot let my regular clients down.'

'I …'

'I'll pay you cash. Ten dollars an hour.'

Hayley swallowed. Ten dollars an hour. A few hours for the time she was here. That would mean not dipping into her minimal dollar pot for entrance fees to all the places Angel wanted to visit. Anything more would be a bonus to tide her over when they got home.

'Right,' she found herself responding. She crossed her fingers.

Rebecca picked up a sheaf of papers and handed them to Hayley. 'Familiarise yourself with everything written on here.' She shook the papers as if to signify their importance. 'The client I'm giving you today has a Diana.'

'A Diana?'

'Yes. We have levels of service at Majestic. The Queen Elizabeth is a deep clean, the full works, from blinds and tracks to baseboards, with everything in between. The Princess Diana is more of a personal service.' Rebecca let out a sigh. 'It's a medium-level clean with the emphasis on the areas of the home that mean most to the family.' Rebecca presented a hand forward, stroking the air. 'It's all about the little touches. The plumping and arranging of cushions, placement of ornaments and decorative features, bed-making, beautifying. With the Diana, the focus is the family, not the dust. We make their house a home again.'

Hayley now felt she needed a hygiene degree to take on this role. When did cleaning become so technical?

'Finally, we have the Camilla,' Rebecca said.

She was almost afraid to ask. She swallowed. 'What's that?'

'A quick whip-round and the garbage taken out.'

Hayley forced a smile and wondered what a Prince Andrew or a Prince Harry might entail. She didn't dare think about a Prince Philip.

The lavender was in her throat again and she coughed. She wondered if Angel had her ear up to the door.

'So, could you start today? I have a prestigious client who needs a Diana at three this afternoon.'

'I, er, well …' The reality of the situation was finally beginning to hit home. She was about to accept a job with no paperwork or permissions. She had no childcare either.

'Is there an issue?'

Hayley shook her head. 'No, no, absolutely not. Today. Three o'clock.'

'I'll go get you a uniform and give you all the details you need.' Rebecca smiled. 'It's like Christmas has come early. My first real English employee.'

Hayley smiled. Angel was going to murder her.

CHAPTER TWENTY-THREE

Drummond Global Offices, Downtown Manhattan

'I'll get some more water.'

'He doesn't need more water. He's drunk two glasses in the last half hour. He probably needs a Scotch.'

'I think I should call the doctor.'

'No!' Oliver put his hands to his head. Kelly and Tony had been talking at pace for the last twenty minutes, and as well as the aching in his chest, his head was starting to throb. He opened and closed his eyes, concentrated on the infographic, ensuring the images were clear. He was going to improve on those percentages if it killed him. The irony wasn't lost.

'How you doin'?' Tony asked, shifting nearer the sofa Oliver was resting on.

He sighed. 'You shouldn't have come over here.'

'Hey, one minute I'm talking to you about the power of thought and the next I can hear Kelly here shrieking like she's a victim on *Stalker*.'

'I didn't know what to do,' Kelly responded.

Oliver observed her pale skin and nervous stance. She couldn't be more than twenty and this was not what she'd signed up for. She gets seconded to work for the boss for a day and he collapses right in front of her.

He swung his legs off the sofa, ignoring the woozy feeling as he sat up. 'Go have a coffee,' he said, addressing Kelly. 'Then make a start on those dictations.'

'But maybe I should …' the girl began.

'You heard the man,' Tony interrupted. 'He goes down again, he's got fifteen stone of Italian stallion right here to pick him back up.'

Kelly nodded in an uneasy fashion and made for the door.

Oliver looked to Tony, shaking his head. 'Was that your idea of flirting with her? You scared her half to death.'

'Talking of that …'

Oliver attempted to get to his feet but sat back down when the effort overrode him. He crossed one leg over the other. 'I'm fine.'

'You don't think you ought to see a doctor?'

'What's the point?'

'Er, to stop you from dying.'

'Will it?' He let out a frustrated sigh. He felt so out of control in this situation and that scared him more than anything. It wasn't the knowing *whether* it was going to happen, it was the not knowing *when*. He'd almost come to terms with knowing his life would be short, but the inability to schedule it in a calendar irked him. If he knew he had two months or two years, even if he knew he only had today, he could make plans. In this limbo there was nothing to do but wait. It was time wasted. Time he probably didn't have. And last night he'd chased a woman through the snow and kissed her.

'I picked up last night,' he stated, sighing.

'Yeah? Way to go! What was she like?' Tony threw himself down on the sofa next to him.

A smile was trying to make its way onto his lips but thoughts of the newspaper article filtered through first. 'She sold me out to a newshound.'

'Whoa. Today's article?' Tony asked.

He nodded, but instead of feeling the gripe of anger that had welled through him earlier all he could recall was how her lips felt embedded in his last night.

'What did you do? Don't tell me you couldn't make her wish come true?'

He swallowed, thinking about the Google search he hadn't completed earlier. Michel De Vos's name would still be blinking at him on his computer.

'Something like that.'

Statue of Liberty, New York

'Did you know there are twenty-five windows in the crown of the statue?' Hayley said as they walked towards the entrance. She shook the guidebook, her head dropping further into it. She'd been quoting snippets of information at Angel since they'd boarded the ferry.

'I know what you're doing,' Angel responded.

'*I'm* educating *you* for a change.' She sniffed. 'Did you know three hundred different types of hammers were used to create it?'

'Mum, why have you got a job as a cleaner?'

'Fashion alert, twelve o'clock.' Hayley pushed Angel's head in the right direction. 'We have a fanny pack. I repeat, we have a fanny pack!'

'Mum!' Angel exclaimed.

'Reasons Christmas is better in New York number 56. We don't have to watch the Queen's Speech.'

'Mum, stop!'

Hayley swallowed. There was no getting away from the topic now. She sighed. 'I know you think I'm being completely weird but …'

'It isn't just weird. It's completely crazy and I don't get it,' Angel said, snatching the guidebook from her.

'I know you don't.'

'What's that supposed to mean?'

What *was* it supposed to mean? She didn't want to tell Angel she had lost her job. That wasn't a worry a nine-year-old should have. But anything else was going to be a lie and she was already holding so much back from her. She took a breath.

'I'm just … a bit short of money at the moment, that's all.' She watched for Angel's reaction. 'The flights were more expensive than I thought and I want us to be able to do everything we want to do here. Like this.' She held her arm up and out like the Statue of Liberty, fixed her face to solemn.

'We could ask Uncle Dean,' Angel suggested.

Hayley shook her head so hard it hurt. 'No.'

'But he has loads of money.'

'Yeah, I know.' His financial stability had always been thrown in her face by her mother.

'He won't mind.'

'*I* mind, Angel. I want us to stand on our own two feet.' She looked down at her boots, wet and covered in snow. 'Four feet. Yours and mine.' She sighed. 'You know what I'm saying.'

'If Nanny was here she'd say you were being stubborn.'

'If Nanny was here she'd be needing the toilet by now.'

'The bathroom. You should say "bathroom" as we're in America.'

'Are you going to do that the whole trip?'

'I'm just trying to behave like a local.'

'Then you won't be needing this, will you?' Hayley snatched the guidebook back. 'Look, here we are, standing below one of the most iconic places in New York and we're talking about Nanny needing a wee.'

Angel let out a giggle of amusement before raising her eyes to the sky. She emitted an awe-inspired sigh. 'I didn't realise how tall it was.'

Hayley's eyes went to the green copper woman, rising up at the edge of the Hudson River, her torch held out like a beacon to everyone below. 'Just how tall? Let me see …' She thumbed the pages of the book in her hand.

Angel made a grab for it. 'Give it back!'

'You mean you don't already know the answer?! Shame on you, Angel Walker.'

'I do know that there's no way you're going to be able to manage a Princess Diana on that house this afternoon. Your idea of cleaning is remembering to unload the dishwasher before we have to use paper plates.'

Hayley stared at her daughter, her mouth falling open. 'You were listening.'

'It was pretty hard not to.'

Hayley nodded. 'Well, maybe you can help me. I mean, Ms Rogers-Smythe said the Diana was all about family. You can plump some cushions and spray some lavender everywhere while I flick a duster round.'

'What if they have a really technical hoover?'

'As we're in America I think you should be saying "vacuum".'

'I'm serious, Mum. I don't know why you've got yourself into this.'

Wise words from the mouth of a nine-year-old. 'I told you, it's a money thing. And it's not something for you to worry about.'

'We could ask Nanny for money.'

'No.' That was worse than asking her brother. 'After we've seen all there is to see here we're going to go and collect my uniform and equipment and we're going to do a Diana. Period.' She sniffed. 'See, how's that for American terminology?'

Angel wrinkled her nose. 'Rad.'

The Riley Club, Lower Manhattan

'Are you sure you're up to this?'

Tony had pulled his red Mustang to the kerb and Oliver had his hand on the door handle.

'I've taken a day's quota of painkillers and hydrated myself to the absolute max,' he replied.

'The finance talk in that place would kill me,' Tony said, nudging his head towards the opulent entrance of the Riley Club.

'I'd better get in there. Andrew Regis is always early for everything.' Oliver opened the door and the chill of the wind slipped through the gap, infiltrating the in-car heating.

'D'you want me to swing by and pick you up later?' Tony offered.

'No, I'm good. You go take care of the restaurant.'

'Restaurants,' Tony added with a grin. 'That's a plural.'

'What?'

'Days away from completion on two more. Part of the Papa Gino franchise.'

'Wow, Tony, that's great news. Why didn't you tell me about it?'

'Well, you had a lot going on and nothing was signed and sealed.' He paused. 'And it's hardly global software.'

Oliver swallowed. Had his best friend really not told him because he thought his family's business was less of a business than Drummond Global?

'I mean, it's just pizza,' Tony added.

'The best pizza,' Oliver said sternly. 'And people will always need pizza. I'm not so sure they're always going to need computers when the zombie apocalypse comes.' He smiled at his friend. 'It's tough times out there and I'm proud of you.'

The sentiment clogged his throat. What had gotten into him? He quickly opened the door some more and shifted himself out.

'Hey, pizza on the house for opening nights,' Tony called out to him.

Oliver ducked his head back into the car. 'I think opening night should be sponsored by Drummond Global.'

'Really?' Tony asked.

'Absolutely. Now get out of here,' he urged. He slammed the door of the car and waved a hand at his friend. The Mustang pulled out into the flow of traffic and Oliver looked up at the Riley Club. He stepped towards the door.

In days gone by all you'd been able to smell in the entrance of the club was the fragrance of cigar smoke. Now the atmosphere was pure testosterone mixed with a dash of Scotch. Oliver hated it. And now, as he stood in the lobby, there was a six foot Christmas tree and a life-size moving Father Christmas. It was ghastly.

Standing on the regal red carpet, Oliver looked into the antique mirror against the gilt wallpaper, adjusting his tie. His father had spent half this life in his place, making and breaking deals, mixing in influential circles. Was that why he detested it so much? Because it had taken so much of his father's time – more time he could have spent with the family? He shook himself. This wasn't any time for sentimentality. This was business. And he was going to lay it on the line to Andrew Regis. He checked his reflection once more. The truth was, he still wasn't entirely convinced by the man's motives. The merger looked good for both businesses on paper, but was it the same in reality? They needed to finalise how it was all going to work once they'd joined forces. Had Oliver jumped on the offer because it was going to grow Drummond Global? Or just because it was a steal of a price? He needed to make sure all his ducks were in a row and get focussed.

Oliver took a step towards the door that led to the Invicta Room. A violinist was playing in the corner of the grand space, partially obscured by a large plant, the lights from the two chandeliers that dominated the room were turned down low and most of the tables were taken up by businessman clones. Formal three-piece suits, the majority of the people wearing them over fifty. One day he would be exactly the same. He swallowed at that thought and inhaled, turning his head a little. If he made it to fifty. It seemed unlikely. Perhaps not turning into one of them was a plus point.

Andrew Regis was sat by the window, his polished bald head instantly recognisable. Oliver moved across the floor towards him and, when he was a few yards from the table, the man got up, extending his hand out.

'Oliver,' Andrew greeted. He grasped Oliver's hand, pumping it up and down.

'Andrew, it's good to see you.' He sat down, instinctively picking up the wine menu. 'Have you ordered drinks?'

'I'm on the Scotch I'm afraid.' He smiled, raising his glass. 'It's been one of those mornings.'

Oliver said nothing but moved his eyes to scan the list of drinks. Like magic, a waiter appeared alongside their table.

'We'll have a bottle of the Australian Merlot.' He looked to Andrew. 'Is that OK with you?'

'That's absolutely fine with me.'

Oliver waited for the waiter to take his leave before he clasped his hands together and angled his body forward. 'Andrew, I'm going to come right out with it. We need to iron out this deal together.'

The man picked up a linen napkin and toyed with it in his hands. 'Straight down to business then,' Andrew said.

'I must have looked through the contract a dozen times now. It seems to me your lawyers are fighting hard to keep themselves in fees. The latest changes are so miniscule ... the whole thing is racking up unnecessary costs and a whole lot of aggravation.'

Andrew nodded. 'Your mother said you would say that.'

The sentence stung like he'd just stumbled into a nettle bush. Heat spread quickly to his cheeks. 'You've spoken to my mother about this?' He blinked. 'Why would you do that?'

Something changed in Andrew Regis's stance. He looked a little uneasy. Oliver watched him press the napkin to his lips.

'She hasn't told you,' Andrew stated, putting the napkin to the table. He shook his head. 'She said she was going to tell you.'

Now Oliver's chest cavity filled up, his heart beating like tom-toms as he frantically tried to decipher the vagueness Andrew Regis was delivering.

'Told me what?' His words were tentative, because he wasn't sure he wanted to know what was coming.

'Your mother and I ... we've been spending a lot of time with each other and ...'

Oliver didn't need to hear any more. Those choice words said everything. The room stared to spin, the violinist grating on his every nerve, the temperature increasing instantaneously. He stood up.

'Oliver, please, sit down.' Andrew got up.

'If you're telling me what I think you're telling me then I have nothing to say to you.' He recoiled from the table, staring at the man opposite, his father's best friend.

'We've kept things discreet for the past couple of months but I said she had to tell you before it got out.'

'I don't want to hear it.'

'Oliver, come on, this is a little over the top, don't you think?'

It was all Oliver could do to keep standing. He wanted to lash out, spray the table settings to the ground in fury. Instead he ground his teeth together and spilled words out. 'If you're telling me that you and my mother are having some sort of romantic relationship, then this merger ...' He took a breath. 'This merger is over.'

Now it sounded like the violinist had ceased playing and everyone in the room had stopped talking. The sounds of fine dining had been replaced by hushed whispers.

'What your mother and I have together has nothing to do with this. The merger is business, Oliver.'

'Yes, it is. My *family's* business.'

'Which is only going to benefit from this mutual joining,' Andrew responded.

Oliver shook his head. 'No.'

Andrew sighed. 'Listen, I've done all the right things. I've bided my time, I've stayed out of things but ...'

'You've bided your time?! What is that supposed to mean?' He laughed. 'You've been hanging on for the moment your best friend met his maker? Jesus Christ!'

'I didn't mean that. I just meant ... Richard's been dead for a while now.'

He couldn't stand this any longer. He wanted to punch Andrew Regis, but if he did it here he would make the front page of the paper tomorrow as well. No, he had to maintain his cool.

He held his hand out to Andrew and waited for a response. 'It was nice to see you again, Andrew.'

The man looked at the offering and Oliver pushed his hand a little closer. Andrew took it, giving it an unsure shake. 'Let's schedule another time to get together, once all this has had a chance to sink in.'

Oliver straightened himself. 'Be in no doubt, Andrew, our business is concluded.' He turned to the waiter who was returning with the bottle of red wine on a silver tray. 'Charge the wine to my account.' He looked to Andrew. 'With my compliments.'

His heart fighting for room to expand and contract, Oliver turned and headed for the exit. The animated Santa leered and swayed and the Christmas lights flickered in his peripheral vision as he fought his way to the door of the Riley Club. He burst through it, out onto the street, desperately pulling in a breath of freezing air.

It took him half a dozen inhalations to feel anywhere near better. With shaking hands he reached into his coat for his cell phone.

He called up a contact and dialled, waiting for a response. 'Hello, Daniel?' He looked back to the door of the Riley Club, half expecting Andrew Regis to be following him. 'Daniel, it's Oliver Drummond. I need you to do some work for me.'

CHAPTER TWENTY-FOUR

Westchester, New York

'I can't believe my Majestic Cleaning name is Agatha,' Hayley exclaimed.

'I can't believe you were thinking of getting the subway here.'

Hayley manoeuvred Angel out of the cab before stepping down onto the pavement behind her. She looked up at the house sitting proud at the top of a snow-covered grassy bank. It was imposing in its size and perfect. White pillars propped up the front entrance and the US flag hung from a pole to the right of the front door. The windows had shutters, giving it a colonial feel. It looked worthy of a cleaner much more accomplished than her. She cleared her throat and turned to Angel.

'Have you not seen the people on the subway? Me dressed in this outfit would not be the craziest costume on there, I can assure you.' Hayley brushed down her burgundy skirt, then adjusted the waistband. The white shirt was made for someone with an AA cup size not a generous C. She felt like an extra on *Nanny 911*.

'The mop would have got some funny looks,' Angel continued.

The driver opened up the trunk and handed her the wicker basket apparently containing all her hygienic needs. Hayley thrust the mop at her daughter and dug into her rucksack for some money for the cabbie.

Passing the cab driver a bill, Hayley caught Angel's expression. Her daughter looked so much like her mother right now.

'Let's just get it done and then we can go somewhere nice for dinner tonight,' Hayley said.

'And spend all the money you made cleaning.'

'Please, Angel, just for once in your life, could you act nine and not forty?'

The atmosphere cooled to well below freezing and, as the cab drove away, the silence and the hot breath from their mouths was all that was left.

Hayley took the mop from Angel and, with the basket nestled tight under one arm, she led the way to the steps at the front of the house.

'OK, here we are. The client's name is Cynthia.' Hayley blew out a breath. 'Do you think that's a made up name too?'

'It's better than Agatha,' Angel responded.

When they got to the front door, the brass letter box and knocker all immaculate, the reality of what she was doing hit her. Working here was breaking the law. It had said as much in the small print of the visa waiver documentation *and* the very serious man at JFK had mentioned it too. Yet here she was, rocking up to a house that looked fit for the Obamas to move into, her nine-year-old daughter in tow. *She needed the money.* Would that wash if immigration caught her? She hoped she didn't have to find out. US immigration didn't mess around. They were all tooled up more than mobsters.

Before she could move, either to flee back down the steps or to knock, the door swung open. A beautifully turned-out woman, possibly in her fifties, stood there. She was wearing a royal blue woollen skirt and matching jacket, patent nude-coloured shoes, her blonde hair set in place and pearl earrings in her lobes. There was no need for fashion advice here. Everything was current. This woman had style written all over her.

'Hello, I'm H … I'm Agatha from Majestic Cleaning,' Hayley greeted, offering her hand forward and dropping the basket to the floor.

'I'm pleased to meet you.' Cynthia's eyes went immediately to Angel and the woman smiled warmly.

'Oh, excuse me, this is … Charlotte.' Hayley swallowed down the lie. 'Charlotte is here on work experience today.'

'Work experience,' Cynthia repeated as Hayley pushed the mop back onto Angel. The woman sounded a little confused and Hayley couldn't blame her.

'Yes, and …' Hayley stuttered.

'My mother is an actress,' Angel blurted out. 'But I want to do something real.' She smiled. 'And the world will always need cleaners.'

Hayley smiled at Cynthia.

'Come in,' Cynthia said, stepping aside.

Hayley gave Angel a glare and moved over the threshold and into the impressive hall. She dragged the basket over the doorway.

The house was show-home ready, with dark wooden floors, pale painted walls and large windows letting in every sliver of light available. If there was any mess or dust, it certainly wasn't in the hall or up the sweeping staircase that trailed a path to a balcony. This might turn into a Camilla and not a Diana after all.

'Ms Rogers-Smythe called and said she had someone new for me. I can't stay, I have a meeting to get to,' Cynthia said.

'We understand,' Angel said, nodding soberly. 'You must be very busy.'

Hayley watched Cynthia study her daughter and wished the woman had to leave now, before Angel could get another sentence out of her mouth.

'Yes and I have a small gathering here tonight, which is why I need the house cleaned this afternoon.'

The shine coming from the floor said nothing but sanitation. Hayley wasn't sure how she was going to get this place any cleaner than it was, unless there was the mother of all destruction in the lounge room.

'Leave it with us,' Angel responded.

'Me,' Hayley jumped in, glaring at her daughter. 'Leave it with *me.*'

Cynthia was looking at them like they were both crazy and Hayley didn't blame her one bit. It was like a scene from a situation comedy, except it wasn't fiction, somehow this laughable situation was now her life.

Cynthia took a black, expensive-looking woollen coat from a dark wood stand and put it on.

'That's a lovely coat,' Hayley blurted out. 'A hound's-tooth scarf would really set it off.'

'Really?' Cynthia responded, looking sceptical.

Hayley felt the blush hit her cheeks. She was as bad as Angel.

'Or a hat,' Angel added, nodding.

Hayley took hold of Angel's arm and squeezed, directing her behind her own body. Perhaps Angel was right about the hat. Maybe her daughter was inheriting her fashion instincts.

Cynthia smiled at them as she buttoned up her coat and took a step towards the door. She turned back. 'If you need anything, just ask Sophia.'

As if she'd been summoned, a short dark-haired woman of something like Puerto Rican origin appeared from another room. Hayley smiled awkwardly. Housekeeper? Couldn't she clean?

'Have a lovely meeting!' Angel said a little too enthusiastically.

Cynthia stopped on the doorstep and Hayley tried to keep Angel behind her.

'Your house is going to be Diana-ed to perfection by the time you're done.' Hayley nodded and dipped her body into a bow. Why had she bowed? Was that in the Majestic remit?

Cynthia was looking even more bewildered now and Hayley didn't blame her. This whole situation was farcical. As Cynthia left the house, Hayley swung the door shut, leaning heavily against it. It took a second for her to realise she was being scrutinised by Sophia. The dark-haired woman was looking at them both with suspicion in her eyes. Hayley straightened up, putting her hands to her hat and adjusting it. Then she clapped her hands together and met Sophia's gaze. 'So, show me the dirt!'

Central Park, New York

Oliver didn't know where he was going but he knew he couldn't go back to the office in this frame of mind. It was like the city was spinning, the high rises falling forward, threatening to spill all over him like some big budget disaster movie. He felt sick, his stomach sat in his chest, pressure crushing him, breathing shallow. Putting one foot in front of the other through the snow-lined paths of the park felt like walking a high wire.

His mother and Andrew Regis. That was what her visit to the office was about the other day. She'd wrapped it up in a Christmas invitation, tested the water, then, when it all blew up, she threw the McArthur Foundation at him and chickened out.

He shook his head, looking across the park to a family playing in the snow. Just like the Drummonds had, all those years ago.

He bent down, sinking his hands into the freezing cold white stuff. He let his fingers rest there until the icy feeling started to burn his skin hot. What was happening to him? He'd never felt more out of control in every area of his life.

He balled the snow up into his palms, rolling it around in his hands, pressing and squeezing, shaping it hard. Maybe he should pretend it was Andrew Regis's head. Did that make him immature? Was it wrong to be so affected by the news his mother was moving on romantically? His father had been dead a while. The emotion knotted in his throat. No, something about it was off. Just how long had it been going on?

He stood up, pulled his arm back and launched the snowball into orbit, not caring where it landed or who it might hit. He punched his reddened hands down into his pockets and watched the ball smash into a litter bin. What would Ben do?

He shrugged his shoulders up and down, attempting to warm his body. Why was he thinking that? It was pointless. Ben wasn't here and they were two different people. *Very* different people. Ben had been adored. He had just been the second child. The add-on. The second screen subscription on *Netflix* no one was really sure they wanted but had anyway, just in case. Just in case what? Something happened to the first one? Well it had, the first one was gone.

His eyes went to the newspaper seller on the corner, where the park met the street. Even from this distance he could still make out his photo. *One Wish in Manhattan*. He shook his head. *Lois. Hayley.* He couldn't imagine why she had done this. To get back at him for making fun of her wish? It seemed extreme. And it hurt. Bad press he could deal with. Her kissing him then selling him out? Well, it burned.

He needed something. A pick-me-up. Just enough distraction to get him through the day. It seemed the welcoming lights of a bar were beckoning him from across the street.

Westchester, New York

There was no pit of doom in the lounge or anywhere else. Nothing was out of place in the entire house. Not one cushion needed plumping, not one rug needed vacuuming and Hayley could see her reflection in all the surfaces. She had no idea what she was supposed to do to make it different. Angel was humming 'Jingle Bells' on a loop, pushing a J-cloth up and down the windowsill and she was polishing the life out of the ornaments that already glittered as much as the diamonds in Tiffany's. Suddenly Angel stopped humming and looked to Hayley.

'There aren't any photos!' her daughter announced.

'What?'

'There aren't any photos in here, or in any of the other rooms,' Angel stated.

Hayley's eyes shot to the main display cabinet and saw her daughter was right. Photos were what made a house a home. Not these stylish, funny-shaped ornaments, the urns of flowers, the chenille cushions and the deep pile rugs. There was nothing in the décor that said anything about the people who lived in the house. The furnishings shouted money but that was all.

'She seemed quite nice,' Angel remarked, a delicate sigh leaving her lips.

'The fact she doesn't have any photos on display doesn't make her horrible.'

'We could look in the drawers,' Angel suggested.

'Angel!'

'I just thought, if it's a Diana, the personal touch, the focus on the family ... We could see if there are some photos and put them out.'

'No, we can't.' Hayley shook her head. 'I've been a member of Majestic Cleaning for only a few hours. I'm pretty sure in all those terms and conditions I haven't read yet there will be a big fat piece about confidentiality, and opening clients' drawers will be punishable by the electric chair.'

'New York doesn't have the death penalty actually. And only five states still use the electric chair. There's Alabama, Florida ...' Angel started.

'How do you even know that?'

Angel put her hands on her hips. 'So what do we do?' She looked at her watch. 'We have an hour left.'

Hayley looked around the lounge. Despite the warm gold, red and brown furnishings, the atmosphere was cold. The cream-coloured mantle surrounded an open fire that didn't look like it had been lit for a while. The ornaments were all square-edged and uniform – they didn't look like trinkets picked up from travels or well-loved reminders of experiences. And there wasn't a sniff of Christmas anywhere.

'*I* could open the drawers,' Angel stated. 'She thinks my name's Charlotte and I'm not technically employed so I technically wouldn't be breaking the rules.'

Was this a bad idea? She should be taking advantage of the fact there wasn't much to do. But, on the other hand, she was a part-time party planner. Fashion, dressing and décor was her thing. She had an excellent eye and there was no doubt this place was certainly lacking in something. She turned to Angel. 'I'll keep that Sophia busy, you check the drawers.'

It was a completely altered space. The fire was pumping out heat, crackling with bundles of twigs Angel had obtained from the garden and some coal Sophia had reluctantly found for them. Hayley was sure the housekeeper thought they were certifiable, especially after Angel had barricaded the door and said she would have no access until they were finished.

Hayley stood back from the flames and admired their handiwork. They'd found votives to put in the bare candle cups, and three framed photographs in a drawer. Cynthia and a man both looking so happy, dressed in bright, flashy clothes, then two bare-chested boys of about ten, arms around each other, ice cream staining their lips, and finally another of the darker-haired boy a little older, a certificate held proudly in his hands. Angel had trailed a string of white lights they'd found in a box of Christmas decorations in the cupboard around the candles and the photos. It transformed the room from something neat, clean-lined but cold into somewhere homely, a house with the family back at its heart.

She looked to her left as Angel let out a grunt of dissatisfaction from her precarious position on something antique-looking.

'Don't you fall off that and break something. It looks expensive,' Hayley said, moving across the room.

'I love your concern for me, Mum.' Angel stretched a little further and looped a green, gold and red garland over the curtain pole.

'If it's remotely Edwardian or Victorian or even from the fifties, I think I'll need to clean for an era to pay for it.'

'Please, Miss Majestic Cleaning. You need to let me in now. Mrs Cynthia will be back at any moment.' It was Sophia's voice from behind the door, blocked off by a heavy nest of tables.

'I wish we had a tree,' Angel mused, getting down from the table and dusting her footmarks off with the sleeve of her top. It was probably the most dust the table had ever seen.

'Here or at Uncle Dean's?' Hayley asked.

'Both.' Angel lifted the magazine rack up from the side of the sofa. 'Where shall I put this?'

Squinting at the newspaper through the slats in the wood, Hayley moved closer to her daughter, her eyes on the photograph on the front page. 'Is that …?'

'What?' Angel asked.

Hayley plucked the newspaper from the rack and straightened it out.

'Miss Majestic Cleaning! I must insist you let me in here now. This is not what happen.'

'Maybe we should let her in now,' Angel suggested.

Hayley didn't respond. She was too busy looking at the photo of Oliver and reading the article about the serial single granting wishes to the female population of New York.

'Mum!' Angel said a little louder.

Something was tugging on her insides. This article was picking him apart, painting him as a megalomaniac, a loner who used women.

'Is that Mr Meanie?' Angel asked, leaning in to get a better look at the photograph.

'Don't call him that, Angel. It's not nice.'

'He doesn't remember the names of anyone who works for him.'

'Do you think Donald Trump remembers the names of all the people that work for him?' Hayley countered.

'Uncle Dean doesn't work for Donald Trump.'

'Miss Majestic Cleaning! Open this door!' Sophia screamed.

Hayley shoved the newspaper back into the rack. 'Put it in the gap between the bookshelves and the fire, it will fit well there.'

She waited until Angel had set the magazine holder down before shifting the nest of tables away from the door.

'Ready, Charlotte?' she asked her daughter.

Angel nodded. 'Ready, Agatha.'

Hayley whisked open the door, preparing for the housekeeper to fall into the room with urgency, only to see her across the hallway with Cynthia. Hayley watched the housekeeper buzzing around the homeowner like an anxious bee whose hive had been invaded. Cynthia slipped off her black woollen coat and hung it on the stand.

'I want to say, Mrs Cynthia, that I had no idea what they were doing and it was not at all like usual,' Sophie spoke as Cynthia strode towards the lounge.

'I hope your meeting went well,' Angel said, stepping into the hallway and closing up the door again as Cynthia approached the doorjamb.

'Very well thank you.' She smiled at Angel. 'So what have you been doing that's got my housekeeper so flustered?'

'We've gone through the house from top to bottom primping and preening and ...' Hayley started.

'Close your eyes,' Angel whispered, looking directly at the older woman.

Hayley held her breath. The tone coating the simple request was heavy with meaning. Angel had enjoyed transforming this room today. It meant something to her. Family. Warmth. The heart of the home. Hayley knew she had done her best to be Angel's family, but she also knew there had always been something missing. A father-shaped hole. She was going to make sure she found the father, the fitting into it was going to be up to him.

Without answering, Cynthia simply shut her eyes and let Angel take her hand. Hayley swallowed and hoped this was going to go down well or the hours they had spent here might not be profitable. There was a chance it could get her sacked. Within twenty-four hours.

Angel swung the door open, leading Cynthia into the lounge. Sophia let out a blood-curdling scream and Cynthia instinctively opened her eyes before she had travelled more than half a dozen steps.

'Why do you do this? You have no right to do this! I am going to call Ms Rogers-Smythe right away,' Sophia exclaimed, her accent strengthening as her voice quickened.

What had they done? The housekeeper was behaving like they had dressed the room with sacrificed animals. It was only a few decorations and Hayley had called a halt to Angel using the snow spray.

Hayley looked at Cynthia. She was trembling, a hand clamped over her mouth, her eyes glistening with tears. This wasn't the reaction she had hoped for. This was a disaster. She looked to Angel. Her mouth was hanging open as she stared at Cynthia.

'We can fix this,' Hayley said, stepping further into the room. 'I will fix this straight away and I won't leave until it's back to the way it was. No, scratch that, until it's better than the way it was.' She headed for the mantelpiece.

'No,' Cynthia said, her voice gravelly with emotion.

Hayley stopped moving, stood awkwardly, not knowing what to do next. A simple cleaning job in a house that wasn't even dirty and she couldn't even get that right. She was a big fat failure.

'Just go,' Cynthia said, the tears finally escaping.

Hayley motioned to Angel to come towards her but the girl was looking like she'd been petrified. Her eyes were like round saucers, her skin pale, her mouth still agape. Hayley leant forward and grabbed her by the shoulder, pulling her towards the door.

'Can I just say …?' Hayley started. She needed to say something. Apologise.

'No,' Cynthia responded. 'You may not.'

Hayley swallowed. That was clear enough. Sophia was looking at them both as if they were devil worshippers who had decked the room with essence of voodoo. She didn't dare say another thing.

She shunted a dazed Angel towards the front door. 'Come on, this is not a tragedy, Angel. It's just something that didn't quite work out. A tragedy is the war in Syria or a tsunami. This is just a blip. And it isn't our fault.'

Angel shook her head. 'No, it isn't *our* fault.' She sniffed. 'It's all mine.'

CHAPTER TWENTY-FIVE

Dean Walker's Apartment, Downtown Manhattan

'Ta da! Here it is!'

Hayley raised her head from the pizza box on her lap to see Dean put something in front of Angel. A tablet. The Globe. Hayley swallowed as she watched Angel make no reaction. She hadn't touched her pizza either.

'What's going on here? This morning you were super excited to see this,' Dean commented.

Angel flicked her eyes over the piece of technology. 'It looks great.'

Dean looked to Hayley then and she shrugged. What could she tell him without giving up her secret life as a cleaner?

'I'll look at it,' Hayley said, reaching out a hand for the tablet.

'Not with grease on your fingers you won't.' Dean snatched back the Globe and hugged it to his chest.

'Surely it has to go through a grease test,' Hayley said. 'Everyday use will involve dirt and grime, toast crumbs and tea … beer spills.'

'You've just told me so much about your diet.'

Angel put the lid back over her pizza and pushed it onto the coffee table. 'I'm not hungry.'

Hayley watched Dean pay greater attention then. 'You're not sick, are you?' He took a step forward and pressed the back of his hand to Angel's forehead.

'She's fine,' Hayley stated quickly. 'It was just full on at the Statue of Liberty, loads of people, an incident in the crown and ...'

'What incident?' Dean looked concerned now. She really did need to stop embellishing her lies too much. She talked herself into trouble rather than out of it.

'Oh, you know, a kid with a giant ice cream, you can imagine the rest,' Hayley said, sighing. She hoped he could imagine the rest because she wasn't sure what came next.

Dean scooted down at the edge of the sofa, his head on a level with Angel's. 'It's a shame you're not hungry, because Vern's invited us over for dinner.'

Very slowly, Angel turned her head ninety degrees and faced him.

'Really?' she asked.

'Really. He was on about making meatballs,' Dean said.

Angel's tongue ran over her lips. 'And will Randy be allowed out?'

'I expect so. That mutt rules the roost over there,' Dean responded.

'Yay!' Angel exclaimed, bouncing on the sofa.

Dean stood up again. 'So how about it?' he asked, directing the question at Hayley.

She chewed up the pizza in her mouth, the melted cheese singeing her tongue as she chowed as quickly as she could to answer. 'Can I take a rain check?'

'Mum! No! I want to go,' Angel whined.

'You can go ... if that's all right with Dean. I just ... there's some things I need to do.' She enlarged her eyes at her brother, hoping he would get her meaning. She needed to call some more galleries about Michel. She'd had no leads since they got here. As discreetly as she could with cheese hanging from her lips, she mouthed the man's name.

Dean gave a nod of acknowledgement.

'Can I come, Uncle Dean?' Angel batted her eyelashes, all depression over what had happened at the house in Westchester disappearing.

'Sure, with one condition,' Dean said, pointing at Angel and adopting a serious expression.

'What?' Angel asked.

'No "Alfie and the Toymaker" tonight and you play this game called Rabbit Nation on the Globe and tell me what you think.'

Hayley watched Angel's concentrated expression, mulling the terms over.

Angel nodded. 'Deal.'

'Right, well, why don't you go and get changed so you're ready to go,' Hayley said, standing up and stacking Angel's pizza box over hers.

'Can I borrow your red sparkly top?' Angel asked, tipping her head a little to the left and giving her the benefit of the eyelash dance.

'To roll around on the floor with Randy?'

'Purrrlllease.'

'Urgh! Go on then,' Hayley gave in.

7th Avenue, Downtown Manhattan

Oliver had had way too much to drink and nothing to eat. Perhaps he was more like his father than he'd thought. Richard had never worried about healthy living. He'd been very much in the club of going with whatever hand Fate dealt him. He never worked out. He had never curbed his carbs or toned down the Scotch. And he'd beaten the curse. At least until his sixties, when it had finally caught up with him. And Cynthia had cried desperate tears, leant over his body and wept for another family member lost, her soulmate taken too soon, leaving her a widow. Andrew had comforted her, Andrew whose wife had succumbed to cancer just a few years before. A constant in their lives for so long. School friends who had struck out on their own, achieving success in the same field.

Oliver carried on, stumbling a little on the slippery streets. This takeover of Regis Software was supposed to be about combining their strengths, achieving a crossover into sectors neither of the companies had entered separately before. Regis Software had cornered the health industry, Drummond Global had strong contracts with NASA. But what if it wasn't about that at all? What if this was all about Andrew Regis staking his claim on Richard Drummond's property?

Maybe this was about Cynthia. Strengthening his position in the business to coincide with his personal life. Now his brain was working overtime. What if they got married? What happened then? He had enough suspicion to set Daniel Pearson to work. He just had to wait and see what turned up.

Now he felt sick and his vision was blurred. Spending the day in the bar had been the best way to avoid the phone calls he was sure had been jamming up the Drummond Global switchboard.

Oliver stopped walking and palmed his face, trying to clear his eyes and his head. He looked up through the darkness and along the street. Just how many blocks away from Dean Walker's apartment was he?

Dean Walker's Apartment, Downtown Manhattan

Hayley had gone through all the M De Vos's on the internet's version of the phone directory. Why she thought she would have more luck here than she had at home in England she didn't know. No one claimed to know or be the Michel she'd met in Vipers ten years ago. But would even the man himself remember her? It was one night. She might remember every man she'd ever slept with, but what if he had a hundred conquests … or more? She swallowed. She didn't want to think that for lots of reasons. Because it made him promiscuous and her not just careless about contraception but downright insane. She also didn't want to think about lots of little Angels or Gabriels around the world if the artist had sown many seeds.

She picked up the glass of white wine she'd poured and took a mouthful. None of the other galleries would be open now unless they had an exhibition. It would be better to call them in the morning.

The intercom sounded, making her jump. She got down from the kitchen bar stool and padded across to the machine on the wall. She was dressed for bed in a red and white polka dot onesie, Angel's cat slipper socks on her feet. It was far too early to be Dean and Angel, besides, Dean had a key. Unless he'd forgotten it. She hoped it wasn't someone she had to let in.

She pressed the button. 'Hello.'

There was the sound of scuffling and she straight away thought it was kids pranking about. But then someone spoke.

'I guess you're happy now.'

She furrowed her brow. The owner of the words was slurring over them. Maybe it was a down-and-out.

'I think you have the wrong apartment.' She was about to let the button go and return to her wine when the man spoke again.

'You're all the same, you know. You all use people to get what you want.'

Familiarity kicked in. It was Oliver Drummond and he was drunk.

'Oliver? Is that you?'

'Now my mother is doing it to me too. She set up this deal and now I know why.'

What was he doing here? How did he even know she was staying here? Had she told him she was staying with Dean? He was drunk and annoyed and she was on her own. In a onesie. But he *was* Dean's boss and she had run away after kissing him last night.

'Listen, stay right there.' She paused. 'I'm coming down.'

She let go of the button and raced out of the room towards the stairs.

He was going to be sick. All he could taste was the amalgamation of beer, whisky and peanuts he'd inhaled from the bowl on the bar. It was all fighting for release and he was swaying, holding onto the plaster of the façade outside the apartment.

The door opened and there she was. Hayley. The woman he'd kissed last night, the woman who had sold him out to the press. What was she wearing? She looked like Santa Claus. A cute Santa Claus. He really *was* drunk.

'You look terrible,' she announced.

He nodded his head in acceptance, then remembered he was supposed to be furious with her and adopted the appropriate facial expression. 'You,' he said, pointing a finger at her, still swaying. 'You went to the newspaper.'

'What?'

'The front page of the *New York Times*. You sold your story to a journalist.'

He clamped a hand onto the stair rail to the left of the short run of steps he was stood at the top of. He raised his eyes and found no shock on her face, just a lot of anger.

'How dare you,' Hayley stated, shaking her head at him.

'How dare I? I'm the injured party here,' Oliver slurred.

'Look at you! Sponsored by Budweiser and rolling up here throwing accusations about.'

He had no response and his eyes rolled back as balance became a real issue.

'Get inside,' she ordered, shifting back from the door and opening it wider. There was no way she was going to have the perfect couple from across the street being witness to this.

'Why would I want to do that?'

'Because if you make an arse of yourself in front of my brother's apartment I'll never forgive you.'

He lost his footing and stumbled off the top step. Suddenly his arm was being grabbed and he was pulled forward, up the step he'd fallen down and over the threshold of the apartment.

'Get up the stairs, go into the bathroom and vomit.' She sighed. 'Then I'll make coffee.'

Just her words made his stomach lurch like he'd come down off the top of a roller coaster. She pushed him in the direction of the stairs and suddenly he was crawling up them at pace, using the wall for support. He wasn't sure he was going to make it.

CHAPTER TWENTY-SIX

Dean Walker's Apartment, Downtown Manhattan

Oliver had been in the bathroom for almost twenty minutes before he finally emerged, pale and perspiring. Hayley watched him shuffle towards her and she picked up the tray she'd prepared and turned quickly. She knew her body language was saying 'angry' but, in truth, she was feeling much more than that. A small part of her was worried about him. He'd obviously been daytime drinking and that couldn't be just down to a newspaper article, could it?

'Sit down before you fall down,' she ordered, nodding towards one of Dean's couches.

'Why does it sound like I don't have a choice?' he asked.

'Because you don't.' She brought the coffee pot, mugs, glass of water, Advil and shortbread biscuits over to the coffee table and put the tray down. Then she sat in the nearest chair and watched him gingerly lower himself to the cushioned seat.

'Feel rough?' she asked, despite being able to see the answer.

'Uh-huh.' He nodded his head then put his hands to it.

'Room spinning? Walls caving in? Mouth like an under-watered pot plant?'

'OK, you can really stop now,' he groaned.

She leant forward on her seat and reached for the glass of water and the painkillers. She held them out. 'Here, drink this and swallow these.' His hand shook as he took the glass and when he offered his other she tipped the pills into his hand.

She watched him put the tablets into his mouth and swallow them down with a couple of gulps of fluid.

'So, you spent the whole afternoon in a bar and then you came round here to accuse me of speaking to the newspaper.'

He just looked at her, blinking his dark eyelashes over those full hazel eyes, nothing but vulnerability staring back at her. He looked lost.

'Can you at least wait until the pills have kicked in?' He leant forward, resting his elbows on his knees and holding his head in his hands.

'If I wait, guessing the alcohol to blood ratio, you're probably going to fall asleep.'

He made a frustrated noise, pulled at his hair and sat back in the chair. 'Why is it so bright in here?'

'That's the disco-ball side of my brother. He likes glitter and sparkles, the brighter the better.'

'Yay.'

'Ooo attitude. A minor recovery.' She reached for the coffee pot and poured herself a mug full. Then she sat back and nursed it in her hands. 'So, let me be clear. I did not contact any journalist or talk to anyone about you. Either another woman did – there must be hundreds of candidates in line – or your office or apartment is bugged.' She took a sip of the coffee. 'This is New York after all.'

He felt his lips work into a smile then. Her Englishness was coming out now. He still had no idea what she was wearing but she looked cute, even through his blurred vision. Her dark hair framed her heart-shaped face and those clear intense eyes did something to him. He drank a little more of the water. She hadn't sold him out. He should have known that. If she was going to tell a story it would have had far more embellishment and a mention of Superman.

'Is that what you think about New York? That it's all espionage and underhand dealings?' he asked.

'After the day I've had I'm thinking it's a cross between that and the *Gilmore Girls*.' She let out a sigh. 'But *I* didn't drown my sorrows in the nearest glass.'

'No?' Oliver said, indicating the wine glass still sat on the breakfast bar behind them.

'That wasn't because I had a bad day. That was just because I like wine.' She put her lips to the mug. 'And anytime you want to apologise for accusing me of being a grass I'm ready to take it.'

'A grass?' he asked, looking blankly at her.

'Spilling my guts. Being a snitch, an informant, you know, telling, ratting you out.'

'I'm sorry,' he told her, his voice soft.

'Yes, you should be.'

'And I am.'

'Quite rightly.'

'Do you ever let anyone else have the last word?'

'Only my daughter, and we really fight like hell for it.'

He laughed then, unable to help himself, despite how terrible he felt. He pulled himself forward and put his water back on the table.

'So what made you ditch work for beer?' Hayley asked.

'Bad meeting.'

'Not the Globe?'

He shook his head. 'No, not the Globe. It was more of a personal thing.'

Should he tell her? About his mother and Andrew Regis? It wouldn't mean anything unless he explained. His head was pounding now. He opened his mouth to speak.

'You don't have to tell me,' Hayley interrupted. 'It's none of my business.'

He nodded. 'I deserve that.'

'What?' she asked, looking confused.

'I came here drunk, yelling like some immature jerk off. I shouldn't expect you to be my counsellor.'

'Is that what you need?'

'Probably,' he admitted.

Despite the smart suit that probably cost hundreds, if not thousands of dollars, Oliver looked so far removed from her idea of one of the world's richest men. He was less confident here, hungover, his demeanour slightly crumpled. Seeing him like this, his defences down, human, made her shift a little in her seat. *An eligible bachelor*, her brain added all by itself. She put her cup on the table. 'I can listen.'

He shook his head quickly. 'No. There's no point.'

'What d'you mean, there's no point?'

'I'll just end up sounding like the selfish asshole I am and you don't need that hassle.'

'I don't like people making judgement calls for me.' She sniffed.

'No?'

'I thought I'd made that clear last night.'

'When I insulted your wish.'

'I'm over that. I thought I made that clear too.'

She swallowed. Despite his dishevelled appearance and the fact he reeked of booze, she was dipping her toe into dangerous waters here. The memory of their kiss in the snow was pushing its way into her frontal lobe. If she let her brain pull her back to that place, she could still recall the texture of his lips on hers, the weight and urgency of his mouth …

'My mother's dating.' He nodded. 'My father's best friend.'

'A little *Dear Deirdre* I guess.'

'It's been over a year. Things move on.'

'But it doesn't sound like you're happy about it.'

'It isn't about her moving on necessarily. It's who it's with.'

She watched him grit his teeth and rock forward on the sofa.

'And I know how that sounds. Like I'm a kid with issues,' he added.

Hayley held her hands up. 'I wish my mother would date anyone, just to stop her watching gardening programmes. No judgement here.'

'Andrew Regis was my father's best friend since school,' Oliver began. 'We've been in discussions about Drummond Global taking over his company and now I know why.'

'You think it's because he's dating your mother?'

'Yeah I think that.' He reached for the coffee pot with a shaking hand. 'And I'm also thinking a lot of other stuff too. Like what are his other motives for this merger. Like whether this relationship started before or after my father died.'

'Oh, Oliver,' Hayley said. She watched him pour himself a coffee then warm his hands with the mug.

'Don't sympathise. A counsellor would just sit and listen and quietly think about bringing the appointment to an end as soon as was reasonable.'

'Shall I yawn and look at my watch?' she suggested.

She saw him smile. 'That might work,' he replied.

'So have you spoken to your mum about it?'

He shook his head. 'There's other things going on with us right now.'

'Like what?'

'You're good at this.'

'Good at what? Conversation? Yeah, I have to admit I do like to talk. Particularly that last word.'

He took a sip of his coffee and settled back into the sofa.

'And that was a highly proficient swerve from the topic,' she said.

'Let's just say she wants me to do something I just don't want to do.'

'Mothers do that. *I* do that with Angel.'

'I don't expect you'd make her stand up in a room full of people and talk about a dead relative.'

'Your father?'

'No, my brother.'

And there was Ben sweeping into his mind again. His short dark hair, his engaging smile, the perfect American-dream poster boy. His jealousy and grief always intertwined so freely, both jarring, both painful to recapture. He'd loved his brother, desperately. He recalled the first time he'd thought they'd lost him. They were out on the ocean just a few hundred yards away from their summer beachside retreat, larking about on the boat when the weather had taken a turn for the worse. He'd done everything his father had taught him to get the boat to shore, Ben had taken charge, tried to quell both their panic. But they just seemed to be drifting further and further out to sea. And then a wave had rocked the vessel so hard it had flipped his brother overboard. He still remembered the waves, smashing against the side of the hull, angry white crests, hiding his brother. He had stared into the water, eyes straining, looking for the bright orange of Ben's lifejacket. What seemed like minutes had ticked by until finally he'd surfaced, spitting, coughing, his arms flailing against the current. Oliver had strained over the side of the yacht, uncaring for himself, holding the wooden oar at arm's length and praying for Ben to reach it. He had and they'd lain on the deck knowing if the elements took them they would be going together. Less than five minutes later, Richard had turned up on a speedboat and they were safe.

Oliver hid his face in his mug of coffee, drinking some of the liquid down and hoping it would settle his intoxication as well as his thoughts.

'Ben died five years ago this week.' He took in a breath. 'My mother likes to ramp up the emotion at this time of year, as if we don't acknowledge it somehow we'll forget about him. I have a different opinion,' Oliver stated.

'What do *you* think?' Hayley asked.

'I don't want to forget him, but sometimes I feel he's hanging over me like something out of *A Christmas Carol*.'

'And your mother thinks you'd be perfectly cast as Scrooge?'

'You got it.'

He looked to her then, watching her shift in her seat, wrapping her fleece-encased legs under herself. Did she understand? Perhaps now, with just the vague outline. But if he told her what he was really, ultimately, afraid of, what would she think then? He swallowed.

'Well, if it's any consolation at all, I'm pretty sure my mother hates me.'

Her voice came out so matter-of-fact, it took him a second to realise fully what she'd said.

'Hates you?' he queried.

'Too strong?'

'I don't know. Do you think it is?'

'She *adores* Dean, but then he's the handsome, intelligent, not-pregnant-at-eighteen one.'

'And you are?'

'I'm the one who does everything wrong. I'm the one who threw away her dreams to have a baby. I'm the one she glosses over talking about at bingo.'

'And that hurts.' He watched her expression. She seemed to mull over his sentence. She brushed her hair back off her face and leant an elbow on the chair, propping up her head with her hand.

'I don't know if it hurts anymore. I've got used to it.'

'Have you talked to her about it?'

'No. We don't do that sort of talking in our family.' She sighed. 'But seeing as I left my ten-year diary at her house, full of angst and issues and referring to her as Grotbags ... well, if she finds it it probably won't be long before she reads what I could never say.' A chill ran through her. She didn't want her mother finding the diary. She shouldn't have left it unsupervised behind the Gonks. The trouble was it was just as dangerous here in New York where Angel could come across it as it was at Rita's home. She unfolded her legs. 'I see what you did there. Nice moves but *I'm* the counsellor here.'

'Who said it had to be a one way street?'

'You're intoxicated. Everyone knows you never take advice from a drunk guy.'

'Everyone knows you always tell the truth when you're drunk.'

'Well then, if that's the case ... why did you kiss me last night?'

Hayley's cheeks caught alight and straight away she wished she had a way of filtering her thoughts instead of letting them blurt out of her lips. She should say something else, lighten the mood. But nothing was forthcoming.

She couldn't stop looking at him and his eyes were locked on hers. And again, his proximity was doing strange things to her insides.

'I kissed you because I couldn't bear the thought of you walking away thinking I was the biggest jerk in the city.'

'Ah,' she said. 'It was a PR exercise.'

He shook his head. 'No, I just ... didn't want to never see you again.'

She swallowed, seeing the truth in his eyes, feeling the sincerity flowing from him. Oliver Drummond, superficial, serial-dating Superman, was as complex as they came and now he was looking at her like he might want to rip her clothes off. How did she feel about that? Crazy excited was the truth of it. But in reality, her stakes were high and she couldn't throw any sort of caution to the wind.

She smiled, trying to dampen down the passion. 'I bet you say that to all the girls.'

He shook his head. 'No, actually, you're the first I've ever said that too.'

'Wow,' she said quickly. 'What was that beer the bar served you?'

'Now who's swerving the topic?' He smiled.

'I'm sober.'

'Pity.'

She smiled and let out a breath. 'You don't want to get mixed up with me.' She stood up. 'I'm here looking for another man.' She sighed. 'There's too many complications.'

'I'm already mixed up with you, Hayley.' He rose to his feet.

They were still a couple of feet away from each other but her body was reacting like a raging inferno was about to burn her to the ground. This couldn't happen. Her mission to find Michel was paramount. Getting involved with anyone was not on her agenda.

'I'm a mess, Hayley.' He moved closer. 'Nothing in my life is how I want it to be right now.' He put a hand to her cheek, let his fingers rest on the skin. 'But then there's you. When I'm with you …'

She could barely get breath inside her. His fingers cupped her jaw and all her pleasure senses engaged at once. She shouldn't let this happen.

'When I'm with you everything else matters a little bit less,' he whispered.

'You're forgetting you came here under the influence, wanting to give me a piece of your mind.' She almost wished she had sold a story to the press. Having him still angry wouldn't be leading to … whatever this was.

He nodded. 'When I should have known the truth.' He brushed her hair with his fingers. 'Because I've gotten to know you.'

She swallowed. 'You only know what I've told you.'

He nodded again. 'And instead of telling me you wanted a trip to Honduras or you longed for a Ferrari, you said you wanted to find Angel's father.'

She took a breath. 'And you hated that.'

'I still do.' He trailed a finger down from her jaw to her neck and the zip of the onesie. 'But you were honest with me. You were real.'

She shivered as his finger fixed over the zipper and tugged slowly downwards. Trust her to be dressed up like a toy room helper from Angel's Christmas storybook when there was a chance she was going to be seduced.

She was getting drawn in by his eyes, her body inching nearer as his fingers pulled her zipper lower. She ought to move away. She needed to just take half a step backwards and achieve even a hair's breadth of distance. Except she couldn't move, didn't want to.

His lips touched hers and she felt the same zing fizzle through her as she had the night before. His mouth was hot, his fingers parting the material of her inappropriate nightwear.

'God, what is this thing?' he asked, tugging at the zipper a little more.

'It's a onesie,' she replied.

'I hate it.'

'Right now, I hate it too.'

He kissed her again, yanking the fleecy material over her shoulder to release some of her flesh.

Then the front door slammed and Hayley jumped like a startled kangaroo.

She clapped her hand to her mouth. 'It's Dean and Angel.' She pulled the zipper back up.

'What do you want me to do? Go? Hide? It's your call,' he told her.

'Hide?' She couldn't stop herself from smirking.

'I don't know,' he said, a small laugh escaping. 'What would happen in the *Gilmore Girls*?'

'There would be hiding, definitely, and lots of talking about random stuff that only highlights the fact that you're here and we've had coffee and …' There was no hiding the number of cups on the table. Hiding wasn't an option. She widened her eyes. 'You have to make this about the Globe. Yes! That's it!

You've come here to ask Dean something about the Globe that couldn't wait.'

'Like what?' Oliver asked, tucking his shirt in.

'I don't know! I'm not the owner of a consumer electronics company.' She thought for a second, almost able to hear the footfalls on the stairs. 'It overheats!'

'What? I can't say that!'

The door to the lounge area swung open and Angel and Dean entered the room. Hayley leapt forward, pulling Angel into an over-the-top embrace, coddling her head to her bosom. 'Did you have a lovely time? Was Vernon's food a-ma-zing?'

'Hey,' Oliver greeted, waving a hand.

Angel struggled from her embrace and eyed Oliver with suspicion.

'Mr Drummond … what are you doing here? I mean … is there something I can help you with?' Dean started, putting a plastic container on the dining room table behind him. 'Oh no … it's the Globe, isn't it?'

Hayley nodded her head up and down, eyes on stalks, willing Oliver to agree.

'Rabbit Nation works fine. I've been playing that all the way there and all the way back,' Angel remarked.

Hayley nodded all the more vigorously, then shot Dean an innocent look, toying with the zipper on her onesie.

'Yes, I'm afraid it's the Globe,' Oliver cleared his throat. 'I think we have an overheating issue.'

CHAPTER TWENTY-SEVEN

Dean Walker's Apartment, Downtown Manhattan

Her brother was still looking at the product like it might explode in his hands as Oliver talked to him about something he'd found out on the electronics grapevine to do with one of the components they had used. Hayley felt bad for making Oliver lie and for getting Dean hot under the collar about the apparent failure of his baby. But the alternative was to try and explain what the billionaire was doing in the apartment with her. The two men were huddled over the Globe on the breakfast bar, Dean talking and swiping and Oliver looking back to her every now and then for a get-out.

'Did you know, Vernon's meatball recipe has been in his family for six generations,' Angel said, appearing at Hayley's elbow, a bowl of ice cream in her hands.

'I didn't know that,' she replied, her eyes still on Oliver.

'I know there's nothing wrong with the Globe,' Angel said, digging her spoon into the dessert and pushing the food into her mouth.

Hayley turned to Angel. 'What d'you mean?'

'There are shortbread biscuits on the coffee table,' Angel said through a mouthful.

Hayley looked to the table. The half-empty coffee pot, the glass of water, the biscuits. Did the scene have incrimination written all over it?

'He's Uncle Dean's boss. What was I supposed to give him when he turned up here? Leftover pizza?'

'Billionaires don't just turn up at people's houses,' Angel continued. 'They make appointments in work time.'

'How many billionaires do you actually know that you're basing that judgement on?' Hayley put her hands on her hips.

'I know what's going on,' Angel stated loudly.

Hayley watched Oliver glance over his shoulder and away from Dean's dissection of the tablet. Her heart was hammering now. She wasn't that transparent, was she? She made certain the zipper on her onesie was up to her neckline.

'You got him to come over here and you're going to ask him for a job,' Angel said, finishing the sentence off with a firm nod.

'I have a job,' she reminded, in a whisper.

'You think? After the way we were almost ordered to leave that house today?'

Hayley let out a sigh. She hadn't heard anything from Majestic Cleaning and she didn't dare call. She shrugged. 'It will blow over.'

'Are you crazy? The woman looked like she wanted to kill us and the housekeeper screamed like she was in a horror movie.'

'Which you are not old enough to watch.'

'Biscuits never lie,' Angel said, looking triumphant.

She held her hands up. 'OK, you got me, I wanted to ask him for a job.'

Angel's eyes grew big. 'And?'

'And you and Uncle Dean burst in and I didn't get the chance.'

'So there's nothing wrong with the Globe?'

'No … I mean yes … I don't know. I mean, I didn't say that.'

Angel's eyes misted over and she slumped down onto the sofa, ice cream spoon still in her hand. 'I really wanted that lady to like what we'd done to her room today.'

Hayley moved, plumping down next to Angel and taking the spoon from her. 'Yeah, me too.' She dug into the ice cream and ate a mouthful.

'I thought it looked beautiful. It was warm and inviting, the fire was cosy and the lights made her photographs stand out,' Angel continued, grabbing back the spoon.

'We did a great job. It just wasn't to her taste, that's all.'

'And you're probably going to get fired because of me,' Angel added, looking glum.

Hayley shook her head. 'No, not because of you, because of me.' She sighed. 'I don't know what I was thinking. I shouldn't be working here. I don't have the right paperwork and this is supposed to be a family holiday. I should be making the most of not working and spending every second with you.' She put an arm around Angel and drew her close.

'But what about money?'

Hayley shrugged. 'We'll work something out.'

Angel moved slightly, turning her head to look at her. 'So no more mopping and silly outfits?'

'No more mopping and no more Agatha. Now go and get another spoon for this ice cream. You can't possibly eat it all yourself.'

'I think Dean would have had me stay here all night taking it to pieces with him.' Oliver smiled as Hayley showed him down the stairs to the front door of the apartment. He felt almost human again after water and coffee and the bathroom visit that lost him half his body weight.

'I'm so sorry. I couldn't think of anything else to say.' She stopped at the bottom of the stairs and put her hand to the gold latch. 'He's not going to rip it all apart and start again, is he? I don't want to be responsible for the crumbling of an empire.'

'I've put his mind at rest I think. Said I wasn't sure of the model number. He'll probably Google it.'

'Or Globe it.'

'Voyage it actually. That's the name of our search engine.'

'I like it.' She nodded. 'All about the journey and no connotation of wild animals.'

He looked quizzical.

'Safari?'

Oliver smiled then. Her eyes were shining as she looked back at him, dewy, alive. 'Can I take you out somewhere?'

She didn't reply and he realised he was holding his breath and his stance. He was almost bracing himself for the negative response.

'I made you stand there for half an hour getting fictitious about a piece of equipment and you want to take me out somewhere?'

'I came round here drunk and behaved badly. Let me make it up to you.' He swallowed, then reached for her hand. He turned it over and gently stroked her palm with his fingers. He couldn't remember the last time he had stroked a woman's hand this way.

She nodded, smiling. 'OK.'

'OK?' He shocked himself by how surprised he sounded. She'd said yes. 'Well, what do you want to do?'

He felt her squeeze his hand.

'No more wishes. You decide,' she replied.

'Are you sure about that? I don't want to take you out somewhere and have you disappointed.' In truth he was playing for time, his brain desperately wondering where he could take her, what he could do, how to make the best possible impression.

'I'm sure, Superman.' She rose up on her tip-toes and planted the lightest of kisses on his lips. She let go of his hand and backed up the first step.

'Well, shall I call you? I don't have your number.' He reached into the pocket of his trousers and drew out his cell phone.

'Ready?' she asked.

'Hold up just a second.' He tapped at the screen.

'077026 415798.' She turned away and headed back up the steps.

'What? Was that seven nine eight or seven eight nine?' he called.

'Bye, Clark.' She stopped walking and turned back. 'By the way, Angel loved the Christmas tree in your lobby.'

CHAPTER TWENTY-EIGHT

Drummond Global Offices, Downtown Manhattan

Oliver took a deep lung full of the frosty air before he pushed the door to the office block. Despite the hangover headache he was managing, it was a good day. He had coffee and he had a plan. Today he was going to create the perfect date for a woman he really wanted to get to know better. And he was going to set Daniel Pearson on another mission. He'd granted lots of wishes and no matter how much it irked him, he was going to try and do something about Hayley's.

He stepped into the reception area and straight away saw Clara. He smiled and made his way over to her.

'Good morning, Clara. How was your day off? If you tell me you spent it anywhere but the bedroom I'm going to be disappointed.'

Clara's mouth fell open and she started to splutter as the receptionists behind her giggled. 'I wasn't aware I had to report my day off activities to the CEO.'

'Absolutely you don't.' He touched his nose with his finger. 'I won't say a word.' He grinned, indicating the elevator. 'Going up?'

'Yes, but ...' Clara started.

'Before you do anything this morning, Clara, could you get the Christmas tree guys back here and have them put it back in the lobby.' He looked at the vacant space, not even a pine needle in sight. 'But get a bigger one. And more decorations.'

He pressed the button for the lift. 'And get a couple of thousand dollars' worth of toys to go under the tree. We'll give them to employees' children and the hospital.'

'Oliver, what's happened?'

He smiled. 'Nothing's happened. I just think we should get the Christmas tree back in here.'

'Because?'

'Because it's nearly Christmas.' He stepped into the lift.

'It was nearly Christmas the other day when you had them take it down,' Clara answered, following him.

'Timing is everything,' he replied, unable to keep the grin off his face.

Clara shook her head as the doors closed. 'I saw the front page of the newspaper yesterday.' She turned to look at him. 'I called in to speak to you about it only to be told you were out of the office.'

'Uh-huh.'

'And when I called again, every hour on the hour, I got given the same message.'

He let out an exasperated sigh. 'It was your day off. What the hell were you doing calling me? I told you I expected you to …'

'Spend the whole day in bed, yes, the whole lobby heard you.'

'And did you? In between phone calls?' He moved himself into Clara's personal space, ducking his head a little to catch her eye.

Clara smiled back at him, a coy expression on her face. 'There may have been some marital harmony at some point during the day.'

He clapped his hands together and laughed. 'Good.'

'And where were you? Did you and Andrew Regis take the meeting to the country club or something?'

He felt his smile slide and he tightened his lips together, drawing in a breath. 'Not exactly.'

'Well, you should know he's been on the phone already this morning,' Clara said.

'OK.'

'Twice,' Clara added. 'And so has your mother.'

'I see.'

'Three times.'

He stood tall, ignoring the weight in his chest. Whatever his mother was up to with Andrew Regis he wasn't going to let it pull him out of this good place he was in right now.

'Reconsidering the tree and the presents?' Clara asked.

'No.' He shook his head. 'The tree comes back, the presents arrive and when the mail is ready I want you to come into my office and tell me the most romantic place in the city to take someone on a date.'

'According to the newspaper, you grant women wishes.' He watched the smirk play on her lips.

'Don't believe everything you read in the press, Clara.' He winked. 'And why don't you have William call someone named Nick in packaging. He needs an assistant manager I've heard.'

He watched the smile arrive on Clara's lips. Today he was unstoppable.

Dean Walker's Apartment, Downtown Manhattan

'No, Peter, I don't really know,' Dean paced around the kitchen, his mobile phone to his ear. 'He turned up here last night, said there was a problem and I've been up all night trying to find this report on the internet.'

Hayley cringed as she sipped at her cup of tea. Angel kicked her ankle from her seat around the breakfast bar and glared.

'You have to tell him,' Angel said through tight lips.

Hayley shook her head. 'I don't know what you're talking about.'

'There's nothing wrong with the Globe.'

'We don't know that.'

'He didn't sleep,' Angel stated, a spoonful of cereal in her mouth.

'How do *you* know? *You* should have been asleep.'

'I'm going to tell him,' Angel said.

'Tell him what?' She raised her teacup in innocence.

'That there's nothing wrong with the Globe and that you're trying to get a job.'

Hayley watched Angel swing her legs to the side, facing her body towards Dean.

'Uncle Dean!' Angel called loudly.

Hayley jumped down from the high stool, spilling tea as she set the cup down and raced to Angel. She put a hand over her mouth and pulled her into her body, muffling the sound. This was becoming a regular tactic.

'Angel, please don't,' she begged.

Angel fought herself free and wiped at her mouth with the sleeve of her sweatshirt. 'You leave me with no choice then.' She reached across the table and dragged the New York guidebook across the countertop.

'Oh please, not one hundred and one facts about the birds of Central Park.'

'Let me see.' Angel thumbed the pages of the book. 'I think … yes … the New York Public Library followed by the Empire State Building and then the Rockefeller Centre.'

'I thought we might have a look at a couple of galleries and can we swap the library for a browse around Barneys or Bloomingdales?'

'No.' Angel crossed her arms over her chest.

'Oh fine, you win.' She stuck her tongue out. 'Go and get dressed then.'

Angel pulled a face and headed towards the door, swinging her hips in some sort of victory dance.

'I'll see you when I get in.' Dean ended the call, putting his mobile phone down on the countertop. He did look pale and harried, and it was all her fault.

'Listen, I reckon Oliver's got it wrong. You know what these MDs are like. What do they know about the grass roots of the business?'

Dean was suddenly looking at her like she had grown a second head.

She looked down at her onesie. Had she spilt something on herself? 'What?'

'You said *Oliver*,' Dean stated.

She swallowed. She'd totally forgotten Dean knew nothing about any of their meetings. She could feel her cheeks turning into a riot of colour. 'Isn't that his name?' she offered.

'Yes, I just …'

She interrupted quickly. 'Angel wants to go to the Empire State today and, after I've phoned as many galleries as I can, we're going to go and visit some more and hope I get a lead on Michel.'

Dean picked up his coffee mug. 'D'you think that's wise?'
'What?'

'Going to the galleries with Angel. I mean, what if he's actually *in* one of them?'

'Don't you think I've thought of that?'

'I don't know. Have you?'

'Yes, I've decided I'm going to talk to her about it at the top of the Empire State, having drunk several strong coffees.' Hayley felt her chest tighten at the thought of broaching the subject with Angel. She carried on regardless. 'I'll tell her I know about her wish and that I'm going to help her find her father.'

A loud bang on the floorboards had Hayley turning towards the doorway. She gasped. Angel was stood just behind her, the special dictionary fallen open on the floor at her feet.

CHAPTER TWENTY-NINE

Drummond Global Offices, Downtown Manhattan

'That was reception again. Your mother has left another message,' Clara said, putting down the phone on Oliver's desk.

'When do you think she's going to give up?' he asked, leaning back in his chair.

'I've known her half my life, Oliver. She isn't going to give up until you talk to her.'

He nodded, filling his chest cavity with a long breath. Clara was right, of course, but he wasn't ready yet.

'Is this about the McArthur Foundation?' Clara asked.

He shook his head. 'No.'

'Then …'

He knew she'd deliberately left the end of her sentence open, the words hanging there, just waiting for him to fill in the gaps.

'So, romantic locations,' Oliver said, pulling himself upright and smiling at Clara.

'You were serious about that?'

'Did you think I wasn't?'

'It's that woman who was here the other day.' Clara smiled. 'Lois.'

He couldn't stop the smile spreading across his mouth. 'Maybe.'

'Oliver, I've never seen you look like that before.'

'Like what?'

'Like you're not running from the world.'

He swallowed, the smile fading a little. Was that what he did? Was that how others saw him? He felt the familiar grip of fear tighten its hold on his heart. Planning a date like this was having faith in something he didn't believe in. This wasn't a casual pick-up. Making a diary entry with someone was as permanent as he'd ever been. A voice at the back of his mind was urging caution. *You are going to die.* He swallowed, tempted to listen. Or did he dare to ignore it? Live life without thinking too hard, like Tony kept suggesting.

'It wasn't a criticism,' Clara said quickly. 'I just know how much pressure you've been under since your father died and …'

He cleared his throat. 'So, I was thinking of a Broadway show. What's best?'

Clara put a hand to the turquoise statement necklace on her chest, twisting the beads between her fingers.

'No?' Oliver asked.

'Well, it's a nice idea but you can't really talk to each other in a show.' She shifted in her seat. 'A first date should give you an opportunity to get to know each other better.'

He nodded. 'You're right. What was I thinking?'

He thought over Clara's statement, watched her cheeks redden because she'd spoken her mind.

'Dinner?' Oliver suggested.

'Where's your originality? Food is good but you need something more.'

'Cocktails?'

'Clichéd.'

'Philharmonic orchestra?'

'You can talk over violins?'

He stabbed his pen at the pad in front of him and picked up the stress baseball. 'Why is this so difficult?'

'Because you care.' Clara smiled. 'What are her interests?'

The question jarred his thought process. He didn't know. They had met three times now, had conversation, kissed, and he had no idea what she liked.

'I don't know.' He felt pathetic. 'She has a daughter.'

'Even *I* knew that. Think, Oliver.'

'She's smart.' He stood up. 'I don't necessarily mean intellectually so …' He sighed. 'I don't know that. But she's a smart talker, knows how the world works, finds the fun in everything. Fights me for the last word.'

'Feisty and fun-loving.' Clara nodded, making notes on her clipboard.

'Am I wasting my time here, Clara?' He turned towards her.

'What makes you say that?'

'Should it be this hard?'

'The very best things in life are the ones you have to fight for.'

He swallowed, a feeling of melancholy washing over him. 'My father used to say that.'

'I know he did.' Clara smiled. 'And then he would tell the story about the boat capsizing.'

The story he had recalled just last night had been told at every networking event his father had attended since he was old enough to go with him to them. It had only been replaced with something else when Ben had died. Then it had been all about life being too short, making the most of what you had, no longer about going out and aiming big, fighting for what you wanted. Richard Drummond's success hadn't dwindled after Ben's death but his outlook on life definitely had.

His eyes lit up as a light bulb went on. 'How about Greenwich Village?'

Clara smiled. 'Now we're getting somewhere.'

Empire State Building, Midtown Manhattan

'Did you know there are a hundred and two floors in this place? Reasons Christmas is better in New York number 55 – exercise whilst visiting iconic buildings,' Hayley said. She breathed in the wintery air and leaned against the barricade of the eighty-sixth-floor main deck. The temperature had dropped below freezing, which meant a wind that bit but no snow and a bright, clear blue sky with a sun doing its best to heat the city up.

'I've waited eighty-six floors for you to tell me about my dad. I'm not going to wait sixteen more.'

Hayley felt the bitterness in Angel's words and saw the anxious expression just visible under Dean's New York Rangers beanie she had borrowed. Acting on maternal instinct, she reached for the collar of Angel's coat and refastened the undone top button.

'Mum,' Angel said, shaking herself away.

'Look out there, Angel,' Hayley pointed to the vast expanse of skyscrapers below them, laid out like a glass and metal picnic blanket. 'Isn't it beautiful?'

'Please, Mum.'

She let out a sigh, her breath hot mist in the air. She'd told Dean she was going to tell Angel up here. She'd kidded herself that she was ready. But Angel overhearing the earlier conversation meant it wasn't something she could hide away in her diary anymore. It was time to face the music, and the consequences.

She smiled. 'Well, I guess it's confession time.' Her voice shook slightly. 'I heard you asking God and Father Christmas to find your dad and that's why we're here. In New York.' She let out a rush of breath. 'And I haven't told you because I wanted to try and find him first.'

She watched for Angel's reaction but there was little except the wide eyes that were growing larger and the fact she was looking less child genius and more vulnerable nine-year-old as the seconds ticked past.

'You've never asked me and I thought maybe you didn't want to know or …' Hayley started. She sunk her hands into the pockets of her coat.

'I didn't want to hurt your feelings,' Angel responded.

'Hurt my feelings? Why would you think that?'

'Because if I told you I wanted to know about my dad, you might think you weren't enough for me.'

She gulped back a knot of feeling. 'Oh, Angel, if you wanted to know, you should have asked.'

'I thought one day you would tell me. I didn't want to upset you.' Angel blinked her dark eyelashes. 'And I used to hear Nanny shouting at you about him. She calls him "that man" and she keeps saying he ruined your life.'

Hayley clapped her hands to her mouth as her stomach fell to ground-floor level. Angel had heard those horrible rows, the arguments about the latest 'dead-end' job she'd got that hadn't suited her mother. The constant reiteration about how she'd had to pay for that first year of college even though Hayley hadn't been able to go. Her dreams being killed. The car crash of her life. Just how much had Angel heard and never told?

She had to compose herself. This wasn't about her mother's disapproval, this was about her daughter wanting to know where she came from.

'His name is Michel,' Hayley began. 'And he's an artist.'

A quizzical look appeared on Angel's face, her brow furrowing. 'Painting?'

'Yes, and photography,' Hayley replied.

'Oils or watercolours?'

Hayley hesitated. 'I'm not sure.'

'And he lives here? In New York?'

'He did.'

'But not now?'

'I don't know. I hope he still does.'

Angel still looked puzzled. 'Can't you call him or email him or something? Say I want to meet him.'

This was where it was going to get difficult. But she wasn't going to lie to Angel, there had been too much hidden for too long already.

'Angel, I don't have his contact details.' She set her eyes on the city and said a mental prayer. 'I *never* had them.'

Angel didn't respond straight away and Hayley zoned in on the dulled noise of the streets from their position in the sky. Normality to the residents of this state, rush, bustle, heading to work or off home, business, pleasure. None of them could be going through the same situation she was.

'But he was your boyfriend,' Angel stated finally.

'Not really,' Hayley admitted on a breath. She turned to face her daughter then. 'We've done the whole how-babies-are-made thing, haven't we?'

Angel pulled a face and nodded her head. 'I'm not stupid.'

'Well, we only did it once.' She let another breath go. 'And I never saw him again.'

She swallowed her guilt and shame and kept looking at Angel. Eventually Angel looked up and met her eyes.

'You mean he doesn't ...' Angel paused and wet her lips. 'He doesn't know about me?'

Hayley shook her head. 'Angel, I'm sure if he knew about you he'd have been to see you.'

He would, wouldn't he? Just like, if she'd known a way to contact him before Angel was born, she would have. Wouldn't she? Hadn't she wanted to? Wasn't it her mother who had told her he wouldn't want to know and she was better off without him?

'So, he's *never* known about me,' Angel repeated, her eyes getting even bigger.

'No, but he's going to. That gallery we went to the other day, before the Guggenheim, I'm sure he exhibited there and the man I spoke to is going to contact some more galleries who are going to help. And I went to the club we met in just the other night and there's a bartender there who might know him and …' Hayley gabbled.

The wind was blowing the strands of hair flying loose from under Dean's hat and Hayley just wanted to envelop Angel in her arms and not let anything touch her. This obviously hadn't been anything like her daughter had envisaged in her mind. She had known her father was out there somewhere, but perhaps she'd imagined a real relationship between her parents, her father knowing about her but having to leave for some reason. This, as Hayley had always thought, was an unkind truth.

'I'm going to find him, Angel.' She struggled to keep her voice steady.

'How?' Angel asked, moving up alongside the barrier and looking out over the sea of grey.

'I told you, we're going to call all the galleries in New York and find someone who can put us in touch or there's the barman at Vipers. Maybe Michel still goes there and he remembers him.' She blew out a breath as a shiver ran over her body. 'I'm not going to stop until we find him.'

'But what if … what if he has another family?' Angel said. 'He might be married. He might have other children.'

Hayley put an arm across her shoulders and drew her close. 'Yes, he might.'

Had Michel met his soulmate? Did he have children? Did they look anything like Angel?

'We just need to find him first. Anything else will have to come later.'

'He might not want to know me at all.'

'And if he doesn't, we tell him what we think of him and we kick him in the Will.I.Am.'

She saw a smirk appear on Angel's face.

'Because that would make him the biggest ... dope,' Hayley said, letting go of Angel and adopting a rapper stance.

'Stop it! People are looking!'

Hayley put her arm back around her, affectionately rubbing her shoulder. 'Angel, I might not know a lot about him but I do know that he was funny and bright and passionate about life.' She recalled their walk through Central Park. The leaves on the trees a russet colour, waiting to fall, the air crisp, the moon lighting their way. 'He told me the world is just one big ball of experiences waiting to be grabbed.'

'Really?' Angel looked unimpressed by the anecdote.

'He had cool hair,' Hayley added.

Angel smiled. 'What else?'

'He had nice eyes, like yours,' she said, reaching for Angel's hand.

'Do you have a photo?'

'Yes!' Hayley said excitedly. 'It's back at the apartment but ... yes, I have a photo.'

Her daughter's smile widened then, becoming more genuine. Right now Hayley would say or do anything to make this easier for her. She couldn't help but feel as if she had let her down along the way to this moment, because of her own cautiousness about the subject … or perhaps her mother's.

'Can we go up to the top?' Angel asked, slipping her hand into Hayley's. It was a small gesture but it meant everything.

'Absolutely. As long as I can re-enact *Sleepless in Seattle*.' Hayley grinned.

Angel snatched her hand back, folding her arms across her chest. 'I am *not* being Tom Hanks.'

'Reasons Christmas is better in New York number 29. Visiting scenes from your favourite movies!'

CHAPTER THIRTY

Drummond Global Offices, Downtown Manhattan

Oliver relaxed the knot on his tie and unfastened the button of his suit jacket as he walked along the corridor.

'What is in that thing?' he asked, looking to Tony, who was devouring something wrapped in paper.

'Pastrami. Want some?' Tony offered it over, strings of meat hanging from his lips.

'No. What I *do* want is to know what you're doing here again.' He pushed open the door in front of them. 'I thought you had two new businesses to oversee.'

Tony nodded. 'I do. I also have a best friend who's determined to kill himself with overwork and malnutrition before his genetic heart condition can do the job.'

'Sshh,' Oliver hissed. He looked over his shoulder to see who might be listening. 'Keep it down.'

'What?' Tony asked, his eyes wide with innocence.

'My condition isn't common knowledge around here.' He lowered his voice further. 'They know my brother died young, there's enough speculation of age and alcohol playing a part with respect to the rest of the family.'

'OK, I get it. Sorry.'

Oliver blew out a breath. 'No, I'm sorry. I'm just strung out about my mother that's all.'

'What's up with Mrs D? She's OK, isn't she?'

'That clarifies one thing,' Oliver said, pushing open the next door.

'What thing?'

'That she didn't have intimate dinners with Andrew Regis at your restaurant.'

'No freaking way!' Tony's eyes came out of his head. 'She's seeing Andrew Regis?'

Just the sentence had Oliver's shoulders tensing in reaction.

'I don't like the guy,' Tony followed up. 'Eyes are too close together. And you should never trust a man who wears that much cologne.'

Oliver stopped walking. 'I need to get on.'

'Oh, sure, me too. I just dropped in to check you were still alive and kicking after yesterday and … thought I might bump into Kelly.' Tony grinned.

'Go and check on those restaurants plural,' Oliver ordered.

'I'm going.' He stopped, waving his wrap in the air. 'Oh and I've had orders from Momma to get you to the restaurant soon. She wants to feed you up. Said you looked too thin in the picture on the front of the *New York Times*.'

Oliver shook his head. 'Tell her I'll pop by soon.'

'She'll expect you this week.' Tony started walking but stopped. 'Oh and the tree in the lobby? Very understated.' He laughed at his own joke. 'No less is more around here.'

'Tony,' he said, smiling. 'Only more is more.'

Tony laughed and began to make his way back up the corridor.

Oliver took a deep breath in before approaching the final door. He had had a productive morning. As well as getting some ideas on date locations from Clara, he had called everyone off the Regis Software merger. By the end of the day both his mother and Andrew Regis would know the deal was officially off the table. And now, down on the tenth floor of his building, he was going on another fact-finding mission.

The dark-haired secretary at the entrance to the level almost spilt her coffee when he stepped onto the floor.

'Good morning,' he greeted, smiling at her.

'Mr Drummond, we … we weren't expecting you,' she replied.

'I wanted to take a walk,' he said, looking through into the work rooms.

'Of course … that's fine.'

'I'm glad.' He smiled again. 'Is Dean Walker around?'

'Yes, I think so.' She looked at her computer screen. 'Would you like me to buzz him?'

'No need. Room Seven, isn't it?' He started walking.

'Yes, that's right.'

'Thank you.' He waved a hand and headed down the corridor.

'Good morning, Mr Drummond,' a young man greeted him as he passed.

'Good morning,' he responded.

He didn't recognise any of these people. Now the company had grown to this level it was impossible for him to sit in on all interviews. But should he know more than he did? Should his employees be more than names on a computer system and faces he didn't know?

He stopped. 'Hey,' he called to the man passing him.

The employee stopped in his tracks and turned to face Oliver. He noted he was already looking concerned.

'What's your name?' Oliver asked.

'Milo Rodriguez, sir.'

Oliver nodded then held out his hand. 'Good,' he said as Milo connected the handshake. 'Well, I'm Oliver and it's nice to meet you.'

'You too, sir.' The guy seemed completely bewildered.

Oliver broke the connection and headed back down the corridor. It was time to stop being the soulless, man-at-the-top and start being someone people liked a little. He only hoped it wasn't too late.

Tilton Gallery, 8 East 76 Street

'Is this it?' Angel asked.

They were stood outside a cream-coloured building that looked more like a townhouse than a gallery. Its towering height only emphasised its lack of width and, if it hadn't been for the Parthenon-style pillars at its entrance, it would have passed for nothing out of the ordinary.

'I guess it is,' Hayley said, looking at the building. She had never been here before but this was another of the places her diary had confirmed Michel had talked about. He had had an exhibition of his work here. He had sold a few pieces. She remembered he'd been excited about it.

'Are we going in?' Angel asked.

Hayley nodded. That's what they were here for, but she was still filled with so much trepidation. Would it be another dead end or would luck be on their side this time?

'I should have brought the photo,' Hayley cursed. 'Why didn't I bring the photo?'

Angel took hold of Hayley's hand. 'It doesn't matter, Mum. If he had an exhibition here there will be a record of it, won't there?'

If he had been telling the truth. That always crossed her mind too. What if he wasn't an artist? That would explain the lack of artists called Michel De Vos on Google and the fact none of the galleries had come up with anything so far. He could have been a hot dog vendor and she wouldn't have known any different.

She smiled at Angel before any of her thoughts seeped out into her expression. 'Yes, there will. Let's go in.' She led the way up the steps.

Drummond Global Offices, Downtown Manhattan

This was the hub of the company, its engine and driving force. This was where ideas were created, world-changing pieces of equipment were devised, revolutionary gadgetry that had the ability to make a real difference to people's lives.

Oliver stood in the doorway of the room and just watched the employees at work. The smell of electronics took him right the way back to the garage and workshop in Westchester. His father had worked late into the night in the early days, a soldering iron never far from his hand, working diligently, every tiny section of each component nurtured by his hands. Then later Oliver had watched Ben working with him too. Ben was always given the first opportunities because he was older. But his outstanding capabilities had also made him the first port of call even when age no longer counted. Still a little jealousy mixed in with the grief no matter how hard he tried to ignore it.

His presence was noticed by Peter Lamont, the head of the department, and the man cleared his throat loudly, making everyone stop what they were doing. It almost looked like they were going to stand to attention and salute. Oliver stepped into the room.

'Don't let me stop what you're doing,' he said, waving their attention away.

'Mr Drummond, if this is about the Globe then I can assure you …' Peter started.

He shook his head. 'No, it isn't about the Globe. In fact the Globe is fine. I need to have more faith in your months of testing and extensive research and not believe everything that's served to me on the internet.' He cleared his throat as a picture of Hayley from last night, dressed in her woollen festive night-wear, came to mind. 'Could I have a moment with Dean?'

Oliver looked to the rear of the room. Dean was already out of his chair and heading towards them.

'Take my office,' Peter said, indicating the side room to the open-plan section they were standing in.

'After you,' Oliver said to Dean.

He followed Hayley's brother into Peter's office and, once they were both inside, he closed the door.

'Mr Drummond, I just want to say …' Dean began.

Oliver held his hand up to stop him talking. He was nervous enough as it was. He just needed to do some straight-talking and get what he came for.

'It's Oliver, please.' He loosened his tie a little more and began to pace the carpet. 'So, the thing is, Dean. Last night, after I met your sister… Lois … not Lois, not at all Lois.' He blushed and felt his resolve crumbling under Dean's scrutiny. Why was this woman getting under his skin so much? This had never happened before and it scared the crap out of him. 'Hayley,' he corrected. 'Hayley.'

Dean was just looking at him like he was the biggest jerk he'd ever met. And at the moment he was filling that role beautifully.

He let out a frustrated noise and swept a hand over a pile of papers on Peter's desk, making them flutter up, some falling from the desk to the floor. He was making such a mess of this, he was just going to have to come right out with it.

'I've asked Hayley on a date and I need your help.' There, it was out.

Dean started to cough and it was so vigorous and breath-impairing that Oliver feared he was having some sort of attack.

'Are you OK?' Oliver asked, moving from behind the desk to beside Dean.

Dean shook his head in a confirming way. 'Yeah, I'm fine,' he said, coughing some more but straightening up. 'I just … I just thought you said you'd asked my sister out on a date.'

Oliver nodded. 'I did.'

Dean's pallor turned mortuary white. He choked out a response. 'You did?'

'Yes. Do I have to ask permission?'

'No, of course not, I … I'm just surprised that's all.'

'Surprised why?'

'Well …' Dean began.

He got it then. Dean had read yesterday's news. He, along with the entire rest of the population of the city, thought he was a serial philanderer who behaved like an Aladdin character. He really needed to get his public relations people onto damage control. He'd ignored all their messages yesterday.

'She has Angel,' Dean filled in.

Oliver tried to compute what Dean meant. He ended up just furrowing his brow as he looked back at him. 'I realise that.'

'Well, with all due respect, she has quite a lot going on right now.'

'She said yes,' Oliver said, in case there was any doubt.

'She did?'

He nodded. 'And I know about her ex. Angel's father. The so-called painter with the artistic hair.'

'You do? Wow, you must have drunk a lot of coffee together before we got home.'

'Yeah, we did.' He pulled in a breath. 'So, I want to take her somewhere special, and that's where you come in.'

Dean was still looking a little bewildered by the conversation. 'It is?'

'What does she like? I don't mean food or wine or cable channels, I mean what makes her tick? Where can I take her? What can we do together that's going to really mean something to her?'

He had to swallow at the end of the sentence as the intensity of it hit him. And Dean wasn't saying anything, he was just looking at him like he might have lost his mind. Had he lost his mind? His heart was beating hard, telling him two things. One that he cared about this woman an awful lot already and two that he was taking chances here, chances he didn't have. Did he have the right to engage in this, with Hayley, and her daughter?

'She's only here for a couple of weeks,' Dean spoke.

'I realise that too.' Somehow that made it better. Whatever connection they had … well thinking about it as just two weeks was much more manageable. He relaxed a little.

'And she's had a lot to deal with over the years.'

'A daughter who talks endlessly and wants to save every lobster in Asian Dawn, if not every Chinese restaurant across the world.'

'You've got it,' Dean stated.

'I've definitely got it,' he said.

Dean seemed to assess him then, his eyes trying to take him apart from the inside. Finally Dean moved, picked a pen out of the pot on the desk and grabbed a notepad.

'She likes fashion,' he said, leaning over the desk and writing. 'B.A. That's Before Angel, she was going to study at a really good college that only accepts the best of the best. She had to give it up.'

Oliver swallowed. Another person whose path in life was altered. But instead of toeing the family line, Hayley had sacrificed her dreams for her daughter.

Dean held out the paper. 'This is her absolute favourite designer, or rather, it was. She doesn't get a lot of time for browsing through anything these days.'

Oliver went to take the note but Dean held on fast.

'My sister's spent half her life feeling inadequate.' Dean sighed. 'Hayley's clever and she's a good person. She's just been dealt a challenging hand and had no acknowledgement of how well she's done raising Angel.' He still held the paper. 'She just doesn't need anyone coming in and letting her down. Even if it's only for a couple of weeks.'

'It's just a date,' Oliver reminded. He smiled, admiring the way Dean wasn't going to be browbeaten on this.

'Hayley doesn't go on many dates.'

'She has Angel,' Oliver said, understanding.

'And Angel is the most important thing in her life.'

Oliver put his fingers to the notepaper. 'I get that.'

Dean released his grip.

'Thank you,' Oliver replied.

Tilton Gallery, 8 East 76 Street

'Do you think the floor is part of the exhibition?' Angel asked, looking down as they walked into the first room of the gallery.

'It could be. This parquet has had much more than an Elizabeth, a Diana and a Camilla done to it.'

The magnificent, glossy wood flooring was in perfect contrast to the bare white walls surrounding them. Further into the room there were two large windows letting in every ounce of natural light possible and ahead were several wire cages Hayley assumed were art. To their left was an ornate fireplace not dissimilar to the one at the house in Westchester yesterday. A wide staircase wove seamlessly upwards.

'Good afternoon. Can I be of assistance?' The accent was French and both Hayley and Angel turned around to greet their company.

A very tall, very slim woman in her mid-fifties was stepping towards them. She was dressed in a roll-neck jumper, a thick tartan wool skirt, black tights and boots. Her silver/grey hair was pinned back in a chignon and on her nose were a tiny pair of gold glasses. She smiled.

Angel dug Hayley in the ribs with her finger, making her jump forward a little.

'Yes, please.' She took a breath. 'We're looking for someone. He's exhibited here before, about ten years ago.'

'I see,' the woman replied.

'I called.' Hayley took a breath. 'A couple of weeks ago and the person I spoke to said they would call back but they didn't and …' She stopped as her mouth dried up. 'I know it's an odd request but we really need to meet with him and just … see how he is,' Hayley continued. 'We lost touch.' *And I had a baby.* She couldn't say that. This woman would think she was completely hopeless.

'Do you have files?' Angel asked. 'Could you look in a book or on a computer and see if you have a phone number or an email address for him?'

The woman smiled at Angel. 'What is this person's name?'

Angel looked up at Hayley, her eyes urging her to make the reply.

Hayley cleared her throat. 'Michel. Michel De Vos.'

The woman nodded. 'I will go and see.' She turned away from them and headed left out of the room.

Hayley blew out a breath. 'My heart's hammering.'

'Mine too,' Angel admitted.

Hayley swung an arm around her shoulders and pulled her close. 'Listen, no matter what she says, it's a positive, right?'

'Right,' Angel agreed.

'Because she'll either have something or she won't.'

'I know.'

'Good.'

'Are you sure this was one of the galleries he talked about?'

'Pretty sure.'

Angel looked up at her then. 'How much wine had you drunk?'

'Angel!'

'Well, you don't remember everything right after you've had wine.'

'It was this one … my ten-year diary said so … I think.'

'Mum!'

'Well, it doesn't really matter because if the lady comes back and says there's no record of him, we have hundreds of others to try. And we *will* try them all.'

She could see Angel was nervous. She was lifting her feet up and down as if they were cold, then shuffling her heels on the floor. The red coat swung around her knees as she twisted and, all of a sudden, she looked so small. This was a huge thing for a nine-year-old to be going through. Hayley had dealt with it very badly. She should have given Angel more credit and told her sooner.

The squeak of shoes on the shiny floor gave them their first indication that the woman was coming back. Hayley held her breath until her chest ached.

The lady stopped just in front of them and, for a second, Hayley wondered if she was going to say anything at all. Then she smiled.

'I have good news.'

'Oh … really?!' Hayley looked at Angel. Her daughter was on tiptoes, cheeks glowing in anticipation. Was this it? Had they finally found Michel. She felt sick. *This was good. This was what you wanted.*

The woman looked at the paper in her hands. 'He has exhibited here … in 2004.'

Angel deflated like a bouncy castle being turned off. Hayley took hold her hand and squeezed it.

'… and again just last year.'

Air gushed from Angel's mouth like someone had turned on a leaf blower.

'Last year,' Angel's words came out in a loud whisper. Her body straightened taller as her enthusiasm gained momentum.

'Well, I …' What was it she wanted to say? 'Do you have a contact number for him?' Hayley asked.

The woman's lips drew inwards. 'No, I'm afraid not.'

'An email address?' Hayley said. 'Anything?'

'I have a website address, that is all.' The woman held a small piece of paper in her hands.

Hayley watched Angel light up like a Christmas tree, eyes twinkling, skin glowing, smile wider than the Hudson River.

'Could you give it to us,' Hayley said excitedly. She swung her rucksack off her back and began scrabbling inside of it for her phone.

The woman adjusted her glasses, looking down at her own writing. Angel started to read out the letters.

'www.oilandwater.org.'

Hayley started tapping the address into the search engine on screen. What sort of website address was that? But out of all the searches on Google, Safari, Bing and Internet Explorer it was definitely one she hadn't tried before. Her fingers shook with each key tap.

As she hit the search button she could feel the nervous energy like static coming out of Angel's every pore. This meant the world to her daughter. She said a silent wish as she watched the blue line creeping at a snail's pace along the top of the phone screen. *Please*.

The line zipped along at last and a mainly white page appeared.

This webpage is not available.

No. Hayley hit the refresh button, angling the phone away from Angel's gaze and fixing a smile on her face. This time the blue line was quick.

This webpage is not available.

Hayley raised her head, caught the expectant look of the woman, the Olympic swimming pool sized eyes of Angel. What was she going to say? She let a small cough start her off.

'Damn 3G never works when you need it to.' Her cheeks were burning like hot oil was coating them. 'I'll check it on the PC when we get home.'

Delaying tactics would have to do for now. She needed to make sure she had tissues and marshmallow hot chocolate before she said anything to Angel.

CHAPTER THIRTY-ONE

Downtown Manhattan

'I need the nearest bodega,' Hayley said as they trudged through the rapidly falling snow on the way back to Dean's apartment.

'Do you have 3G yet?'

Angel had phrased this question in ten different ways since they got off the subway. Hayley was still wondering how to reply. She knew she had to tell her daughter. She knew she'd promised honesty. She just wanted to get her back to the apartment, in a safe, confined place before she told her it was another dead end.

'He could be right here in New York,' Angel continued, her eyes rising to the height of the buildings all around them.

Hayley grabbed her arm as the stream of people hurrying along the street thickened. The inclement weather and the rush-hour city traffic were converging together in a congested mix that was making her head spin. She really did need fizzy wine.

'Do you think he's in New York now?' Angel asked above the engines of the long line of cars and the beeping horns.

'I don't know.'

'But he must still be in America,' Angel continued. She was full of excitement or nervous energy. Maybe a little of both.

She was in a no-win situation. She made a non-committal noise that didn't affirm anything.

'He could be living just a few streets away from here,' Angel said, starting to skip.

'Angel, stay close,' Hayley begged.

'There might be a phone number on his website. We could call him and ...'

'Angel, stop.' Hayley pulled her to a halt, swinging her out of the throbbing wave of commuters and into the doorway of a bakery. The scent of freshly baked confectionary filled her nose. Wafts of spun sugar hit her hard as Angel lifted her head, eyes large. All her daughter's hopes and dreams about meeting her father coated her expression.

'I just ...' Hayley started. She swallowed. 'Just don't get your hopes up too much.'

'Why?' Angel asked bluntly, putting her hands on her hips.

'Because ...' Could she put this off any longer?

'Because what?' Angel's voice was softer now, faltering.

Hayley squeezed her eyes tight shut, trying to ignore the street sounds, shut out the smell of road traffic, simmering hot dogs and mustard sauce, icing sugar and fondant from the bakery. She had to do this now. She swallowed, feeling like someone about to pull the head off a favourite teddy bear.

'The website didn't exist.'

A truck had stopped next to the sidewalk with a whoosh of hydraulics and Hayley wasn't certain Angel had actually heard what she'd said. There was no change in her daughter's expression, no lip-trembling or tears welling up. Should she tell her again?

'The website ...' Hayley started.

Angel nodded then, her chin defiant. 'I heard what you said.' Now there was a slight wobble to the voice.

'I'm sorry, Angel,' Hayley whispered out.

'Why?' Angel shook her head. 'We're trying every gallery in New York, aren't we?'

'Yes.' Hayley nodded, determined.

'It's just one stupid website. He probably bought another one.'

Her daughter was trying to be brave and it hit her heart hard. *That's my girl. Never give in.*

'Absolutely.' She nodded. 'And we're going to find out what it is and we're going to find him.'

A guy dressed in a Santa suit began strumming out 'Feliz Navidad' as the snow started to fall again. Hayley slipped her arm around Angel's shoulders. 'Let's go get us some popovers.'

Hayley's phone began to ring, Beyoncé's 'Single Ladies' sounding out through the material of her rucksack.

Hayley unzipped her bag and dipped her hand into it.

She looked at the display. It was an unknown number. She pressed to answer and put the phone to her ear.

'Hello.' She swallowed down her rising heart. Angel dragged at her arm.

'Miss Walker? It's Rebecca Rogers-Smythe.'

'Oh hello.' She knew what this was. She didn't need to be as clever as Angel to know she was going to be sacked. Her only surprise was the fact this hadn't happened sooner. The shouting from the housekeeper and the look on the woman's face the previous day had been an obvious indicator. One of them, or perhaps both, would have been on the phone requesting that Agatha never darken their door again.

'I've had a call from the client you cleaned for yesterday.'

Hayley closed her eyes. She would jump in first and resign. It had been a ridiculous idea anyway.

'Ms Rogers-Smythe …' she started.

'She would like you to drop in this evening if possible.'

'I can't … wait, what did you say?' She creased her brow and looked out, past Angel and onto the darkening street.

'I realise it's an unusual request but I can only assume she was pleased with what you did.'

'Pleased? You mean she didn't ...' The word complain was on the tip of her tongue but something told her to stop.

'I'm really hoping you could fill her twice weekly spot,' Rebecca interrupted.

'I could ... head over there now if that was convenient.'

Angel screwed up her nose and folded her arms across her chest, tapping her foot on the floor.

'I'll give her a quick call back and confirm. Toodle pip!'

Hayley ended the call and dropped the phone back into her bag. 'Cheer up, genius kid. I think your fairy light arrangement might have just scored me the cleaning job.' She inhaled the winter air. 'Either that or we're about to see a rich woman go all Wrestle Mania.'

'We're not going to a bodega?' Angel asked.

'No, we're going back to Westchester.' She took a step out onto the sidewalk and stuck out her hand. 'Taxi!'

Drummond Global Offices, Downtown Manhattan

'So ...' Oliver leant back in his chair and squashed the stress ball with his right hand. 'Where are we with the woman who was threatening court action on the maternity leave issue?'

Clara tried to stifle a yawn but he caught it. It was after five. She'd worked her butt off today.

'Was it twins or triplets?' Oliver continued. 'Huey, Louie and Dewey?'

'Sorry?' Clara shook her head and dropped her eyes down to the notepad in her hands, looking for the information. 'I'm not quite sure.'

'Clara, pack up, you're going home.'

Clara shook her head. 'We have two other employment issues to go through.'

'Not today. Go home.' He stood up. 'What's the name of the employee who wants to extend her time with her children?'

'Kate Vickram.'

Oliver nodded. 'Agree to it. In fact, get Mackenzie and her team to make it standard in all the contracts.' He paused, looking to the windows where snow was flashing past like a rushing white fog. He turned back to Clara. 'And send her a care package. Good stuff. Things for her, things for the babies and get her husband some beer. He's going to need that.'

He watched Clara's jaw drop a little away from the rest of her face. 'Are you sure?'

'Yes, Clara, I'm sure.' He raised a finger in the air. 'And tomorrow I want flash cards.'

'Flash cards?'

'You know those things kids use to learn letters and words? A is for apple etc. Well I want employee photos and names.'

'You want employee photos and names,' Clara repeated.

'It's time I invested some time in the people that work for me,' he answered.

There was a knock on the door and Clara looked at her watch.

'Are we expecting someone?' Oliver asked, striding towards the door.

'I'm not,' Clara replied.

Oliver threw open the door and Delaney Watts dropped her hand, adopting a glossy smile to greet him. This was one person he *did* recognise. Blonde, perfectly turned out, with the nose of a bloodhound. Delaney took care of his public relations with the ability to sniff out bad press quicker than a gossip columnist.

Except the headlines in the news yesterday, which she was still getting to the bottom of.

'Oliver,' she said, putting her hand out to him.

He shook it and opened the door wider. 'Do we have another problem?'

She let out a tinkle of a laugh. 'What makes you say that?'

'Good news comes via a PowerPoint presentation in the boardroom, bad news is delivered here with paper evidence.' He indicated the file she was clutching to her chest.

She smiled.

'Know who sold me out to the *New York Times*?'

'I'm still working on it.' Delaney smiled at Clara. 'Hey, Clara.'

'Hello, Delaney.'

Oliver returned to his seat, putting his hands behind his head as Delaney sat in the chair next to Clara, crossing her slim legs. 'So, go on, tell me what devastation is about to fall on the company.'

He watched Delaney's expression change. The confident smile was wavering a little, her pupils sharpening. He swallowed and waited.

'I got a tip-off from my contact at *Business Voice*.'

This wasn't going to be sugar-coated. Delaney had on the voice that had delivered uncomfortable news many times before. Oliver coiled his fingers around the arms of his chair.

'Andrew Regis has done an interview. It's going to press tomorrow.' Delaney uncrossed her legs. 'He's going public on the collapse of the deal and he's using sound bites like "the end of an era for the companies' relationship" and "a bond destroyed by Drummond's fears for the future".'

Oliver tightened his grip on the chair as his heart began an uncomfortable beat. He hadn't been expecting this. With whatever was going on between Regis and his mother, he hadn't anticipated an attack on the family name being on the cards. What was the idea behind that? What would his mother think about the Drummond name being dragged through the dirt? The thoughts circled around in his mind, colliding, smashing together, weaving and interlocking until they were one horrible mess.

'Now we have a couple of options,' Delaney said, opening up the file on her knee. 'We can …'

'Let it run,' Oliver said. He cleared his throat, trying to remove the emotion.

'Oliver, I'm not sure that's the right choice,' Delaney responded quickly.

He stood then, taking a deep breath and trying to quell his rapid heartbeat. 'How confident are you with your source? Because I don't believe it.'

'We've worked together for a couple of years now.'

'How do you know this isn't a test?' He looked to Clara. 'What if all this is a fabrication to cause me to make a knee-jerk reaction.'

'That isn't really my source's style. He's passed me considerable information in the past – all accurate.'

Oliver put his hands to his forehead. 'He wouldn't do this. He's dating my mother.'

'What?!' The word came out of the women's mouths at the very same time.

'Is that true?' Delaney followed up. 'Is that why the merger isn't going forward?'

'No,' Oliver shook his head. 'That would be an emotional decision and not a business one.'

He saw Clara toy with her necklace out of the corner of his eye. She knew all too well how emotion could cloud his judgement. Was it all about not being able to cope with this change in circumstance? Or was there real foundation to his pulling out of the deal? He'd had enough suspicion to employ Daniel Pearson. Didn't that alone say enough?

He picked up the stress ball from the desk and palmed it from hand to hand, the eyes of the women on his every movement.

'Do nothing, Delaney. If it's true and that article is anything like you say it's going to be, his union with my mother is going to be very short-lived.' He launched the ball across the room and watched it hit the framed infographic.

CHAPTER THIRTY-TWO

The Drummond Residence, Westchester

'Fashion alert on the cabbie back there. Double denim and a paisley shirt,' Hayley said as she and Angel mounted the steps towards the grand entrance of the imposing Westchester house. She was trying to lighten the mood for herself as much as for Angel. She had played through the various outcomes of this visit on the cab ride over. The very worst one was Cynthia standing at the door alongside US immigration officers with guns and handcuffs. The best one was the housekeeper being allowed free rein of the fire poker.

'And he sang out of tune,' Angel added.

'Like you,' Hayley said, nudging her arm.

'I sing in tune!'

'I've heard dolphins love it.'

'Mum!'

'Oh damn it!' Hayley stopped walking. 'What am I wearing?!'

'Jeans, a cream coat you've had since forever and a T-shirt that isn't really cool for your age.'

'What's wrong with telling the world I like Coca-Cola? Don't you know the holidays are coming?' Hayley began to chant the theme song from the Coke advert until Angel put her hands over her ears.

'I meant I'm not wearing my uniform,' Hayley stated once the joke had worn thin.

'I wondered why it was easier getting here. There was no adjusting your hat or ducking for doors.'

'Is she going to call me Agatha?'

'Is she going to call me Charlotte?'

Hayley let out a breath.

'There's only one way to find out,' Angel said, indicating the door in front of them.

Hayley raised her hand then stopped. 'Something's different.' She turned to Angel. 'The garland on the door here.' She knew it wasn't a touch they'd added. She reached out and put her fingers to the round fir pine cone and lace ornament hanging on the door. 'Did you put it there?'

Angel shook her head.

The door opened and Hayley immediately dropped her hand from the decoration to greet Cynthia. 'Hello ... sorry, we were going to knock straight away but we started to admire your garland on the door.'

The woman smiled at them both. This was a good start. There was colour on her cheeks, she was wearing a vibrant pink dress with navy blue piping and she wasn't waving a fist.

'Won't you come in?' Cynthia said, opening the door wider.

Hayley pushed Angel in first.

'Wow!' Angel stated, her head tilting backwards as they stepped into the hall. Hayley found her head tilting back too as she took in the transformation. The cavernous, expensive-looking hall of bright tiles and wooden cladding had been transformed into something warm and welcoming, straight out of an upmarket alpine lodge. There was a huge, real Christmas tree towering up towards the ceiling, its branches decked with coloured lights, red bows, balls and baubles. Swags of velvet hung from the stair rail, the scent of pine, marshmallow and mint filled Hayley's nostrils and Angel was already walking over to a tweed chair in which a fat Santa Claus doll was sitting, his head turning left and right and his animated cheeks glowing.

'Come through,' Cynthia said, opening up the doors to the lounge.

Hayley took Angel by the arm, pulling her away from Father Christmas and trying to direct her attention back to the task in hand.

'Wow,' Angel stated again as they entered the other room.

'Enough of the wowing,' Hayley said through gritted teeth. She levelled a smile at Cynthia who led the way over to the sofas.

Their hard work to transform the room into a more homely space had been left untouched by the house owner. There was even a second Christmas tree by the fire, more ornaments and fripperies, a couple more framed photos.

'Won't you sit down,' Cynthia said, dropping into an armchair.

Hayley plumped for the two-seater sofa opposite and Angel followed her lead.

Cynthia smiled. 'Would you like some tea?' She indicated the pot on the coffee table between them.

Hayley shook her head. 'No, thank you.'

Cynthia nodded. Hayley watched the woman toying with her hands as they rested in her lap. She seemed nervous.

'So, I've asked you here today to say thank you,' Cynthia began.

Hayley swallowed. Was she serious? A thank you hadn't figured in any of the possible scenarios she'd thought up. This was the very last thing she'd expected.

'I have to admit, the moment I set eyes on what you did in this room …' She paused, so many emotions present in her expression. 'Well, I didn't see it for what it was right away.'

'I apologise … I'm new at the company. It was my very first Diana. In fact, it was my very first anything at all …' Hayley began.

'And my name isn't Charlotte,' Angel blurted out.

Cynthia burst out laughing then, leaning forward in her chair, her hands on her knees, her chest vibrating with sound.

Now Hayley felt uneasy, like Ant and Dec were about to burst out and declare she was the victim of a *Saturday Night Takeaway* prank. She swallowed.

Cynthia smiled. 'All these years I've had Majestic Cleaning no one has turned my living room into exactly that – a *living* room.' She drew in a breath. 'It was just what I needed at exactly the right time.'

Hayley was still unsure what to say.

'I've been not living for so long I'd almost forgotten what it was all about, what's most important.'

'I love the Christmas trees,' Angel said, jumping up from the sofa and going over to the tree by the fire.

'Me too,' Cynthia answered, smiling.

'I don't really understand,' Hayley admitted.

'I lost my husband not so long ago, and my son.'

Hayley felt the woman's grief thicken the air between them.

'But you can't mourn forever or else mourning is the only connection you have with the people you've lost.' Cynthia stood then, moving to the mantelpiece and picking up a framed photo. 'They were both such life-loving, vibrant characters. They would hate the fact that I've been moping around here just because my other son won't move on.' Cynthia showed Angel the photo she was holding.

'That's my husband there. Handsome, wasn't he?'

'*He's* cute,' Angel said, pointing at another person in the picture.

'Ah, that's my son, the one who passed away.'

'And that one?' Angel asked.

'That's Oliver, my other son. He's the stubborn one.'

Hayley watched Angel's eyes go out on stalks as she turned to face her. Her daughter mouthed 'Mr Meanie' and Hayley stood up, nudging the coffee table with her leg and making the cups roll together and chink.

'Oliver Drummond?' Hayley was taking the photo from Cynthia's hand before she was truly aware of it.

Cynthia was Cynthia Drummond, Oliver's mother. The people in the photo were Oliver's father and his brother, the two people he'd talked so passionately about last night. She swallowed. Suddenly being here had taken on a different dimension entirely.

'I'm not surprised you've heard of him. That article in the news yesterday ...' Cynthia shook her head.

'My uncle works for him,' Angel said.

'Angel ...' Hayley began.

'Angel? Is that your real name?' Cynthia smiled. 'It's very pretty.'

'My uncle is in charge of the Globe,' Angel continued, grinning.

'Which we *do not* talk about *at all* to anyone, because it's top secret,' Hayley said sternly.

'How are things going with that?' Cynthia asked Angel, looking at her with sincere eyes.

'I love Rabbit Nation.'

'But will it be as addictive as Candy Crush Saga?' Cynthia asked seriously.

'Encouraging children to love their rabbits is better than encouraging them to look at sweets.'

'That's a very good point,' Cynthia agreed.

Hayley looked again at the family photo in her hand. Happy, smiling faces at the beach. Cynthia was there in jeans and a T-shirt, long hair loose, her husband, a tall, well-built man with a wide smile and sparkling eyes, was on one side of a surfboard stuck in the sand and the two boys were knelt in front. Oliver's brother was dark-haired like his father and, even as a youth, was archetypally handsome. Oliver had his arm around his brother and he was grinning like this moment was the happiest of his life. Hayley raised her eyes to look at Cynthia. Had she really given up on Oliver? Maybe she should send Angel on an errand to find lemonade and come clean that she knew him, tell Cynthia how he felt about the Regis Software merger ... how he felt about Andrew Regis. The words weren't coming. It wasn't her place.

Cynthia smiled at Hayley. 'I bought a hound's-tooth scarf yesterday.'

Hayley put the photo back on the mantelpiece. 'You did?'

'I did. And you were right. It does go beautifully with my coat.'

'Well, I...'

'Mum's great at fashion tips,' Angel jumped in. 'She works at a dry-cleaners and she plans parties for people.'

'Angel ...' Hayley felt her cheeks glowing.

'Parties. I'm so pleased to hear that.' Cynthia clasped her hands together. 'I'll cut right to the chase.' The woman took a long breath before continuing. 'I'd like you to work on a project with me.'

'A project?' Hayley asked.

'Yes. I work with a charitable organisation whose annual fun-draiser is in need of pepping up a little. It's a cause very close to my heart and I really want this year to be extra special. The lady who usually helps me has gone down with glandular fever. She can't work, she can barely speak and …'

'I really don't think …' Hayley interrupted.

'Please, hear me out.' The plea in Cynthia's tone tugged at her. 'It's one night, at the Crystalline Hotel, three hundred people, a three course meal and entertainment, plus awards and speeches.'

Cynthia continued. 'What you did here yesterday … you have an eye for detail and that's what I need. I need someone to come in and make that ballroom special.'

'You mean décor? Table settings?' Hayley asked. Her heart was thumping in her chest. Was it panic or passion being ignited?

'Yes and party favours. Plus I definitely need something more entertaining than last year's barber shop quartet.'

'You want me to organise the whole event?' Now her stomach was pumping bile and adrenaline in equal measure.

'I'll be there to help, but I'd like you to coordinate everything.'

'It sounds so cool,' Angel remarked, eyes bright.

'With any outside companies you decide to use, of course, and a very generous budget,' Cynthia continued.

'When Angel said party planning … it's a small business, local.' She wet her lips. 'It isn't New York,' Hayley stated.

'Don't forget you put on that big fashion show for my school and the fete last summer.'

She was so lucky to have a daughter who remembered everything. However, she could tell this event was in a completely different league to a local fair and juniors wearing Roman costume.

'I'll put a team of assistants at your disposal and I'll be on hand or at the other end of a phone to help you. Plus I'll pay you twice the going rate for a New York event organiser,' Cynthia continued.

Hayley shook her head. This was crazy. 'You could hire any of them. All of them much more capable and experienced. Why me?'

Cynthia took a breath. 'I've had people coming into this house since my husband died and not one of them did what you did the other day. You picked up on what was missing and you delivered it. That's what I want for this fundraiser. I want people to feel the human touch, go away knowing the aims of the foundation, feeling hopeful for the future, celebrating the past, not crying into their eggnog over those they've lost. We're still living, we shouldn't be ashamed of that fact.' Cynthia's words couldn't have been more impassioned.

It was a huge responsibility. And this woman was Oliver's *mother*. How did that sit in the equation? It didn't. It was so utterly awkward it made her feel sick. Then again, she hadn't actually heard from him yet. Maybe he'd been a lot drunker than she'd realised. Perhaps he had no intention of really following through on this date idea. Why was that thought kicking her so hard?

'Please, Agatha, say yes and make my Christmas,' Cynthia begged.

Hayley looked to Angel. Her daughter had wide eyes resembling a pleading cat desperate for food, her hands clasped together like a starving orphan from *Oliver*. She had to say no. She had no papers to work here. She knew things about Cynthia she really shouldn't know if she was going to work for her. Plus, she'd already told Angel she was giving up the cleaning job. She was on a mission to find Angel's father. She didn't have time for bolts out of the blue. She swallowed, the pressure in the room getting to her. But it was exciting. It would challenge her in a way she hadn't been challenged since Angel was born. It was short term, one event – huge, terrifying – but the thought of it was making her heart sing. She would have a chance to use her flair and imagination *and* it was for a good cause. Should she question how the opportunity had come her way? Or just go with it?

She sucked in a breath, ions fizzing around her body in reaction. 'My real name's Hayley. I have absolutely no idea why you would give me a chance like this.' She paused. 'And I also have no idea if I can actually pull this off, but if you're really sure I'm what you need … '

'I am sure,' Cynthia insisted.

'Then … I accept.' She swallowed, not believing she had really said the words. She nodded. 'I'll do it.'

Angel let out a squeal and grabbed her mother's hands, shaking them up and down until she thought her arms might drop off.

'Thank you,' Cynthia said, her words full of sentiment.

'I have no idea what I've let myself in for. You'd better show me the layout of this Crystalline Hotel ballroom,' Hayley said, a nervous laugh falling from her lips.

'I can do better than that. I'll take you there tomorrow.'

'Great,' Hayley nodded. 'So, when is this big night? How long do I have to organise the extravaganza to end all extravaganzas?'

'Oh you have plenty of time,' Cynthia said, moving towards the coffee table and reaching for the pot of tea. 'It's in five days.'

CHAPTER THIRTY-THREE

Dean Walker's Apartment, Downtown Manhattan

Hayley poked a whole handful of crisps into her mouth at once and chewed them up over Dean's laptop, spattering crumbs over the keyboard. Her ideas book was open on the central island, two pieces of material sticking out of the pages. One was platinum coloured with a matt finish, the other a gold gauze. It was part of the décor for a party she'd organised at the local city hall. The Guggenheim dress design hadn't been progressed but she had much bigger things to focus on now. Her hope was some of these scraps of ideas were going to leap out and help kick-start the plans for the fundraiser.

'Did you know the Crystalline Hotel is one of the oldest hotels in New York City?'

Hayley opened her mouth at Angel's statement, more crisps scattering, and she turned her head to where Angel was sat on the sofa with Dean.

'Hang on. How do you know that? I have the laptop right here,' Hayley exclaimed.

'And I,' Angel began. 'I have the Globe. The whole world at my fingertips.'

Hayley watched her daughter poking the screen of the tablet like an old hand and shook her head.

'So, I'm not really sure how you've ended up organising a Drummond family function,' Dean said, turning his head to Hayley.

'Sshh! Don't call it that! It isn't that!'

She had already decided that she couldn't tell Oliver anything about this. He still hadn't called so maybe it wasn't even going to be an issue. She knew his relationship with his mother was complicated at the moment. If she heard from him, if they *did* go out, she was just going to have to keep the two things separate. That's what you had to do when there was a conflict of interest wasn't it? Or were you meant to come clean? A shiver of acknowledgement that lying to either party wasn't the right answer ran through her. She'd have to cross that bridge when she came to it.

'Well, first of all Mum got a cleaning job and had to wear this …' Angel started.

'Haven't you got rabbits to play with?' Hayley interrupted.

'You got a job? What job? When? Why?' Dean pumped out.

'Please say a word that doesn't begin with a "W".'

'Hayley …'

'Agatha,' Angel chipped in.

'Kiss goodbye to any more ice cream, missy!'

Dean put his hands to his head, looking completely bewildered. 'A job? And now this thing for Cynthia Drummond? You're supposed to be on holiday and … the other thing.'

'Looking for my dad,' Angel offered.

'I know this,' Hayley replied. 'And I'm not doing the job any more, just this other thing for the mother of your boss.'

'We needed the extra money,' Angel said, leading with an expression that said poverty.

'I think we need to talk.'

Hayley swallowed. Dean's voice was verging on stern. A tendon in his neck was pulsing, his face on the edge of puce. Dean usually only did comedic camp angry. This wasn't good.

'Shall I shut my ears?' Angel chirruped.

Hayley got down from the bar stool and flounced out into the hallway, knowing her brother would follow. She backed herself up against the wall, her head level with a framed photo of Shirley Bassey. There was so much he could say and she wasn't sure which bit scared her the most.

Dean arrived in the hallway and closed the door behind him. He folded his arms across his chest.

'Very nightclub doorman,' Hayley remarked.

'This isn't a joke.'

'Which bit?'

'Exactly!' Dean let his arms drop then flourished them upwards. 'The fact you said that says everything.'

'Just get it over with.' Hayley dropped her eyes to the carpet.

'Oliver Drummond came to see me today. He told me he'd asked you out on a date.'

Her heart skipped. He *was* going to follow through. He was thinking about her. He'd meant what he said. She swallowed. Why did she feel so awkward about it with Dean?

'How has that happened?' Dean asked again.

'If I told you it all began in an alleyway would that make me sound like a ho?'

Dean shook his head at her. Perhaps fighting her corner with humour wasn't the best idea when he was in this mood. Her mother always hated it.

'Should I have said no?' she asked Dean. 'Is there an employee family no-go zone or something?'

'I didn't realise you were looking for a relationship.'

Her brow creased as her brain tried to catch up with the meaning behind her brother's words. 'I can't even begin to understand that.' Her head nudged Shirley Bassey. 'I wasn't looking for a relationship, but what you just said indicates I *shouldn't* be.

Only the other day you were commenting on the fact I hadn't had many dates since I had Angel.'

'That wasn't what I meant.'

'Well, what did you mean? First of all you don't want me to be a nun, then you want to drag me to the nearest convent? Mixed messages here, Dean!'

'Hayley, you're being over the top …'

'Over the top? Wow!'

'What about Michel?' Dean asked.

'What *about* Michel? We went to the other gallery he said he was exhibiting at when I met him and the only thing they had was a website address … which doesn't work!' she yelled. 'Before you came home from work I called forty-eight galleries and got nothing, but still Angel thinks he's going to come running into her life like a dreamy, schmaltzy movie on the Disney Channel.'

'I just think …' Dean started.

'And what does me trying to find Michel have to do with Oliver? *If* Michel gets in contact we're not going to rekindle the one night of romance we had and morph into Brad and Angelina.'

'You don't know that.'

'I do know that. Because I don't want that,' she said with determination. 'Anyway, he could be married. Or … he could have realised he's gay.'

She gave a satisfied nod as that sentence settled into Dean's conscience.

'I'm not looking for a relationship. I wasn't even looking for a date but … he asked and … he's funny and stupid and irritating and … I'm on holiday for the first time in nine years and in between the searching for an ex-lover I wouldn't mind having a bit of fun! And … I like him.'

A conscious pang of heat took her by surprise. She *did* like Oliver. It was obviously casual, but not casual enough to dismiss entirely.

Dean sighed. 'Well, what about this job? You know you can't work here without a permit.'

'Yes I do know that.'

'So ...'

'So I needed some extra cash because I quit my job, and I took a chance. I thought I could see how it went and ...' Hayley stopped.

'And what?' Dean asked.

'I don't know.' She sighed. 'After the boss finally put his clammy, wandering hands on me one too many times I thought maybe ...' She sighed again. Dean would think she was certifiable if she admitted she'd hoped to see if New York's streets were paved with opportunity for them when they got here. 'It was stupid.'

'There are harassment laws to stop that sort of thing.' Dean shook his head.

'I know. I just couldn't bear the hassle of all the paperwork and the meetings. It was just easier to leave.'

'He could do that to the next girl. How could you be so stupid?'

'All right! I don't need it rubbing in my face from the golden child.'

The second the words were in the air Hayley regretted them. She wanted to say she was sorry or retract the fierceness of the statement, instead she nudged the photo of Shirley Bassey with the side of her head and it fell off its nail and hit the floor.

Hayley bent down, retrieving the picture and brushing the glass with her fingers. 'Sorry ... I'm sorry.'

Dean snatched the frame from her. 'It doesn't matter. It's just a picture.' He slipped it back into position on the wall. 'I'm worried about you.'

'I'm fine,' Hayley responded quickly.

'You're not fine.'

'Aren't I?'

'I know what it is,' Dean said with confidence.

'You do?'

'Angel's coming up to secondary school age. She's growing up, getting more independent, it's making you re-evaluate everything.'

'Who made you Dr Phil?' She tutted. 'It's really not that.'

'You think you need to strike out a little.'

'There's nothing wrong with doing that anyway. You said so yourself. Or did you mean something more like crochet?'

'I think you know that in a few years' time Angel's not going to be occupying so much of your time and you think you need to fill it with something else.'

'*Don't* I need to fill it with something else? Don't I *deserve* to fill it with something else?'

'A job here?'

'Well, why not? How about a life of my own? Doing things I want to do. Things that don't involve Angel.'

'Like dating my boss?'

'Well, why not that too? I mean, what's so wrong with that? Why shouldn't I go out with him? Or is a lowly single mother with no college qualifications not good enough for your precious boss?' She sized Dean up, tilting her head at an angle. 'Is that what it is? Are you ashamed of me?'

'That is the most ridiculous thing I've ever heard,' Dean snapped back.

'Is it? Because from where I'm standing all you've done is insinuate I'm mentally challenged for wanting more from my life than a child. All this women must stay at home and nurture is totally out-dated and sexist, neither of which I thought you were!'

'Hayley ...'

'No, I'm not going to apologise for taking this fundraiser job.' Hayley put her hands on her hips and struck a pose. 'And I'm not going to feel remotely guilty about accepting a date with one of the world's more eligible bachelors.' She nodded. 'And if you have a problem with any of that then maybe ... maybe Angel and I should stay at a hotel.'

The thought that all their dollars would evaporate in a couple of nights if they stayed anywhere but a youth hostel triggered an involuntary swallow. She moved, shifting down the hall before Dean could say anything else.

'Hayley, where are you going?'

'Out,' she responded, not looking back. 'I'm being branded as the bad mother so I may as well act the part.' She crashed down the stairs and headed for the front door. Grabbing her coat from the hook on the hall wall, she roughly put it on then flung open the door with full force. She bowled over the threshold, stepping out into the night.

CHAPTER THIRTY-FOUR

Washington Square Park, Greenwich Village

Hayley's angry stomps had lessened in ferocity, her pace finally turning into a gentle stroll as she headed towards the arch. The snow falling from the sky was so dense she could barely see anything in front of her. Focussing on the near-replica of the Arc de Triomphe, she carried on, trying to sort out the mess of her muddled mind.

Dean did have a point. But he had no idea of her discontent at home. He had thought this was just a winter holiday, a chance to get together and catch up. Then she'd dropped the mission to find Michel on him. Taking on a job would sound crazy to someone who didn't know it was ever on the agenda. And Oliver. Romance of any kind, no matter how tentative the status, that had never crossed her mind either. But now there was adult male company on offer and the owner had to-die-for bone structure and eyes she regularly got lost in, why should she turn it down?

She stopped at the base of the arch, looking up through the snow and admiring its stature. She had been here before. In the early morning, just as the sun rose, she and Michel had stood underneath the arch letting the first rays of light touch their faces after their night together. At eighteen it had seemed romantic. Spending the night with a stranger. A good-looking foreign stranger who painted and took photos for a living. It would be a story to tell to her children. She hadn't thought it would be a story she would tell the child she'd made that very night. Now when she thought of what she'd done, all she wanted to do was warn Angel about her own stupidity, tell her never to drink or go off with strange men she knew nothing about.

Hayley shivered and drew her coat closer. There was no way she was leaving this city without finding him.

Restaurant Romario, Greenwich Village

Oliver put his lips to his bottle of beer and took a sip of the cool liquid. He'd had the breath taken from him by Tony's mother and father when he'd come by the restaurant and they'd force-fed him and Tony several dishes from the menu. Protesting seemed rude and, in his opinion, the food was the best Italy had to offer in New York. The restaurant was busy, couples and families dining on the traditional pizza and pasta fare along with several 'secret recipe' dishes Mr Romario had concocted over the years. Red and white check cloths, candles set in empty bottles of Pinot Grigio, the wax dripping down in bubbling strands, coating the glass. It all made for an authentic Italian experience. There was festive cheer thrown in too. Silver and gold tinsel hung over the old wooden window frames and a small Christmas tree sat on a table in the corner, a set of porcelain nativity figures in front of it.

'I have a date,' Oliver said, turning his attention back to Tony.

'Sorry, man, I don't think I heard you right.' Tony narrowed his eyes and looked at Oliver with suspicion. 'Did you say you have a date?'

Oliver nodded, a smile invading his lips. He still hadn't worked out all the details of the night yet. But he knew he wanted to make it unforgettable. The knowledge of that was killing him as much as exciting him. That was the reason he hadn't called her yet. He wanted everything to be perfect and he also needed the time to sit with the idea of going out with someone he cared about.

'As in, with a woman? Someone you've met once and arranged to meet again?' Tony clarified.

'Kissed too actually. More than once.'

'Wow, and did you hold hands?'

Oliver stretched across the table, buffing Tony's shoulder with his hand. 'Funny guy.'

Tony laughed, undoing the top button of his shirt and leaning back against the red and white check upholstered booth they were sitting in. 'So, where did you meet this one?'

'At the Chinese restaurant actually.' He smiled again. 'When I was escaping from the woman in the red dress.'

'You dog!'

Oliver was quick to shake his head. 'No, it wasn't like that. She bailed me out big time.'

'And that made you want her even more,' Tony scoffed.

'It's complicated.'

'Shit, she's married?'

'No,' he paused. 'But she does have a daughter.'

'Oh man, stay out of that.'

'What makes you say that?'

'Kids, exes, they're complications you definitely don't need.'

'The ex isn't on the scene right now.'

'Then she'll be needy. And boy, single mothers can smell a billionaire from a mile away,' Tony said, swigging from his drink.

'Hey, when did you get so judgemental?' He felt a niggle of anger digging in his stomach.

'I'm just telling it like it is.'

'You haven't met her yet,' Oliver defended.

'Have you asked her what her wish is? Bet it's a loft in Tribeca.'

Oliver squirmed in his seat. At the mention of Hayley's wish a gnawing feeling started in his chest. He'd called Daniel Pearson earlier for an update on Andrew Regis and to see if he'd made any progress finding Michel De Vos. There was nothing yet, in either respect.

'Her wish was to find her child's father,' Oliver breathed out.

'Holy shit.' Tony's eyes enlarged. 'That's what she wished when she could have anything?'

Oliver nodded. She'd been honest, true to herself, passionate. All the things he admired. All the things he'd forgotten how to be.

'You like this woman,' Tony said, his tone even.

Oliver opened his mouth to reply but, for a second, couldn't. There was that voice again. *You're going to die. This date is pointless. You can't fight fate.* How could he throw his hat in the ring when she was destined to leave and he was going to die?

But this was his best friend, the guy who knew him better than anyone. He had to be honest despite everything else. 'Yeah,' he said, nodding. 'I like her.'

Vipers Nightclub, Downtown Manhattan

Hayley had meant to go straight back to Dean's. He'd already sent two messages and left a voicemail. He was worried. Stroppy her was thinking *so he should be*, sensible her was thinking she might have overreacted a little and storming off into the night wasn't behaviour befitting of someone her age. But the nightclub was on her route back and standing outside, feeling the throb and pulse of the music from inside, had transported her back ten years again. With purpose in her stride she headed to the entrance.

'Excuse me! Is Artie here?' She had to shout above the music and squeeze her way in between patrons waiting to be served.

'Artie doesn't work until Friday,' a girl called back, stopping in front of her, using the bottle opener to de-lid a bottle of Bud.

'Someone told me that, I just thought he might have picked up a couple of extra shifts.' She needed a lead on Michel. It was driving her crazy. She needed something solid to give Angel.

The bartender passed the bottle to the customer and took payment before giving Hayley her attention. She flicked back an abundance of curls and smiled at Hayley.

'Artie's married by the way,' the girl told her.

'Oh,' Hayley said. 'I wasn't thinking of hitting on him.' She slipped her phone from her pocket and tapped the screen until the photo she'd taken of the photo of Michel was displayed. 'I'm looking for someone.' She turned the screen to the bartender. 'His name's Michel De Vos. He, er, we met here ten years ago and I'm trying to find him.'

The girl took the phone from Hayley and studied the photo up close. Hayley swallowed as she watched the woman taking in the picture. There was no look of recognition on her face but that didn't stop the whirling sensation in Hayley's stomach from taking hold.

'I've seen him in here,' the girl said finally, passing the phone back. 'His hair's the same.'

Hayley fought to get her words out over the knot that had strangulated her vocal cords. 'What? When?'

The girl took another order and began swirling vodka into the cocktail shaker. 'A month ago? Maybe more.'

She couldn't believe it. *A month ago. Michel was in New York.* She wet her lips. 'Are you sure?'

The barwoman nodded. 'Yeah, he came in every night for a couple weeks. Sometimes he sat here at the bar. Said he was an artist.' The girl smiled. 'Probably just a line.'

Tension flooded her gut. If only she had been as streetwise as this girl in 2005. The bartender made to move off, shaking the mix of drinks up.

'Wait,' Hayley said. She grabbed a paper coaster. 'Have you got a pen?'

'One second.' The barwoman poured the drink into a long glass, added an umbrella, a cherry and a slice of pineapple and finally a straw. It didn't look dissimilar to the cocktail Coke Angel had made with Vernon.

The girl passed a pen over and Hayley grabbed it like it was an antidote to a lethal snakebite. She began writing furiously on the paper coaster until the whole circle was full.

'If you see him again …' She paused to take a breath. 'These are all my contact details.' She held on as the girl took hold of the paper. 'Could you tell him Hayley Walker, the girl in the pink dress who liked fashion, really needs to see him again?'

The bubbling in her stomach was like a chemical experiment where no one knew quite what was going to happen. Hayley finally relinquished the paper and smiled at the bartender. 'Thank you.' She stepped back from the bar, a little light-headed. She let the music seep into her, gently allowing her eyes to get used to the strobe and glitter ball reflections. If Michel was here a month ago he could still be here now. Angel might just get her wish. And how Hayley felt about that, she still didn't really know.

CHAPTER THIRTY-FIVE

The Crystalline Hotel, Downtown Manhattan

'Uncle Dean thinks you aren't talking to him,' Angel whispered.

They were stood in the lobby of the most impressive hotel Hayley had ever been in, waiting for Cynthia to arrive. The carpet was gold-flecked and the chandeliers threw out shapes of light that bounced off the walls. The green of the Christmas tree was completely over-embellished with blingy ornaments and lights that faded in and out to carol songs.

'Why would he think that?' Hayley responded.

'Because the only words you said to him over breakfast were "we're out of bagels".'

'We *are* out of bagels.'

'Are you fighting because I told him about Majestic Cleaning?' Angel asked, her eyes wide.

'No of course not.'

'I'm sorry I told Uncle Dean,' Angel said, her eyes moistening.

'It isn't your fault, Angel. Let's just forget it. I'll calm down, he'll calm down and someday soon we'll be back to sharing tales of Vernon's cooking.'

'Someday soon? They say that in books when it's going to be a really, really long time.'

'It won't be that long.' Hayley checked her watch.

'Is it likely to be more "shortly" or more "soon"?'

Her mobile began to ring and she swung her rucksack off her shoulder, unzipping it. She located her phone and looked at the number. It wasn't recognised. Perhaps it was a lead on Michel.

'Hello.'

'Good morning, Lois.'

Oliver's voice had her toes curling and her cheeks heating up in appreciation. She turned her body away from Angel in case she read the body language. 'Good morning, Clark.'

'So, I remembered your number.'

'It seems so.'

'And I'm hoping you're still free tonight.'

'I have to admit, Dean has excellent cable channels.'

She could tell he was smiling.

'Then he should also have a DVR.'

Now she was smiling. 'What time will I need to be setting it?'

'I'll pick you up at 7.30.'

'And what should I wear? Formal? Casual?'

'Cute sleepwear?'

'That's funny, Clark.' She looked to Angel who was now paying her all her attention. She didn't want to let on this was a date. Her daughter had enough going on. 'I'll dress for business.'

'My imagination is running wild.'

'Cynthia's here!' Angel announced, jumping up.

'I've got to go,' Hayley spoke quickly. 'I'll see you later.' She ended the call, dropping her mobile phone into her backpack. She brushed her hands down her front. She'd dressed to impress this morning. She'd cobbled together a pair of smart black jeans, her boots, a cream chemise and a red jumper she'd cut up the middle to create a make-shift jacket. She'd spent the early hours of the morning sewing it into place when she hadn't been able to sleep.

'Good morning, how are we today?' Cynthia greeted, holding her hand out first to Angel and then to Hayley.

The woman looked immaculate in a grey two-piece suit, her hair and make-up as perfect as ever.

'We're really well. How are you?' Hayley answered.

'A little flustered I have to say but …' She paused. 'I'm really looking forward to showing you this room. Shall we?'

Cynthia held out her hand and ushered them into the main body of the hotel. Hayley looked back, taking a moment, her eyes roving over the immaculate décor of the lobby again. This function, like the hotel, was going to have to be perfection. Just what had she taken on?

Drummond Global Offices, Downtown Manhattan

Andrew Regis had done it. The interview was on Oliver's desk in front of him. The man had told the world the merger between the two companies wasn't going ahead because of Oliver's reluctance to embrace the future. He'd called him a control freak and a megalomaniac. He said he had none of his father's belief in mutual support creating stronger foundations. And Andrew had formally announced his personal relationship with Cynthia. His mother must have known this was on the cards and she hadn't told him. That stung more than the article itself.

'Oliver.' Clara's voice invaded his consciousness. He looked up to see his personal assistant still sat in her chair opposite his desk. How long had he been staring at the words? He didn't even remember the last thing Clara had asked him.

'Yes,' he said in reply.

'Shall I order some coffee?' she offered.

He shook his head. 'No, I'm good.'

She tutted out a noise and reached for the magazine article. 'I never liked that man. I know he was your father's best friend but, I don't know, I never really trusted him. There's something about his eyes.'

'My mother obviously thinks very highly of him.'

'But not after this, surely!'

'Why not?' Oliver asked. He reached for the stress baseball.

'Because none of this is true.' Clara shook the magazine.

'Isn't it?'

'No, Oliver.'

'So I'm not power-crazed?'

'No.'

'A control freak?'

'That one maybe a little.'

'Not a team player.'

'We all have certain strengths and weaknesses.'

'You should have been a politician, Clara.' He stood, the force of his movement sending his chair shooting backwards to hit the wall. He paced towards the windows, looking out at the skyline.

'You know why he's done this,' Clara said.

'To belittle me? To undermine my decision in public so the whole board question it? To discredit Drummond Global?'

'No. This isn't a man who's acted with his business head on. This is him bitch-slapping you for not welcoming him into the family with open arms. This is all to do with Cynthia. It's personal. He feels threatened.'

'Did you just say "bitch-slap"?' Oliver turned back to face her.

'I believe I did. I apologise.'

'No, don't apologise.' He took a breath. 'What do you think I should do?'

'I really don't trust the man,' Clara said. 'Something about all this doesn't add up.'

'Which bit?'

Clara adjusted her body in the chair. 'Can I speak freely?'

'Of course, Clara.'

'Well, the merger from the beginning was always driven by the relationship he had with your father. Yes, they were friends, for a very long time, but I can't help thinking that there was a reason your father never went into business with Andrew Regis in the first place.'

'I have thought about that, Clara. I assumed, initially, when they were both starting out, they were working towards different goals, maybe sparking off the rivalry a little.'

'Regis Software has nothing like the contracts Drummond Global has.'

'I know that. But they have expertise in areas we haven't broken into.'

'And why hasn't Drummond Global broken into those areas?'

'Because we've been focussed elsewhere.'

'Maybe. But like I said, I don't trust the man.' She shook her head. 'And this relationship with Cynthia ... what's his play there?'

'You don't think it's genuine.'

'Your mother is a very powerful woman on the board here.'

'You think he wants that power.'

'I'm not going to say that outright but I would just keep your mind open to all possibilities where Andrew is concerned.'

Oliver gritted his teeth. The thought of Andrew Regis having dishonourable intentions towards his mother made his blood boil more than thinking he had *honourable* intentions towards her. He still hadn't heard anything from Daniel Pearson. If there was dirt to be found Daniel would find it. Perhaps there was nothing there. Maybe Andrew's motivations in all areas were genuine.

'What do I do about this?' Oliver asked, indicating the magazine Clara was still holding.

'You could call Delaney and get her to manage it with a retort in their rival's edition tomorrow.'

'But you wouldn't do that?'

'No. I'd play Mr Nice. I'd invite Andrew and your mother out to dinner, congratulate them on their relationship, see how the land lies and try and get a feel for what he's up to.' She threw the magazine down onto the desk. 'You know what they say about friends and enemies.'

Oliver nodded. 'Yes.' He sucked in a breath. 'Yes I do.'

The Crystalline Hotel, Downtown Manhattan

'It's gorgeous! I can't keep my eyes off of it!'

Angel had been squeaking with excitement since the second Cynthia had opened the doors into the Crystalline's ballroom. The room had an arched ceiling with diamantes embedded in every inch of the plaster. Light streamed in from the Art Deco windows and when the many spotlights connected with the tiny sparkles they produced pinpricks of light on the mellow duck egg blue walls and the vintage parquet floor.

'What do you think?' Cynthia had addressed Hayley and she turned to the woman, her eyes alive.

'I think it's a beautiful setting.' She swallowed. 'My mind's buzzing with ideas to make it even more perfect.'

'I knew it would be,' Cynthia said, smiling.

'Did you know that Fred Astaire and Ginger Rogers once danced here,' Angel announced, twirling around on the dance floor, her arms in the air, one leg cocked at an angle.

'Did they really?' Cynthia asked, clapping her hands together and looking delighted.

'You'll have to excuse my daughter, she's a bit of a walking encyclopaedia,' Hayley said, unzipping her rucksack and getting out a notebook.

'I think she's a doll.' Cynthia sighed. 'I longed for a daughter but it wasn't to be.'

'Well, if it's any consolation, she's not even ten yet and she already raids my wardrobe. So …' She looked up from her pad. 'How do you usually have the setting arrangements? Round tables? Long ones?'

'Usually round. Businesses tend to buy a whole table or two.'

'And they would sit all together?' Hayley asked, writing notes.

'What do you mean?'

Hayley looked up again. 'Well, if they all sit together that would mean that every year they sit next to the very same people, all from their own companies.'

'That's usually what happens.'

'It isn't very good for talking to other businesses though, is it? I mean, as well as the charitable cause, this is a great networking opportunity, a social gathering. I'd want to talk to people I don't know yet, meet some new friends.'

Cynthia put her hands to her mouth, her eyes growing bigger as she looked at Hayley.

'Have I said something really stupid? Because I can retract it and just go back to thinking how we can decorate this place.'

Cynthia shook her head. 'No, you're absolutely right. Why has no one ever thought of that before? We don't want people being insular all night, we want interaction and cooperation, making new acquaintances. We can sell tables but we can mix up who sits where. Can we make a note?' Cynthia asked, striding into the centre of the floor where Angel was still dancing.

Hayley scribbled as she followed Cynthia. She also made a note about getting drapes around the windows, creating a more intimate setting without making it feel small. The room had a presence all of its own. She was going to ensure any enhancements she made were in keeping with the era of the building but definitely noticeable. It was going to be classic and classy. The platinum and gold could definitely work.

'So, do you have a speaker all lined up?'

'You should get someone really cool like Michelle Obama or maybe Miley Cyrus. She's interesting,' Angel said.

'Shall I write down "wrecking ball" as well as "glitter ball"?' Hayley shook her head at Angel.

'I was hoping Oliver would speak this year,' Cynthia stated.

Hayley swallowed. She wanted to shut her ears. If she didn't hear anything it wouldn't influence the other area of her life she was keeping separate from this one. She started to hum 'Stop The Cavalry' in her head.

'Is he too busy?' Angel asked.

'He says he is, but I know it isn't that.'

'What is it then?' Angel asked again.

It was no good. She could hear everything. She shot Angel a warning look.

Cynthia sighed. 'As much as Oliver supports the foundation, I know he hates it in equal measure. He didn't deal with the death of his brother or his father very well and he hates to be reminded of it.'

'My nanny hates to be reminded how old she is,' Angel said. 'She also hates being reminded that she started using Oil of Olay when it was called Oil of Ulay.'

'How do you *know* that?' Hayley asked.

'You were the one that told me!'

'I didn't expect you to remember.'

'Do you know me at all?'

Cynthia burst out laughing. 'You two are hysterical. If I don't find another speaker I think you should do a comedic double act. Right, shall we meet the chef? See what suggestions he has for the catering?'

'Yes, let's talk cuisine instead of complexion,' Hayley agreed, glaring at Angel.

closed his eyes. 'Thomas Mitchell! That last guy you showed me is Thomas Mitchell from technical support.'

'Congratulations, Mr Drummond, you're getting to know your staff.'

CHAPTER THIRTY-SEVEN

Dean Walker's Apartment, Downtown Manhattan

Hayley blew at the clear gloss on her fingernails and took a sneaky peek at her watch again. It wasn't long until Oliver would be coming. She'd been buzzing since their phone call that morning, wondering where he was going to take her and how the night was going to go. She shook her hands in the air to speed the drying process. She was really nervous, which was completely ridiculous. She'd spent more time with this man than she'd spent with Angel's father. And they got on. Really well. Better than she'd got on with any man. They had a vibe, they bounced off each other, it was a good connection. With only a few weeks before she had to face unemployment back home, it was nice to be in a New York bubble where she had a job and a night with a good-looking guy to enjoy.

The door of the bedroom opened and Angel burst forward. 'I got triple bunny points and unlocked a golden chicory!'

'So much excitement over vegetables! I wish you were the same when they're on your plate,' Hayley exclaimed, waving her arms in the air.

'Wow. You look really nice.'

'Do I?' Hayley asked, brushing her hands down the front of the red dress she'd last worn to a work Christmas party a few years ago. She didn't know why she'd even packed it in her case but now she was very glad she had

'What are you going to do with your hair?' Angel asked.

'I've done my hair!'

'Oh.' Angel's response wasn't encouraging.

Hayley stared into the mirror. She'd brushed and blow-dried. What more could she do when it was in that in-desperate-need-of-a-good-cut phase?

'Uncle Dean!' Angel hollered. 'Did you say Vernon used to be a hair stylist?'

'Angel, stop!' Hayley put her finger over her lips and tried to shush her.

Dean appeared at the door of the room. 'You yelled ... oh Hayley, you look nice.'

'Why is everybody sounding so surprised?' Hayley asked, folding her arms across her chest and dropping down to the bed. Things were still a little tense with Dean.

'She needs her hair done. This is an important business dinner,' Angel said in serious tones.

'An important *business* dinner eh?' Dean said, giving Hayley the benefit of a shamed look.

'Can Vernon come over and cut it real quick?' Angel asked.

'That's *really* quick in British English,' Hayley commented. 'Wait a second, no! I don't need a haircut and Oli ...' She stopped herself quickly. 'The person I'm having a business dinner with will be here in less than an hour.'

'It shouldn't take that long to zhoosh it up,' Angel said.

'What word was that? Zhoosh?! There is no way that's in your special dictionary.'

'Actually it is. Z-H-O-O-S-H. It means to make more exciting or attractive.'

'Hmm, you mean like the time I gave Mrs Farmer a makeover *and* got her into a peplum?'

'Vernon is on his way here,' Dean responded.

'Ooo tell him to go back for his scissors!' Angel ordered.

Oliver Drummond's Penthouse, Downtown Manhattan

'Man, will you chill out?

Tony was gulping his best Scotch like it was water and Oliver didn't even care. He was nervous. More nervous than he'd ever been before, which was ridiculous. It was just a date. And just because he didn't do dates very often it didn't ramp up this date to a higher ranking. It was just a night out. Casual.

'I'm fine,' Oliver replied, although the tone of his voice said otherwise.

'So this chick is English. She's the sister of someone who works for you. She's got a nine-year-old daughter and an ex she wants to find.' Tony sucked in more Scotch. 'I have to say the last bit of that sentence is just plain weird.'

'It's for her daughter,' Oliver said, looking at his reflection in the mirror.

'So she says.'

'What reason has she got to lie?' He turned to face his friend then. 'Wouldn't it have been easier to say she wanted a Porsche or an island in the Indian Ocean?'

'You still don't know for sure it wasn't her who sold you out to the *New York Times*.'

'I do actually,' Oliver said with a nod. 'Delaney found out I've had a journalist on my tail for the past month. He was sat right behind me that night we went to Vipers.'

Tony shook his head. 'How did she find that out?'

'With Delaney it's often better not to ask.' Oliver turned to face him. 'How do I look?'

'Like you're ready for a fashion show.'

Dean Walker's Apartment, Downtown Manhattan

'I know Angel said you *used* to be a hair stylist but how long ago is "used to be"?' Hayley cringed as the scissors clipped another section of hair and she felt it fall from her shoulders.

'It must be about ten, eleven years or so ago,' Vernon said, removing a clip from her hair.

'Gosh, that long,' Hayley stuttered out the reply.

'It's like driving a car. Once you learn it's there with you forever,' Vernon said, snipping some more.

Hayley grimaced. 'The technique maybe, perhaps not the styles. I know the Jennifer Aniston was really popular back in the day but …'

'Why are you so nervous?' Vernon asked with a smile.

'Oh, I don't know. I have someone coming to pick me up in twenty minutes and I haven't had my hair cut in like two years. I'm concerned he won't recognise me. I'm concerned *I* won't recognise me.'

'Relax, Hay, I trust Vernon implicitly,' Dean stated, putting a mug of coffee on the breakfast bar.

'Does he cut your hair?'

'Heaven's no! I go to a little Asian man in Greenwich Village.'

'Let me out of this chair!' Hayley screamed.

'Mum, for goodness' sake. You're in charge of organising a big Christmas charity fundraiser and you're acting like a baby over a haircut. If I were you I'd be more worried about getting that finished on time, not a few split ends.'

'I wasn't worried about split ends. But at the rate my hair's falling on the floor there might be none left to worry about.'

'Dean, go and get me some of that wax you use and the blow-dryer,' Vernon instructed.

'I'm fine. It's fine. We can be done now, can't we?'

'Mum, you're meant to enjoy make-over transformations,' Angel said, sinking her teeth into an apple from the fruit bowl.

'Is that what I'm having?'

'It certainly looks like it from where I'm standing.'

'Dean! Bring me a mirror!'

Oliver Drummond's Penthouse, Downtown Manhattan

'I have to say you're going to a lot of effort for someone who lives on the other side of the world,' Tony stated as Oliver buttoned up his coat.

'Just because things can't be permanent doesn't mean you shouldn't make an effort.'

'Spoken like someone living on borrowed time.'

Oliver swallowed. There was the reminder that it wasn't just Hayley living an expanse of ocean away that would stop this being any more than a string of dates. It was the fact of his own ticking time bomb. That was why he didn't make plans. That's why every night he let himself blow in the wind, end up wherever the mood, circumstance or his best friend took him. There would be no putting down roots or long-term connections for him, that's why everything in his personal life stayed casual. Just like this. Tonight was absolutely no different except it was planned fun – with someone he knew – rather than spontaneous fun – with someone he didn't. That's what he kept telling himself.

'I didn't mean that,' Tony said quickly. 'I let the Romario mouth take over for a second without engaging the brain.'

Oliver smiled, shaking his head. 'That's OK. I know what you're doing.'

'What am I doing?'

'Looking out for me. Like you always do.'

'Come on, Oliver, that sounds way too much like sentimental crap to me.'

He nodded. 'You're right and I need to get out of here.' He swallowed. 'So remember, table for two, the one in the corner about ten o' clock.'

'It's all arranged, man. Momma's been flitting around the kitchen since I told her you were bringing someone over.' Tony smiled. 'You might only have temporary on your mind, but Momma's never seen you with a girl … she's expecting marriage.'

Dean Walker's Apartment, Downtown Manhattan

'Close your eyes,' Vernon said.

'I think I'm going to be sick,' Hayley said, shutting her eyes tight.

'Don't puke, it will ruin your dress,' Angel said, guiding Hayley by the arm towards the gilt framed mirror in the hallway.

'OK. Are you ready?' Vernon asked.

'I very much doubt it.'

'Open your eyes!' Vernon ordered.

Hayley snapped back her lids, fully expecting to be horrified by what she saw. Instead she choked on a lump of emotion that had jumped up from nowhere. Staring back at her was the reflection of someone she barely recognised. Her mid-length hair had been cut to just below the chin in an inverted bob, sleek, shiny and perfect. She put her hands to it, ready to feel some of the glossiness. Vernon took her hand.

'You mustn't touch it, darling. You'll ruin it.'

'I … don't believe what you've done.'

'You look gorgeous, Hayley, utterly gorgeous,' Dean said, wiping at his eyes.

'Oh no, I'll go and get the Kleenex,' Angel said, disappearing back towards the kitchen.

'I don't know what to say.' Hayley looked to Vernon and then to Dean.

'You just go out and have fun with that gorgeous man,' Vernon said. 'I've got a project for Miss Short Stuff while you're out. We're going to beautify Randy.'

'Thank you, Vernon,' Hayley croaked out.

'You're welcome. I'll set to it,' Vernon said, rubbing Dean's shoulder as he passed.

Hayley admired her reflection in the mirror again, taking delight in the way her new hair moved.

'I mean it, Hayley, you look absolutely stunning,' Dean said.

'Good enough for a billionaire?'

She hadn't meant the sentence to come out hard and she swallowed, waiting for her brother's reaction.

'Listen, Hayley, about last night … everything I said to you just came out wrong.' Dean sighed. 'I am so incredibly proud of you but I'm also an overprotective brother who lives on the other side of the world and worries.' He paused. 'You've gone through so much and sometimes I just want you to slow down and … maybe share what's going on in that head of yours.'

'I'm not sure you'd really want to know,' Hayley said, smiling.

'I do, Hayley. I *do* want to know,' Dean insisted.

She nodded. 'Well, I need something other than Angel in my life now, Dean. I came over here for Christmas because she wanted to find her father but when I thought about coming here I wondered if I might find something for myself too. Even if it was only inspiration, you know, a starting block.'

'Like the job with the uniform I'm not going to ask about.'

'Yes, like that ... but look what that led to. I'm event-managing one of the most prestigious charity events in the city ... and now I've said that out loud I feel really, really scared.'

'And there's a billionaire about to pitch up at my door and whisk you off for a night of excitement I really don't want to think about.'

Hayley smiled. 'I don't know what's going to happen with Oliver but I like him and he likes me and we make each other laugh.'

'He laughs? Seriously? I'm going to have to put that on a notice board at the office.'

The intercom buzzed and a fizz of anticipation crackled through Hayley's body. Oliver was here.

'I wish I'd opened some wine,' she said, her lips juddering out the words. 'It's got cold in here.'

'It's just nervous anticipation. Where's he going to take you?' Dean asked.

'I have no idea.'

'Well, listen to me,' Dean said, putting his head close to hers and turning them both towards the mirror. 'You get a chance to go to that penthouse then you take it. It's the weekend, Vernon and I can do that awful Christmas story and breakfast in the morning.'

Hayley looked at their reflections and turned her face to kiss Dean's cheek. 'Thank you.'

'You're welcome. Now, go on down, before his footman buzzes again.' Dean let her go.

'Angel!' Hayley shouted. 'Don't you make Uncle Dean read that Christmas story more than three times and only two bowls of ice cream!'

'Three times!' Dean exclaimed.

'Goodnight. I'll be good!' Hayley said, pounding down the stairs, tucking her sequinned bag under her arm.

'Don't be good. Just be careful!'

CHAPTER THIRTY-EIGHT

Outside Dean Walker's Apartment, Downtown Manhattan

Oliver put his finger to the intercom button again, ready to push it for a second time. She had changed her mind. He swallowed. How did that make him feel? *Disappointed.* He took his hand away from the button and blew some hot breath onto his fingers. It was freezing tonight but inside he had been crackling with anticipation for what was to come. Maybe he should go. Accept that between this morning and now she had had second thoughts.

The door whipped open and there she was.

'My God,' he exclaimed, his eyes bulging in appreciation.

She looked even more heavenly, if that was possible. It was her hair. It was different. It now showed off her petite features, that heart-shaped face, highlighting more of that soft neckline he wanted to get better acquainted with.

'I'm sorry, I should rephrase that quickly.' He reached for her hand. 'You look stunning.' He brought her hand to his lips and placed a delicate kiss on her skin. 'I've never seen business wear quite like it.'

'Why, thank you, Clark. I have to admit you scrub up quite well yourself.' She blushed.

'Shall we?' he asked, indicating the black town car waiting at the bottom of the steps.

'Can I know where we're going now?' Hayley asked, taking his arm.

'No.'

The Metropolitan Opera House, Lincoln Center Plaza

Hayley had sat herself back into the heated leather seats of the car and spent the entire journey surveying the sights and sounds of the Big Apple through the tinted glass window. The buildings on the drive ranged from giant international stores and smart hotels, to bodegas and brownstones. Lamp posts cast a glow over the snow-covered vehicles parked on the street, strings of fairy lights hung from trees and roofs, the faint scent of ginger snaps was in the air. It was the first time since she'd arrived in the city that she was actually able to take it in in all its glory. Because there *was* beauty in the bustle of life here, like the arch in Washington Square Park last night, old and new blending together to create one perfect heady mix of a culture she'd once thought was hers for the taking. Concentrating on the scene outside had been better than the alternative. Focussing on her companion. Her nose had been filled with the musky scent of his aftershave and they'd sat so close the heat from his body had seeped its way into hers. Gazing at the city sights had stopped her falling under the spell of those hazel eyes and admitting what his presence did to her.

The car had dropped them five minutes or so ago and now they were walking, the shoes she had packed but never expected to wear starting to shave the skin off her little toes.

'Is it far?' she asked Oliver, trying her best not to limp.

'No,' he responded. 'It's just over there.'

Hayley followed his line of vision to a fountain just ahead, its water bright white, bubbling up like a newly found oil well. Just behind, five arched windows stretched up from sidewalk to sky, ethereal light making them look like heavenly guardians protecting whatever was within.

'What is this place?' she asked, unable to stop the anticipation spreading over her face.

'It's the Metropolitan Opera House,' he answered.

'Wow!' she breathed out quickly. *Opera.* She couldn't show any disappointment. It might be good. It wasn't Maroon 5 but it was a new experience. She swallowed.

He grinned at her. 'You love opera, right?'

She nodded so much she was afraid her head might roll right off her shoulders when she was done. 'Yeah, of course! Who doesn't love opera?! Men and women singing in a language I don't understand. I'm all about the soprano and the not understanding the plotline.' She swallowed. 'That was a joke by the way. This is a really great idea for a date.'

Oliver let his laugh go. 'I hate opera.'

'You do?' She couldn't help the gasp of relief. 'You really had me going there for a second.'

He offered her his arm. 'Come on, let's get inside out of the cold.'

Hayley slipped her arm through his, her fingers taking a hold of his black woollen coat, the solidity of his forearm prevalent under the fabric. This was happening. This was her going on a date. A date she wanted to be on, with someone who made her insides curl up in ways she'd forgotten about.

They walked across the paving, their breath hanging hot in the freezing air, following groups of people ahead all starting to congregate outside the entrance.

Hayley tugged on Oliver's arm, making him turn his head. 'So if this isn't opera, what is it?'

He smiled then, his eyes creasing at the corners, and Hayley held her breath. There were those oh-so-kissable lips she really wanted to get to know more intimately. God, it was like she was on heat. One sniff of a date and she was ready for anything. She was supposed to be being cautious here, not turning into a man devourer just because she hadn't had a man for a while. Albeit a long while.

'You'll just have to wait and see,' he replied, tapping his nose with his finger.

She wrinkled up her face in disapproval. 'Has anyone ever told you you're deeply annoying?'

'Would you like all their names and zip codes?'

The look on Hayley's face when she saw the banner announcing what they were going to see was priceless. Her mouth had sprung open, her jaw hanging, eyes unbelieving. She turned to stare at him, unspeaking, seemingly lost for words which, for her, was a definite rarity. He felt pure unadulterated joy welling up inside him. This was what it felt like to do something for someone you cared about. And then something stung. He didn't do caring like that. It only led to pain. He kept the smile on his face and put a hand to his chest to quell the spasm that had occurred in apparent protest. This had to be light and casual. He ground his teeth together. He was living in the moment. *Just* the moment. Nothing else.

'I know about this … I mean … I knew it was in New York soon and I hoped I'd be able to catch some of it on TV. I mean, people like me don't get tickets to this sort of thing,' Hayley gabbled.

'People like you?' he questioned, drinking in the sight of her in the perfect dress, the ends of her new hairstyle just touching her delicious jawline.

She shrugged. 'It's one of the most famous fashion collaborations of the year. All the greats are here, Alexander McQueen, Versace, Galliano and …' She took a breath like she was steeling herself for something. 'Emo Taragucci.'

'Who's that?' Oliver asked, his face a blank canvas.

'Who's that?!' She flipped around on him, looking mean. 'I can't believe you said that.'

'To be honest, I'm kind of a Tom Ford guy.'

He watched Hayley approach the poster, looking up at it like it was something to worship at. 'Emo Taragucci has been … was … an inspiration to me.'

He wet his lips. Was she about to open up to him now? He'd known the flashes of spirit she had shown him were only the tip of the iceberg. Underneath the responsibilities of being a mum there was a frustrated spirit waiting to break out. He held his breath, wanting nothing to get in her way.

'I dreamed I'd be designing clothes like this one day,' Hayley said, the words floating from her mouth almost subconsciously. 'I thought … hoped … one day my name would be up there.' She indicated the poster with a shaking finger. 'Somewhere like this.'

This was her wish. When he'd asked her at Vipers she had totally ignored her own dreams and desires and told him what she wanted for her daughter. But this was it. This was what she wanted the most for herself. His Adam's apple bobbed in his throat as he remembered his own life plan he'd had to give up.

'It's never too late,' he whispered, stepping close to her until he knew she could feel his breath on the nape of her neck. He watched her visibly shiver in response. What he wouldn't give to touch that delicate skin, the shorter hair leaving it bare to the world.

She shook her head. 'No. I missed my chance. Flying off to Milan and creating my show for London Fashion Week is never going to happen for me now.'

'That's defeatist.'

'It's reality. I have Angel.'

'If you fold her up a certain way I think she could class as hand luggage.'

Hayley laughed. 'The special dictionary alone covers that. Add all the guidebooks and I may as well pay for her seat.'

He reached out and touched a strand of her hair before removing his hand quickly. Where had that come from? It was way too intimate. He cleared his throat. 'Shall we go in?'

The opera house was, without doubt, the grandest place Hayley had ever set foot in. The tiers of sumptuous red upholstered seats were just like the Albert Hall. Looking upwards she marvelled at the unusual circular design of the ceiling and the Art Deco-style starburst lights, their arms shooting out like radiant rays of stardust. Even in the best dress she had to wear she felt conspicuous. Oliver, on the other hand, couldn't have fitted in better. His winter coat was over his arm now and the charcoal suit he was wearing tapered in all the right places. She really needed to stop looking at him like he was a piece of meat ripe for the barbecue. But she couldn't deny there was a part of her warming to this man in quite a significant way. Bringing her here wasn't about showing off his ability to get tickets that had probably sold out the second they went on sale. Somehow he knew this meant something to her.

She watched him saying hello to various patrons along the way. He was a well-known businessman; he probably knew half the room. She, on the other hand felt like a fish out of water. She really needed to learn to walk a little taller, remember the social skills she used to possess before the only thing she had to focus on was Peppa Pig. In a few days she was going to be mixing with the rich and the beautiful at the McArthur Foundation fundraiser. And she really needed to tell Oliver about that.

Right on cue he turned back to catch her gaze. 'We're here,' he stated, holding an arm out, indicating the very front row.

The front row. Of course he had got them tickets for the front row. Where else would a billionaire trying to impress his date sit? She threw a glance over other guests already in their seats and almost choked on the air she couldn't swallow down.

'Oliver, don't look now, I think Victoria Beckham is sat two rows behind us,' Hayley hissed.

She watched him look then wave a hand of acknowledgement. 'Ah good, I've been meaning to catch up with David about youth sports sponsorship.'

'Are you kidding me?' Hayley said, her voice an octave too high.

'What?' Oliver responded with a laugh of innocence. 'If you're impressed by sitting in front of Victoria Beckham what are you going to think about sitting next to Emo Taragucci?' He indicated the seat to Hayley's right.

Suddenly she felt like she was holding the winning lottery ticket and didn't have a clue what to do.

From the second the music started, Oliver watched Hayley give every ounce of her attention to the show going on in front of them. She clapped and whooped, whistled in appreciation and watched steely-eyed as model after model made their way down the catwalk on stage towards them. It was evocative. *She* was evocative. His eyes hadn't been on the stage, they'd been on only her. He swallowed as that thought travelled over his brain.

Hayley pointed. 'Look at that. See how she creates the illusion of length. And those colours!'

'I'm not even going to pretend I know what I'm looking at.'

'Oh come on, Oliver, you appreciate the female form, don't you?'

'It has been known.'

'Well, Emo Taragucci dresses women in a totally unique way. All her designs are ultra-feminine, sexy, strong, everything a woman should be.'

'Hear, hear,' Oliver answered.

Hayley punched his arm. 'You'd better mean that.'

'I do, I swear,' he laughed.

'Ooo, look at that one … it's beautiful,' Hayley said, admiring a black dress printed with tiny Japanese blossom.

Her excitement and enthusiasm was catching. Her joy in the fashion show made him feel the same elation as winning another billion-dollar contract or scoring a winning touchdown on the football field. He swallowed back the feeling, something pinching. There had to be at least an arm's length. She was leaving. He was dying. He couldn't do complex.

'I squeezed Emo's leg,' Hayley whispered, her face close to his.

'You didn't!'

'I didn't mean to, I just got overexcited. She took it well. She is coming back after her section of the show isn't she?'

Oliver laughed. 'How hard did you squeeze her?'

'Do you think it would be too much to ask for a selfie?'

CHAPTER THIRTY-NINE

Greenwich Village, New York

'So this is Greenwich Village,' Oliver remarked after the car had dropped them off again.

Hayley sucked in some of the cold air, including a mouthful of snowflakes, one hand deep in her pocket, the other intertwined with Oliver's. She was still on cloud nine after the fashion show. Seeing a production like that, something she would never normally have been able to get invited to, had been unbelievable. Sitting next to her absolute, number one icon in the fashion industry had been on another level. By the end of the evening at the theatre Hayley had felt confident enough to speak instead of squeeze and she'd complimented the designer on all her favourite collections since she'd become a fan.

Hayley sniffed. Scents of incense, spruce, chocolate and mulled wine filled her nose. There were different flavours on every corner. A man was selling Christmas trees up ahead and it reminded her that Dean still didn't have one in the apartment. He had always been far more into Christmas than she was until Angel came along and stoked up her excitement. When Angel was little she'd always made a paper fairy for the top of the tree. Hayley suspected making tree toppers was way too infantile for a nine-year-old now. Her daughter was growing up so fast. Then Michel came to mind. He'd walked her through Greenwich Village in their twelve hours together. He'd seemed right at home with the bohemian ambience.

She came to a stop outside a store where Christmas music was coming from the window display. There were animatronic animals moving to the sound of 'Rockin' Robin'. A stag was in the middle, his mouth opening and closing in time to the lyrics, two penguins sat in front, their wings lifting up and down, then there was a trio of rabbits – knitted red scarves wrapped around their necks – and half a dozen small mice, spinning round and round in circles. Fake snow was filtering down upon them and a troupe of Nutcracker soldiers moved up and down the window frame on a track, pink wooden cheeks glowing, arms shifting forward and back.

Hayley laughed. 'Angel would love this.'

'What does this store sell anyhow?' Oliver asked, trying to look for merchandise. He stepped back, looking at the sign. 'Pet supplies,' he remarked, shaking his head.

'Can we go inside?' Hayley asked him.

'You want to go shopping for pet supplies?'

'We enjoyed the display, Dean's partner has a dog, come on,' Hayley encouraged, stepping towards the door.

Oliver checked his watch. 'We have a dinner reservation.'

'Five minutes, I promise.' She pulled a face she hoped was like one of Angel's when she wanted something. It always worked for her.

'I really hope this dog likes sequins.'

'It isn't really for Randy,' Hayley responded, tucking the paper bag containing a silver sequinned waistcoat and bow tie for the pooch under her arm. 'It's for Angel. Fussing over that dog and dressing it up is going to take her mind off finding her father.'

Oliver swallowed. Daniel Pearson hadn't been able to find any trace of Michel De Vos which even the private investigator thought was unusual. He was going to keep looking, try a different tack, report back as soon as he had something.

'Still nothing?' he asked her. Should he tell her he was looking? How would she feel about that? Pleased that he wanted to help? Or was it too much and none of his business?

She sighed. 'I went back to Vipers last night. Another bartender there said she'd seen him recently, like in the last few weeks. I left my details.' She swallowed. 'Last night it felt like all my Christmases were coming at once but in a city this big it's still a long shot.'

'Hey, don't underestimate the outside chance. Drummond Global has made a fortune on some of those.' He smiled. 'We're here.' He held his hand out indicating the building they'd stopped at.

'Restaurant Romario,' Hayley said, reading the sign.

Oliver took it all in, like he was seeing it for the first time. Not much had changed since he was a kid. The window frames and door had been given a fresh lick of paint but the green and red canopies over them were still the originals. His stomach rolled as if it could already taste the delicious Italian feast about to come their way. Breadsticks and olives followed by a garlic-infused lasagne.

'I'm starving,' Hayley announced. 'I want the biggest pizza they've got.'

Oliver smiled, stifling the laughter with a hand to his mouth.

'They do *do* pizza don't they? This isn't one of those restaurants where I won't know the name of anything is it? I went to a Christmas meal once where they did *heirloom* tomatoes and something called a mackerel escabeche. I was too scared to order anything but turkey.'

Oliver pushed at the door. 'One thing I can tell you is, you won't want the biggest pizza they've got.'

'Are you sure about that? I'm a big eater.'

'It takes two people to carry it,' Oliver responded.

Hayley watched Oliver push open the door and a bell chimed above as he moved over the threshold. Heat hit her as she stepped up into the entrance and smells of oregano, parmesan, olive oil and freshly baked dough infused her nose. As she relieved herself of her coat, shaking snowflakes off the material and folding it over her arm, she watched Oliver being swallowed up in the embrace of a short, dark-haired woman in her sixties. The woman was speaking in hurried Italian and Oliver was responding, kissing both her cheeks with real affection. This was somewhere he knew well. And it was nothing like the opulent surroundings of Asian Dawn. This was a cosy restaurant, somewhere you would come to feel at ease. It wasn't the sort of place Hayley had imagined eating dinner at tonight and, as she watched Oliver in this relaxed atmosphere, she realised that was a good thing.

The older woman shuffled forwards, dark eyes shining at Hayley. Before she had a chance to do or say anything, the woman had taken her hands and was clutching them tight in a move that suggested she was thrilled to meet her.

'You are a very beautiful girl, very beautiful,' Mrs Romario said, still holding on to Hayley's hands.

'Thank you,' Hayley said, a little embarrassment creeping in.

'Hayley, this is Anna Romario, this is her restaurant,' Oliver introduced.

'Oh, it's so lovely to meet you,' Hayley replied, shaking the hands that were holding on to hers with more affection.

'This one needs a good girl,' Mrs Romario continued, her eyes moving to Oliver.

'Whoa there, Momma, I think that's enough of the match-making right now.'

Hayley looked to the newcomer. He was taller, late twenties, with dark eyes and hair to match. He smiled and held out his hand.

'Tony Romario,' he introduced himself. 'And actually this is my restaurant now, along with two others from the Papa Gino franchise.'

'You're not at a networking event,' Oliver said.

'She's cute,' Tony whispered back.

'Thank you,' Hayley replied. She shook Tony's hand.

Oliver smiled. 'Hayley this is my best friend, Tony. Tony, this is Hayley Walker.'

'Charmed,' Tony said, smiling. 'Now, please, let me show you to your table.'

Hayley followed Oliver through the restaurant to a booth at the back next to a window looking out onto the street. Oliver pulled out a chair for her and she sank down into it, looking to the view outside. A group of carol singers stood across the road, the tune of 'Ding Dong Merrily On High' just audible through the glass. A couple walked by, wrapped up in hats and scarves, taking turns to nibble on a doughnut.

Hayley turned back to the room and watched Oliver take his seat opposite.

'A menu for madam and one for sir,' Tony said, passing them out. 'Can I recommend a wine or perhaps some champagne?'

'You keep working that charm,' Oliver joked. 'Hayley? What would you like to drink?'

'I do like fizzy wine. It doesn't have to be champagne. Sometimes fizzy wine is actually better,' she responded.

'Got any fizzy wine for the lady?' Oliver asked, looking amused.

'Only Bollinger,' Tony replied, not missing a beat.

'Bollinger it is then,' Oliver answered.

'I'll be right back. Oh, the specials are on the blackboard but we're all out of the arrabbiata.' Tony left the table and headed towards the bar area.

Hayley let out a laugh, putting her hand to her mouth. 'I'm sorry.'

'What is it?'

'I had no idea you were going to bring me somewhere so … so normal.'

She watched Oliver shift in his seat and knew instinctively she'd said the wrong thing. She followed it up quickly. 'I didn't mean that how it came out. This place, it's lovely.' She looked at the other booths behind them, the round tables covered in gingham cloths, the wine bottle candles shimmering. 'I just thought …'

He interrupted. 'I'd take you to a soulless restaurant on a rooftop somewhere and we'd pick over heirloom tomatoes and mackerel escabeche?'

She nodded. 'And that was me putting my foot in it.'

He pulled in a long breath. 'I could have taken you somewhere like that. That's what I would usually have done but …'

Her heart was racing. The velvet texture of his tone was settling on her like a layer of snow, but warm, welcome.

'I've not brought anyone here before.' He swallowed. 'This place is …' He reached his hand across the table and picked a breadstick from the glass in the centre. He broke it in two. Hayley could sense his hesitation. For whatever reason, he was finding this difficult.

'My mom and dad, me and Ben, we used to come here every Friday night without fail. It was one of the only times business was switched off and we talked about other stuff that was going on.'

Hayley leant her elbows on the table and inched herself closer. 'Like what? School?' She smiled harder. 'Glee club?'

Oliver smiled. 'No one in our family was in Glee club.' He broke the breadstick again, pieces landing on the small plate to his right.

'So what did a young Oliver Drummond do at school? Don't tell me … you were president of the debating society?' She could see him doing that. Commanding other students, leading a healthy argument about the state of the world.

He shook his head. 'No, that was my brother.' A sigh left him. 'I was on the football team.'

'A jock.' Hayley couldn't help the surprise touching her reply. 'And I suppose we're talking a funny-shaped ball rather than the kind David Beckham uses.'

He nodded, pushed a piece of breadstick into his mouth. That gave her every reason to focus on those gorgeous lips that looked just as good no matter what expression they were wearing.

'So,' she recovered. 'When did you stop with the ball games and start with the hard drives?'

She watched a wistful expression appear in his hazel eyes. It seemed like his thoughts were flying far away from the Romario's restaurant. She waited, hoping he was going to say something.

'When I ripped apart my shoulder and couldn't make it as a professional.'

That wasn't the answer she'd been expecting.

'Here we are, Bollinger, a 2004 vintage. Does that meet with sir's approval?' Tony asked, appearing at the table, red-faced, a bottle opener between his teeth.

'Just get it open, Tony,' Oliver answered.

CHAPTER FORTY

Restaurant Romario, Greenwich Village

'It was always Ben's dream to work for the family business. I was the one who always went against the grain,' Oliver said as they shared a plate of olives, sardines drizzled with lemon, fresh bread and a garlic butter.

'There's nothing wrong with wanting your own path,' Hayley said, trying to delicately skewer an olive. 'I wasn't going to be a housewife like my mother or a bricklayer like my dad and I wasn't ever as clever as Dean.' She scoffed. 'I definitely proved that by getting pregnant young and ruining all my plans.'

'I think you're too hard on yourself.'

'Maybe you are too,' she responded. The mood had shifted. This was easier, safer territory. 'So, were you really good at football? Like Jonny Wilkinson was to rugby?'

'Something like that. I take it he's good,' Oliver said with a smile.

'I can just see you in the outfit.'

'Uniform,' he corrected.

'Tight white pants, bigger shoulder pads than Joan Collins …'

'I looked hot in that uniform.'

'I'm not saying otherwise.'

The thought of him in tight pants was causing an involuntary reaction. She was hotting up from the tips of her toes and the flush was moving upwards at a rapid, unrelenting rate. He was looking right at her, sultry, like if they weren't in a populated restaurant he might rip all her clothes off.

'Is that your boardroom face? Because it's totally working on me.' She shifted in her seat. 'Right now I'd do anything for you,' she whispered. What had come over her? Was this the wine talking or her innermost thoughts jumping out of her lips? Her heart was racing now.

She watched his composure drop away and he wet his lips. Before she knew it she was slipping off her shoe and stretching her leg out under the table until she connected with him. Keeping her eyes on his, she slowly began to inch her toes up his calves, past his knee and up onto his thigh.

'You are a bad, bad, girl,' he whispered, his eyes not leaving hers.

She jolted in her seat as she felt his foot on her, moving latently upwards.

'We shouldn't be doing this in a family establishment,' she said, swallowing as she felt his foot slip up onto her chair and begin parting her thighs.

'Absolutely not,' he agreed.

Her delicate foot was kneading his groin and he was powerless. He was raging with lust, completely out of control. He should stop but it was too good, erotic, sensual, something more than that all at once. He pressed his foot forward, inch by inch, knowing he was so close to the most intimate part of her and wanting to feel it.

'Have you still got the uniform?' Hayley asked, her voice raspy.

'What do you think?' he whispered.

He watched her squirm as his toes made contact with her. He pressed a little harder.

'Is it getting hot in here?' She fanned a hand at her face as she looked back at him.

'You tell me.' He felt her furl and unfurl her toes on him and he knocked his knife off the table with his elbow.

'Ditto,' she said, eyes wide, lips parted.

'A large Capricciosa and a Tre Gusti,' Tony announced, slamming their plates down with no finesse at all.

Oliver shot his leg down from Hayley's chair. His face was flushed and he made a grab for his napkin. 'Thank you, that's great.'

'Fast service around here,' Hayley remarked.

'Almost a little too quick,' he replied.

Oliver watched her, tearing apart her pizza and eating it like she was a famine victim. There was nothing superficial about this woman. She wasn't sat there putting on a show for him, she was who she was and that was a breath of fresh air. Everything about her invigorated him. Everything she had going on in her life and she was still able to be so … natural, so free. If it wasn't so stimulating he would probably feel jealous.

'This pizza is so good,' Hayley said, wiping a sheen of grease from her lips with a finger before grabbing a serviette.

'It's the best pizza in the whole of New York in my opinion.'

'So,' she took a sip of her champagne. 'Why did you stop coming here?'

She didn't pull any punches. And he didn't have an answer ready. Why had the Drummonds stopped coming here? Ben had died and the whole family had fallen apart, not feeling whole when one of them was missing. Maybe that was the problem.

They hadn't clung to each other, they had all done everything they could to get away. Richard with the business, him too – the only person who'd tried was Cynthia. And she was still valiantly trying now.

He shrugged, sitting back in his chair. 'Ben died. It didn't feel right I guess.'

'But you and Tony are friends, *you* still came here on your own.'

He shook his head. 'Not for a long time. And Momma Romario never lets me forget it.'

'I wouldn't want to be on the wrong side of that one. She has the grip of a strongman.' She picked up another piece of pizza and gazed out onto the street. Two children were building a snowman on the sidewalk, their parents helping gather up piles of snow. It reminded her she'd promised to make Angel a snow president.

'Angel loves Christmas,' she remarked.

'She's a kid. All kids love Christmas.'

'I always like the food more than the presents,' Hayley said, poking in the pizza slice.

He laughed. 'You surprise me.'

'So do you do the whole going to church thing at Christmas?'

'When I was a kid. Not now.'

'Me neither. I'm not sure I know what religion's really about. I'd just like a world where everybody respects everybody, for who they are as people, not anything else.'

'Thought about running for office? You'd definitely get my vote.'

'People make life too complicated,' she mused.

'There's just never enough time,' Oliver stated.

'It's us not *making* time that's the issue,' Hayley corrected.

'Sometimes it isn't that simple.'

'And that's my point. It *is* that simple … if you want it to be.'
She looked up at him. 'Like, if you knew your father and Ben
were going to die what would you have done? Would you still
have done whatever you did or would you have spent more time
with them?'

'It isn't an ideal world.'

'And you haven't answered the question.'

'Of course I'd want to spend more time with them.'

'And you know you should have.'

'That's not really fair, Hayley.'

'I wasn't talking about you.' She sighed. 'I was talking about
me.' She kicked the table leg. 'My father died just after I had
Angel and, unlike my mother, he didn't think I was a waste of
space, or a let-down because I'd made a mistake. I took him for
granted, Oliver. I assumed he would always be there. I didn't
cherish things, I didn't spend enough time living in those moments and I wish I could go back and change that.'

'He wouldn't want you to be feeling guilt about it. No one
knows how long they have here.'

Oliver swallowed as the conversation hit close to home. He certainly didn't know how long he had here. He was supposed to be
all about the moment. He'd always tried to pack everything he
could in to however long he had left. But in an entirely different
way to what Hayley was suggesting. In a detached, solitary way
that meant nothing to anyone. Hayley would hold her loved
ones close, not push them as far away as possible like he was. He
took a sip from his glass.

'My mother told me at my father's funeral that me getting
pregnant and having Angel had aged him. She practically accused me of putting the nail in his coffin.'

'She's wrong, Hayley and you know that.'

'Is she?'

He reached his hand across the table, slipping his fingers in between hers. 'Yes, she is.' He used his other hand to raise her chin with his finger, forcing her to look at him. 'And I'm betting anything if your father can hear you now he's hammering his fists on whatever cloud he's on, telling you you're letting him down thinking this kind of crap now.'

Hayley sniffed and he saw the tears in her eyes. He just wanted to pull her towards him, envelop her body with his.

'What d'you think your father would be saying?' she asked him, gently

He sucked in a breath. That was a hard question to answer. How would Richard feel about the situation with Andrew Regis and his mother? The course he was steering the company on with the Globe? How he'd lived his life since his death? Hayley? Richard would definitely have liked Hayley. He smiled then.

'He'd be saying "Oliver, you have a beautiful woman right here with you, why are you wasting your time thinking about me".'

He felt a laugh come from her and she unlinked their hands. 'I'm sorry, I made this kind of deep, didn't I? I blame the carol singers out there.' She nudged her head towards the scene outside.

'I blame the extortionately expensive champagne.'

'But I'm worth it.'

'The jury's still out on that one, Lois.'

She swiped a hand out, catching him on the shoulder.

'Ouch, that hurt.'

'Sorry, was that the injured shoulder?'

'No, that was my baseball arm.'

'I bet you're a pro at that too.'

'Of course. And NHL and NASCAR.'

'I *do* know what those are.'

He laughed. 'No you don't.'

'I could try and guess. I'm good at abbreviations.'

'Go ahead, I might LMFAO.'

'You are so annoying!'

She was looking across at him, her cheeks flushed, her eyes bright, that infectious smile on her face. She was so beautiful, sat there sparring with him. He blew out the candle and leaned across the table, taking her face in his hands. Slowly, he brought her lips to his, needing to feel her mouth. She softened beneath his fingers, warm and open to his every move. Deepening the kiss, he lost himself, letting everything he was starting to feel for her flood over him. He slipped his hand into her hair, drawing her nearer still, driven on by the heat of her mouth and the intensity of her responses.

And then he broke the connection, needing to breathe. He carried on looking at her, trying to read her eyes. He swallowed as she matched his gaze and finally he was able to speak: 'I want to take you home tonight.'

'I thought that's what the town car was for,' she replied.

'*My* home,' he said, his eyes not leaving hers. His heart was leaping like a child on a pogo stick, bouncing so hard it was starting to hurt.

She smiled at him, grazing her fingers down the fine stubble along his jaw. 'A lady cannot accept an invitation to the penthouse on the very first date.'

'Screw that,' Oliver said, taking hold of her hand.

'Why, Mr Drummond, what language in front of a lady!' She smiled before continuing. 'Last time I spent the night with someone in New York things got really complicated.'

He watched her drop her eyes, her mind somewhere else. He tilted her chin with his finger again. 'We'll keep it safe in the red room, I promise.'

CHAPTER FORTY-ONE

**Outside Oliver Drummond's Penthouse,
Downtown Manhattan**

'This is where you live?' Hayley looked up at the glass and chrome building in front of them. It was imposing, somehow stood out amongst the other premises of equal stature around it. The snow was falling heavily now and her teeth started to chatter. She wrapped her arms around herself, holding onto the sequinned bag like a lifebuoy.

'This is where I live. Come on, let's get inside before you freeze,' he said, heading towards the doorman. 'Hey, Bosco.'

'Good evening, Mr Drummond,' the doorman responded.

'Hello, Bosco, I'm Hayley.' She waved a hand at him.

'Good evening, Miss.'

'I bet Bosco has seen some action, whisking in your Wish Women,' Hayley said as they entered the lobby. 'This looks just like your offices. But where's the Christmas tree? This is so bare.'

Everything was chrome and grey, modern, functional but a little bit dull. There was nothing to suggest the holidays were fast approaching.

Oliver pressed the button for the elevator. 'It's a multicultural building. Some of the other residents don't celebrate Christmas so we don't have a tree.' He reached for her hand. 'FYI – that's another abbreviation right there – I don't bring my Wish Women here. And don't call them that. They aren't a thing.'

'Double W I think the Twitter hashtag is. Rumour has it that particular edition of the *New York Times* sold big.'

'You're making it up,' he said as the elevator doors opened.

'Maybe, but it's never going to get old,' Hayley said, stepping into the lift with him.

'I think you're forgetting the rather amazing fashion show I took you to tonight.'

'Which could only have been bettered by having Adam Levine come and sing in the interval.' She sighed. 'But I did meet Emo Taragucci, in the flesh, actually there for me to squeeze,' Hayley said, hugging herself.

Oliver smiled. 'I'm glad you enjoyed the evening.'

'It isn't over yet, is it?' she asked. She watched the numbers of the floors on the display going up slowly and she looked to Oliver, a smile playing on her lips. 'Ever done it in a lift before?'

'What?'

She shifted closer towards him. 'I said, have you ever done it in a lift before?'

She watched him swallow and finally catch on to what she was suggesting.

'I have a five-million dollar penthouse on the twenty-fifth floor and you want to do it in the elevator.'

She licked her lips. 'I don't know if I can wait twenty more floors.' She unbuttoned her coat and shrugged it off her shoulders, then, slowly, she lifted the hem of her red dress, dragging it up her body revealing stockings and her best black silk and lace panties and matching bra.

'Jeez, Hayley, what are you doing to me?'

'Looking a little overdressed over there, Clark.'

In one move he lost his coat and in the second and third he unfastened his buttons and ripped his shirt away from his body.

'I knew you were trouble, the very second I set eyes on you by that fire exit,' he breathed. He claimed her mouth with his, pushing her body up against the mirrored wall. She tasted of chocolate and coffee and that something he could never quite put his finger on. He was pretty sure it involved vanilla but right now all he could taste was lust – whether it was his or hers he couldn't tell.

She wrenched her lips from his. 'You knew *I* was trouble? I think that's a bit rich.'

'Stop talking!' he ordered, his mouth at her neckline, his tongue tracing the length of her shoulder.

'Get these things off,' Hayley said, her hands at the belt of his trousers.

He stood up straight, his hands on top of hers. He held her fingers as she weaved the leather through the buckle, his eyes on her, wanting to watch her expression and feed off of it. They lowered his zipper together, he slipped a condom from his pocket and then she took over, yanking at the material so he had no choice but to kick his trousers off and away.

He appraised her, her chest rising and falling, her nipples tight against the silk of her bra. The condom packet between his lips, he reached forward with both hands, looping her back and unfastening the clasp until the fabric slackened and he pulled her bra forward, letting the straps slip down her arms and off.

Voluptuous breasts greeted him and the kick of arousal stung. He wanted to touch her, taste her, own every inch of her. He held off, just watching. She slipped her fingers inside her panties and he watched her, teasing, toying, easing her hand backward and forward.

'God, you are so hot.' He removed his jockey shorts, made sure he was safe and took a half step nearer to her.

She slipped her panties off and pressed her back against the mirrors that lined the lift, pulling him with her. She kissed his mouth, the edge of her teeth nipping his bottom lip. This was driving him crazy. He had to get inside her. He had to take her now.

He slammed his hand on the elevator buttons, hoping it would buy them some time and then he lifted her up in his arms, his hands clasping her buttocks as his mouth dived into hers.

A gasp left her as he lowered her down so he could slip inside. The heat that met him intensified every ounce of passion he was already full of.

'Do it,' she whispered in his ear. 'Move me.'

Hayley was aching all over, trembling, itching for a need to be fulfilled. All the flirtatious banter, the teasing, the kissing in the snow, no one had ever got to her like this man had. This complex billionaire no one seemed to understand except her. She saw him. All of him. His worries and concerns were so similar to hers. They were like two parts of the same Christmas cracker. And right about now she was ready to be pulled apart.

She braced herself against the wall of the lift, her hands on his chest as he made love to her, fast and urgent, then slowly, thrusting long and deep, until she dug her nails into him and begged for release.

She kissed his mouth, looking into his eyes, wanting to watch as he came apart, as he pulled her to pieces with him. And then it was happening, it was like being catapulted through the air at a million miles an hour and not knowing where you were going to land. Stars pricked her eyes as Oliver called out, his hair damp between her fingers, his skin shining with perspiration. Tiny pleasure sensors were sending happy signals to her every part. She didn't want to let him go. Then one of her legs buckled.

'Ow, cramp,' Hayley said, shifting a little but not wanting the connection to end.

Oliver kissed her lips. 'You OK?'

She nodded, putting a hand to his cheek. 'You?'

'Spent,' he responded, still catching his breath.

She laughed. 'A billionaire with nothing in reserve.'

'I didn't say I had nothing. I just think maybe a change of location could be in order.'

'Ah, the infamous red room. Finally I'm going to see it?' Hayley asked as he stroked her hair back from her face.

'You really think I have one?'

'I'll be disappointed if you don't.'

CHAPTER FORTY-TWO

Oliver Drummond's Penthouse, Downtown Manhattan

Hayley opened her eyes and blinked at the unfamiliar shapes in the half-light, trying to recall where she was. *Oliver's penthouse.* A fuzzy, furry feeling spread through her as she remembered the previous night. The fashion show, the lovely meal, the lift … the balcony overlooking Central Park. Now, here she was, wrapped up in Egyptian cotton feeling like she could conquer the world. She turned onto her side, facing Oliver. There was just one little thing eating away at her. The McArthur Foundation fundraiser. She should tell him she was organising it. *Not* telling him was virtually lying to him. But she knew how it would make him feel. If she told him, it would impact on what they had together and she didn't want that. The time she spent with him was just about them. It didn't involve Angel or Michel or Drummond Global or Cynthia. She didn't want to burst that happy bubble just yet, especially after last night.

She mussed his tawny hair and watched him open his eyes.

'Good morning,' she greeted. 'What do you have for breakfast round here?'

'God, Hayley, you must have one hell of a metabolism.' He sat up, rubbing at his eyes. 'Either that or you're going to just wake up twenty stone one day when it catches up with you.'

'And if I did?' She asked, looking cross.

He smiled. 'Obviously I'd love you just the same but ...' He stopped. 'By "love" I meant, you know, care about you, as a person and ...'

'You love me!' Hayley exclaimed, bouncing her body on the bed. 'Oh I'm going to be Mrs Drummond! Bosco, the doorman! Send for Emo Taragucci to design my wedding gown! Book Romario's for the reception and order Maroon 5! We're going to get married!' she shrieked.

Oliver shook his head as he watched her theatrical performance. 'You're crazy.'

'Your #DoubleWs will be devastated. I might have to hire personal security and carry mace.'

'God help anyone who tries to attack you.'

'What's for breakfast?' she said, diving over him and knocking him back into the pillows.

It was like his chest had been hit with a steel bar. Oliver couldn't reply. He shifted his body into a full sitting position and tried to take a breath. It wasn't coming.

'Oliver?' Hayley asked, pulling the sheet up around her and looking straight at him. 'Wow, did I hit you that hard? I obviously don't know my own strength, Man of Steel.'

This couldn't happen now. He tried to raise his chest but everything was compacting down like someone had placed a railway sleeper on his ribcage. The beads of sweat were at his forehead already and his vision was starting to blur. This wasn't like the last time. This was much, much worse. He fought to regain control.

'Oliver?' Hayley said again. There was concern in her voice.

'I'm OK,' he breathed out, the words scratching and jarring.

'Oliver, please. You're scaring me.'

Her eyes were wide and pricked with tears as she stared at him. She reached a hand out for his and he moved it away. He needed to manage this on his own. He didn't want to let this touch her.

'Really, I'm OK,' he whispered through dry lips. His body's reaction was continuing to tell him the exact opposite.

'You're not OK. I can *see* you're not OK. Tell me what to do or I'm going to call an ambulance.'

He didn't want to die. He especially didn't want to die now, after a night that had meant so much. There was no denying he was falling hard for her and maybe this was telling him he was a fool to even think of it. What good was a dying man to her? What good was a dying man to anyone?

His heart galloped in response, pulsing the blood through his veins until it was all he could hear in his head. This was really happening, right here, right now, when he was probably the happiest he had been since his father died.

He used his arms to push himself to the edge of the bed, trying his best to shut out the pain and Hayley's piteous scrutiny. He needed to get up. Somehow he needed to find the strength.

'Right, that's it,' Hayley said, grabbing his robe and wrapping it around herself. 'This is crazy. I'm calling an ambulance.'

'Hayley, please …' The words barely made it from his mouth. 'Please, just go.'

'Go?! Are you completely insane? I'm not going anywhere.' She picked up her sequinned bag and pulled her phone from inside. He watched her thumb move across the screen. *911.*

His throat was starting to get tight now and his head was filling up like someone was tipping liquid cotton candy inside then letting it grow and morph. The pressure in his chest was unbearable. It would be easy to give in. Just let his body have its own way, sink into the pain, give in to it all. No more worrying, no more stress, just peace. As he tried to get up from the bed he felt his eyes start to close.

'Hello? Yes, I need an ambulance … I need an ambulance now.'

St Patrick's Hospital, Manhattan

Oliver was in the same room and attached to the same machine he'd been strapped to the time Clara had accompanied him here. Hayley was sat where Clara had been sat but instead of spinning the beads on a statement necklace she was chewing at her nails. They'd been left alone but he didn't know what to say. What was there to say? Now everything was complicated. Ruined.

'Didn't think the morning after the night before I'd end up in the hospital,' Hayley remarked. 'I've done police stations before but never hospitals.'

'You should go,' Oliver said, his voice tight.

'Why do you keep saying that?' Hayley asked. 'What is it you're not telling me?'

Her voice told him he'd hit a nerve. How was he going to play this? Where was he going to go with this situation now? Last night he had had one of the best nights of his life, it had felt as close to real as he was ever going to get. Not just physical attraction but warmth, tenderness. The hot sex in the elevator had been one thing but when they'd come together on his balcony overlooking Central Park she'd come apart so completely, so honestly. What the hell had he been thinking? He had absolutely nothing to give her. He was like a convict on death row, biding time, just waiting to die. He had made this situation. He had let himself care. He had let *her* care. He'd had no right to do that. *Asking* her to leave now was too late. He'd just have to *make* her and he knew exactly how he was going to do that. However much it would hurt him it was his own stupid fault.

He put his hands to his chest and ripped a sucker from it.

'What are you doing? Don't do that,' Hayley said, her jaw dropping.

'Any second now a very attractive Dr Khan is going to walk through that door.' He ripped another sucker away. 'She's going to look me up and down and tell me I have stress and I work too hard.' Another sucker came off. 'She's told me this week already.'

He reached over the cabinet for his T-shirt and pulled it over his head.

'Is that what it is then?' Hayley asked. 'Stress?'

'So they say,' Oliver answered.

'What's that supposed to mean?' She pushed some errant hair back behind her ear. 'You really scared me in the apartment. I thought you were … having a heart attack or something.'

He wanted to laugh now. Make light of it. Tell her she was being ridiculous. He didn't have the energy.

'I'm fine,' he said, sliding himself off the bed.

'Are you sure?'

'I'm still breathing. Today must be my lucky day.' He used every last ounce of reserve energy he had to stand straight. The muscles in his abdomen rippled in response but he kept his expression neutral.

'Well, are you going to go back home? I can call us a cab,' Hayley suggested, getting to her feet.

'I can call a car,' he responded, taking the pulse monitor from his finger. 'You should get back to Angel.'

'Right, yeah, I should probably do that.'

Hayley's tone had his stomach squeezing hard. This was the right thing to do. The only thing. He gritted his teeth together.

'Have I done something wrong?' she asked.

He couldn't look at her. He didn't want to see the hurt expression he knew she would be wearing. What was he doing? This was practically killing him. He shook his head. 'No.'

'Then what the hell is going on here?'

'Nothing.'

'Oliver, last night I thought …'

'Listen, Hayley, last night, it was fun and …'

That had been overly flippant. He didn't want to hurt her. But maybe hurting her was what it would take.

'*Fun.*'

She had spat the word out. Those three letters felt so sharp. Each letter spiked his insides like a shard of ice. He looked at her then, out of the corner of his eye. She didn't realise now but he was doing it for her and she would one day see that. Because the second he had started to care, instead of arranging a date, he should have backed right off. Now, at the hospital, after this latest dramatic and unwelcome visit … he wasn't prepared to put her through anything like that again. And the one thing he could guarantee was there *would* be a next time.

'I've got a lot of business stuff going on at the moment so …'

'Of course you do,' Hayley said. She got to her feet, stuffing the clutch bag under her arm. 'And business is so important when seconds ago you were wired up to a heart machine.'

'Hayley …'

'No, there's … something wrong with you … in the head. I have no idea what it is and I don't want to know.' He watched her wet her lips. 'I thought last night … you were someone different. The guy I've got to know away from the captain of industry mantle and the power suit. The one who makes me laugh, the one who fights me for the last word.'

Her words were hitting every part of him like tiny poison darts sent to deliver a killer dose. He wanted to stop her. He wanted to smother her mouth with his and kiss her like he had last night. Show her how much she meant to him already. But he couldn't do it. It would be a selfish act and he had to be more unselfish than ever in this situation.

'But now I know it was just an act and I'm still just as naïve as I was all those years ago when I fell for the charms of another man.' She sighed. 'But at least he didn't pretend to be someone he wasn't.'

He swallowed. She couldn't have been more right about that. Not even *he* knew who he was. He had an idea of who he *wanted* to be, but with time running out did it even matter anymore?

'There's something you should know,' Hayley stated, flicking her hair back and adjusting her bag under her shoulder.

He looked at her directly then, giving her his full attention.

'I'm helping your mother organise the McArthur Foundation fundraiser.' A sigh left her. 'I didn't tell you because it's only just happened, quite spontaneously, and I knew that's where your mother had asked you to speak and how much you loathed it. And I thought if I kept *that* and *this* completely separate it could somehow not collide together and I could make it work.' She sniffed. 'But now I realise there is no *this* and perhaps I should have focussed on more of *that* and right now I definitely know I should have run the other way the second you asked me what my wish was.'

She was organising the McArthur Foundation fundraiser? His chest tightened all over again. Why would she be doing that? And she *knew* his mother? It gave him all the fuel he needed to hold onto his clenched jaw and his decision to end this.

A tear escaped her eye and began to slowly slide its way down her cheek. 'Goodbye, Clark.'

He watched her turn towards the door then she walked through it, disappearing from sight and slipping right out of his life.

CHAPTER FORTY-THREE

St Patrick's Hospital, Manhattan

'What the hell happened?' Tony burst through the door of the room where Oliver was still sat on the bed.

'Can you take me home?'

'That ain't a proper answer and don't we need to sign you out or something?'

'I've ended things with Hayley.'

If he said it out loud then it would become real and he could move on. He couldn't get the look on her face out of his damn mind. He'd made her believe she was no better than one of his Wish Women. Just thinking about the title she'd made up hit him where it hurt.

'You have got to be kidding me? Why? What happened? Tony exclaimed, running his hand through his hair.

'*This* happened!' He raised his hands to indicate his medical surroundings. Dr Khan had been in during the time it had taken Tony to get here and offered him more advice, including the one thing he was never going to consider. Why the word 'risk' scared him so much more in health than in business he didn't know.

'She stayed the night ... and this morning you did your whole collapsing thing and ... what? She freaked out?' Tony pieced together.

He shook his head. 'It was more like *I* did.'

Tony put his hands on his hips, sucking in his chest. Oliver could feel the displeasure from his friend. He didn't want a dressing-down here. He was perfectly capable of doing that himself. He just wanted to get home and focus on something else.

'I got it,' Tony said nodding. 'You met someone you actually care about. Someone you wanted to give more than one night to.'

Oliver took a stride towards the door of the hospital room. 'Really, Tony, I don't need to dissect it, I just need you to take me home.'

'Now she's seen you at your weakest. And she still stuck by you …' Tony continued. 'You're scared, if you make this more than one date, you're going to have to tell her the rest of it.'

Oliver turned on him then. 'And so what? She's better off without me. Everyone is!'

The volume of his voice shocked even him. He watched Tony close his mouth as if he had thought better of saying anything else. He didn't want to say anything else either.

'Please, Tony, no lectures. Just take me home,' he begged.

With that said his cell phone began to ring from the pocket of his jeans. He slid it out looking at the display. *Daniel Pearson.*

'Oliver Drummond.'

'Mr Drummond, it's Daniel Pearson.'

'You've got something for me?' He tightened his core.

'I've just spent a very interesting twelve hours shadowing Andrew Regis.'

'Go on.'

'Let's just say he didn't spend the night alone and I think you'll be very interested in who he shared his time with.'

'Let's meet,' Oliver said, biting his bottom lip as he looked at his friend.

'Just name the time and place.'

'Give me an hour and I'll meet you at Carly's Coffee House. D'you know it?'

'Yeah I know it.'

'Good,' he paused. 'Anything on Michel De Vos?'

Dean Walker's Apartment, Downtown Manhattan

Despite more snowfall and the freezing temperatures, Hayley had walked block after block before finally having the strength to go back to Dean's apartment. All the signs of Christmas – the trees on sale, the scent of apple, cinnamon and spiced wine, the carols coming from every store and street entertainer – seemed to be mocking her. *Happy Holidays! Why on Earth have you wasted your time messing about with a guy when you should be focussing on the whole reason you came to New York in the first place. Your daughter. The very first thing you saw him do was run out on a date. How could you be so naïve and think he would treat you any differently?*

She pushed back her shoulders and lifted her chin defiantly to the voices in her head. But it didn't stop a depth of sadness cloaking her. She had only known him a short while, but despite all her mental pep talks she had really liked him. *Really* liked him.

She braced herself before pressing the intercom of Dean's apartment. Angel didn't need to know anything about this and she could gloss over the details for Dean's benefit like she'd done so many times to get out of trouble when she was younger. Oliver Drummond was coming completely off her radar and her entire focus was now going to be on finding Michel and organising the McArthur Foundation fundraiser. Her priorities had become temporarily screwed and she was never going to let it happen again.

'Hello,' Dean's voice greeted. A yapping noise ensued, meaning Vernon and Randy were also there. Great! The whole lot of them scrutinising her and asking about the night before.

She put on an enthusiastic tone any voice artist professional would be proud of. 'Hey there, big brother! I'm back! And I've seen some bargain Christmas trees down the street. Isn't it time we got one?'

Carly's Coffee House, Downtown Manhattan

Daniel Pearson had passed Oliver the envelope a few minutes ago and the images were already starting to swim in front of his eyes. He looked hard at the photographs, barely able to believe what he was seeing. It couldn't be true, it was too outrageous, worse than anything he had imagined. He slipped the photos back into the envelope and threw them to the table. Taking a deep breath, he picked up his coffee cup.

'I don't believe it,' Oliver stated.

'I have all the audio you need. They made it really easy for me. They talked and did just about everything in his car.'

Oliver closed his eyes. 'Please, spare me.'

'What do you want me to do?' Daniel asked him.

'Nothing else, not yet. I need to deal with this personally,' he stated.

'Fine by me.' Daniel passed him a second envelope. 'The audio files are on a memory stick in there.'

Oliver shook his head. 'I just can't believe this.'

'You were suspicious of him, now you have your answers,' Daniel said.

'Yeah, I do. I'm just wondering how I'm going to tell my mother.'

'Rather you than me,' Daniel said, sipping at his drink.

'Exactly.' He hesitated for a moment, what he was going to ask next affecting him far more than it should. 'Any luck with the other issue?'

'Michel De Vos?' Daniel queried.

'Yeah.'

'Actually, yes,' Daniel answered.

A shiver ran over Oliver like a cold, uncomfortable sweat breaking out.

'He changed his name a couple of years ago. Now goes by Michel Arment. He's moved around quite a bit in the last few years but I should be able to get contact details by the end of the day.'

Oliver nodded. He almost had all the answers, not that it mattered any more. He drew his cell phone out of his pocket. 'Thanks, Daniel. The money will be in your account as usual and, as always, discretion is paramount here.'

Daniel nodded. 'It goes without saying.' He stood. 'Have a good afternoon.' He held out his hand and Oliver took it.

'You too.' He called up a number on his phone and pressed to dial. 'Hello, Dean?' He wondered whether he was public enemy number one right now in the Walker household. He deserved it. He'd made Dean a promise. He breathed out. But this was business. 'Dean, it's Oliver Drummond. Listen, can you spare me a half hour?'

CHAPTER FORTY-FOUR

Dean Walker's Apartment, Downtown Manhattan

Hayley had Dean's laptop, her phone, her idea's book and the Globe all set out on the breakfast bar, tapping at whichever appliance was going to give her the answers she needed.

'I want to go and get the Christmas tree now,' Angel announced, looking up from where she was brushing Randy.

'Maybe when your Uncle Dean gets back we can go and get it,' Vernon suggested. He turned the page of the broadsheet he was reading and tapped the seat of the sofa next to him. Randy jumped up and sat down and Angel tracked his every move with a brush.

Hayley bit the pen in her mouth. Her mind wasn't in this. It was still in a hospital room at St Patrick's. What had happened there? How had things gone so wrong so quickly?

She turned her attention to the drawing in her ideas book. The Crystalline Hotel ballroom, a rough draft of how she envisaged it looking. She really had no idea how she was going to be able to coordinate this fundraiser in so short a time. So far she had come up against every hurdle known to event managers. Things she wanted were out of stock, the chef was having issues no matter what she suggested and apparently balloons in New York didn't come in platinum.

Her phone rang and she checked the display eagerly. *Unknown number.* Had she really been hoping for Oliver? After everything she'd told herself about him, she was still subconsciously hanging out for his call. She needed to wise up. She pressed to answer just as Randy let out an irritated yelp.

'Hello.'

'Hello, is that Miss Walker?'

She didn't recognise the voice.

'Yes, are you calling about the flowers?'

'Er, no I …'

'You're from the lighting company?'

'No …'

'The radio equipment company?'

'I'm calling from the Fanway Gallery.'

'Oh!' Hayley's eyes immediately went to Angel who was already scrutinising her. 'Hello.'

'I'm just responding to your call the other day. I'm afraid we're not at all familiar with anyone by the name of Michel De Vos.'

Her heart sank for the second time that day but this time it went to basement level. Another dead end in the search. She was starting to think Michel had disappeared off the face of the planet. *Daily Planet. Hypnotising hazel eyes.* She needed fizzy wine. *Bollinger.* Why was her mind determined to crucify her?

'Miss Walker?' the caller asked.

'Sorry, thank you for … for taking the time to call back,' Hayley said. She ended the call, put the phone down and dropped her head with it. Why was everything so difficult?

'Who was on the phone?' Angel asked.

Hayley flipped her head up quickly, rubbing at her eyes. 'Oh just some woman about the thingy for the fundraiser.'

'What thingy?' Angel said, her attention now firmly away from the dog.

'The …' She had a list of things right in front of her. Why couldn't she think of one single thing to say? 'The … the …'

'Table displays?' Vernon offered, putting down his newspaper.

Hayley pointed at him. 'Yes! Exactly that!

'Maybe I can help.' Angel got to her feet and Randy jumped down from the sofa, walking to heel.

'You've already done so much, Genius Kid,' Hayley said, slipping an arm around Angel's shoulders and pulling her in for a hug.

Angel got up onto the stool next to her and looked at what Hayley had on the screens of her devices. She began to read aloud.

'*Oliver Richard Julian Drummond is the CEO of billion-dollar technology company, Drummond Global. He is the ...*'

Hayley snapped down the lid of the laptop before Angel could say anything else.

'*Michel De Vos, Argentina. Michel De Vos, Libya.* He isn't there, is he?' Angel exclaimed, reading the screen of Hayley's phone.

'I don't know where he is! That's why I'm looking!' She knew her voice was strained, but despite saying she was going to concentrate all her efforts on the fundraiser she hadn't been able to stop thinking about Oliver and the Finding Michel issue.

'*The McArthur Foundation – supporting parents, carers and sufferers. We are dedicated to enhancing the lives of the living and caring for the families who've lost.*'

Hayley turned the Globe upside down so its screen was facing the marble of the breakfast bar.

'Why were you reading about Mr Meanie?' Angel asked.

Hayley shrugged. 'Just getting some background information, that's all.'

'I wish Ben Drummond was still alive. He sounded way more fun,' Angel remarked.

'That's not nice, Miss Meanie,' Hayley told her.

'Cynthia liked my idea of creating the menu around the favourite foods of the family members who died,' Angel informed her, propping up her head with her hand.

'She did?' Hayley asked.

'Yeah. She said Ben loved shrimp.' Angel twirled her hair around her finger. 'Some weeks, when he was my age, they had to have barbecue every day.'

Hayley thought about Oliver this morning. He'd looked in so much pain before the ambulance arrived. She'd had to help him into a T-shirt and jeans. He'd leant on her for support and then he kicked her to the kerb the second he was feeling better. What was that all about?

'Can we go and get a tree now?' Angel asked again, batting her eyelids.

'What?'

'Angel, listen, you let your mom get on with her work and I promise we'll get the biggest tree that can fit in here, we'll take Randy for a run round the park *and* I'll shout us all waffles at Bernard's,' Vernon spoke up.

'Waffles? With chocolate and honey and ice cream?' Angel asked, turning her head to the man in the room.

'Whatever you want,' Vernon responded.

Hayley looked to him, catching his eye before mouthing a thank you.

Her phone made a bleep and her eyes shot to the screen.

Mother

Her eyes widened as she read the message, each word hitting like pins being poked into a newly-designed dress. She thought this day couldn't possibly get any worse. It just had. A lot worse.

I found your diary. Why are you trying to find that man?

Carly's Coffee House, Downtown Manhattan

Dean was practically ashen with shock at the business news but had been surprisingly polite. Oliver had expected nothing short of animosity over what had happened at the hospital. He couldn't believe Dean wouldn't have an opinion on it – boss or no boss – so he could only conclude that Hayley hadn't told him anything. Yet.

Regarding the business issue, Oliver had known deep down Dean would know nothing about it, but he'd had to check. He needed to be certain he could trust him with what came next.

'I don't believe it,' Dean uttered, his hand shaking as he reached for his coffee cup.

'Neither did I but there are photos and audio files.'

Dean cleared his throat. 'What do you need me to do?'

'I need you to come into the office with me and check all this out. There must be more evidence there.' He paused. 'I want to know everything about this relationship. I want to know how long it's been going on, the extent of it, the damage it's done and how we can rectify it all as quickly as possible without the company losing face.'

Dean nodded.

'I'm going to be asking you to hack into personal accounts. Can you do that?'

'Absolutely. You're the boss. And, if this has been going on right under my nose then I have a personal interest in putting it right.'

Oliver smiled. 'Thanks, Dean.'

'No problem.' He smiled. 'So, Hayley's keeping pretty tight-lipped but … how was your date last night?'

Masking the feelings that were erupting like an active volcano he reached for his coffee cup. *Empty.* A pang, like the snap of a rubber band, pinged in his chest. That was his confirmation that she hadn't told her brother what a dick he'd been. So just what did he say to it? The truth? That it was one of the best nights of his life? Or the other truth? It was one of the best nights of his life which he'd fucked up to protect her?

He smiled, putting on the best performance he could manage. 'You'll have to ask her about it.'

CHAPTER FORTY-FIVE

Pop-up Christmas Tree Lot, Near Central Park, New York

The text from Rita had been the last straw. The apartment had suddenly got claustrophobic. Words and sentences on all her devices had started to swim in front of Hayley's eyes. She needed to breathe, ground herself into the city. But it seemed as if the whole world was out buying Christmas trimmings. As she stood by the tree lot, she again took in Central Park in the afternoon. Just outside the gates were the lines of horses, carriages attached, waiting to take couples and families on a romantic tour of the city's sights. Just along from them were slightly less romantic open-top buses to do the same. The smell of hot dogs and sauerkraut made her lick her lips and remember that she hadn't eaten all day. It took a lot for her to go off food but Oliver's kick to the gut had done it. The only upside to the day was getting colour-coordinated drapes that weren't going to cost a wealthy sheikh's fortune.

'What about this one, Angel?' Vernon asked, pointing to a rather large, bushy spruce.

Angel wrinkled her nose. 'Not tall enough. You said we could get the biggest.'

'He said what?' Dean erupted.

Hayley watched Vernon laugh and move along the line of trees for another look.

'So how's it going with the fundraiser?' Dean asked, slipping his arm through Hayley's. This was it. Dean was warming up to asking her about the date with Oliver.

'It's going. Whether it all comes together for the night I have no idea. It needs to be perfect. I need to live up to a professional event planner who is still phoning Cynthia every four hours even though she can barely speak.'

Dean laughed. 'That's New York for you. People here aren't so good at letting go.'

'Hmm,' Hayley responded, her mind immediately going to Oliver.

'And what about Michel? Any luck there?' Dean had lowered his voice deliberately and Hayley shot her eyes to Angel who was scooping Randy up into her arms.

Hayley shook her head and put her hands into her hair as if a stress headache was about to burst forth at the mention of his name. 'I don't know what to do next, Dean. The only thing I can think of is getting a radio or TV announcement like they did in *Annie*. Knowing my luck it would be equally unsuccessful.'

'And Oliver could play the part of Daddy Warbucks?' Dean offered.

'That isn't funny.' Hayley pulled her hair at the mention of Oliver. And the fact her brother had just slotted him into a step-father role. That was never going to happen. And it was all proof that keeping her distance from dates in the past was the right thing to do.

She changed the subject slightly. 'How can a man just disappear like that? I'm coming to the conclusion that Michel gave me a false name. I mean we've all done it.'

'Have we?'

'I used to go out and tell men my name was Terri and I test-drove cars for Vauxhall.'

'You didn't!'

Hayley let out a heavy sigh. 'What am I going to do if I can't find him, Dean? I made Angel a promise, a promise I meant with all my heart. But what am I going to do if I can't deliver?'

Dean slipped his arm around her shoulders. 'She's had nine years without him. You're doing all you can. There's only so many stones to be upturned.'

'She might be intelligent but she's still nine and that isn't going to wash.'

'Well,' Dean started. 'There's only one other thing I can think of.'

'Anything. As long as it isn't appearing on Oprah.'

'It would be costly, but you could hire a private investigator,' Dean said.

'Are you kidding me? Is that really what people in New York do?' Hayley shook her head. 'I was thinking you were going to suggest looking at microfiches in the library.'

'Do they even exist anymore?'

'This is the one!' Angel yelled, one arm stuck inside the branches of a tree to rival the one in the lobby of Drummond Global. 'It's called Bruce!'

'Holy crap,' Hayley stated. 'Bruce the Spruce.'

Dean squeezed her arm in his. 'Listen, if you want to hire the P.I. then I can help you out with the money.'

'I couldn't do that, I …'

'You wouldn't be asking. I would be offering.' He patted her arm. 'Think about it.'

Hayley watched Angel dancing around the tree like it was a beloved totem pole and she was Hiawatha. Looking back to Dean she sighed. 'So, tell me about your day.'

'My day,' Dean said, a loaded sigh leaving his mouth. 'If I told you, I'd get fired. Which is pretty much what I thought was going to happen when I asked Oliver about your date.'

She hadn't got away with it at all. Dean still wanted to know and she was running out of other suitable topics. Mother might be her only other option. Hayley turned her face away from her brother as her cheeks reacted. She did not want to talk about it. The hurt and humiliation were way too fresh.

'Well, that sounds a lot easier to handle than getting a text from mum saying she's found my ten-year diary.' That should do it.

'Oh.My.God,' Dean said, putting his gloved hands to his face.

If Rita had started from 2015 and worked her way back ten years there was far worse to come than Hayley's search for Michel. And although it was all true – exactly how she'd really felt when she wrote the words – thinking of her mum, alone, near Christmas, reading the hurtful comments and quips was punching her with guilt. She'd thought about texting back, pleading with her not to read it, or calling and begging, but she knew it wouldn't do any good. The book had been opened and so had the can of worms.

CHAPTER FORTY-SIX

Dean Walker's Apartment, Downtown Manhattan

Hayley watched Angel flying around the newly erected Christmas tree like she was competing in a contemporary dance competition. Her arms stretched high, garlands of gold, silver, blue and red tinsel dripping from her fingers, then moving low, slipping bauble after bauble onto the outstretched boughs of the tree.

Mac Sullivan from the apartment next door had had to saw the bottom of the trunk off for them to even get it into the building. Angel's face had been a picture. Her words full of concern. *Don't hurt Bruce. That's more than thirty centimetres. Don't bend his arms.* Hayley smiled, watching Angel pat Randy on the head as she collected another sparkling decoration from Dean.

While her daughter was distracted Michel wasn't in her thoughts, but the closer Christmas got, Hayley knew the questions would be coming thick and fast. *Why haven't you found him? You promised.* Hayley put a line through another museum address on her print-out and picked up her phone.

The intercom bleeped and Dean got up off the floor to respond to it. 'Can we try and get it a little colour-coordinated?'

'Dean, it's a Christmas tree,' Vernon responded. 'Not an ornament.'

Pressing the button, Dean answered. 'Dean Walker.'

Hayley watched her brother raise his eyes as Vernon passed Angel a tacky, garish-looking fairy.

'Hey, Dean, it's Oliver,' the voice came back.

Hayley's stomach plummeted to somewhere close to down-the-escalators-at-Waterloo-Underground-Station level as she heard the voice that had been sending her erogenous zones into overdrive almost since she'd met him. She swallowed, quickly remembering it was also the same voice that had sent her packing this morning.

'Has something else happened?' Dean asked in a panicked voice.

'No, we're all good. I'm on my way to deliver the news actually.'

Something was going on with the business that she didn't know about. She wasn't privy to any of that now she was no better than a one-night stand. Again.

'Is Hayley there?'

Now her stomach was rushing, diving through the tunnels of the subway without stopping at any station along the way. What did he want? Hadn't he said all he needed to say earlier?

Dean looked over to her then, as if waiting for some sort of response. Hayley knew what he was thinking. She hadn't told him any of what happened the night before, but the very fact she hadn't waxed lyrical, or come out with any hilarious anecdotes told its own story. She should be shaking her head right now. She should be waving her hands and signalling that she wasn't there.

'Er…' Dean made the non-committal noise, his eyes widening as every millisecond ticked by.

'It won't take a minute, I promise,' Oliver said.

Huh, a promise meant little at the moment. And her physical reaction to his voice was betraying the level-headed side of her.

The side of her that wasn't going to let her guard down for any-one ever again.

'She's here. She's coming down,' Dean finally spoke.

Hayley sent her eyes out on stalks. Why had he done that? Hadn't he got the message that she didn't want to see him? Now Dean had taken the decision out of her hands. Now there was nothing she could do about it. She had to go and see what Oliver wanted. The most annoying thing about all of that was the flutter of something in her stomach that was utterly unwelcome. *Desire.* She now officially hated herself.

She slipped down from the bar stool. She could do this. She would go down there, let him say whatever he had come to say and be done with it as quickly as she could. Like a doorstep conversation with an election candidate.

'What's going on with you two?' Dean asked her.

She sighed. 'Let me pass on answering and I won't ask a thing about whatever is going down at Drummond Global.'

Dean closed his mouth like a drawbridge at a castle under threat of invasion and Hayley headed for the door.

Oliver was going to deliver this message and nothing else. When she walked out this morning he was adamant he wasn't going to see her again. Just being here was screwing him up, but he didn't have a choice. He sighed as he waited. He wasn't going to look into her eyes or drop his gaze to her lips or admire her defiant jaw which, under these circumstances, would definitely be defiant. He'd hurt her. At a time when she least needed it. She was vulnerable, in an unfamiliar country, looking for her daughter's father and he had treated her so badly. He pulled in a breath as the cold started to seep through his woollen coat and sink its way into his bones. He had to carry on treating her badly. It was the only way forward.

The door creaked open and light from the hallway framed her image. It was like someone had put his insides into a blender. He was turning into pulp right there on the step.

'Hi,' he greeted when the power of speech had come back to him. He cleared his throat, trying to get back on task.

'What are you doing here?'

It was the very to-the-point question he'd been expecting after everything that had happened at the hospital. He held out a gift bag.

Hayley shook her head. 'What's this? Something from Tiffany's to buy back my affections?'

He cleared his throat again. 'It's the bow tie and waistcoat we bought for Randy.'

He watched her expression change and she took hold of the bag, accepting it.

'Oh … thank you.'

She looked directly at him then, those eyes meeting his. He hurried on. There wasn't time to be distracted.

'So, I just wanted to give you that and also to … to give you this.' He passed forward the brown envelope he'd had tucked under his arm all the way here. It had felt like a bomb on a timer because, despite his honourable intentions, he was in deep and dire conflict about it. Half of him wanted to tear the papers to shreds and let them never see the light of day. The less selfish side of him, the pieces of the Oliver he aspired to be if he ever got his head straight, was urging him on.

Hayley took the envelope but, instead of looking at it, or tearing at it, she left her eyes on him. It was as if she were trying to see inside him and translate the contents without actually having to look.

Was she going to make him say the words? He blinked, breaking their connection for just a second. They shouldn't matter so much. He needed to think of it as a business deal. Fulfilling wishes was what he did after all.

'I found Michel,' he stated.

Hayley grabbed the railings at the top of the stone steps, immediately snapping her hand back as the frozen metal burnt her fingers.

'When I say found, I mean … someone I work with,' Oliver took a breath. 'Someone I use for difficult situations … I asked him to find Michel and in the envelope are his latest contact details.' He swallowed. 'There's an address, here in New York, and … a number.'

She looked at the envelope in her hands, disbelieving. Was the answer to Angel's dearest wish really held inside? After months of searching every place she could think of – every directory, every website, every different web provider – it seemed too good to be true. And all this was being delivered to her by the guy who stamped all over her heart only a few hours earlier. She smoothed her hands over the paper. Was this a trick? She jerked her head up then, facing Oliver.

'Is this for real?' She narrowed her eyes. 'Because I have a little girl up there I made a promise to and if this is just false hope …'

'It's not,' Oliver said. 'My source confirmed the location.'

'Can you please stop speaking "spy"?'

'He's spoken to his neighbours and he's seen him.' Oliver let out a sigh. 'It's an address in Brooklyn.'

Hayley shook her head. How could that be possible? How could he have been so close yet so impossible to track down? She couldn't stop the tears from spilling from her eyes, feeling so many sensations all at once. Hope. Joy. *Fear*.

As the salty tracks of her tears started to crystallise on her face she looked up at Oliver. She watched him put his hands in the pockets of his coat and tighten his jaw.

'Thank you,' she breathed.

He nodded. 'Well, I have a reputation for making women's wishes come true.' He swallowed. 'I couldn't let this one beat me.'

She watched him bite his bottom lip, as if he was thinking about what to say next. Why had he done this? Had he thought better about shutting her down at the hospital? She felt weak for even considering it.

'Listen,' he started. 'I just wanted to say … about the McArthur Foundation fundraiser.' He wet his lips. 'It's a great cause and … no matter how I feel about it … even though it's not my bag …' He stopped, like he didn't know what he had started to say. 'You're going to make it an incredible event.'

She needed to say something. He had come over here with Angel's wish in his hands. His hazel eyes were full of emotion and those pert lips she'd kissed so hungrily looked more delicious and tempting than an open tin of Quality Street. If she took a step towards him what would he do? She slid one foot through the dusting of snow.

He stepped back and her heart fell. This was goodbye.

'Well, I'd better head off … lots to do' Oliver smiled at her. 'Goodbye, Lois.'

She swallowed the knot of emotion clogging up her throat. Her heart and libido were telling her to stop him as she watched him take the steps down to the pavement. He turned back and she held her breath. He waved a hand then pulled the handle of the waiting town car and slipped into the back seat. She sighed, watching her breath spiral in the freezing air and whispered into the night. 'Goodbye, Superman.'

CHAPTER FORTY-SEVEN

Mancinis Restaurant, Tenth Avenue, Manhattan

Oliver had picked a booth in a back corner of the restaurant. He'd ordered a Scotch and a jug of water then spent the last five minutes straightening everything on the table into a slightly different place. How was this going to go down? The images were etched on his brain but the betrayal bit him more than anything. His father's best friend. When had that stopped counting for something?

'Oliver.' His mother's voice drove him from his reverie and he got to his feet quickly.

Cynthia looked effortlessly chic as always in an ice blue shift dress that brought out the colour of her eyes. Oliver leant forward, kissing her first on one cheek, then the other.

'You're early,' he remarked, his eyes shifting to Cynthia's companion.

There he was. Andrew Regis, wearing that old-school three-piece suit combination he always wore. Head glossy, cheeks coloured by spidery red veins. He thought the extent of his betrayal was this relationship with his mother and that article in the magazine questioning Oliver's leadership. How wrong he'd been.

'Andrew.' Oliver held his hand out to him, going against everything his body's engine was telling him to do.

'Oliver,' Andrew responded, grasping the offering and giving it a firm, professional shake.

Both men waited for Cynthia to slip into the booth before taking their seats. Oliver poured his mother a glass of water and went to offer the jug to Andrew's glass.

Andrew put his hand over the tumbler. 'Why don't we have a nice bottle of red?'

'What a good idea,' Cynthia agreed, picking up a menu. 'Then we can clear the air properly and start moving forward.'

Oliver swallowed, not able to raise a smile at his mother. How was she going to feel about this? Her first venture into the relationship arena since Richard's death and this! He wasn't going to soft soap the business side of things. She was on the board. It was her right to know, just like all the other members he was going to have to explain it to. The other part ... He put his hand to his tie and slackened the knot. He didn't think he could do it to her. He forced a smile. 'I couldn't agree more.'

Cynthia had done an excellent job of keeping the flow of conversation going until the starter arrived. Now, every mouthful of the mushroom-filled ravioli was turning Oliver's stomach. He shouldn't be sitting with this disgusting liar of a man. He should be dragging him out into the street and giving him the kicking of his life.

'Only a week until Christmas and they say the weather is going to turn,' Cynthia continued. 'I'm hoping the forecasters are wrong. A little snow is traditional this time of year but a storm cutting off the city is something no one wants.'

Oliver nodded his head up and down. He'd been doing that a lot. He wasn't sure he could offer up niceties in the circumstances.

'Brings everything to a halt. Workers can't make it to work, nothing gets done,' Andrew chipped in.

Silence descended again and Oliver forced another forkful of food into his mouth.

'Right, well, seeing as the atmosphere here is decidedly frostier than it is outside, I think it's time we addressed this head on.' Cynthia threw her napkin down on the table.

Oliver put his fork down onto his plate and leaned back against the fabric seat of the booth. He watched Andrew's movements. The man picked up his glass of red wine and put it to his lips. The lips no amount of lies had fallen out of.

'No one got anything to say? Fine, I'll start,' Cynthia said, a heavy breath coming from her lips. 'Oliver, I owe you an apology.'

He sat up a little more and pulled the cuffs of his shirt into line.

'I should have told you about my relationship with Andrew personally and I should have told you weeks ago.' Cynthia looked to Andrew, reaching for his hand. Oliver clenched his teeth tight together at the show of solidarity as Cynthia continued. 'It's a difficult time of year for us all and I thought it was better to wait until the New Year before going public.' She swallowed. 'But that wasn't fair on you, Andrew.'

It felt as if Jesus' tombstone was clogging his airway. He couldn't sit here and listen to much more of this, watching Andrew create this fantasy right in front of him.

Andrew patted Cynthia's hand, looking into her eyes like a lovesick puppy. The ravioli started to repeat. He'd had enough.

'I have something I'd like to say,' Oliver spoke up. He cleared his throat and picked up the file of paperwork on the seat next to him. He flicked the pages, his thumb making the dust between the sheets fly up into the air.

'I'm hoping it's going to be that you're putting the merger of the two companies back on the table,' Cynthia stated.

Oliver shook his head. 'No.' He looked to Andrew. 'But that will be perfectly OK with Andrew because he never really wanted it in the first place.'

He held the older man's gaze, looking to see if these first words would start everything dropping into place.

'Oliver,' Cynthia said. 'Why would you say something like that? That article in *Business Voice* was nothing but bravado. Andrew knows it was the wrong thing to do and he's going to print a retraction as soon as the deal is back on the table.'

'You're not listening, Mom.'

'He's right,' Andrew responded. 'I had my doubts at first.'

Oliver baulked. Was he about to confess? He hadn't been expecting that.

'I wasn't sure to begin with, Cynthia. You know Richard and I always had very different views on the direction of our businesses.' He sighed. 'That was always the reason we never worked together. But when you raised your concerns about Oliver's ability to carry the company forward, I knew I had to look at it again.'

'You liar!' Oliver let every drip of loathing come out along with the words. 'That isn't true.'

'Oliver.' The plea came from Cynthia.

He was hit by the expression on his mother's face. She did have concerns but not about Andrew, about *him* and his ability to run Drummond Global. This was so wrong. He couldn't delay the inevitable any longer.

'Don't say anything else, Mom.'

'Oliver, I know you've found things tough this past year and all the support the board has tried to offer you've categorically turned down. I didn't know what else to do,' Cynthia continued.

'If you or the board had a problem you should have come to me,' Oliver stated.

'You always shut me down.'

'That's just not true.' Oliver shook his head.

Cynthia sniffed, tears forming. 'I was trying to protect you, hoping you would work it out for yourself. I know running this business isn't what you dreamed of but it's your father's and Ben's legacy. I thought at least that meant something to you.'

It was like his mother had stamped on his chest with her court shoes on. Was that how she really felt? Did she think that he didn't care because it wasn't his dream? Before the Globe, his father and Ben were the only reasons he had for driving the company on.

'The two companies merging was for your benefit, Oliver, not mine,' Andrew stated, looking pious.

Oliver drew his lips into a firm line. 'Bullshit.'

'Oliver!' Cynthia exclaimed.

He snapped open the file of papers and pushed them past the water jug, into the middle of the table.

'The merger was a distraction, nothing more. He never wanted it to happen. The only reason he got so distressed when I called a halt on it was because he wasn't sure he had enough time to implement his real plan, the one he's been working on since my father died.' Oliver glared at Andrew. 'If I hadn't pulled Drummond Global out of the deal, you would have done it yourself. Because it was all fabricated.'

'What?' Cynthia said, looking to Andrew.

'As is your relationship with my mother,' Oliver continued. He was gritting his teeth now, trying to maintain his cool but wanting to reach across the table and grab this excuse for a man by the scruff of his neck.

'I have no clue what you're talking about,' Andrew said, throwing his napkin down onto the table.

Andrew looked rattled now. His cheeks a little redder, his forehead beading with perspiration. The man was finally starting to realise what was about to go down. Soon, when all his deception was laid bare, he was going to be on his knees begging for mercy.

Oliver found the relevant page in the file on the table. 'Mom, the whole merger was simply a distraction. It was all just a diversion tactic so we were both off our game. You'd be caught up in your love affair and I'd be caught up looking at clauses that didn't matter, while Andrew here used one of my employees to pass him classified information.'

He watched Cynthia's reaction, saw her shift her hand away from Andrew's. 'What is he talking about, Andrew?'

'I have no idea, but I'm not going to sit here and be accused of something so absurd.' Andrew got to his feet. 'I wasn't sure about coming tonight but your mother insisted. And,' He drew a breath. 'It's that time of year – reconciliation, peace and goodwill to all men and all that jazz. I thought I owed you the chance to apologise …'

'I have nothing to apologise for,' Oliver exclaimed. 'You on the other hand …' He narrowed his eyes at Andrew. 'I've been through Peter Lamont's emails. He may have deleted, emptied and cleared history and all the usual kind of stuff, but I found all the evidence I need.'

'Show me,' Cynthia said. 'Sit down, Andrew.' Her tone was fierce.

'This is preposterous,' Andrew stated, sinking down into his seat.

Oliver looked to his mother. 'Mom, I don't think you should be reading the emails.'

'Why not? If he's been deceiving me I want to see it with my own eyes.'

Oliver pulled the file back towards him. 'All you need to know is Peter Lamont has been passing him details of the Globe in order for him to launch his own tablet before we do. Similar specifications, slightly modified, but basically a carbon copy of something my technicians have been working on for the past year.'

Now Andrew was the colour of someone who might explode at any moment. Cynthia dragged the file towards her, her eyes roving over the text.

'I've nothing to say,' Andrew started. 'This is all a big mis-understanding. We were about to become one company, Peter Lamont was simply pre-empting what was going to happen in a few weeks – the merger, the two companies joining forces and aligning their plans.'

'That wasn't for you or Peter Lamont to decide and it's too late. I know *everything*.' He emphasised the word 'everything' to leave no doubt.

His mother was still looking at the emails, if she turned over too many pages she would get to the photographs. He didn't want her to see them. Oliver put the flat of his hand over the file and pulled it back towards him.

'Mom, you've seen enough,' Oliver said, swallowing.

Oliver shifted his eyes sideways, looking to Andrew, who was at least having the decency to appear awkward and uncomfort-able now.

'Just believe me that whatever you think you had with this man, it wasn't real,' Oliver stated.

Cynthia turned in her seat, her eyes boring into Andrew, him looking straight ahead into the mid-distance.

'I want to know, Oliver,' Cynthia said, her voice determined yet mixed with fear.

Oliver picked up his glass of red wine and swallowed it in one gulp, then he took a deep breath and reached across the linen cloth for his mother's hand. He gently pressed their skin together in, what he hoped, was a show of solidarity.

'He wasn't just having business dealings with Peter Lamont.' Oliver swallowed. 'He's been sleeping with him.'

Andrew leapt up then, his wine glass falling to the floor, the table rocking so much the plates all shifted. Cynthia took back her hand, plastering it to her mouth as shock set in.

'I've never heard anything so ridiculous in my life and you need to keep your voice down because accusations like that are very dangerous things to make,' Andrew said, pointing a finger at Oliver.

Cynthia was starting to cry, hiding her face away in a napkin, her body directed towards the wall. He wanted to ease her pain but he wasn't sure what he could do now apart from get rid of Andrew as quickly as possible with the minimum amount of fuss.

'Unfortunately for you, and for me, because I had to listen to it … I have full audio detailing far more than I ever wanted to know.'

A sob came from Cynthia then and Oliver got to his feet.

'I will make this very public by tomorrow unless you put a halt to your copycat production plans. You will go on record retracting that article shaming me and my company and you will cite stress as the cause of your mental breakdown that led to the merger folding. Other than that I don't care how you spin your way out of this, but you do not slander me, my mother, or Drummond Global or I swear to God I will be handing a memory stick over to my PR girl and she will finish you with it!'

Oliver was shaking violently, his whole body tremoring as fury shot from every pore. This man disgusted him. If his father could see him now, his best friend, lying and cheating, betraying Cynthia, dragging the Drummond name through the dirt, he wouldn't be able to stop himself physically attacking him.

'Go!' Oliver ordered. 'Get out of this restaurant and get out of our lives. I don't want to ever see your face again!'

He held himself steady as Andrew turned to look at Cynthia. The man opened his mouth to speak but, perhaps thinking better of it, he slid himself out of the booth. Oliver watched him collect his coat from the rack on the back wall and walk towards the door.

'He's gone,' Oliver said, his voice barely more than a whisper.

'Oh, Oliver,' Cynthia said, the tears flowing freely.

'It's OK, Mom,' Oliver said, sitting down and reaching for her hand once more.

'I had no idea. You have to believe me. When he did that magazine article I was furious and ...' Cynthia started.

'Sshh, it's OK, I know.' Oliver swallowed. 'He fooled us all.'

He squeezed his mother's hand and swallowed back the bile in his throat. This was what happened when you put your faith in someone and took your eye off the ball. He was never going to make the same mistake again.

CHAPTER FORTY-EIGHT

The Crystalline Hotel, Manhattan

Hayley hadn't slept at all and was operating on sugar-infused lattes a waitress was bringing her every hour. She held a tape measure up to the window, popping up on tiptoes to reach the top.

'I can help!' Angel exclaimed, leaping up from a chair and slamming shut her special dictionary.

'It's OK,' Hayley said, her spine straining as she stretched.

'Let me,' Angel said. She began pulling a chair across the parquet floor, the noise jabbing at every one of Hayley's irritation senses.

'It's fine, Angel. Stop doing that before you scratch the very expensive floor.' Her eyes went to the sleek wooden blocks. A scratch about twelve inches long stood out like Rudolph in the reindeer pack.

Hayley put her hands into her hair, preparing to scream. This was all she needed. Her deliveries for the fundraiser hadn't arrived and now her daughter was intent on wrecking the venue. Did she dare called Rebecca Rogers-Smythe and ask how best to remove a scratch from vintage parquet?

'I'm really sorry, Mum,' Angel said, her eyes going from the mark on the floor to Hayley and back again.

This was all Oliver's fault. She shook her head. No, that wasn't fair, it wasn't Oliver's fault. What he'd done was thoughtful and amazing but that hadn't stopped the contents of the brown envelope practically searing her skin the entire night. After Oliver had left, Hayley had slunk to her bedroom and stared at the envelope. While screams and shouts came from the living room, where it sounded like Randy was trying to tear down Bruce the Spruce, she'd tore open the seal and taken out what was inside.

There were only three pieces of A4 printer paper. One piece detailed contact information for a Michel Arment. The other was a copy of a driving licence. The third was a photo. Hayley didn't need to look at the photo for long. There were no doubts. This man was the one she'd spent a night with. Angel's father.

'It's OK,' she breathed, putting an arm around Angel and pulling her into an embrace. 'I've been cranky since the orchid lady didn't show up.' She stroked a hand over Angel's hair. Did she tell her daughter yet? Should she call Michel first? There was so much riding on what she did next it was almost too much to cope with.

Angel lifted her head, smiling as she looked up at Hayley. 'Randy looked so cute in that outfit you bought him, didn't he?'

Hayley smiled. 'No fashion alerts needed for that pooch. And I think Uncle Dean was secretly jealous of the waistcoat.'

Angel laughed. 'That's what Vernon said.'

Hayley's eyes went over to the scratch on the wood. 'Listen, why don't you go and sweet-talk the waitress into getting me another latte and I'll see if I can find something to get rid of the mark.'

'I could see what my special dictionary suggests,' Angel offered.

'Good idea.'

The Drummond Residence, Westchester

Oliver opened his eyes, blinking at the unfamiliar surroundings for a moment, until the night before came back to him. He was at home, his family home in Westchester. His old bedroom.

There was still a poster of the New York Giants from 1994 on the wall. He sat up and smoothed his hands over the shadow of stubble on his face. He felt like he'd drunk a bottle of Scotch and then been run over by a snowplough.

There was a soft knock on the bedroom door and he pulled the covers up a little. It would be Sophia with coffee.

'Come in,' he called.

The door opened a crack and Cynthia popped her head around it. 'Good morning.'

'Hey, Mom,' he greeted.

Cynthia stepped in. He was surprised to see her dressed in casual slacks and a Rangers sweater. He couldn't remember the last time she'd dressed down. But it wasn't just her clothing that was slightly off, she looked exhausted, obviously worn from everything that had happened last night.

I brought you some coffee,' she stated, moving to put the mug down on the nightstand. 'I thought you might need it.'

'Thanks,' he responded. 'It was some night.'

'Yes, I won't disagree about that.'

He picked up the mug, taking a drink, before returning it to the nightstand.

'So, we talked about Andrew all last night.'

'Yes we did.'

'Now how about we talk about you?' Cynthia suggested.

The question made him shift in the bed, his hands going back to the mug and lifting it again. 'You said it yourself last night, you and the rest of the board don't have confidence in me to lead Drummond Global.'

'Oliver, that isn't quite what I said.'

'I'm not saying you're wrong either.' He put the mug back on the nightstand. 'I admit, these last few months my focus has shifted.' He swallowed. 'And my health hasn't been so good.'

He waited for his mother to react. She had no clue about anything that had happened recently. He watched her take it on board.

'Tell me, Oliver.' There were tears in her eyes. 'I can't help you unless you talk to me.'

What was he going to say here? He didn't want to put any more on her plate after the shock of last night. But was it fair to hold off? He knew he would likely cause his mother more anxiety by keeping it to himself rather than laying it all out there.

'I've been having pains … in my chest … shallow breathing … rapid pulse.' Just thinking about it felt like he was calling on an attack.

Cynthia's hands went to her mouth and she stifled a sob. 'Oh, Oliver.'

'Mom, I think it's only a matter of time.'

New York Public Library, Bryant Park

After a morning filled with organisation for the McArthur Foundation fundraiser, Hayley had spared the afternoon to tick off one of the "must-sees" on Angel's list of New York sights. The New York Public Library. Following this visit her plan was to leave Angel with Dean while she checked out the intel on Michel. She wasn't going to be one hundred per cent convinced of anything until she saw Michel in the flesh, here, actually in New York. After so many dead ends and false leads, she was still cautious and she wasn't sure quite how to feel. Of course it was what she wanted. Finding him for Angel. But piece by tiny piece it was becoming reality and she wasn't sure what happened after that.

I never realised I was such a "witch dressed by Debenhams".

Her mother had sent another text. Rita was starting to get to the good stuff. In some ways it was a relief the diary had been found. She swallowed. Did she really mean that? Had she always wanted Rita to know what she was thinking? Being an ocean away made it slightly easier to deal with and there was so much going on right now it wasn't riding high on her list of priorities.

'You do know you're not supposed to have your mobile on in a library,' Angel whispered.

'Show me the sign,' Hayley responded.

'Sshh!' Angel hissed as they walked into the Rose Main Reading Room.

'I know books are important and interesting but why was it you wanted to come here?' Hayley asked, touching icons on the screen of her phone.

'Wow!' Angel said, looking up and around her.

At her daughter's exclamation, Hayley took her eyes off the phone and looked too. Light flooded in from the arched windows on both sides of the grand room. Chandeliers hung from a ceiling that was ornately carved, paintings of cloud and blue sky at its centre. Ancient-looking wooden tables and chairs filled the floor space and underneath the large windows were rows and rows of books occupying a full-length balcony and the walls below.

'It looks like something out of Hogwarts,' Angel said, her tone awe-coated.

Hayley jumped as her phone began to trill, prompting a death stare from Angel.

'Wait right here, I'll find a place I can talk. Don't move,' she ordered, rushing to the door they had just walked through.

'Hello? Yes, this is Hayley Walker … oh hello Sally-Anne, how did you get on? Can they do what I want with the lights?'

When Hayley returned to the reading room, Angel was sat at a table, a giant book open in front of her.

'Is that a really big bible?' Hayley joked, pulling up the chair next to her.

'Actually it's an encyclopaedia.'

'This is what we used to use before we had Wikipedia,' Hayley informed. 'Does it have "aardvark" and "anteater" with pictures?'

Angel looked up. 'Did you never get past the "A" section?'

'"Bison" and "buffalo". See if they have two separate entries for what's basically the same thing.'

'Who was on the phone?' Angel asked, turning a page.

'Sally-Anne from the lighting company. It's a go for that effect I wanted.'

'The one *I* suggested, you mean.'

'OK, clever clogs, it was all your initial idea but I followed it through.'

'And is the menu all done? You know, the idea *I* had about including food the family members loved?' Angel batted her eyelashes at her.

Hayley folded her arms across her chest. '*I* came up with the slogan.'

Angel patted her arm. 'So how much else have you got to do?'

'Not as much as I had to do yesterday.'

'That's good then,' Angel responded. 'So apart from Nanny being mad with you, everything is fine.'

'How do you know Nanny's mad with me?' She coughed. 'Not that she is or anything.'

'Uncle Dean got a text this morning. It said something about a lifeguard and how could he have kept secrets about you from her.'

Oh God. Daytime television had definitely been sacrificed for diary reading.

'She isn't happy about us looking for my dad, is she?' Angel stated. 'I saw the other message she sent you. She called him "that man" again.'

Hayley closed her eyes, taking a second before opening them again. 'I've never really listened to what Nanny had to say about most things.' She sighed. 'And about your dad … she's wrong.'

The details about Michel were in her rucksack. She could pull them out now and tell Angel he'd been found. But she knew what would happen. Dancing would ensue, eyes brightening like a neon bar sign, mouth opening in wonder as if she was Dorothy in *The Wizard of Oz* discovering the Yellow Brick Road. She had to play this carefully and protect Angel. Above all, she needed to tell Michel he had a daughter before they came face to face. A shiver ran over her.

'Nanny's met a man called Neville,' Angel informed her matter-of-factly. 'He plays bowls.'

'What?' Hayley shook her head, trying to get her mind back in the moment.

'She told Uncle Dean that before she started getting mad about a lifeguard.' Angel's voice echoed around the cavernous room.

Dean was going to kill her for writing about the lifeguard. 'Sshh!' Hayley said. 'We don't want to be chucked out of the library. They probably inform that scary man at the desk at the airport and he has our fingerprints.'

'Did you know that the fingerprinting system for criminals was introduced in New York in 1906?'

'I didn't know that.' She swallowed. Who was Neville? She knew she didn't listen to everything her mother said but mention of bowls and a man would have spiked her radar. 'So, anyway … about your dad.' She cleared her throat as quietly as she could. 'Nanny only says things like that because she worries about us.'

'So she likes my dad?'

'Angel, she doesn't know your dad.' Hayley paused. 'But she does know us and she doesn't want either of us to get hurt, that's all.'

Angel wrinkled her nose. 'I don't know if I agree with Nanny playing bowls with Neville.' She sniffed. 'We don't know him at all.'

'No, we don't,' Hayley agreed. 'But, like us, Nanny's going to do what she feels is right.' She sighed. 'Let's just hope Neville likes gardening programmes.'

Neville could be a good thing. So could bowls, no matter how that sounded. A little social activity, her mother getting out of the house and away from re-runs of *Escape to the Country*.

Hayley turned her attention back to her phone. She typed out a text, being careful not to show Angel.

Dean: Can you have Angel for me later? Got a lead on Michel.
P.S. Sorry Mum knows all about the lifeguard xxx

CHAPTER FORTY-NINE

Kingston Avenue, Brooklyn

Hayley checked the address on the paper again. This couldn't be where Michel lived, it was too … big. The brownstone she was looking up at had one large door at its centre and an arched window either side. Above were two more storeys. It had to be converted into apartments, didn't it? Either that or he was a highly successful artist or something else now. She swallowed and thought about phoning him again. Three calls before she'd set off from Dean's apartment had proved fruitless and she couldn't bring herself to leave a message. *Hi, I'm Hayley. You might not remember me, but we met ten years ago and I had your daughter.* Ringing the bell and having a face to face was the only way.

She walked up the steps to the entrance and drew in a heavy breath. What was she going to say? How did she start? Would he even remember her? This situation called for every ounce of bravery she had.

She pressed the bell and waited. Beyoncé's 'Single Ladies' erupted from the bottom of her rucksack. She ignored it, looking through the glass of the door for any signs of movement. The phone persisted, the whole of the first verse and the start of the chorus. No one was coming to the door. Hayley unzipped her rucksack and ferreted her hands around the contents to retrieve the phone. *Dean.*

'Hello,' she answered.

'Hey, er, you need to come back here,' Dean said without further explanation. He sounded guarded, like he couldn't speak because someone was holding a gun to his head. Or something bad involving Angel had happened. Her heart jumped at that thought.

'What's happened? Is Angel OK?' She put a hand to her chest as palpitations threatened.

'Angel's fine ...' Dean lowered his voice. 'You won't believe this, Hayley.' He whispered. 'Michel is here.'

Manhattan Wheelers' Football Ground, Manhattan

'Come on, Danny! Hurt them!'

Oliver had heard Tony's voice as soon as he started mounting the bleachers at the game. Every step he took towards his friend in the midst of the middle row brought back memories. The grass was still speckled with snow where ground workers had cleared it, and the bright white lines on the turf were freshly marked. He inhaled, smelling the grease of the burgers and fries from the catering van, just a hint of liniment and sweat. The shouts from the players and the barracking from the stands had once been comforts, now they just taunted him.

He excused himself past other spectators until he was next to Tony. His friend was red-faced, Manhattan Wheelers beanie on his head and half a hot dog hanging from his mouth.

'Room for another one?' Oliver asked, already sinking to the bench. He pulled his hat further down his head and blew on his fingers.

Tony dropped his hot dog roll to the floor. 'Jeez! Are you trying to give me a heart attack?' He stuffed the remaining sausage between his teeth. 'No pun intended there by the way.'

Oliver shook his head, a smile on his face. 'What's the score?'

'They're getting their asses kicked and Danny's playing like he's never seen a ball before.' Tony got to his feet, gesticulating hard to one of the players. 'What the hell was that? Are you insane?!'

Danny was Tony's fifteen-year-old nephew who had always been touted by Tony as the star player of the outfit. But Oliver also knew that Uncle Tony was hard to please.

'So what are you doing here? You haven't been here since …' Tony started, retaking his seat.

'Since my father died,' Oliver stated. For a long time after his dream of playing professional football was gone he'd come along to these small-time games with Tony and Richard. He knew it made his father feel better, thinking they could share something that wasn't connected with Drummond Global.

'Well, if I'm honest with you, you haven't missed that much.' Tony stood again. 'Will you look at that, referee?! You're killing me right now!'

Oliver waited for Tony to sit back down before speaking again. 'One of my employees was giving Andrew Regis the heads-up on my new tablet.' Oliver put his hands into the pockets of his woollen coat. 'He had no intention of merging with Drummond Global he just wanted to steal our ideas.'

'The sneaky bastard! I knew he couldn't be trusted. Didn't I say he couldn't be trusted?' Tony exclaimed. 'So what happens now?'

'I don't know really. I try to get my life in order I guess.'

'You're going to suck it up and go home for Christmas?'

'Maybe. Sophia and Pablo were both there this morning doing their very best to convince me.'

'And you're gonna book a couple of tables at the McArthur Foundation fundraiser? Put me down for two seats, I'm sure I can score a plus-one by then.'

The fundraiser was the only thing Oliver and Cynthia hadn't discussed. He knew she would still want him to speak and he wasn't prepared to change his mind about that.

'I'm going to take some time out.'

'Yeah, of course you are,' Tony said. 'And that was Santa Claus right there, flying over the Hudson.'

Oliver smiled. 'I'm serious.' He needed to do what was best for the company and, more importantly, he needed to do what was best for him. He didn't want to spend whatever time he had left being so dissatisfied with everything that he made himself and every single person around him miserable.

'Oh, jeez, Oliver, you're not going to make a bucket list are you? I'm not freaking asking you what *your* wish is.' Tony leapt up again. 'Danny, that quarterback is making a monkey out of you.'

'I thought I might try making pizzas for a while. You got any work going?'

Tony laughed out loud. 'You're freaking me out now, man.'

Oliver slapped him on the back.

'So, tell me, where does Hayley feature in these "time out" plans?' Tony focussed all his attention on Oliver then.

He swallowed, still a little surprised that the mention of her name moved him so much. Had she called Michel? Of course she had. Finding her daughter's father was her whole reason for coming to New York.

'Listen, I spent an evening watching you with her. You lit up like the Rockefeller Christmas tree just from conversation,' Tony told him. 'And then there was the whole foot thing.'

Oliver shot him a look of disdain. 'Tony Romario, you are perverted.'

'Yeah,' Tony nodded. 'Maybe I am. But you're a fool.' He rubbed his hands together. 'Tell the girl you're dying and let her make her own decisions. Not ones you've made for her.'

CHAPTER FIFTY

Dean Walker's Apartment, Downtown Manhattan

Dean opened the front door and Hayley bowled through it. 'You'd better tell me exactly what he said to you and what you said to him and what Angel said to anybody.'

'Slow down,' Dean said. 'Take a breath.' He followed her towards the stairs.

'Take a breath?! He's up there with the daughter he doesn't know he has. Why didn't he just ring?! Why did he have to turn up here? What's he even doing here?'

'I know, it's Sod's Law.'

'I want to kill Sod right about now.' She put a hand to her head, trying to press away the tension with her fingers.

'What do you want me to do? Do you want me to take Angel out somewhere so you can talk to him alone? I'll do whatever you want me to do. Just tell me,' Dean said.

'What have you said to him? What have you said to Angel?'

'He knocked on the door, he said he was looking for you, that you'd left this address at Vipers.' Dean sighed and put his hand to his head as he recalled the scene. 'I asked him in, I said you wouldn't be long, I made him a coffee, I told Angel he was a friend and …'

Hayley clamped a hand to her mouth. 'Oh my God, no, Dean, she knows it's him. I showed her a photo!' She ran up the stairs, taking them two at a time, and burst into the main room, her breath catching in her throat. The scene before her stole what little breath she had left.

Angel was sat on the arm of the sofa holding a foolscap pad and there he was, Michel, Angel's father, sat next to his daughter, sketching with her. He looked completely unchanged. He was wearing jeans and battered Converse sneakers, a tie-dye T-shirt, his hair still tousled.

'So,' Hayley started, making herself move. 'What's going on here then?'

Angel looked up, a serene yet slightly scary smile on her face. 'Michel is here.'

'I can see that,' Hayley stated, stepping closer.

'Hello, Hayley,' Michel greeted, putting the pad down and standing up. He stepped forward and quickly kissed her on both cheeks. Angel started to clap and Hayley shot a look to Dean for some help.

'So, Angel, let's go find Randy and Vernon and take them for a walk,' Dean offered, taking his niece by the arm.

'But I don't want to. I want to stay here,' Angel protested, pulling a scowl.

Hayley swallowed. 'Angel, please, go with Uncle Dean.'

Michel had walked into this situation with absolutely no prior warning. She needed to tell him in a controlled way, so he had a chance to react to it without Angel being here. He deserved that at the very least.

Angel folded her arms across her chest and looked indignant. 'It's not fair.'

'Double waffles and hot chocolate?' Dean tempted. 'Let's get your coat.' He shepherded Angel from the room and Hayley collapsed into the chair opposite Michel. How did she begin? When she eventually found the strength to meet his eyes, he was gazing back at her.

'You have done something a little different with your hair,' he started.

'You haven't.'

He smiled, put a hand to it. 'It has been a long time since we saw each other last.'

'You do remember then?' Hayley asked. 'One wild night under the influence of wine and vodka.'

'But, of course. It is impossible to forget someone who wore a neon pink dress and danced so crazy.'

She blew out a breath. That was something. Not that it would make it any easier. 'You changed your name.' *And it was agony trying to find you*, she wanted to add.

'Yes, for my job. It was a suggestion from my agent. He thought Michel Arment had more appeal.'

'Wow,' Hayley stated. 'An agent.'

'So, you live here now? In New York?' he asked her. 'With the man that was here?'

She shook her head. 'No. Dean's my brother. I'm just visiting.' She swallowed. 'I still live in England. *We* live in England.'

He nodded. 'I have travelled quite a lot. I go back to Belgium for a time, then to France, but I come back here two years ago. My art goes well here, people like it and they buy it.'

'That's good,' Hayley nodded.

She watched Michel's eyebrows knit together as he looked at her. 'You want to catch up? To go out together?' he asked. 'That is why you try to find me?'

She shook her head. 'Not exactly, no.'

'Then ...'

She squeezed her eyes tight shut. If she could pay someone to come in and deliver this news for her then she would. Like a kissogram service but not. He was here. It was what she'd wanted. She needed to get it over with.

'There's no easy way to tell you this.' Hayley drew in a breath that had her ribs bursting for relief. 'Our night together all those years ago … we didn't just make love, Michel, we made a baby.' She screwed her eyes shut again. 'I got pregnant and I had your baby.'

There. It was done. Out in the open. The only thing to be afraid of now was his reaction.

She dared to open one eye and watched the colour fall from his face. He leant forward, put his face in his hands, dragging his fingers down the skin, eyes wide with shock. He wet his lips and opened his mouth to speak. 'The girl who was here …'

Hayley nodded. 'Yes, that's her. That's Angel.'

He shook his head. 'I do not believe this.'

'I know it must be a shock and I never had any intention of getting you involved, but Angel, she has this dream to meet her father and I just want to make her happy. That's all I've ever tried to do.'

'I mean … how could you do this?'

'What?'

'Ten years ago you have a child and … I do not … I cannot.' His voice was raising in volume and his agitation was clear to see. He got to his feet, kicking at the wooden flooring and heading towards the Christmas tree. He threw his arms up in the air, bells on Bruce's branches reacting as his fingertips swiped at them.

'You say you were careful … I ask you this!'

'I was drunk, Michel! And young and stupid!'

'Ten years, Hayley,' Michel stated.

'I know how long it's been.'

'You do not find me when you know you are pregnant.'

'Well, no, I mean, you were here and I was in England and we were both young. You wouldn't want to settle down with a child. You had dreams to paint and take pictures, see the world.'

'So you do not tell me?'

'I …' Hayley moved her eyes away. She didn't know what she had been expecting but it hadn't been this. So much anger and accusation.

'You do not give me the choice?'

'It was my problem.' She swallowed, instantly regretting the word 'problem'. Her mother had told her what to do and she had let her, too ashamed, too overwhelmed to have an opinion. *He wouldn't want to know. He was on the other side of the world.*

'I didn't think …' she began.

'That is obvious.' He made a noise of irritation like someone had pushed past him on the street.

She tried to even out her voice, taking a breath before continuing. 'Listen, we have to deal with the situation as it stands now. I have a nine-year-old daughter who made a wish this year to meet her father. *Your* daughter. Now, it's up to you.'

She waited for her words to sink in, watching him shift his feet, rubbing one trainer up against the other. He turned to face the window and Hayley watched him as the snowflakes flashed past the glass. What was he going to do?

He turned around to face her and she swallowed.

'I am allowed to have a decision now, yes?' Michel spat.

She opened her mouth, unsure what was going to come out. 'Yes … of course … I …'

She watched him suck in a breath that filled his wiry frame, rocking him slightly until his hair fell over his face. What was he going to say?

'I can't deal with this, Hayley.' He put his hands into his hair, wrapping it around his fingers until he was pulling it like someone in complete turmoil. 'I just can't deal with this.'

'Listen … I know it's a big thing … a huge thing but … nothing has to change for you. I mean, we can …' She was talking so quickly none of the words were coming out how she wanted them to. She just needed him to know that Angel just wanted the chance to get to know where she had come from.

'Nothing has to change?!' He shook his head, his hair responding to the motion. 'You tell me I have a child! Everything has changed!'

She could feel the tears at the very edge of her eyelids. One blink and they would be slipping down her face. She had to hold it together.

'I'm sorry.' He strode towards her but moved past, heading for the door. 'I can't do this.'

'Michel, please,' she begged, reaching for his arm.

He shook her off and before she was really fully aware of it, she was hearing footfalls on the stairs and the slam of Dean's front door.

CHAPTER FIFTY-ONE

Dean Walker's Apartment, Downtown Manhattan

Hayley couldn't believe he'd walked out. Was her mother right? Was that what would have happened if she'd told him ten years ago? She was hurt and disappointed. Yes, she'd only known him one night back then, but he'd been kind and decent and hadn't behaved like someone who was going to run the second something unexpected happened. This was all her fault. From beginning to end it had been a disaster and now Angel was going to be bearing the brunt of all those mistakes. It was even worse that Angel had actually met him. Now she would think he didn't want to know her. She had meant to protect her from that.

She wiped at her tear-stained eyes and blew her nose as she heard sounds from downstairs. Angel, Dean, Vernon and Randy were back. She had no idea what she was going to say. She couldn't tell Angel the truth. What was the truth anyway? Michel had just been told he had a nine-year-old daughter. You didn't get over that in a New York minute. He couldn't leave things how they were, could he? He would come round. He had to.

Hayley rushed to the sink, splashing cold water on her face and rubbing it dry with the Union Jack tea towel. She had this situation.

And then the door opened and Randy burst through it, his claws skittering over the wood floor towards her, bow tie shining from his furry neck. The dog leapt up at her knee and she stroked its head.

'Hey,' Dean greeted cautiously.

'Hey! Did you have double waffles and hot chocolate?' Hayley asked like she was an excited children's television presenter.

Angel was already pouting, her eyes roving over the empty lounge room. 'Where's Michel?'

'Michel?' She put a question mark at the end of his name which was an instant mistake. She wet her lips and tried again. 'He had to go. He had an exhibition to get ready for tomorrow.' *More lies.*

'Why don't we read Randy your favourite Christmas story?' Vernon suggested to Angel.

'Did you tell him about me?' Angel asked.

The look on her daughter's face was killing her. So much hope was written there, so much love too. This meant everything to Angel and she wasn't about to rip that apart until absolutely necessary.

'Yes,' Hayley said, eyes shining with more tears. 'Yes, I did.' She swallowed. 'It's a big thing … a really big thing to take in and … he's doing so well with his art and he's really busy right now.' She paused. 'We just need to give him a little bit of time.'

It sounded lame and nowhere near enough.

'So we just need to sit tight and wait a little bit longer, OK?' Hayley asked Angel.

Angel nodded. 'OK.' Her voice was soft, lacking in any real emotion.

'OK?' Hayley checked.

Angel nodded again. 'His eyes are just like mine aren't they?' she stated.

Hayley smiled. 'Yes, they are.' She said a mental prayer in the hope God was watching this and that he could send a team of disciples to give Michel a kick up the backside.

Restaurant Romario, Greenwich Park

'So, what are you thinking of doing on this sabbatical?' Cynthia asked. She slipped an olive into her mouth and watched Oliver from across the table.

'I have no idea. Try and stay alive long enough to enjoy it, I guess,' he responded, grinning.

'That isn't funny, Oliver.'

He took a swig of his beer. 'I need to sort out the unholy mess at the company first. Peter Lamont's dismissal, the Regis Software episode…' He looked at his mother then, wanting to gauge her reaction. She had been stronger than he could have imagined over Andrew Regis and he knew how much it must have hurt to have her trust and loyalty betrayed.

'Cole is quite capable of stepping up to the plate,' Cynthia said.

'I know,' Oliver replied. 'I'm just not quite ready to hand over the reins just yet.'

'And if you had another focus? Something else to concentrate on in the meantime?'

Her last sentence made him realise where this was heading and he was shaking his head with a whole lot of certainty. 'No.'

'You don't even know what I'm going to say,' Cynthia said, picking up her wineglass.

'I definitely do know.'

'I want you to speak at the McArthur Foundation fundraiser, Oliver.'

'Mom, we've done this before. I don't want to get into another fight about it.'

'Neither do I,' Cynthia responded, putting her glass back down on the table. 'So, why don't you tell me about Hayley Walker?'

Oliver fumbled with his beer bottle and it slipped from his hand, spilling some of its contents on the red and white tablecloth. He reached for his napkin and began to mop up the fluid. His mother had thrown him. He didn't know what to say. Had Hayley told his mother about them? How else would she know?

'Oliver, I still come here with Janice and Linda.' She reached across the table and lay a hand on his arm. 'Anna told me you brought someone here, how you were with each other … Tony filled me in on the rest.'

Oliver's eyes shot to the bar area where Tony was making drinks for other tables.

'Don't worry, he didn't give you up easily. I did have to threaten every bad teenage photo I have of him, blown up to poster size and put on the windows of his new restaurants.'

Oliver blew out a breath. 'There's nothing to say. We had one date and then I realised it wasn't going to work.'

And he'd been reliving every moment of their time together ever since. Her laugh, the way she talked at a hundred miles a second, her enthusiasm for life. And there it was. How could someone so full of life be forced into his pity party?

'You know she's helping me organise the fundraiser?'

He nodded. 'Yeah, she told me.'

'She's doing an excellent job.'

'She's an excellent person.' He raised his eyes to his mother then. 'Very capable.'

Cynthia let a sigh leave her lips. 'It doesn't have to be this way, Oliver.'

'It doesn't have to be *what* way?'

'Running from your feelings doesn't make them go away. All it does is make you sad and the person you have feelings for even sadder.'

He picked up a slice of pizza from his plate, thought about eating it, then dropped it down again. 'I can't do what you did with Dad and Ben.'

'What did I do?' Cynthia asked. 'Except love them unconditionally?'

'There! That. Exactly that.' He wiped his fingers on the napkin. 'How can I expect someone to care for me unconditionally when the truth is I could die at any time?'

Cynthia shook her head. 'I was in a very dark place when we lost Ben. We all were. But your father, he held us all together as best as he could, knowing his number could be up at any time.' She placed the flats of her hands on the table as if she was garnering strength from its solidity. 'He told me that everybody in this world could die at any time and he was right. All of us are dying, Oliver. I could get run over in the street, or be gunned down by that gang over in the housing project, there's risk just getting up in the morning.' She smiled then. 'But we can't all stay in bed. *Netflix* wouldn't cope with demand.'

'Mom …' Oliver started.

'You need to stop being so afraid and contact the consultant, Oliver. And then, tell Hayley everything.' Cynthia paused. 'If she's the person you think she is then it won't matter one bit.'

CHAPTER FIFTY-TWO

Dean Walker's Apartment, Downtown Manhattan

'I can smell burning,' Angel remarked, padding into the kitchen dressed in a fluffy cat onesie.

'No burning here, just golden brown waffles.' Hayley served the food onto a plate. 'Grab them while they're hot.'

Hayley watched Angel eye the charred offerings like they were offensive. 'What?! Black is the new golden brown. Everybody's doing it.'

'Where's Uncle Dean?' Angel asked, climbing up onto a bar stool and pulling the orange juice carton towards her.

'Work. He had to go early. He said something about it being a big day. That could mean something crucial about the Globe or it could mean he's going to his favourite restaurant for lunch.' Hayley slipped onto the stool next to Angel. 'Eat up.'

'Could we phone Michel?' Angel asked.

Hayley stiffened. She'd called Michel half a dozen times the night before and left messages. There had only been endless ringing and the bleep of the answerphone. It was up to her to try and make it right. She'd apologised over and over, she'd tearfully begged and told him how much Angel wanted this until she'd run out of words.

'Listen, I think we should just give him a minute to get used to things. I mean, before yesterday he didn't know about you, Angel.'

'I know but he was really nice and …'

'Hey, I promise we'll call him tomorrow, OK? Besides, I need your help today. I've got a million phone calls to make about the fundraiser and emails to chase up and I need to meet with Cynthia.'

Hayley stopped talking. She had promised Angel two things on this holiday, one was she would find her father and the other was to spend quality time with her. She'd found the man but he'd run off, she'd wasted her time with a billionaire and she'd got a job. She was scoring so badly on every count. She swallowed down a mouthful of overdone waffle. What was running through Angel's overactive mind right now? She'd wished for her father for months and now they'd found him he'd run out on them. She wanted to hold her daughter close, shut all the doors to this harsh side of life and protect her from everything and everyone. It had worked for so many years. This was her fault. She had invited in this heartache.

She smiled at Angel. 'Listen, I promise, if I get all the things on my list done by this afternoon, we'll go skating at the Rockefeller Centre.'

'Yay!' Angel exclaimed. 'And can we get a Hillary Clinton bobble head? I promised I'd bring one back for Jessica.'

'I'm scared that those even exist.' Hayley smiled through a mouthful of waffle.

The intercom buzzed and Hayley slipped down off her stool. Had she ordered something for the fundraiser to be delivered here? She needed to get her list in order. She'd drawn butterflies all over her writing last night plus an idea for a dress she was never going to get to make.

'Hello,' she answered.

'Hayley?'

Michel. Her heart jolted and immediately her eyes went to Angel who had juice drizzling down her chin.

'Yes ... I'm here ...' She swallowed.

'About last night, I …'

'Sshh, la la la la la, it's OK, don't speak any more. I'm coming down.' She shut the intercom off before Michel could say anything else. The last thing she wanted was for Angel to know how he had bolted from the flat like his clothes were on fire.

She saw Angel open her mouth to speak but she pointed, warning her not to. 'Wipe your face. I'll be back.'

Drummond Global Offices, Downtown Manhattan

It was just nerves this time. Oliver's heart was pounding hard as he pumped the stress ball in his hand. He felt sick and clammy. He couldn't concentrate.

'Do you want me to get Delaney to draft something for the press?' Clara asked.

He hadn't heard what she'd said. What were they talking about now? Had they moved on from Peter Lamont?

'I'm sorry, Clara. What were we discussing?'

'All this stuff with Andrew and Peter is getting to you, isn't it? How could it not? I just can't believe it of Peter. His poor wife and the children.'

'What I told you about that, Clara, it goes no further.' Oliver let out a sigh, his chest burning. 'Peter has been fired for leaking confidential information to a competitor, nothing else. His private life stays that way, for Andrew Regis too. This whole thing is already killing my mother.'

'How *is* she?'

'Throwing herself into the McArthur Foundation fundraiser. I don't think it's fully hit her yet.'

He put his hand to the knot of his tie and loosened it a little. Was it hot in here? Outside the windows he could see the snow was falling again. What was Hayley doing right now? Was she with his mother organising the fundraiser he couldn't be part of or was she with Michel? The last thought stung. He cared about her, really cared about her, but he had to let her go. Whatever this guy turned out to be, Oliver could almost guarantee he didn't have a life-limiting condition going on.

'And what about you, Oliver?'

'Dean Walker has been made head of department. He was in charge of the Globe anyway so it makes sense …'

'You haven't answered the question.'

'I think that's the boss's prerogative.'

The sentence was out of his mouth before he'd thought about it. Clara didn't deserve his sarcasm. She had been there for him, sucking everything up, since his father died. She'd been unfailing in her support no matter how badly he'd treated her.

'I'm sorry, Clara.' He sat back, the leather chair reclining. 'I didn't mean that.'

'I know you're the boss, Oliver, but I worry for you.' Her hands went to the necklace at her throat.

'I know you do.' He nodded, reaching for the baseball stress ball again. 'And I've decided to take a little time out.'

'You have?'

He nodded. 'Once this scandal has been dealt with, once the Globe is launched, I'm going to take a minute, do some things I haven't done for a while.'

'Like what?'

He smiled. 'I don't know. Not make plans for one thing. Maybe take a vacation.'

Clara smiled. 'And Lois? Will she be someplace in these not-making-plans plans?'

'No,' he responded, squeezing the ball tight. 'I've burned my bridges there.' He sighed. 'And it's no more than I deserve.'

Dean Walker's Apartment, Downtown Manhattan

Michel's dark hair was covered in snow and Hayley was sure the faded denim jacket he was wearing was the same one he'd worn ten years ago. His eyes were ringed by dark circles, hinting at a lack of sleep the night before. She was almost pleased. How many sleepless nights had she endured when she'd found out she was pregnant, then the sleepless nights with a crying baby. She swallowed. Single parenthood had been her choice. The noise of the city going on around them – cars, bikes, Santas with handbells – all faded away as if knowing the importance of this moment.

'I am sorry,' he started, his blue eyes meeting hers.

She didn't know how to respond to the statement. What was he sorry for? Leaving? The things he'd said?

'No, Michel, I'm sorry. I should have done everything differently. I realise that.' She sighed. 'But I can't go back.'

'I know,' he whispered.

'What do you want to do?' Hayley asked, bluntly.

'I would like to meet my daughter,' he replied, the sentence wrapped with emotion.

Hayley nodded, the enormity of it all hitting her with a vengeance.

Michel shook his head, flakes of snow scattering. 'I do not know what I am supposed to do.'

'Listen, I'm not asking you to marry me and fly to England. All she wants is to meet you, to know who you are. Anything else is going to take time.'

He put his hands in his hair. 'This is life-changing.'

Hayley nodded. 'I know.' She let out a breath. 'But Angel, she's the brightest thing in my life. She's clever, exceptionally so, and she's funny and she makes me laugh a hundred times a day … and she has your eyes, Michel.'

There were tears in those eyes now as he nodded his head. Maybe she hadn't been wrong about this man after all.

'Come on,' she said. 'Come in.'

She wanted this so badly for Angel. It didn't have to be formal, nothing set in stone or permanent plans for the future, it just had to be a beginning, a chance for Angel to know her father.

She led the way up the stairs to Dean's apartment, Michel following and her heart beating like an enthusiastic little drummer boy. Pausing at the top of the staircase, Hayley took a breath then pushed open the door that led to the kitchen.

And there Angel was. Cleaned face, eyes expectant, the hood of her cat onesie pulled over her head so the ears stood upright. She marched past Hayley and held her hand out to Michel.

'It's very nice to meet you again,' she said. 'Mum says you have "busy" hair, but I like it.'

Michel laughed, his eyes crinkling up, his mouth open in genuine amusement at Angel's comment. Hayley remembered that expression and her body warmed in response. She carried on watching as Michel took hold of his daughter's hand and gave it a small shake. 'It is very nice to meet you too.'

'I'm glad you came back,' Angel continued, her eyes fixed on Michel.

'Me too,' he responded, his voice coated with emotion.

'My friend at school wants me to bring home random things from New York.' She reached for her sketchbook on the breakfast bar and pulled it into her arms. 'We need to finish that picture.'

'I'm not sure you need me to finish it. You are an excellent artist,' Michel said.

'Well, Mum can only draw dresses and stuff, so I guess I must get it from you.' She smiled, holding out a pencil to him.

Hayley's heart swelled as Michel accepted the pencil. It was a start.

CHAPTER FIFTY-THREE

Dean Walker's Apartment, Downtown Manhattan

Hayley had been making phone calls all morning to organise the McArthur Foundation fundraiser whilst keeping one eye on Michel and Angel. They'd drawn quietly for half an hour or so, Angel looking up from her pad every now and then, blinking like she couldn't believe Michel was real. Hayley had also seen Michel doing exactly the same thing. When he looked at his daughter it was as if he were gazing at an object of wonder, something beautiful he couldn't quite believe was so close, something he didn't quite understand yet. And now, as it neared lunchtime, they were going ice skating. Angel had thrown that out there with all the finesse of someone who was used to getting their own way and, as Michel had shown no obvious signs of wanting to leave, Hayley felt duty-bound to give in.

'What do you think?' Hayley asked, twirling around in the kitchen. 'Ice skating chic or ice skating chic?'

'Those aren't gloves,' Angel remarked, staring at Hayley's hands covered by long woollen sleeves.

'No, I gave you my gloves. These are hand-warming couture.' She stretched them out for Angel to see.

'They look like sleeves off a jumper.'

'Ha! But the people of New York won't know that. They will think, "ooo look at that fashionista wearing hand-warming couture".'

'Are you OK with doing this?' Michel asked her.

'Of course,' Hayley said. 'I've got my hand-warming couture which is going to stop me getting my fingers sliced off. I'm all good.'

'Thank you,' Michel whispered as Angel focussed on buttoning up her coat.

'What for?'

'For this second chance,' he said. 'I behaved so badly last night and ...'

'See that girl over there?' Hayley interrupted. 'She hasn't stopped smiling since you walked in here this morning.' She laid a hand on Michel's arm. 'That's all I want.'

He nodded as if he understood.

'OK then,' Hayley said, addressing Angel. 'Let's get this over with ... I mean ... let's go and have some fun.'

The Rockefeller Center Ice Rink, New York

'Have you skated before?' Angel asked, holding onto the side of the ice rink, her feet as still as she could keep them.

'Of course,' Michel answered, turning his body and expertly moving backwards like a winter Olympian.

Hayley hadn't even taken a step onto the ice yet. This small patch of white in the middle of the brick, steel and chrome of the surrounding buildings was almost surreal. As was the giant tree towering over them like a triffid and the gilt statue of some old god surrounded by a waterfall.

'It's Prometheus,' Angel said, looking at Hayley.

'Is that another word for freezing?' Hayley asked, her teeth chattering together.

'No, it's the name of the statue you were looking at. Prometheus. He's a Greek god and this one is actually made of bronze, not gold.'

'Angel, you are coming to skate?' Michel called, beckoning her.

'Go on,' Hayley said, still not making any moves. 'Go and skate.'

'Reason 23 why Christmas is better in New York, ice skating next to a Greek god,' Angel said, slowly removing her fingers from the edge of the ice rink.

'Yup, pretty cool. So, off you go,' Hayley urged.

Angel stared at her, unmoving. 'You're going to wait until my back's turned and then you're going to sneak off to the café.'

'How very dare you! As if I would!'

Her daughter knew her far too well. The skates were already pinching her toes.

'Come on!' Michel shouted. 'We come here to skate!'

Hayley pulled a face. 'I don't remember him being this bossy.'

'Come on, Mum. I'll hold your hand,' Angel said, gingerly moving on the ice, her hand held out to Hayley.

'I'm not sure ice skating is going to be me,' she said, putting one foot in front of the other but pausing before the ice.

'I'm not sure green vegetables are really me but you still make me eat them. Come on!'

Angel pulled her forwards and, before she could do anything to stop herself, she was on the ice, her feet slipping and sliding away from her like a newborn fawn.

'Angel! Don't you let me go!'

'Stop pulling on me! You'll stretch my new coat,' Angel screamed.

'I can't stand still!'

'It's ice skating, you're not supposed to stand still!'

'This is all wrong. It's unnatural I tell you!'

With her arms flailing and her legs kicking, Hayley screamed as Michel took her arm and she grabbed him with both hands in desperation.

'Whose idea was this?' she exclaimed, her fingers digging into his coat as he held her up.

'Angel wanted to come,' Michel reminded her.

'The child is evil,' Hayley said, narrowing her eyes at her daughter.

'Come on,' Michel said. 'I will help you.' He skated backwards, letting her hold onto his arms.

'Wait for me!' Angel shouted, trying to follow them without falling.

Oliver had followed them. He'd left Clara and the office behind with the sole intention of … what? What had he really been thinking when he left Drummond Global and headed for Dean Walker's apartment? He wanted to see Hayley again. Why? To torture himself? To remind him what he'd had for a short time? What he'd let go? What he'd given up on? Or did he really want to do something he'd never done before?

He watched them from the sidelines. To any onlooker they would appear to be the perfect family. A couple, the man helping his partner, their child trying to keep up with them. Maybe they could be in time. Perhaps that was what Fate had in store for Hayley. Was this his final visual message to leave well alone?

He let a breath go, watching it thicken in the air. He could leave, right now, and she'd never know he'd been here. With Michel and the McArthur Foundation fundraiser she already had so much going on in her life. It wasn't fair to burden her with something else. What they'd had had been fun, exciting. She didn't need what he would bring to the table. It was selfish to tell her, wasn't it? It would be for his benefit. To prove he *could* tell someone? That wasn't fair.

He watched her, letting go of Michel and trying to move of her own accord. Hair poking out from under a red woollen hat, some crazy jumper sleeves over her sweater, knees bent inwards. She was smiling. She was happy. He should go.

And then it happened, their eyes connected. Across the ice, skaters circling around the rink between their locked vision. His mouth dried up, along with his resolve. He couldn't look away.

It was Oliver. Standing on the edge of the rink, looking back at her. Her stomach contracted, she wobbled on her skates and before she could right herself her bottom met the ice with a bang.

'Mum, are you all right?' Angel skated up to her, now moving like a professional.

'Yes, I'm fine. This part is well padded.' She flicked her legs, shifting her feet to try and get traction. 'Get me up.'

Angel bent double, taking Hayley's hands in hers and straining to shift her.

'Hurry up, Angel.' Her heart was racing. Oliver was here, at the ice-skating rink? Why? What was he doing here? Was he here to see her? She needed to find out. Despite everything, her body was urging her to get off the ice and go to him. She looked again, across the ice, twisting her head to reconnect with him. He wasn't there.

'I can't move you! You're too heavy!' Angel screamed. 'It's all the fizzy wine!'

'Let me help you,' Michel said, appearing beside them with a stop on the ice that Robin Cousins would have been proud of.

'No, it's too late.' Hayley began to unlace her boots. 'These are coming off.'

'What? You cannot do this,' Michel told her.

'Mum! What are you doing?'

'I … just … I need to run.' She wrenched the boot from her left foot. 'I can't run in these. I can't even skate in these.' She pulled at the second boot. 'Hold onto them for me.'

She thrust the blades at Michel and started sprinting in her socks across the ice rink, much to the amusement of the other skaters.

Her heart was driving the blood around her body as the freezing surface beneath her feet scalded her soles. She ran like she was treading on broken glass, hopping off the rink and scouring the onlookers for Oliver.

'Oliver!' she called, seeking out anything familiar that would lead to him. His dark coat, the tawny colour of his hair, his stance, the shape of his shoulders. She skidded past a woman carrying a tray of coffee and mince pies, her eyes metres ahead, picking off strangers, frantic to find him. And then she saw him, walking briskly towards the exit. She injected more pace into her run.

'Oliver Drummond! Don't you leave!' she yelled at the top of her voice. 'Stop right there!'

It was like someone had hit a pause button on life. Everything halted. Chatter stopped, the sound of Michael Bublé quietened, people turned to look at her and the only sounds still audible were the blades of the skaters on the ice.

She was breathing hard as she watched him stop. Then he turned around, his eyes finding hers through the crowd. She stepped on, quickly closing the gap between them as everyone around went back to what they were doing.

She looked up at him, suddenly filled with nervousness. She wet her lips.

'So, you thought you'd come here and show off your silky skating skills huh?' She forced a nervous smile.

'I've been kept amused for the past ten minutes by yours,' he stated.

'I aim to please. It's all deliberate. It's a new genre of ice dance, a bit like body-popping,' she replied, putting an arm out then letting her forearm dangle from the elbow.

He nodded and the atmosphere cooled. She didn't know what to say but she had to say something. And not something verging on the ridiculous. Something real. She didn't want things to be how they were between them.

'Michel's here,' she stated.

'I saw,' he replied. 'I'm glad.'

'What you did, finding him I mean, it was such a wonderful thing and ...'

He shook his head. 'You don't need to thank me.'

She watched him swallow, agitation in his stance.

'I was never completely honest with you, Hayley.'

She frowned then. 'You weren't?'

He shook his head. 'No.'

'O-K.'

'I'm not sure I really want to be honest now but ... I feel I owe it you.' He smiled. 'Do you want to get a coffee?' He looked down at her feet. 'And maybe your shoes?'

CHAPTER FIFTY-FOUR

The Rockefeller Center Ice Rink, New York

Hayley ditched the jumper sleeves and let the cardboard cup warm her hands as she watched Michel with Angel on the ice. Holding hands, laughing, getting faster with every circuit, her daughter was having the time of her life.

'He seems to be taking to it,' Oliver remarked. 'Fatherhood.'

She looked at him. 'It's like a first date. Neither of them really know what to say or do. I'm hoping there'll be a second but it's a difficult situation.' She sighed. 'And it takes a lot more than skating and hot dogs to make a parent.' She smiled, her eyes on him. 'What is it you need to tell me?'

She watched him put his coffee cup to his mouth and take a sip of the liquid. He turned to her, adopting a serious expression then clearing his throat. 'It's about my Wish Women really,' he stated. 'And, the reason I meet women that way.'

She could see he was struggling to get the words out and she clamped her lips shut before something inappropriate spilled out.

'The truth is, Hayley … I can't give anyone a future with me,' he stated.

Hayley nodded her head up and down. 'I understand. We're not dissimilar. I've not introduced any man to Angel for the very same reason. There are no guarantees and if you're going to put a lot of time and effort into something there has to be some sort of assurance, or at least definite intentions. Dates and one nights are OK as long as everyone is on the same page.'

'It isn't that.'

'Oh.'

'This is so hard.' He put his cup down on the wooden railing.

'Just tell me, Clark,' she begged. She was nervous. Whatever he had to say sounded serious. 'Just take a deep breath and get it out there.'

'OK,' he agreed, filling his lungs with the chilly air. 'OK.'

She waited, letting the steam from her cup caress her cheeks as she watched him.

'The reason Ben died was because he had a defective gene.' He sighed. 'Ready for the science bit? Well, there's something called a calmodulin protein, which is a kind of sensor that measures calcium in the heart cells and regulates heart rhythm. Ben's didn't work properly and it caused a sudden cardiac arrest.' He took a shaky breath. 'And he died.'

'I know all about that now,' she said softly. 'I read his story on the McArthur Foundation website.'

He nodded. 'Of course you did.' He put a hand to his hair, raking his fingers through it. 'Hayley … I have the same defective gene.' He swallowed. 'And because of that … I don't know how long I have to live.'

His heart was kicking him right this second. Drumming hard and irregular beats as he watched for her reaction. Right now she was looking confused, gripping the cardboard cup a little too hard, her eyes small, as if she was trying to understand exactly what he'd said. He needed to hammer home his point. She needed to be clear. If anything it would make her see how much better an option Michel was.

'My brother had it, he died before he was thirty. My grand-father too, dropped dead at the same age, he had it. And my father only made it to sixty-five. It's what the Drummonds do. We work ourselves into the ground and then we die.'

Hayley was shaking her head, tears bubbling up in her eyes. This was what he'd wanted to avoid. Her pain. This reaction right now. He could feel the tearing of her insides, the kick to her gut and the punch to her heart.

'Listen,' he said, reaching out for her hands. 'It's OK.'

'This is what happened wasn't it? In your apartment, after our date, when I had to call the ambulance …'

He nodded. 'I should have told you then. But all I could think about was how much faith you'd put in me just going on that one date and that I'd somehow duped you into being there. Because, despite the crap I came out with at St. Patrick's, that date meant something to me, Hayley.' He paused. 'And the more it meant, the worse the situation was. So I did what I always do when faced with anything remotely emotional, I switched off, I pulled back and …' He looked to the ice rink. 'I found you a replacement.'

Her tears were falling now, dripping down her face, her red-dened cheeks bitten by the harsh New York weather. He wanted to kiss her tears away, make her pain stop but he held off.

'Don't cry,' he whispered, moving a strand of her hair away from her face.

'I *want* to cry.'

'*I* don't want you to cry.'

'Well they aren't your tears so I'll do what I want with them.'

He held onto her hands, locking their fingers together until they were bound tight. 'I'm sorry I lied to you, Hayley, and I'm sorry I let you down.'

'Shut up. Just stop talking,' she ordered. 'I don't want to hear any more sorrys from someone who's been living a half-life, picking up random women and having an intimate relationship with an android tablet.'

'Ouch.'

He watched her close her eyes, then she tightened her grip on their interlocked fingers. She was so beautiful. He would happily spend the rest of his life just looking at her. He swallowed. He had given up on that chance, but at least now he had finally been honest. All he wanted was for her to be happy. Maybe with Michel she could be.

She snapped open her eyes, holding his gaze.

'I actually think it's pretty presumptuous of you to assume I wouldn't be interested in what we have just because you have a rapidly expiring eat by date.'

'Eat by date?'

'Short shelf life. Use by.'

He shook his head, unable to keep the smile from his lips. 'Food.'

'It scares the hell out of me, Oliver.' Her voice shook. 'And … I have to think of Angel.'

He watched her swallow, drop her eyes for a second. Of course she was right. What good was a dying man to a nine-year-old? Especially one who had spent her whole life without a father figure. The child needed more than he could ever give her.

'But I also know that I've spent the last nine years on my own with my daughter and I'm not about to pass up something special just because I might end up being alone again some day.' She sighed. 'I thought that for a minute when Michel almost didn't come through. I thought maybe it had to be just me and Angel, two girls road-tripping through life, not letting anyone else in. But … life's all about taking chances isn't it?' She wiped her eyes with the back of her hand. 'We all know the end destination, it's all about the stops along the way.' She smiled. 'And how boring would it be if everything was calculated like Sat-Nav?' She squeezed his hands again, bunching them tightly in hers. 'The Oliver I know isn't afraid of anything. And he's clever and funny and ever so slightly sexy and …'

'Whoa, hold up there a second. *Ever so slightly* sexy?' He twisted their fingers together. 'I challenge that.'

'I challenge you back. I challenge you to take a chance on me, because however this pans out I want to start something with you … here, now … then via Skype, seeing as there's a little distance issue, but …' She paused. 'I want to be more than just the woman you called Lois once. That's what I deserve, not this talk of replacements and switching off.' She held his gaze. 'And it's what you deserve too. Me and Angel, two crazy chicks who won't bore you with wishes but might want you to join in singing to *Lip-Synch Battle*.' She smiled. 'Something real.'

He gazed into her eyes, seeing her feelings for him so openly displayed. He swallowed. He was a fool to think he could live without trying to love. And he *did* love her. He *loved* her. Whatever time he had left he wanted to fill it with feelings just like this.

He pulled her into his embrace, wrapping his arms around her, loving the way she fell against his body. 'God, how could I think I could live without you?'

'Yeah, how could you?' She took a step back from him, picked up her jumper sleeves and wiped her eyes with them. 'Multiple uses. I should patent these.'

He swallowed, then let out a breath. 'I am scared, Hayley.'

'I know,' she replied. 'Me too. But the way my ice skating's been going today there's every chance I'll be dying before you.'

'Do you look on the bright side of everything?'

'Is your glass always half empty?'

He smiled. 'I'm not going to win this one, am I?'

'You know how I am with the last word.'

'I remember.'

'Good.'

'So, there we are.'

'Yes.'

'I'm not letting you have it.'

'Oh yes, you are.'

'We'll see about that.'

He cupped her face with his hands, pressing his lips to hers and pushing her body back against the Perspex surround of the rink. He'd never met anyone like her.

Hayley was feeling that deep pull of longing again, just from the touch of his mouth. He was stripping her bare with his kiss, setting fire to her heart. She wound her fingers through his hair and dragged him closer still.

'Mum!'

Angel's voice had her falling away from Oliver and jarring her elbow on the railing. 'Ouch!'

'Why are you kissing Mr Meanie?' Angel hissed as Michel skated up to join her.

'Mr Meanie?' Oliver said.

Hayley smiled. 'Michel, this is Oliver Drummond.'

Angel pulled a face and folded her arms across her chest.

'It is nice to meet you,' Michel greeted, holding his hand out to Oliver.

'Likewise. I've been watching your moves on the ice there. Did you play hockey?' Oliver asked, shaking Michel's hand.

'Oh no, in Belgium we skate just for fun,' he answered. 'You are coming on the rink?'

'I don't think so, I …' Oliver began.

Hayley tugged at his sleeve. 'Why not? Didn't you tell me you were an expert on skates?'

'I may have exaggerated a little and I haven't done it for years,' Oliver added.

'Well, you can't be any worse than me. In fact if there is anyone worse than me I'd really like to meet them,' Hayley said.

'OK,' Oliver said, clapping his hands together. 'Now I've been put on the spot I think I ought to get out on the ice and show you what I've got.'

'Oh my God are you going to wave your hands in the air like you just don't care?' Hayley asked, slipping on her jumper sleeves.

'Only if *you* do. Wait, *you'll* need both your hands to hold on to the barrier,' he teased.

Angel laughed. 'That's funny.'

'Right, that's it! You're going down, mister!'

CHAPTER FIFTY-FIVE

Dean Walker's Apartment, Downtown Manhattan

Angel had been standing in front of the mirror in Dean's hall for the past twenty minutes. First her hair had been down – brushed flat – then it had been parted and palmed into position – then it had been swung up into a high ponytail. Now she was trying to plait it but Hayley could see she was all fingers and thumbs.

'Do you want me to …'

'No.' Angel shook her head.

'I'll do it really quickly.'

'That's the problem. It won't look right.' Angel let out a heavy sigh.

Hayley knew what this was because she was feeling exactly the same. It was trepidation. Angel's very first outing alone with her newly found dad.

Without asking, Hayley stepped forward and began braiding Angel's hair.

'The one thing we can't have happen is Michel turning up and you looking like a walking, talking fashion alert,' Hayley stated, trying to lighten the mood.

She lifted her eyes from the plaits and looked at Angel's reflection. Her daughter was tight-lipped and lacking the enthusiasm that had oozed so readily when this trip was planned after ice skating.

This was going to be the only real time she had let Angel go. She was about to entrust a man she barely knew to take her daughter into the heart of a heaving, over-populated metropolis. The school day trip to the science museum in London had set her teeth on edge when Angel was seven, but this was something else completely.

'So where did he say he's taking you?' Hayley asked, slipping the three strands of hair together.

She knew exactly where Michel planned to take Angel. There was no way she'd let him have her without knowing every stop on the agenda and a definite time to be back home. But she wanted to hear it from Angel. Hope the planned activities would reignite her spirit.

'On a horse and carriage ride and then lunch at the House of Sandwich,' Angel said, her voice monotone.

'Let's have a little more feeling for those horses. They work hard every day of the year. Do you want to take a carrot?' Hayley suggested.

Angel shook her head.

'Keep still or these plaits are going to fall out and you might end up with the soft perm look like her.' Hayley moved her eyes towards the photo of Shirley Bassey.

'What are we going to talk about?' Angel blurted out.

Hayley let out a rush of air as she tied one plait into place. 'Angel Walker, if there's one thing you've always been excellent at it's talking.' Hayley smiled. 'I've been coaching you in this area for years.'

Angel met her eyes in the mirror then. 'We've only talked about drawing and stuff … and you were there last time.'

Hayley let go of Angel's second pigtail and put both of her hands on her daughter's shoulders.

'Is that what you're worried about? Being with Michel on your own?' Hayley asked softly.

'No,' Angel answered immediately. It was obvious the real answer was yes.

Hayley swallowed. What should she do here? Her maternal instincts were telling her to bundle Angel up in a hug and tell her she'd come along too, the other part of her was advising she didn't do that just yet.

'Well, you always tell me about school. I bet Michel would love to hear about the time that boy brought in a photo of the Chelsea football club owner when you were doing about the Romans.'

The beginnings of a smiled formed on Angel's lips.

'Or you could tell him about the brilliant firework display we went to this year. Eating toffee apples until our teeth stuck together.'

Angel shook her head.

'Keep still. I'm nearly done.' Hayley tied up the plait.

'Will you come with us, Mum?'

Angel's plea tugged at her but she maintained what she hoped was an unreadable expression as Angel surveyed her in the mirror.

Oliver was seeing his mother tonight so Hayley planned to stay in with her ideas book and notes for the fundraiser then Dean's cable channels until Angel got home. The ice-skating had been so much more than circles around the rink. It had seemed to start a new phase for everyone. Michel had delighted in Angel. Father and daughter with pink cheeks and excited eyes as they raced each other around the ice and Oliver had joined in too. He and Angel had paired up to beat Michel when the cones came out and a slalom ensued. He was good with her. He made her laugh. He was making it look like he wasn't trying too hard. And it seemed natural, no matter how crazy the whole situation really was. And it *really* was. She swallowed. There were moments when she thought about what it would be like to lose Oliver, if this faulty gene claimed him. She tightened the band on Angel's hair. She tried not to let those thoughts seep too deep. She'd only just found him. She wasn't about to give up easily.

The buzz of the intercom broke the silence.

'He's here,' Angel whispered.

Hayley turned her daughter around to face her.

'Listen,' she paused. 'This is exciting! This is your dad, taking you out!' She took another breath. 'I searched for months for him and … Oliver looked too,' Hayley added.

'He did?' There was surprise on Angel's face.

'Yes he did. So, you see, a lot of people have been wanting to get you your Christmas wish, Angel.'

'It isn't that I don't want to go. I really do. It's just …'

Hayley knew how Angel was feeling. Until a few days ago her daughter had known nothing about the search for Michel. Now he was here and it was all very real.

Hayley smiled. 'I know. It's OK.' She squeezed Angel into a hug. 'If you want me to come, I'll come but let's go and answer the door.'

Horse and carriage – Central Park

The horse was called Marco but Angel had decided to call it Snowy given it was a dappled grey who had almost been camouflaged against the snow on buildings, street and trees when they'd boarded. A white carriage, red and black canopy up to stave off the winter weather and a driver dressed in top hat and tails. Only in New York!

Now Hayley was sat on a red velveteen seat, close to Angel, snuggled under a tartan blanket, her teeth chattering as a strong wind blew snowflakes at them as they trotted through the park.

Central Park looked like the icing on top of a rich Christmas cake, with tree decorations sparkling with frost. Compared to the towering buildings encasing them, it was a patch of serenity, the only noise being the faint beep of car horns, Marco's hooves and a saxophonist playing jazz who was braving the inclement weather.

'This is the best way to see this part of New York,' Michel stated. He was sat on the seat opposite them, a rug over his knees, snowflakes settling on his coat and in his hair.

Hayley smiled. Michel had been fine about her coming with Angel. She could tell he was nervous too and she didn't blame him. This was a big step forward in their relationship. 'When do we have to stop to pick up Marco's poop?'

'Mum!' Angel exclaimed.

'What? Did you not see the buckets hanging underneath the carriage?' She turned to Angel. 'You're so good at doing that for Randy, maybe you could volunteer.'

Angel pulled a face and then quickly smiled at her father. 'What's your favourite New York building, Michel?'

Michel rubbed his hands together and blew some hot breath onto his fingers. 'That is a hard question.'

'Oh it isn't,' Hayley said. 'It has to be the Statue of Liberty. She's strong, she's feminine and she's green. What's not to love?'

'Mum, the Statue of Liberty isn't a building,' Angel corrected.

'Well, landmark then. She's my favourite landmark.'

'I like the Brooklyn Museum,' Michel answered. 'It's near to where I live.' He directed a smile at Hayley. 'There is a replica of the Statue of Liberty there.'

'Can we go there?' Angel asked.

'Yes, of course.' Michel looked to Hayley again. 'If this is OK with your mum.'

Hayley smiled as the carriage came to a halt.

'Angel,' Michel said, sitting forward in his seat and holding a bag out to her. 'You would like to feed the horse?'

Angel's face lit up. 'You brought carrots? Mum said to bring a carrot but …'

'Apples actually,' Michel interrupted.

Angel didn't need to be told twice. She grabbed the bag and jumped down from the carriage, heading across the snow to the horse up front.

'Can you see her?' Hayley asked, moving to the side of the carriage to keep Angel in her line of sight.

'Yes, I can see her,' Michel said. 'Why don't you come and sit over here?' He patted the banquette next to him.

Hayley stood up, holding onto the blanket and dropped down next to Michel, settling when she could clearly see Angel offering an apple on the flat of her hand to Marco.

'She was nervous for today,' Michel remarked.

'You guessed,' Hayley said. She sighed. 'Yes, it wasn't me being overprotective, although I seriously am. She was just a little apprehensive, worried about what to talk about, that sort of thing.'

'Me too,' Michel admitted. 'It is all so very different and I want things to go well.'

'I know,' Hayley answered.

'I feel as if every small moment is magnified a thousand times.' Michel let out a breath. 'This carriage ride through the park, feels like something monumental.'

'You mustn't overthink it,' Hayley said. 'That's what Angel's doing too. You both need to relax. Just be yourselves.'

Michel ran his hand through his hair, snowflakes fluttering into the air as he moved. 'I feel I have so much to make up for.'

'No,' Hayley shook her head. '*I* have so much to make up for.' She pulled the blanket up over her body. 'I should have told you when it happened.'

'We said we would not talk about the past,' Michel reminded her.

'I know I just …'

'Cannot ever stop talking?' Michel said, smiling. 'I remember this about you.'

She nodded. 'I'm taking memorable as good, seeing as we had a child together.' She watched Angel petting the horse, slipping her fingers between the hairs of its mane.

'You are getting serious with Oliver?' Michel asked.

His question surprised her for a second and she had to stall a little, playing with the fringing on the rug before she made her answer. Despite Dean's first remarks insinuating she might be looking for Michel with a view to the whole mother/father/daughter package there was no reignited spark. Michel was still an attractive guy but there was no chemistry fizzing. Was that why he was asking about Oliver? She looked to him then, analysing his expression. No, there was no flicker of desire from what she could tell.

She sighed. 'We have a distance issue. He's here in New York and I live in England.' She put a finger to her lips, biting on the nail before continuing. 'But I haven't felt for anyone what I feel for him.' She laughed then. 'Which is completely crazy because it's so new.'

Michel shrugged. 'Some of the best things in life are new and come out of the blue.'

Hayley watched his eyes go to Angel then and her heart warmed. This was going to be OK.

CHAPTER FIFTY-SIX

Restaurant Romario, Greenwich Village

Angel speared an olive with her fork, missed its centre and sent it flying off the table and onto the floor. Hayley raised her eyes at her daughter and cast a glance out the window at the worsening weather. The snowfall had continued relentlessly the last few days and now there was a good couple of feet in places that hadn't been cleared by the ploughs. Michel had started to become almost a constant in their lives much to Angel's pleasure. Finally, just yesterday, Angel had gone out with him alone, to the Brooklyn Museum. Angel having her father in her life had also softened the edges around the conversation they'd had about Oliver being a little more than Dean's boss. Angel hadn't said very much and Hayley hadn't pushed the subject. Her daughter was having to take on so much at the moment it wasn't fair to expect her to adjust to everything overnight. But she knew Hayley and Oliver were dating and for the time being he was still called Mr Meanie. Hayley still didn't know when she was going to explain Oliver's health issues, if at all. The truth was, they hadn't talked about it much themselves. They'd spent the last couple of days just enjoying being together. Eating burgers bigger than dinner plates, browsing the shops on Fifth Avenue, taking in the sights and sounds of a city gearing up for Christmas. Oliver's heart condition and the McArthur Foundation fundraiser – those two topics were strictly off the agenda for now.

'More garlic bread, Angel?' Tony asked, winking at her.

'Tony, if you give that child any more garlic bread she's going to be keeping vampires away for the foreseeable future,' Cynthia stated, raising her head from her leather portfolio.

'My dad likes garlic bread. We had some for lunch the other day,' Angel informed.

'Want to see how we make it here?' Tony offered. 'Special, secret recipe dough,' Tony informed.

Angel stood up, scraping back her chair. 'Can I, Mum?'

'No eating it,' Hayley warned.

'Come on,' Tony encouraged. 'What happens in the kitchen stays in the kitchen.'

Hayley took a sip of the white wine she badly needed and pushed a piece of paper towards Cynthia. 'Here's the details of the table magician.'

Subtle, she'd found, was the best way with Cynthia. The woman looked at the print-out with a dubious expression on her face.

'He comes highly recommended. I spoke to three hotels that have had him work there. He's been on TV and he even supported David Copperfield back in the day.'

'And you think the fundraiser attendees will find this appealing?' Cynthia asked with scepticism.

'Have you ever had a table magician before?'

'No and there's probably a very good reason for that.'

'Illusion is really on trend, Cynthia, I promise you.'

'Is he expensive?'

'No, and with *my* magical skills of persuasion I reckon I can get him for a song ... well ... a trick ... you know what I'm saying.'

Cynthia sighed and let the paper drop to the tablecloth. 'It's futile to oppose, I'm guessing.'

Hayley grinned. 'You won't regret it.'

Cynthia gave her a warning look over the top of her designer reading glasses. 'No live animals.'

'I promise,' Hayley said, slipping the magician's details into place.

'So,' Cynthia said, closing her folder and taking a grip of her wineglass. 'You and Oliver.'

Hayley swallowed. They hadn't talked about this at all. She knew Cynthia knew and she was sure Cynthia knew Hayley knew she knew but she didn't know how to broach the subject. She had gone from terrible hygiene operative to fundraiser planner then to the girlfriend of Cynthia's son in such a short space of time. They'd only talked business. There had been a lot to organise. And she had been avoiding it.

'Yes, it's becoming a thing since the embarrassing ice skating photos made the papers.'

Cynthia smiled. 'I haven't seen him look so happy in years.'

Hayley nodded and clutched her wine glass a little tighter. Oliver's condition was at the forefront of her mind. She took a breath. 'How did you do it?'

'Do what?'

'Love someone who wasn't going to live a long life and not let it seep into everything.' Hayley shook her head. 'When he first told me it didn't make a difference. I care for him so much it just seemed unimportant …'

'And now?' Cynthia asked.

'Nothing's changed, I still want to see where this is going and I feel more for him than I've ever felt for anybody, but knowing what I know makes me question everything.' She sighed. 'Is this going to be the last burger we share together? Could this kiss goodnight be it for us? Should he be running around the park or should he be taking things easy? What happens when Angel eventually accepts him and gets too close?'

'Never, ever think about it during sex,' Cynthia stated.

'Whoa!' Hayley said, clapping her hands over her ears. 'Table magician, table magician.'

Cynthia laughed. 'Listen, although Ben and Oliver's grandfather died young, before we lost Ben we didn't know about the gene. I've had most of my life not having to think about it. Which is why you have to persuade Oliver to do the sensible thing.'

'The sensible thing?'

Cynthia sucked air in through her teeth. 'I knew he wouldn't have told you all of it.' She shook her head, her set blonde hair moving only slightly. 'There's a chance he might not have the gene,' she stated. 'There's a test.'

Hayley was mid-sip and she coughed, trying to hold onto her wine. 'What?'

'Last year, just before Richard died, we had a letter from a consultant, a heart specialist. His team had done extensive research into the condition and they had come up with a test that can detect the abnormality. They offered Richard and Oliver the chance to take it, to rule out or rule in the condition.'

'And they didn't take it?!' Hayley exclaimed.

Cynthia shook her head. 'Neither of them. Both extremely stupid and very selfish. She sighed. 'I think, getting to sixty-five had surprised Richard already. He felt he'd had a good life and he was going to go out any way the good Lord saw fit. Oliver … well he's been convinced he's dying ever since Ben died.'

Hayley shook her head. She couldn't believe this. He had a chance. He might not have the gene and he wasn't going to find out one way or the other. It was crazy. And he was selfish! Why wouldn't he take the test? He could find out once and for all that he didn't have this condition! She looked at Cynthia. 'Did Richard have the defective gene in the end?'

Cynthia nodded sadly. 'No one knows how he survived as long as he did but I'm grateful for it every day.'

Marvin's Ice Cream Emporium, Downtown Manhattan

Today, in the middle of a snowstorm, ice cream was a big thing. Oliver let a breath go, watching it mix with the freezing air and twist with the exhaust fumes of the slow-moving traffic just in front of him.

Hayley was trusting him here. Showing him that what they had started together really meant something to her. He had his first official date with Angel and he was petrified. He had no idea how to be, or what to do and he was now competing with a new father on the scene who, from all accounts, was adapting excellently to his new role.

A yellow cab crawled up alongside the kerb and stopped. The back door opened and out Angel came. Winter boots on her feet, jeggings and a red woollen coat covering the rest of her. Her brown hair was tied up in two ponytails, reindeers on the elastic bands. She looked to him, wrinkling her nose slightly. He smiled, waved a hand. Angel just carried on looking.

Hayley got out of the taxi and closed the door behind her, waving a thank you to the cabbie. His insides clenched at the sight of her, like they always did. He smiled and she didn't respond either.

'Hey,' he greeted as they approached the entrance of Marvin's Ice Cream Emporium.

'Hey,' Hayley responded, a frosty note to her tone.

He clapped his hands together. 'All ready to fill ourselves with the good stuff?'

'We ate a lot at Romario's at lunchtime,' Angel informed.

He frowned, pushing open the door for them. 'You went to Romario's?'

'It was a business meeting, with your mum, about the fundraiser I'm not allowed to mention,' Hayley stated, sweeping past him.

'I didn't say you couldn't mention it.' He took her arm. 'What's going on?'

'I don't know, Oliver, you tell me.'

Her expression was hard and he really had no idea what he'd done to warrant it.

'Ooo, Mum, they've got hundreds of different toppings!' Angel exclaimed, excitedly, stepping onto the black and white tiled floor of the shop and looking to the counter.

'Well, if you've got room around that loaf of garlic bread in your stomach then you go for it.'

'Hey, Angel, let me show you what I always had here when I was your age.' He stepped away from Hayley and led the way into the shop.

'You came here when you were nine?' Angel asked, looking up at him.

'I started coming here before I could walk. My brother liked it,' he stated, staring through the glass at the different containers of ice cream and toppings.

'More than shrimp?' Angel asked, fixing her gaze on him.

The question took him by surprise. 'How did you know he liked shrimp?'

'Cynthia told us. We're having shrimp for the starter at the McArthur Foundation fundraiser.' Angel smiled proudly. 'It was my idea. The main course is Mrs Futcher's daughter's favourite food and the pudding is a special cheesecake Mr Wright's wife used to make before she got ill.'

Oliver swallowed. It was wonderful and heart-breaking all rolled into one. Just like the foundation itself. He put a hand on Angel's shoulder. 'And you came up with that idea all by yourself? Your mom's always telling me how smart you are. Now I really know.'

The smell of toffee, caramel, chocolate and cream was so powerful it was almost sending Hayley into a sugar coma on its own. But despite the sweet ambience it was difficult to be here, sharing this first proper meeting between Oliver and Angel, when she was so mad with him.

'Can I have another bowl?' Angel asked, looking up at them both, a chocolate button stuck to her chin.

'Angel, you've had three already,' Hayley reminded her.

'I know but I really wanted to try the mince pie flavour and that's limited edition. It mightn't be here after Christmas Day.' She batted her eyelashes at Hayley then turned the eyes on Oliver.

'One more?' Oliver asked, the question directed at Hayley.

'She's playing you,' Hayley told him.

'I know. I don't care. It's almost Christmas,' he responded, grinning at Angel. 'Go get yourself some more.'

Angel leapt up and rushed to the counter while Hayley finally let out the sigh she'd been holding in for an hour.

'Are you going to tell me what's going on?' Oliver asked, picking up his coffee cup and cradling it in his hands.

Hayley folded her arms across her chest, her eyes going to Angel, ensuring she was far enough away not to hear.

'When you told me you were going to die young you ne-glected to mention quite a crucial little thing.' She stared at him.

'What?'

'That there's a test you can take to see if you have the rogue gene.'

Oliver shook his head. 'My mother told you that.' He put the coffee cup down. 'She had no right to.'

'She had every right to. I've put my faith in you, Oliver, you're meeting my daughter right here, in the capacity of some-one I care deeply for, you should have told me.'

'What difference does it make?'

'You might not have the gene!'

He shook his head again. 'Don't do that, Hayley. I've told you how things are. Don't hang on to any false hope that I'm going to be drawing an annuity, because my condition is *hereditary*. My brother had it, my father had it, Grandpa Drummond …'

'Oliver, for God's sake, there's a test to take. Even if you *do* have the condition at least you'll know for certain.'

'I *do* know for certain. I've been having warning signs for months now.'

'Then take the test and get a little piece of paper that says you're going to die young. It's clarity. It's being prepared. It's …'

'Being reminded.'

'You're being bloody-minded and selfish,' Hayley spat. 'I want to know. I want to see it in black and white. Because until I do I'm always going to be hoping it's not true.'

He let out a sigh. 'You told me you could deal with this.'

'I can, but that doesn't mean I have to like it. I'm still into the *Miracle on 34th Street* kind of thing.' She sighed. 'And you of all people should still have some faith in wishes.'

She watched his reaction to her words, hiding her lips in her cup of hot chocolate. She knew confirming what he thought would be hard for both of them but there was a tiny part of her still gripping tight to the belief that life couldn't be that cruel to this family, or to her.

'When they wrote to us, the test was still in its early stages. They used the words *experimental* and *risk*.'

'Anything's got to be better than nothing, hasn't it? And things will have moved on.'

She watched him, his eyes looking into the mid-distance, as if a hundred thoughts were invading his brain at once. Was she asking too much of him? In a week she would be returning home and what happened to their relationship then? There was only so much you could do on FaceTime.

Finally he nodded. 'If it means that much to you …' He reached for her hands and joined them with his. 'If clarification is what you need then … I'll do it, I'll take the test.'

Joy filled her up and she smiled, squeezing his hands tight. 'Thank you, Clark.'

'Oliver!' Angel called. 'Shall I have rainbow sprinkles or chocolate chips?'

Oliver smiled at Hayley, letting go of her hands and getting up from his chair. 'Are you really asking me that question, smart kid? You know the answer, have both!'

CHAPTER FIFTY-SEVEN

Oliver Drummond's Penthouse, Downtown Manhattan

Oliver watched Hayley sleeping. Flat on her back, mouth open, gentle noises coming from her nose, her now shorter brown hair a shaggy, yet attractive, mess on the pillow. He couldn't believe she was still here, still with him. Knowing everything now. She was right. He'd ignored the test for far too long. If, in his heart, he already knew the outcome, there was nothing to lose. And Hayley needed this. Until she saw it for herself, on a report, she'd still be holding out for that Christmas miracle. If they were going to be together then she needed definite clarification about what she'd signed up for. He'd arranged the hospital appointment. Today.

He reached out to her, weaving his fingers into her hair, then softly moving strands from her face. Whatever the outcome he wasn't going to run from his future anymore. Living every moment didn't mean only embracing frivolity. It was focussing on what mattered. *Who* mattered.

Hayley smiled, her eyes remaining closed. 'What's for breakfast?'

'Anything you want,' he whispered.

'Anything?'

'But don't you have a meeting with my mom at the Crystalline?'

Hayley's eyes sprung open then. 'What time is it?' She sat up, looking for the bedside clock.

'It's a little before eight.'

Hayley threw off the duvet. 'I have to get up. I have to go. Dean has work and I need to get Angel and I wanted to call the woman about the flowers and …' She made to spring from the bed but he held her down.

'I hear Dean has a very understanding boss.'

'Who now knows the name of every member of staff thanks to flash cards.'

'It's all about the team.'

'I know. And that's why I have to get up.'

'Stop,' he ordered, moving over her. 'Take a breath.'

'I don't have time to take a breath. If I waste time taking a breath there won't be time for coffee.' She batted her eyelids. 'Make me coffee?'

'When you've said a proper good morning.'

He looked down at her, waiting for the flicker of understanding to reach her expression. He held himself over her, pausing for her reaction.

'I thought I spent quite a lot of time last night saying goodnight,' she responded, grinning.

'It was the best goodnight I've ever had.'

'I don't know if I have the energy for good morning too.' She stretched her body upwards, leaning forward and clasping her arms around his neck, pulling him into her.

'You could skip coffee,' he suggested, kissing her lips.

'Hydration is important,' she said, dropping the lightest kiss on his mouth.

'It's minus five out there not a thirty degree heat wave.'

'I'll be late for your mum.'

'Blame me.'

He kissed her hard, pushing her back against the sheets until she gave in, matching his passion with her own, her hands reaching over his shoulders, her fingers tracing the contours of his back.

She pulled away and looked at him with suspicion in her eyes. 'What's going on?'

'What?' he asked.

'How come you have all this time on your hands? Don't you need to be sorting out the Regis Software mess and dealing with the firing-the-traitor debacle and protecting the Globe like you have been the rest of the week?'

'Not this morning.' He swallowed.

'You have the morning off?'

'Not exactly.' He sighed and shifted his weight from her, turning back to the other side of the bed. He was going to tell her. Of course he was going to tell her. He just knew as soon as he did it would be the only thing she was focussing on.

'Well? You have to tell me.'

He settled himself back on the pillows, dragging the duvet up his body a little self-consciously. He let out a sigh as the seriousness of what he was going to do today hit him hard. 'I'm going to the hospital.'

The air thickened and the seconds seemed to pass by so slowly. Finally she spoke.

'Don't you mean *we* are going to the hospital? Because I'm taking a guess you're not going for a tetanus shot.'

'No,' he said, nodding.

'Then I'm coming with you.' She moved in the bed, shifting onto her knees so she was facing him.

'You don't have to do that. I said I was going to take the test and I am.'

Hayley laughed then. 'You think the only reason I want to come is to make sure you go through with it?' She thumped his arm with her knuckles. 'I want to support you. I want to find out. I want to be there when you get the results.'

'Yeah,' he said. 'That's kind of the reason I wanted to go alone.'

'Well, that makes no sense unless you're going to run for the hills and say we're over.' She frowned at him. 'Is that what you were going to do?'

He shook his head. 'No, of course not.'

'Then I'm coming with you.' She slipped out of bed, grabbed Oliver's Knicks T-shirt and pulled it over her head. 'What time is the appointment?'

'Eleven thirty.'

'Good. I'll grab Angel, I'll meet with your mum and I'll meet you at the hospital.' She padded towards the kitchen on bare feet. 'Same hospital where you were mean and cruel and I swore I was never going to forgive you?'

'Yeah, St Patrick's. What are you doing?' he called, watching her.

She turned back to face him. 'Making sure we're both hydrated. Do you have any bacon?'

He smiled, pulling the duvet up around him. Just what had he done to deserve this woman?

Dean Walker's Apartment, Downtown Manhattan

'Is that eggs I can smell? Because I haven't had eggs this morning and …' Hayley burst through into the kitchen but stopped talking at the sight of Michel by the hob, Angel at his side. 'Oh, hello. Where's Dean?'

'Hi, Mum. We're making eggy bread.'

Michel turned to face her. 'He had to go to work early.'

'Oh, well he didn't ring me.'

'He said he did call but you didn't answer. Angel, you hold this very carefully, it is very hot,' Michel instructed, passing the fish slice to her.

Hayley delved into her rucksack for her iPhone. There were five missed calls. She checked the side. It was switched to silent.

'So, Dean called you?' Hayley asked.

Michel shook his head. 'I came here to speak to you. I wanted to take Angel to another gallery. Dean said you were not here, he needed to go for work, I offered to come to be with Angel until you got here.'

Hayley let out a sigh and put her bag down on the breakfast bar. She needed to stop being so suspicious of everyone's motives with Angel. Michel was her father and for the past few days he had been a walking, talking vision of what a good dad should be. He hadn't pushed or raised expectations or made any promises he hadn't kept. It was going well. He was a good man doing his very best with this new situation and perhaps she ought to give him more credit for that.

'Everything is OK?' Michel asked, coming over to her.

'Yes … sorry.' She swallowed. 'It's just all this is very new and very different and so much is going on at the moment.'

'I understand. I feel the same way.'

'The edges are going brown,' Angel called.

'That is OK,' Michel said. 'Just move the bread gently with the spatula.'

'I hope there's enough for me,' Hayley called. 'But I'll have to eat it on the run.'

'You are busy today?' Michel asked.

'Yes, the McArthur Foundation fundraiser is tomorrow night and I have a tonne of things to do for that and I also … need to be somewhere at eleven thirty.'

'I will have Angel,' Michel said.

'Oh no, Michel, you don't have to do that. I can take Angel with me and …'

'This is stupid. I want to take her to the gallery. I wish to show her some of my work. I can do this. I can take her for lunch. We can visit the Museum of Modern Art maybe?'

Hayley nodded. She needed to let go. She knew that. And Michel had this. But it was harder than she had ever thought. Being solely in charge for so long it was still so difficult to pass over some of the responsibility.

'I love to spend time with her, Hayley,' Michel said quietly, his attention turning to Angel. 'I have missed out on all these years before.'

'I know,' she whispered, feeling a pang of guilt take hold.

'And when you go home, I want to make arrangements to visit. I can come to England or you could come here.' He let out a sigh. 'I do not want to lose this connection now.'

'Going darker brown now!' Angel shouted.

'I will come,' Michel called back. He gave his attention back to Hayley. 'You are her mother. You are the one calling the shots, of course. I just wish to have some more time with her in the future. If you are happy with that.'

'Michel!' Angel screamed. 'There are black bits!'

Hayley looked at him. 'We will work something out.'

He smiled. 'Good. Now, you will take this eggy bread and you will go to your meetings. Angel and I will be fine.'

'Dad!' Angel yelled. 'It's burning!'

A lump shot up into Hayley's throat at the way Angel had addressed him. She looked to Michel and saw an expression nothing short of pure elation. She reached out, taking hold of his hand and squeezing it in hers. 'We will work something out.'

CHAPTER FIFTY-EIGHT

The Crystalline Hotel, Manhattan

'*Platinum* and gold not silver! Yes, there really is a difference and it's one I explained to you when we met, Mr Viceroy.' Hayley paced the ballroom floor as she spoke into the phone. 'Can you get me one hundred and fifty *platinum* balloons and one hundred and fifty gold-coloured balloons by tomorrow afternoon? No? Well, that's great. Thank you so much for that excellent service.' She ended the call and let out a scream that had everyone working in the room reaching for their ears.

She dragged her hands through her hair and bent over, her hands on her knees, her breathing jagged.

'A problem?' Cynthia asked, appearing at her side.

Hayley pulled herself up and fixed a smile on her face. 'No, no of course not. No problem at all.' She had to get this right, especially now. She didn't want Cynthia to think she was incapable in a professional or personal capacity.

'Hayley, I'm here to help.'

'Yes, I know, but this is my project and you're paying me very well to manage it, so manage it I will.' She let out a breath that could have filled three hundred balloons then looked at her watch.

'Is everything all right?' Cynthia said, still observing her.

Did Cynthia know about the test? Maybe Oliver had called her or, more likely, he hadn't wanted to worry her. She swallowed, not wanting to bear the weight of a secret. 'Oliver's having the test today.' She blurted it out before there was any going back.

Cynthia remained virtually impassive but Hayley could see her bottom lip was quivering and there were the beginnings of tears in her eyes as the words took effect.

'He wanted to go on his own but I wouldn't let him,' Hayley continued. 'It's at eleven thirty.'

Cynthia nodded. 'And there's no way either of us are going to stay away.'

Hayley smiled at the woman. 'Good. Well, I'll fix us up with some alternative balloons and then we'll go.'

'We'll stop for coffee on the way. That cardiac unit stuff is like engine oil,' Cynthia said, patting Hayley's arm. She smiled. 'Thank you, Hayley.'

'I'm sure he would have told you. I just …'

Cynthia shook her head. 'No. Thank you for getting him to do this.' She paused. 'You're the reason he's doing it and I'm so glad.'

The atmosphere was thick with emotion and Hayley could feel the tears pricking at her eyes. She cleared her throat and quickly moved back to the middle of the ballroom, looking at the stage. The logo she'd designed for the event was being displayed on the big screen and the turquoise-coloured globes containing warm yellow lights hung from wires right across the length of it. The theme she'd gone for was classic with a homely twist. The room was going to be full of understated exuberance but also stuffed with touches relating to supporters of the foundation who had lost a member of their family or were living with life-altering issues.

'It looks wonderful,' Cynthia told her. 'And it's going to be very special.'

'You like it?'

'Like it? I love it!' She clapped her hands together. 'This is exactly how you changed my home that day. That's why I knew I had to have you for this project.'

Hayley looked at her handiwork, delighting in the way she and the team of people helping her had pulled this together. 'I've never done anything like this before.'

'Would you like to do it again?'

'You have another event?' Hayley asked. Excitement was already bubbling through her core at the very thought of it.

'Not me. Not yet anyway. But when I drop your name into every conversation I have tomorrow night, you're going to be a woman in high demand,' Cynthia told her.

What was Cynthia saying? That she could have an employment future here? In New York? There was no doubt this project had given her her spark back. She may have abandoned the Guggenheim dress in her ideas book but now the pages were packed full of sketches and templates, table settings, swatches of colours. The thought of doing that all over again for something else, another blank canvas to fill with plans and ideas, was more than she could imagine. She swallowed. The reality was she didn't live here and the date on the ticket home was drawing ever closer.

'I don't know about that. And ... I leave next week.'

'Do you?'

Hayley turned at the questioning tone, catching Cynthia's gaze. 'Yes. I mean I live in England.'

Cynthia nodded then let out a light breath. 'I guess I was hoping you might stay. Because of Oliver.'

At the mention of his name Hayley's cheeks gave away every feeling she had. She didn't want to leave him.

'I have Angel to think about. There's her school and her friends and ... my mother.'

She swallowed. Another text had arrived earlier. *I never realised how you felt.* A band of guilt began to tighten in her stomach. She hadn't replied because she didn't know how to. That sentence contained more emotion than she'd felt from her mother for years.

'I shouldn't have said anything. Forgive me.' Cynthia said, patting her shoulder. 'I just see how happy you're making my son and how much he's like the old Oliver right now. I don't want that to disappear if you go.' She smiled. 'And I'll miss you too. And that dear girl of yours.'

'I'll miss you too.' Her voice cracked slightly as the nearness of her departure became all too apparent. She couldn't dwell on it yet. She had to concentrate on the fundraiser. Even if she didn't manage to source the balloons, everything else was coming together. It was going to be a night to remember. She just had to persuade Oliver to be the speaker. Then it would be perfect.

A phone began to ring and Cynthia slipped a hand into her pocket to answer it. 'Cynthia Drummond … oh my God! Have they said anything? Do they know anything?'

Hayley turned back to Cynthia, the woman's anxiety prevalent.

'We'll be there.' Cynthia ended the call, tears forming in her eyes.

'What is it?' Hayley asked. 'What's happened?'

'It's Oliver. He's collapsed. He's at the hospital,' Cynthia informed.

Hayley didn't need to hear anything else. She grabbed hold of Cynthia's hand and ran for the ballroom doors.

St Patrick's Hospital, Downtown Manhattan

The traffic had almost been on lockdown because of the rising snow on the streets and it had taken them twenty-five minutes to get across the city. When they arrived in the emergency room, Clara was sat in a chair in the waiting area just in front a row of cubicles all with their curtains closed. The woman looked pale and concerned and was toying with the diamantes on her necklace.

'Clara,' Cynthia greeted, as they rushed up. 'Where is he? Have they said anything?'

'Hello! Is there a doctor around here! We need a doctor! Where is Oliver Drummond?' Hayley called, starting to part curtains and walk into cubicles.

'It all happened so fast,' Clara started. 'One moment we were talking about Andrew ... well, Regis Software and the next he just went down on the floor.' Clara wiped at her eyes with a tissue. 'But it wasn't like the last time. This time he looked so pale, he was sweating, his breathing was shallow ...'

'The last time?' Cynthia asked.

'Hello! Please, can someone tell us something? You!' Hayley said, grabbing the arm of a nurse.

'What seems to be the problem, ma'am?'

'It was a couple of weeks ago,' Clara said. 'We came here and the doctor diagnosed stress causing hyperventilation.'

'He collapsed on me too,' Hayley added before turning to the nurse. 'Listen, we're the family of Oliver Drummond. He was brought in less than an hour ago by ambulance ...' She looked to Clara for confirmation. 'We want to know what's going on.'

'Just give me a second and I will try to find out for you,' the nurse said.

'Sit down, Hayley,' Cynthia ordered.

'I can't. We don't know what's happening. If I knew what was happening I might feel a bit better, but he could be ... he could be ...' She stopped talking when the enormity of what she'd been thinking got the better of her. This was her fault. This was because of the test. She had pushed it and he was worried about it and now … there might not even get to be a test. The tears were dripping from her eyes already.

'Take it from someone who's spent a lot of time in these places.' Cynthia dropped to the chair beside Clara. 'They need to be looking after him not us.'

Hayley began pacing. 'I need to do something. Shall I get coffee?'

Both women looked at her like she was crazy.

'Yeah, I know it's meant to be bad but …'

A female doctor approached them, a clipboard in her hand. 'You are here for Oliver Drummond?'

'Yes. Yes we are,' Hayley stated.

'I'm Doctor Khan.'

'How is he?' Cynthia asked as she got to her feet.

'He's resting,' Dr Khan answered.

'What does that mean exactly?' Hayley blurted out. 'Asleep? Unconscious?'

'Was it a heart attack?' Cynthia added.

'He isn't unconscious,' the doctor reassured. 'And he hasn't had a heart attack.'

Hayley couldn't help herself. She grabbed Cynthia's arm and squeezed. 'He's going to be OK. I knew it.'

'What happened to him?' Cynthia asked, putting her hand over Hayley's.

Clara got to her feet. 'It was another panic attack, wasn't it? Hyperventilation,' she stated. 'Like the last time.'

Doctor Khan smiled. 'You can see him now, but one at a time. He's a little dehydrated.'

'I told him about that this morning,' Hayley said, shaking her head.

He felt like an idiot. All this fuss again for nothing more than … He didn't even want to think the words *panic attack*. It still made him feel like he was a teenager, afraid to speak in public, worrying about exams or asking a girl to the prom. It wasn't supposed to be in the make-up of a head of industry.

'Knock, knock.' Hayley's head appeared around the curtain. 'My turn now. How's the patient?'

'Not patient at all. I hate hospitals.'

'Me too. Full of ill people like you.' She sat on the side of his bed. 'You dressed under there?'

'If I'm not?' he asked, a grin spreading across his face.

'You are too sick to be making lewd suggestions.'

'You've not spoken to Doctor Khan yet then?'

'She may have mentioned the words "stress" and "panic". You don't have to worry, if it affects your libido we can deal with it together.' Hayley patted his hand.

'Is that supposed to be funny? I'm in here, perspiring and struggling to breathe. Kick a man while he's down why don't you?'

She slipped her fingers in between his then. 'You know I didn't mean it.'

'I know you did.' He smiled but let a sigh pass from his lips. 'I don't want to keep doing this. Because every time it happens I think …'

'You're going to die,' Hayley finished.

'You got it.'

'You work too hard. And you've coiled things up inside for so long you're tighter than … I don't know … tighter than a Botoxed actress.'

'I'm not sure how I feel about that.'

'You need to do this test and then you need a break, whatever the outcome.' Hayley smiled. 'I can think of a few things to occupy your time, Clark.' She walked her fingers up his bare chest.

'I bet you can.'

Someone cleared their throat and Hayley yanked her hand away and turned her head to greet Cynthia.

'Sorry,' Hayley said, slipping off the bed.

'Oliver, the doctor from the cardiac unit is going to come here to see you. For the tests,' Cynthia spoke. 'But, he said you don't have to do this today if you're not feeling up to it.'

Oliver shook his head. 'No. I want to do it, Mom. Whatever happens, I can't be in limbo anymore. Tell them I'm ready, Mom.'

CHAPTER FIFTY-NINE

Dean Walker's Apartment, Downtown Manhattan

'Easy does it. Mind the top step. That's it. Nice and slow,' Hayley said as they climbed the stairs to Dean's apartment.

'Will you quit talking like that or I'm going home,' Oliver snapped.

'Calm thoughts. You don't want to stress yourself out.'

'Hayley, I'm fine.'

'You're not fine. You've had needles in here and lines in there and lots of pills …'

'Just another day in the life of a junkie.'

She slapped his arm.

'Ow, that was one of the needle holes.'

'Was it? Sorry … I'm so sorry. I'll make you hot chocolate.'

'Does Dean have any Scotch?'

'You can't have alcohol.'

'Why not? I've used it to manage stress for a considerable number of years.'

Hayley pushed open the door to the living area. Angel and Dean were sat at the breakfast bar staring at them as they came in.

'Hel-lo. You look like you were waiting for us,' Hayley remarked.

'We could hear you all the way from the bottom of the stairs,' Dean said.

'Are you all right?' Angel asked, looking Oliver up and down. She hadn't called him Mr Meanie and her expression was one of concern.

'I'm fine. Your mom worries too much. She thought I was going to go back to my home and have a medical emergency.'

'In the bath, with Scotch. I'd be freaking out about it all night. You're much safer here where we can keep an eye on you.'

'Did you know that a heart attack is the number one cause of death in the United States?' Angel asked. Perhaps Hayley's thinking that Angel was getting used to her relationship with Oliver had been premature.

'Wow, that's a statistic we could really do without right now,' Hayley said quickly.

'I did know that,' Oliver replied. 'But I haven't had a heart attack so we're all good here.'

'There are also some studies that link the use of tablets and computers with heart attacks,' Angel continued.

'Dean, have you been letting her have unrestricted access to your laptop?'

'Don't blame me for what she knows,' Dean said, holding his hands up.

'I don't think that's true,' Oliver said, holding Angel's gaze. 'But I've heard they can fry your brain and, if you play Rabbit Nation too long, you can go blind.'

A look of horror started to cross Angel's face.

'Then you grow big ears and fur and two long teeth,' Oliver finished off. He was holding his own with her. This was good.

Angel scowled. 'That's not funny!'

'Gotcha!' Hayley said, pointing at Angel.

Dean got down from his stool. 'Shall I make some coffee?'

Oliver pulled a face at Hayley.

'Actually, I was wondering if you had any whisky.' She looked to Angel. 'And no comments about alcoholism killing the people that don't die from heart attacks.'

'Oliver, would you like to read me a Christmas story?' Angel asked, blinking her eyelashes and pouting.

Hayley stood at the door of Angel's bedroom listening to Oliver read the 'Alfie and the Toymaker' story. Angel was grinning, shouting out Alfie's dialogue and getting grumpy when Oliver didn't read the words quite right. This was exactly the same as what she did with Hayley. Oliver was getting the whole, crazy, Angel Walker experience. It meant her daughter was definitely warming to him.

'All right, I think that's enough.' Hayley entered the room. 'The amount of time Oliver's been in here it must be at least the fifth read-through.'

'It's the sixth actually,' Angel responded.

'I'd lost count,' Oliver answered.

'OK, well it's time to do some sleeping,' Hayley said, pulling the duvet up over Angel as Oliver shifted off the bed.

'Are you coming to the fundraiser tomorrow night?' Angel asked, dragging the quilt back down and looking at Oliver.

'Time for sleep, missy,' Hayley interrupted.

'I'm not sure,' Oliver answered.

'The room is going to look amazing. Mum's coordinated all the colours perfectly, the menu is going to rock and there's even a jazz band coming. *And* they're using the logo I drew.'

'You designed a logo?' Oliver looked impressed.

'It's a …' Angel began.

'Sshh, it's supposed to be a surprise for tomorrow. You haven't been telling everyone have you?' Hayley asked.

'Only Uncle Dean … and my dad and maybe Vernon.' Angel grinned. 'And Randy but he doesn't really count.'

'Angel!' Hayley exclaimed.

Oliver looked to Hayley then. 'Can you give us a second?'

'You're kidding right?' She put her hands on her hips. 'I leave you in here a second longer she's going to make you read that book again.'

'I'll take my chances.'

'Why don't you go and open some fizzy wine and some low cholesterol snacks?' Angel suggested.

'What are you plotting?' Hayley asked.

'I just want to ask Angel something about Rabbit Nation. You'd be bored in a millisecond.'

'You're not wrong.' She took a step towards the door. 'Five minutes then I'm coming back in.'

Oliver waited for the door to close behind Hayley before he sat back down on Angel's bed, a serious expression on his face.

'This isn't about Rabbit Nation, is it?' Angel said, worry etched on her brow.

'No, Angel, this is much more serious than that.' He let out a sigh. 'So … you know my brother, Ben …' he began.

'Your mum told us he was brilliant at just about everything.'

'Yeah,' Oliver replied. 'He was.'

'And you miss him.'

'Yes, I do.'

'And you won't speak at the fundraiser because you're afraid you might cry,' Angel said bluntly.

Her words almost stole the breath from him. Children had no filter. They were truth tellers. He nodded his head. 'Something like that.' He cleared his throat. 'But, after these last few days of spending time with your mom and our visit to the ice cream store my stomach is still bursting from, I've decided that

I do *want* to speak.' He sighed. 'I owe it to a lot of people to talk about how a sudden death has affected the life of my family and the people around me and how we can try to live with it.'

He knew Hayley hadn't told Angel about the heart condition. Looking at her now, so cute in her cat pyjamas, her hair tied in bunches, he couldn't imagine wanting her to know anything that might break her heart.

Angel put her hand over his. 'Yes, you do. And I can help you.'

He smiled. 'I was hoping you were going to say that.'

'But I have a condition,' Angel said, tilting her head so her pigtails fell to one side.

'How did I not guess that?'

'You have to promise to dance with my mum at the party.' Angel wore a deadpan expression. 'Proper dancing not just stepping from side to side. She likes Maroon 5.'

'Yeah, I know that, although I think it's only the lead singer she's really interested in.'

'Do *you* have any tattoos? Adam Levine has loads!'

'Not yet. But it could be a look for the future.' He smiled. 'So … dancing. I guess, if that's the price for your help then I can do that.'

'Really?!' Angel's eyes lit up.

'Did you think I was going to say no? I'm desperate here, Angel. And dancing with your mom is going to be fun.'

'You haven't seen her dance,' Angel said, laughing. 'OK, what do you need?'

'I need to see that logo and the new slogan.'

'You know it's top secret, right?'

'I promise I won't show another soul.'

Angel nodded then and reached for her sketch pad. As Oliver reached out for it she held on tight, as if she wasn't ready to let go. 'Mum said you helped to find my dad.'

Oliver swallowed. He hadn't been prepared for that and a tingling sensation started to creep over him. He finally nodded. 'Yes, I did.'

Angel put down the pad and threw her arms around Oliver's neck. She was clinging on so tight he almost couldn't breathe.

'Thank you,' she whispered.

Tears pricked his eyes at her show of affection and he hugged her close. 'You're welcome,' he replied.

'I thought you'd got lost.' Hayley patted the orange sequinned cushion next to her on the chenille sofa as Oliver came back into the living room. 'You didn't read that book again, did you?'

'No, but she did show me her special dictionary.' Oliver sat down.

'I swear I am going to burn that thing.'

He smiled. 'She's one bright kid.'

'Yes she is,' Hayley replied, pride in her tone. 'So, what did you talk about?'

'I can't tell you that.'

'I hate secrets!'

'And apparently, you have a mustard allergy.'

'It isn't an allergy, it's an intolerance and I hate intolerances so I ignore it. God, what else has she told you?'

'You once lost your shoe on Brighton beach and you were chased by bees and donkeys on the very same day when you went for a picnic.'

'That's the very last time I leave you two alone. Ever.'

Oliver laughed and Hayley smiled at the way his body reacted to it. After the day he'd had it was nice to see him looking a little more relaxed. But there was an elephant in the room, prodding her hard with its tusks.

'When will you find out?'

That had killed the laughter. She swallowed, regretful at her timing, but it had been on her mind all day. She knew her sentence needed no further explanation as she saw Oliver fall still.

'It's supposed to take weeks.' He swallowed. 'I paid to get it back in twenty-four hours.'

'Tomorrow,' Hayley said, the word dying on her breath.

'Yeah, tomorrow's a big day for us all.' He put an arm around her shoulders, pulling her close.

'The fundraiser is nothing compared to you getting news that could change your life,' Hayley said. This was happening. And it was *all* happening tomorrow. Now the answer was so close it was terrifying her. She cared about him so much, more than she had cared about anyone. And knowing that, knowing how fast and hard she'd fallen only made it worse.

He shook his head, his fingers smoothing through her hair. 'That isn't true. Most of the people there tomorrow have all had their lives changed. They get out of bed every morning and there's a giant hole in their hearts and their homes. We all get news that's going to change our life at some time.' He kissed her head. 'Bet it was life-changing when you found out you were having Angel.'

'Are you kidding?! I passed out in the doctor's surgery and ate a whole bag of custard doughnuts.'

'My point is proven.'

'I'm still not going to be able to concentrate on food and décor and the trumpeter's issue with the spotlights though,' Hayley stated.

'Yes you are, because I don't want to see you tomorrow.'

'What?' She sat up straight, looking at him in shock.

'I want you to focus on the fundraiser. You and my mom have worked so hard to make this night a success. All the tickets have been sold, it's going to be the best and most profitable night the foundation has had. Tony has a date ... and I'm going to be there.'

She couldn't help the breath leaving her. 'You're coming.'

'How could I not? Angel says you have a table magician.'

'She hated that idea.'

'Well, I love it and so will the mayor and the police commissioner.'

'I hope so.'

'So you have to promise me, no calling, no messaging, no thinking about anything but the fundraiser.'

Hayley screwed up her face. There was no way she was going to be able to do it. 'I can't.'

'Promise me, Lois.'

She looked into his eyes and saw the need for her to give him this. Smothering him when he didn't want it wasn't going to change the outcome of the result. She just had to hope and pray for good news and let him bring it to her when he was ready.

'Arrrrgh, I'm going to say this really quickly before I change my mind.' She closed her eyes. 'I promise.'

As the two words left her lips, his mouth was on hers, kissing an insistent path across her jawline and slipping down her neck. She giggled as his mouth touched a ticklish spot.

'So,' he whispered. 'You know how you like a magician?'

'Yes, Clark.'

He raised his head, his eyes dark and full of longing. 'How about I make your clothes disappear?'

'Why, Mr Drummond, is that a magic wand in your pants or are you just pleased to see me?'

CHAPTER SIXTY

The McArthur Foundation Fundraiser – The Crystalline Hotel, Manhattan

Hayley looked at her watch. There were less than thirty minutes before the doors would open and the very first guests would start to come into the room. She held her breath, looking at the layout in front of her. The tables were heart-shaped and Cynthia had mixed up attendees so everyone would be sitting with someone they weren't overly familiar with. The table cloths were turquoise, the plates bright white, the tableware shining silver and the glasses all polished so you could see your reflection in them. White and turquoise orchids stood in glass vases in the centre of each table together with platinum, gold and turquoise balloons. Turquoise and platinum drapes hung across the windows with beaded butterfly decorations in the middle of each one. The pastel globes across the stage were lit up, shadows of butterflies fluttering inside every piece. It was everything she had wanted and so much more.

'It looks wonderful, Hayley,' Cynthia said, standing at her shoulder.

'You got the balloons I wanted.' She turned to face her. 'How did you do that?'

'Ah well, the Drummond name still carries a little weight around this city,' Cynthia answered, smiling.

Hayley checked her watch again. 'Have you heard from Oliver?'

Cynthia shook her head. 'He said the same to me as he told me he said to you.'

'This is so frustrating. I just want to know.'

'I know.' Cynthia put an arm around her shoulders. 'But let's look at it this way. The worst outcome is nothing changes.'

That was true but she was praying for something else. A miracle at Christmas. Or perhaps she'd had her fair share of those already with Angel and Michel. Earlier she'd had a phone conversation with Rita she thought she'd never have. She had cried, her mother had cried and both of them had said things to each other they'd left unsaid for far too long. There had been a full on thawing over tissues on both sides of the Atlantic and whether it was just Rita reading her diary or perhaps Neville from the bowls club softening her, Hayley was glad.

'The shrimp is lovely,' Angel said, arriving next to them.

'I can see that. You've got half of it over your face. Come here,' Hayley said, licking her fingers.

'Oh no, no, no. Not mum spit!' Angel screamed, skidding away.

'I'll get a wipe,' Hayley said, about to head across the room to where she'd left her bag.

'Hayley, wait. I can clean Angel up,' Cynthia said. 'You need to change into this.' She took a couple of steps towards a package on the plinth at the side of the stage. Hayley watched as she brought the box over to her.

'It's a clown costume, isn't it?' Angel folded her arms across her chest. 'I told you clowns were a bad idea.'

'It's from Oliver,' Cynthia said, passing it over.

Hayley swallowed. She knew what this was before she even removed the paper. 'It's an Emo Taragucci, isn't it?'

'Is it?' Angel asked, eyes ballooning.

'I think you ought to take it to the restroom and try it on,' Cynthia encouraged.

'I can't wait to see it!' Angel exclaimed.

'Hold up there a second, Miss Shrimp Face, we have wiping to do,' Cynthia said, taking hold of Angel's hand.

Hayley smoothed her hand over the light silk as delicate as a feather. The black fabric, bright pink Japanese blossom falling effortlessly over every inch, was like it had been created just for her. She'd never dreamed she would ever own an Emo Taragucci design. The dress cost thousands of pounds but, what made it all the more special, was Oliver knowing which one had been her favourite. He had chosen so perfectly.

She was at the doors to the ballroom waiting for the glitterati of New York to arrive. Through the glass, Hayley could see the snow was still falling, the sky an inky blue, breath from the mouths of the doormen visible in the night air. A woman entered.

'This is it,' Cynthia said through gritted teeth. 'This is Madeline Fisher from the foundation. She'll be the one inspecting our party favours.' Cynthia beamed a smile. 'Madeline! Welcome, welcome! You look wonderful.'

Hayley swallowed, her mouth dry. She checked her watch again. She'd promised not to think about Oliver but it had been on her mind from the minute she woke up. By now he had to know the outcome of the test results. Would he still come tonight? What if he was home right now, on his own, with the truth no one wanted?

'Madeline, this is Hayley Walker. She's the event planner I've been working with to coordinate the fundraiser,' Cynthia introduced.

Hayley stretched out her hand. 'It's lovely to meet you.'

'You're English,' Madeline noted, shaking her hand.

'Yes, but don't hold it against me.' Hayley laughed, then shut her mouth up as Madeline failed to react.

'I heard about poor Aimee. Fancy breaking her foot taking the trash out. I mean doesn't she pay someone to take the trash out?' Madeline asked, her attention back with Cynthia.

'I'm afraid the gossips are a little off, Madeline. She's actually got glandular fever. The poor dear can barely whisper,' Cynthia responded.

Hayley spotted Angel handing out goody bags to guests.

'Excuse me one moment,' Hayley said, heading towards her daughter.

She picked up a bag and held it out to a guest as she walked past the table. 'I need you to cover me,' Hayley said to Angel, her smile fixed.

'What d'you mean? Where are you going?' Angel curtseyed at a lady in an orange ball gown. 'Welcome to the McArthur Foundation Christmas fundraiser. I hope you enjoy the party bag …'

'Favours. Party favours,' Hayley jumped in. She turned to Angel. 'It's not a party bag. Party bags are full of Haribos and cheap plastic crap mums feel they have to buy. There's gift vouchers and jewellery in these. And that's not the kind you can eat.'

'Is there?' Angel asked, her eyes dropping into the bag she was holding.

'I need to call Oliver.'

'Oh no you don't. He told me you're not allowed to call him because he's busy with work.'

Her daughter had no idea about the severity of this situation. She should be handling it better. She checked her watch again. 'It's almost half past seven.'

'And he's going to be here any minute.'

'How do you know that?'

'Because he made me a promise and if he doesn't keep it I have a lifetime's free golden chicories on Rabbit Nation.'

Hayley palmed her face. 'The suspense is killing me.'

'I heard one of the waitresses say the menu from every corner of the world is killing the chef. You're just going to have to be patient, Mum.' Angel smiled at another guest. 'Welcome to the McArthur Foundation Christmas fundraiser.'

Outside the Crystalline Hotel, Manhattan

This was, without any doubt, the hardest thing Oliver had ever done. His hands were shaking as he looked at the piece of paper in his hands. So much was going to change and it scared him.

The car stopped outside the Crystalline Hotel and he looked to the front doors, the two Christmas trees at the entrance, lit up in platinum and turquoise. He checked his watch. It was edging towards nine. Everyone would have eaten, just like he planned. Before he said anything to his mother or Hayley, he wanted to address the room, like he should have done every year since Ben died.

The car door opened and the driver was there waiting for him to disembark. He should move now, get out, put one foot in front of the other through the snow. His legs were shaking so much he didn't know whether he was going to be able to do it. He needed to man up. Own this moment more than he'd ever owned anything before.

He stepped out onto the white sidewalk and slipped the piece of paper into his coat pocket.

CHAPTER SIXTY ONE

The McArthur Foundation Fundraiser – The Crystalline Hotel, Manhattan

'Ladies and gentlemen, thank you one and all for attending this year's McArthur Foundation fundraiser. It's a pleasure to see so many faces, previous attendees and newcomers, here tonight to enjoy this fabulous event and celebrate all the good work the foundation has undertaken this year,' Cynthia said.

The crowd all clapped their hands again and Oliver could feel the sweat on his palms as he stood in the wings. He was more terrified about this than he'd been about his first full meeting with the board of Drummond Global. He'd thrown up in the men's room before that encounter. That was another reason he hadn't got here for the meal, he just wouldn't have been able to stomach it.

'It's five years since we lost my eldest son, Ben, and there isn't one day that passes where he's not thought of. He left a huge dent in our family but tonight's McArthur Foundation fundraiser isn't about dwelling on our pain and suffering ...' Cynthia paused. 'Our loss ... It's about coming to terms with their passing and celebrating the lives of our loved ones ...' A murmur grew from the audience and his mother stopped speaking. She looked to her left and saw him stepping out onto the stage. People in the audience started to clap their hands and he willed his legs to keep holding him up. There were tears in Cynthia's eyes as he met her, leaning to kiss her cheek. So many questions were written in her expression. He couldn't answer them yet. The applause died down and, as he pressed the piece of paper to the stand, Cynthia left. He was entirely on his own.

'Good evening everyone. I'm Oliver Drummond, the CEO of Drummond Global.' He paused. 'Tonight, just Oliver.' He put his hands to the lectern. 'Firstly, I want to apologise for interrupting my mother just then. I think I scared her half to death … because I was the very last person she was expecting on stage tonight.' He cleared his throat. 'Because … since my mother asked me to speak at this event I've been thinking of every excuse I can to get out of it.'

There were a few rumbles of discontent and a couple of laughs before he carried on.

'For me, heading up a billion-dollar corporation and dealing with difficult international negotiations on a daily basis is a piece of cake compared to standing here in front of you good people and telling you what this foundation means to me.'

He took a breath, looking out into the audience. He needed to find Hayley. He wanted to know she was listening to this.

'For a very long time I despised this organisation and I hated what it stood for. Everyone connected with it was still grieving, wallowing in death and illness and making plans to die. I have to say that scared the crap out of me. Why would I want to tell everyone about my feelings? Why would I want to drag up memories of my brother when all it does is rip my heart out?' He paused. 'For so many years I wanted to forget him. I wanted to forget his death, pretend it never happened, because it tainted everything. It crushed my mother, it practically killed my father and it turned me into some sort of control freak in an ivory tower so high Rapunzel would have needed hair extensions to get out of it.'

There were chuckles of appreciation and he picked up the glass of water on the stand and put it to his lips. He recomposed himself and started again.

'Until today I've been living a careless, meaningless, cheap kind of a life where nothing mattered to me other than where the next buzz was coming from.' He swallowed. 'I was afraid to make any connection that mattered, on a personal level and on a professional level too. I'm ashamed to say that apart from my closest team, I didn't know the names of anyone that worked for me. And, what was worse than that was, I didn't care.'

Hayley was shaking as she watched him, completely transfixed, everyone else in the room fading away. He knew the results of his test and he was stood on the stage pouring his heart out to a room full of strangers whose only connection was the failed health of someone they were close to.

Angel slipped her hand into hers, twisting her small fingers into the gaps to bond them tight as Oliver started to speak again.

'I put work ahead of everything else. I wanted to waste my life on exuberance, because, without my brother, without my father, it all seemed pointless.'

Hayley watched Oliver look out into the crowd and she shifted on her chair, leaning forward a little, wanting to meet his eyes. Finally their vision connected and she offered him a tentative smile, her eyes welling up with tears.

'And then something changed,' he said. 'I met someone.'

'It's you!' Angel whispered loudly, removing her hand from Hayley's and doing jazz hands.

Hayley batted her vibrating fingers away, her attention solely on Oliver.

'This person came into my life like a tornado – completely unexpected, going a hundred miles an hour and whirling up a whole lot of crazy.' He took a breath. 'And she saved me from myself without really even knowing it.'

Her heart contracted at his words. They were food to her soul, warming everything.

'Just being with her made me see that I didn't want my life to be meaningless anymore. I couldn't carry on treating my staff like crap, ignoring my mother because she reminded me of the family I'd lost, being emotionally absent from every single day. I had to make peace with what had happened, I had to embrace whatever future I had and I had to make the most of every minute. With the people I care about.'

The first tears were falling and she tried to push them back into her eyes with her fingers. She knew then what he was telling her. He had the same condition as Ben. It was confirmed. But he was now going to suck the life out of every moment he had left. With her.

'The McArthur Foundation isn't something to be feared, it's something to be very proud of. With your donations and your publicity and your volunteering efforts round the clock, you've raised millions of pounds for essential research into all kinds of life-limiting illnesses and diseases. You've also funded the very first holiday home for bereaved families to go spend some time together after they've lost a loved one. I'm in awe of everything you've achieved this year. Thank you so much for your continued support.' He put his hands together in applause and the crowd followed his action, all clapping their appreciation.

Hayley sniffed, wiping her nose on her arm as she stopped clapping.

'So, without further ado, I want to introduce someone special to you all … the designer of the logo for the fundraiser tonight which is now going to become the logo of the McArthur Foundation. Miss Angel Walker.'

Hayley spun round to look at Angel. 'What the … are you …'

'Relax, Mum, I'll give you credit for the slogan,' Angel said, slipping out of her chair as the crowd began to clap again.

A sob of pride slipped out as she watched Angel move through the tables, the spotlight picking out the sequins on the silver party dress she had jazzed up with beads and diamantes yesterday. Angel mounted the stairs and held her hand out to Oliver. He gave it a business-like shake.

Angel put a clenched fist to her mouth and cleared her throat. She leant into the microphone like a professional. 'Ladies and gentleman, I give you the new logo for the McArthur Foundation and the new slogan. My mum helped with that by the way.' Angel paused until the audience were quiet. 'Every single beat.'

The big screen behind them flashed on and Angel's butterfly drawing had been turned into a platinum and turquoise graphic, its wings beating and flexing. With a bang like fireworks going off, thousands of glittering butterfly shapes began to fall from the ceiling of the room and people started to exclaim. There were joyous cries and hundreds of hands clapped together as the room was filled with as much thudding and stamping as a football stadium.

Oliver spoke over the noise. 'Ladies and gentlemen, the McArthur Foundation isn't about grief, it's about courage. And just like the butterfly, some of us might not get long in this world, but we need to make sure that every single beat counts. Thank you.'

There was a roar of appreciation and people began to bang the tables with their hands, knock cutlery against glasses, anything they could to get their emotions across.

Hayley couldn't wait any longer. She pushed past chairs, slipping her body past tables and clapping guests to get to the front of the room. Oliver was coming off the stage with Angel, Cynthia hot on his heels. She needed to know. She just needed to hear the words from his mouth and she would deal with it.

Oliver could see her heading towards him in the dress he'd ordered for her. It was perfect and she had never looked more beautiful, her sleek dark hair shifting as she hurried past people, her eyes wide, those pert lips slicked with pink gloss.

'Oliver, please,' Cynthia begged.

'Remember your promise,' Angel said, tugging at Oliver's jacket. 'Proper dancing.'

He smiled at her. 'I haven't forgotten.'

Hayley rushed the last few steps and practically threw herself at him. 'Tell me, God damn it. Tell me right now! I'm ready for it, whatever they said I can handle it.'

Oliver could see the tears were leaking from her eyes and he looked away, towards his mother, reaching for her hand. He pulled Angel in close and took Hayley's hand before he dragged in a breath that seem to take a long time to fill his lungs.

'I don't have the gene.'

'Oh my God! Oh my God!' Hayley looked to the ceiling. 'I can't believe it! Thank you, thank you!' She threw her arms around him, clinging to him like a boa constrictor.

He looked to Cynthia and saw the release of years of worry in teardrops on her cheeks, an almost serene expression on her face. He squeezed her hand as Hayley hugged the life out of him.

'I knew God couldn't be that cruel,' Cynthia said, slipping a tissue from her sleeve and dabbing at her eyes. 'I'm so pleased for you, Oliver.'

'Mum, it's getting embarrassing now. You need to put him down,' Angel said, folding her arms across her chest.

Hayley took a step back and Oliver smiled at her.

'You OK?' he asked.

'I am now. I mean, I tried to concentrate on name places and the balloons and the butterfly net but all I could think about was you!'

'Come, Angel, let me introduce you to some people,' Cynthia said, clasping the little girl's hand.

Angel made a V with her second and third fingers, putting them to her eyes and then directing them at Oliver as she moved away from them. Hayley flinched a little, looking confused.

'Was that a threat?' Hayley asked him.

'Kind of. We made a deal last night.'

'Oh no. What sort of deal? You know she has a poker face, right?'

Oliver took her hand. 'I hope the jazz band can play some Maroon 5.'

'I have no idea what you're talking about.'

He looked at her, savouring the vision and breathing long and deep. It felt like a whole new world had been opened up for him. He didn't have the rogue gene his brother and father had, he just needed to manage his stress better. He was going to do something he never believed he would be able to do and sign up for some counselling. Because he valued himself and he wanted a new start ... with Hayley.

'I know you're meant to leave in a few days,' he stated.

'Yeah, back to England, jobless and facing a mother who has now read my ten-year diary.' She was concerned about seeing her mother, raking over old ground, facing up to everything she'd written. But after their heart-to-heart on the phone she was hoping things could move forward. Maybe notes about the past would forge a new beginning.

'I don't want you to go.'

He watched for her reaction, wanting to see how she felt about his statement.

She swallowed, affection for him written all over her face. He kissed her lips, softly, slowly, wanting to melt into the moment.

'Stay. At least a little longer,' he begged, smoothing her hair with his fingers.

'I can't. Angel has school and we have a ticket home I can't afford to replace.'

He laughed then, loud and hard. 'Hayley, I'm a billionaire.'

'And you're not going to stay that way if you keep spending it on unnecessary things.'

'Oh believe me, it's necessary.' He smirked.

'What about Angel's school. She's excited about showing off her collection of random objects.'

'I'll get her one of Donald Trump's wigs.'

'Seriously?'

'No.' Oliver laughed. 'Come on, Hayley. How hard is it to say yes? Whenever you need to go home … *if* you need to go home, I'll pay for your ticket. I'll fly you in a private jet if you want, I'll get a tutor for Angel … unless.' He stopped talking. 'Unless you really don't want to stay.'

He watched her eyes, took in the indecision, prepared himself to be let down.

'Are you kidding? Of course I want to stay! I haven't set foot in Bloomingdales yet and I need to get better at ice skating. But I'll need some proper gloves because the hand-warming couture might have looked cool but it was lacking in just about every other area.'

'Stop talking,' Oliver ordered, leaning into her.

'But I have to have to last word.'

'Not tonight,' he told her.

He pressed his lips to hers, slipping his hand around her back and pulling her into him. This was where he wanted to be, the room warm, the sound of happy voices, his suit covered in multi-coloured foil butterflies, jazz music starting up from the stage and the woman he loved in his arms. Lois and Clark. Together. Making every moment count.

EPILOGUE

Christmas Day – The Drummond Residence, Westchester

Hayley slapped Angel's hand as she reached across the table. 'Oh no you don't. Those popovers are for everyone.'

Angel pulled a face, slipping her tongue in front of her bottom row of teeth and pushing it forward.

Hayley put a hand to her throat. 'Swearing! At the Christmas dinner table!'

'Angel, darling, you have as many as you like,' Cynthia said. 'I can always make some more.'

Cynthia was smitten with Angel. She was like the daughter Cynthia never had and Angel truly had the woman wrapped around her little finger.

Hayley looked around at the grotto of a dining room. Outside the snow was two feet deep and set to increase overnight, inside they were all surrounded by garlands of bells, wreaths of holly, pine cones and red bows, a Christmas tree that almost reached the ceiling and Michael Bublé's Christmas album coming out of the sound system. How different a home it was from the empty, soulless space she'd entered as Agatha. Her, Angel, Dean, Vernon, Oliver and Cynthia – with Randy howling for attention in the hall.

She looked at Oliver opposite her, wearing the Superman T-shirt she'd bought him, sipping at the cheap fizzy wine she'd grabbed at a bodega on the way over. She loved him. She knew that now without a shadow of a doubt. She'd agreed to stay longer but in a week, two, however long it was, she was going to have to leave him. She swallowed, popping a forkful of turkey in her mouth.

'I'd like to give thanks and propose a few toasts,' Oliver stated, raising his glass.

'I think that's a wonderful idea but I'd like to start,' Cynthia said.

'And then me, because it's women and children first,' Angel interrupted.

Everyone laughed.

'Right, well, I would like to give thanks to everyone around this table. Dean and Vernon, it was so wonderful to meet you at the Christmas party last week and I'm so glad you could come today,' Cynthia began.

'Thank you for inviting us, Cynthia,' Vernon said, raising his glass.

'Oliver, I know how hard things have been for you these past few years and I know we've talked it out a number of times but I just want to say … your father would be so proud of the man you've become.'

Hayley watched Oliver swallow and shift his eyes to his plate of food.

'And last but not least,' Cynthia said, looking to Hayley and Angel. 'I would like to propose a toast to Agatha and Charlotte. Who came into my house and reminded me it was a home.' Cynthia raised her glass. 'To Agatha and Charlotte.'

'Agatha and Charlotte,' everyone chorused.

Her cheeks flushed as Oliver caught her eye and mouthed the words 'Agatha and Charlotte?' not understanding at all. She shrugged and mimed glugging from a bottle, nodding her head towards Cynthia.

'My turn!' Angel announced, munching up half a popover like a hungry guinea pig.

'Be respectful and don't mention George Washington,' Hayley suggested.

Angel cleared her throat. 'Did you know that the tradition of Christmas lunch in America came from our traditions in the United Kingdom? And in medieval times a pheasant or boar were served up instead of a turkey.'

'I didn't know that and my life was a lot poorer for it,' Hayley said, nodding.

'I'd like to give thanks for my mum,' Angel continued. 'Because she helped me find my dad, even though she really didn't want to see him again, because she didn't really remember much about him but she did it anyway and now I'm getting to know him and he's getting to know me.' Angel blushed as she finished the sentence. 'And he's cooking me a second Christmas dinner tonight and I can't wait to stay over and thank you, Mum, for letting me. And Oliver, you can take my place in Mum's Christmas night tradition.' Angel turned her gaze to Hayley. 'Share nicer than you do with me.'

'Is this a good tradition? I'm a little scared right now,' Oliver said, looking to Angel.

'We're talking sausage rolls,' Hayley said. 'You'll be fine.'

'We're all really pleased you found your dad, Angel,' Dean said, smiling at his niece.

Oliver raised his glass. 'I'd like to give thanks to your mom too.'

'Oh stop, you'll make me redder than the cranberry sauce,' Hayley said, picking up her napkin.

'I had no idea that a chance meeting around the fire exit at a Chinese restaurant was going to turn my life upside down.' He smiled. 'But I do know that trying to escape that night was the best move I ever made.'

'Slushier than a Slush Puppy,' Angel remarked, rolling her eyes but smiling at the same time

'And I want to make a toast to Angel.' Oliver looked at her. 'For letting me see the logo before the fundraiser so I could get my speech just right.'

'You!' Hayley exclaimed.

'What can I say? He needed direction,' Angel responded.

'To Angel. Who might need some help putting together a model replica of the White House later on,' Oliver toasted.

Hayley watched Angel's eyes poke out of her head. 'I've got one?!'

'To Angel,' everyone chorused.

Hayley began to cough loudly, clearing her throat and banging her hand on the table. 'I thought it was women and children first and you jumped the queue, Clark.' She smiled at her companions. 'Now it's my turn.'

She took a breath. 'I want to say thank you to my brother and Vernon for putting up with all the high drama I seem to have brought to New York with me. I'm just hoping spending time with Angel has made up for it.'

'It's all been a pleasure, darling,' Vernon stated.

'I love a bit of high drama,' Dean said.

Hayley looked at Cynthia. 'Thank you to Cynthia for giving me a wonderful opportunity to use my creativity and also for having faith that I could pull it off. I wasn't sure myself until the foil butterflies fell from the ceiling and we recaptured the magician's rabbit, but we did it and it raised loads of money and the press raved about it.'

Everyone clapped their hands together and Hayley did a half bow before sitting still, looking to Angel.

'What can I say about my girl here? She's everything to me, my daughter, my best friend and sometimes the biggest pain in the …'

'Do you know there are at least eleven different words for bottom,' Angel stated.

'I was going to say neck,' Hayley filled in, smiling. 'She has been the best thing in my life for nine and a half years and I don't know where I'd be without her.' She sniffed. 'And I'm so glad you got your wish. Michel, like me, is so lucky to have a wonderful daughter like you. '

Hayley waved her hand in front of her face as the tears began to fall.

'To Angel,' Oliver offered, lifting his glass.

'No! Hang on! I haven't finished yet.' She composed herself. 'I want to give thanks for you, Oliver.' She swallowed. 'I've never met anyone like you. You're warm and you're funny and equally complex and completely irritating but you get me and I get you. And when I talk about random things you just instinctively know what to say. I've never had that before and I know how challenging I am and ... I just want to say ...' She swallowed again, struggling to get the words out. 'To Oliver.'

'To Oliver,' everyone repeated.

'Do you wanna build a snowman?' Oliver asked later that afternoon.

'Oh my, *Frozen* humour? I think that's been slightly overdone,' Hayley responded, yawning from her seat on the couch.

'We can't move right now. The White House is at a critical stage and it's only an hour until my dad comes to pick me up,' Angel exclaimed, her eyes on the building she, Dean and Vernon were constructing.

'Come on, Hayley, forget *Frozen*, humour *me*. You've got new gloves, remember?' Oliver encouraged. 'Mom?' He looked to Cynthia.

'I'm good here, watching Angel create this masterpiece. I might move in when it's finished,' she responded.

'Come on, up, off the sofa,' Oliver said, grabbing Hayley's hand and wrestling her off the couch.

'This is bullying. We haven't even opened the chocolates yet,' Hayley moaned, following him out of the room.

He encouraged her along the corridor towards the back of the house.

'You do know it's minus five outside? It's more likely we're going to be making an ice man not a snowman.'

'We're not going outside,' Oliver said, pausing by the door to the sun room.

'We're not?'

'No.' He pushed open the door and let Hayley be the first to look into the room. He watched her clap her hands to her mouth as she saw the decorations all around. Everything she had used to adorn the ballroom of the Crystalline Hotel was here in Cynthia's garden room. The turquoise drapes at the windows, the balloons, butterfly-shaped candles flickering on every surface, sparkly foil butterflies on the tiled floor. She stepped into the room, a glowing haven from the flakes of snow flurrying down around the house through the dark of the night.

Oliver pressed a button on the sound system and the sound of Maroon 5 filtered out of the speakers.

Hayley nodded. 'You got me Adam Levine. Finally, you got me Adam Levine.'

'That's not all I got you,' he said.

He stood in front of her, his eyes matching hers, as he reached into the pocket of his trousers and pulled out a turquoise blue box.

Hayley gasped. 'That box is too small for a necklace.'

He nodded.

'And it's way too tiny for a bracelet, even.'

Oliver opened it up, his eyes on her, as he revealed the butterfly shaped diamond ring. He heard her intake of breath and he moved then, slipping the ring from the box and holding it, his hand shaking.

'I know you might think this is too soon but I'm still making every moment count.' He paused. 'But for all the right reasons this time.'

'I don't know what to say,' she whispered.

'Say you'll stay. We'll work everything out. Angel's schooling, you becoming an event planner, a designer, whatever you want. I just can't have you going back to England, not even for a minute. I love you, Hayley.' He dropped down to his knee, the ring between his fingers. 'Will you marry me?'

The question hung in the air and he waited, watching every nuance of her breathing, looking for an answer of any form.

'I have a condition before I answer,' she finally said.

'Anything. Anything at all.'

'No more wishes. Only honest promises and taking each day as it comes.'

'Absolutely. Hand on my heart,' Oliver said, putting his left hand to his chest.

Hayley smiled. 'Then the answer is yes!'

'Yes!' he exclaimed. 'Yes!'

'Give me the ring then,' Hayley encouraged, shooting her left hand forward.

Oliver carefully slid the ring into place and admired the stones dazzling against her skin as he got to his feet.

'I love you, Lois,' he said, drawing her into his embrace.

'I love you too, Superman.' She sighed. 'So, where are we going to live because Angel isn't going to like cosying up in the one-bedroom penthouse? And if my mother is going to come and visit, you know, after she's scalded me about my diary, which she will do even though we had a heart to heart, she's definitely going to want an en-suite.' She drew her head away from him and gasped. 'We could get a Red Room.'

He grinned. 'I don't know about that, but wherever it is, I'm going to make damn sure it has an elevator.'

'Mr Drummond!'

He let her have the last word and then, as the snowflakes began to settle on the windows, he pressed his mouth to hers.

THE END

LETTER FROM MANDY

I hope you have tears streaming down your face right now, but also a big grin too! I really hope you enjoyed your holiday in New York with Hayley, Oliver, Angel and the rest of the characters. I have a soft spot for Oliver's tireless PA, Clara!

THANK YOU SO MUCH for buying *One Wish in Manhattan*!

If you enjoyed the book I would LOVE you to leave me a review on Amazon. Hearing what readers think means everything to us authors. Who was your favourite character? Do you know someone like Hayley or a crazy kid like Angel? Was it a perfect Christmas read? Reviews can spread the word to so many more readers – and a gorgeous billionaire like Oliver Drummond needs to be shared!

And, if you liked this book, perhaps you want to read more! I love connecting with readers on Twitter, Facebook, Goodreads, Pinterest – in fact *One Wish in Manhattan* has its own Pinterest board full of snow scenes in Central Park, Manhattan skylines and where to go, what to do and obviously what you can eat. Come and join me!

To keep right up-to-date with the latest news on my new releases just sign up to my mailing list on my publisher's website: www. bookouture.com/mandy-baggot.

Here's to more feel-good fiction and hot heroes!

Mandy xx

Printed in Great Britain
by Amazon.co.uk, Ltd.,
Marston Gate.